DIE FOTOGRAFIE

A NOVEL

by Phillip Martin Johnson

with William Thomas Loesch III

First Edition: February 2021

Cover and book design by Jonathan Netek.
www.kinetekdesign.com

ISBN 979-8-711546-30-6

Published by Phillip Martin Johnson, Houston, Texas.

www.diefotografie.com

While many of the events, dates, and characters are historically factual, this is a work of fiction. Names, characters, businesses, events and incidents are the products of the author's imagination. Any resemblance to actual persons, living or dead, or actual events is purely coincidental.

The cover art includes images from the Remember Me project at the United States Holocaust Memorial Museum. These images are in the public domain and are not intended to depict any specific individuals but rather, to represent fictional characters from the story.

Visit the project at **rememberme.ushmm.org**.

For my mother. Though you left me seventeen years ago, you continue to be my guiding light and my inspiration.

This book is dedicated to all the innocent young lives who became unwitting victims of the monsters in the Nazi concentration camps in the name of "medicine."

This book is further dedicated to the gay, lesbian, bisexual, transsexual, intersex, and queer people in Nazi Europe whose lives were destroyed by the Holocaust. I sincerely hope that this fictional account raises awareness of these underreported souls so their deaths might not be in vain.

Chapter 1

Freda approached *Anhalter Bahnhof,* the train station in the middle of Berlin that was the pride of the city. Every day, over forty thousand German citizens and several thousand foreigners passed through the impressive arched doorways. Rows of arched windows lined all sides of the modern stone structure and once inside, the grand entryway opened into the largest indoor space Freda had ever seen. She tried not to look up in dumbfounded admiration as she had seen nearly every foreigner and child do, yet it was difficult to imagine the scope of the interior. Beautiful tapestries hung from each pillar supporting the outer walls, but the interior of the space had no supports. Its span arched over the trains, the people, and the platforms, so high up that it seemed to recede into the distance.

As people flowed around each other with determined faces, carrying suitcases, handbags, briefcases, and other personal effects, Freda was struck by how clean and orderly everything and everyone was, except for one man. It seemed odd that the man she was following would be trying so hard to hide that he actually stood out more. The medicine bag he carried was made of old, worn leather and his Fedora was tipped forward so that it hid much of his face. Even with his face hidden, Freda was certain she knew the man. What she could see of his face was so familiar. Could they have worked together before? Maybe he was a scholastic colleague from medical school?

Over the melee of heads and hats, Freda could see one of the trains loading its passengers. The stately wooden railcars were trimmed with gold around the doors and windows with a wide band of gold at the top on which rested an arched green ribbed roof. As women were assisted up the short steps and men climbed in behind them, Freda knew she must get to the stranger before he could slip away, though she could not fathom why this felt urgent to her.

Without warning, the ocean of colorful suits and dresses seemed to part between Freda and the man and he began to turn his head slowly toward her. As quickly, but unobtrusively as she could, she averted her gaze toward a crying child who had apparently been left alone on the platform. Kneeling to care for the distraught child, she stole a glance through the crowd at the man just as her view was obstructed by passengers crossing this way and that. He hadn't seen her. He appeared to be looking over people's heads, as if assuring himself he was not being followed.

Freda stroked the little girl's hair. "My goodness," she remarked inwardly. This girl looked so much like Helga...but that was impossible. Helga was almost twenty years old. This must be some relative like a niece...that looked so similar she could be Helga's twin. The child stopped crying and looked directly into Freda's eyes, the despair melting away and her expression brightening with recognition. A peaceful feeling washed over Freda and she sighed as she placed both hands on the girl's shoulders. She was about to reassure the child when an angry woman blustered up to them, complaining loudly and scolding the child, roughly taking her by the hand, pulling her away, and giving Freda a sour look. As the child stumbled to keep up with the woman's long stride, she smiled Helga's smile back at Freda. That smile could only be Helga's, but as Freda reached for the girl, her arm was roughly pushed aside by passing coats and a briefcase that smacked her sharply on the wrist. She drew her arm back into a protective cradle and stood, turning to where the man was a moment ago. He wasn't there.

She realized that she was scanning the crowd so she lowered her gaze and pretended to fix her heavy woolen skirt. Feeling her short-barreled Luger pistol just within reach through the folds of her skirt, Freda smoothed the fabric and looked up again. As she scanned the room, she tried to look through the crowd rather than standing on tip-toe to try to see over it. She didn't see the man anywhere. Suddenly, she felt a blunt stab of pain in a rib on her left side, just behind her heart. She would have yelped in surprise, but the flash of pain prevented her from taking a breath. She knew if she moved she would die instantly.

"Wieso folgst du mir?" ("Why are you following me?") growled a deep male voice directly behind her left ear. Now she was absolutely certain she knew the man but she could not recall where she might have met him. His clothes smelled of antiseptic, the way the inside of a hospital smells.

"Tue ich nicht..." ("I am not...") she began to answer with as much innocence as she could muster knowing she was seconds away from death when the crowd, which had grown unexpectedly dense, suddenly thronged, shoving them both to the side. There was a flash and a loud sound Freda felt through her core more than heard. Her eyes sprang open but she was no longer in the train station.

A gray, diffuse morning light filtered in through dingy lace drapery across the tiny room. Her cheeks were sore from holding a pained expression. The lines on her face were deep and oily and her forehead was beaded with sweat. With a resigned sigh, Freda drew the sheet and woolen blanket aside. Pausing, the memory of the dream she had been having for several years pressed at her mind. She tried to relax for a moment to calm her rapid breathing and slow her heartbeat. Then she sat up and turned to face the day, the room rocking slightly, her head aching. She had stayed up too late the night before, sitting alone, sipping gin, mulling over the various treatment scenarios she was dealing with at the hospital.

Her twin bed was pushed against the wall, old calico wallpaper behind her with seam edges lifting slightly, delicate colors faded with history. Motes of dust floated through shafts of gray light forming a box at her feet, but no warmth. Nothing in this place ever seemed warm. As she placed her feet into faded yellow slippers at the side of the small bed, the frame and wires underneath heaved their disapproval. The bed gave out an occasional thwang as she shifted her weight toward the edge. Gathering her gown around her, she rose and stepped into the dusty sunbeam, turned, and drew the covers over where she had been sleeping. She had never been one to make her own bed. No one ever visited her rooms and no one ever asked, so why make the effort? Freda wasn't a sloppy woman by any standard, but she applied her efforts selectively.

Her evening ritual of gin and solitaire seemed to take a greater and greater toll as the years passed but she was not the type to drink around others. She was no socialite and knew that her small circle would probably not understand why she drank the way she did. It would be frowned upon in the medical community and could call her fitness as a psychotherapist into question. She didn't relish the start of each day, but it was better than the alternative. Sometimes she envied those of her patients in deep depression. It seemed some could sleep for days at a time, dreaming in repose until they had their fill of care-free rest. Of course that wasn't really the case. Some were truly suffering and she wouldn't wish that on herself no matter how bad her dreams were. With a huff of conviction, she stepped across the short distance to the counter taking care to step around the cart in the center of the small room. Lifting an old tea kettle in one hand, she removed the lid and turned the handle on the faucet. Placing the kettle on a towel to the side of the small gas stove, she took a match from a white shaker and struck it on the cast iron grate. A practiced flick of the knob and the burner whoofed alight. In a few minutes, a mounting hiss from the broken tea kettle announced it was ready to pour out. A splash of gin in her tea would help the night's indulgence fade a little faster. She kept her morning gin in a special bottle she had found in a pile of rubble outside a collapsed orphanage many years ago. It was the typical wine bottle shape with a porcelain and wire closure, but when examined closely in the light, dainty little calico flowers appeared etched into its surface along with rabbits in various poses. It was a small treasure she kept for herself, unlike the rest of her life which was completely devoted to her patients and her mission. In fact, she poured her entire being into helping her patients, sometimes at the cost of her own peace and health.

Dressing for a day of travel, she selected a muted wine-colored jacket to complement her gray woolen skirt and comfortable beige shoes. She knew she would be walking more than usual today and it wouldn't do to be sore later, but she should also make herself presentable for Dr. Nowitz. She was certain that her appointment was the reason her dreams had been more disturbing than usual. Dr. Wilhelm Nowitz was an accomplished friend and colleague Freda met with each Tuesday. Wilhelm first met Freda when she was having a particularly stressful response to a case of a young girl who had been so tortured by her non-psychopathic transsexualism throughout her life and the way others reacted to her behaviour, that she had taken her own life despite Freda's feeling that the girl had been improving. Though she knew that the suicide rate among transsexual youth, both pre- and post-operative, was particularly high, she felt that she should have been able to detect the depth of the girl's despair through the various defense mechanisms the girl had developed over the years. Unfortunately, the girl proved an expert at hiding the intensity of her emotions, even from an experienced professional such as Freda.

When Freda and Wilhelm met, she was questioning her ability to help those under her care and appeared to be making a physical effort to keep her feelings contained. When he had invited her to a private counseling session, she was rigid as a statue and his impression was that she could be broken at any moment by a sufficiently unfortunate circumstance. They spent most of their first session, which he refused to charge her for, sitting in silence, exchanging the occasional nicety. She admired his supremely steady patience as well as his thoughtful and peaceful nature. She looked forward to seeing him, not so that she could rant about the week's difficulties, but so she could experience the peaceful energy around him. It was as if his counseling space were shielded from the outside world by an impenetrable shell many metres thick.

She began to pack her medicine bag for the day being careful to arrange the gin she carried in a grain alcohol bottle so that it would not clink against anything or be seen by the casual observer, Freda gathered her *Ausstattung*: the stethoscope she had kept through medical school, a couple clean hand towels, tourniquet, syringes, and various vials including Morphine, Phenergan, and Phenobarbital to help calm agitated patients. She could easily pick out the gin by its blue ceramic cap. She wrapped her hair with a pale blue scarf, took up her bag, and headed for the *Langendreer* station.

Her pace up *Lünsender Straße* was brisk, though she knew she would be early to the station. Each neighbor she passed greeted her with a wave and a smile but Freda never stopped or slowed to exchange pleasantries. With a brief smile and a slight nod, she kept on her way, head down but with a clear view forward. She didn't fear her neighbors, though that had been normal behaviour in Germany for many years after the war. Rather, she had no patience for the small talk she heard people on the street engaging in as she passed. She had a grave purpose that required someone serious and focused to accomplish. Time was slipping away, yet the work could not be rushed. As she came to *In Den Langenstuken* she turned left at Frau Olsen's street-side cafe, then took an immediate right onto *Im Uhlenwinkel* which led to the *Langendreer* station. She passed through a familiar row of mismatched flats, some old, some new, curved around the old station house, and entered the newly constructed station to the right. As she neared, she saw the customary throng arriving for their early morning commute.

She liked to play a private game while traveling. What if he, selecting some random man of the proper age, were one of them? She would practice observing the stranger, learning about his mannerisms, his ticks, making mental notes of his clothing reading his lips if he had a conversation. She saw many people she had spoken to in the past moving through the station. A smile and cordial *"Hallo, wie gehts?"* was rarely answered, but acknowledgment was the socially acceptable thing to do and if she were to remain unseen, she should practice often. As the train pulled into the station, the din of the crowd rose to compensate for the noise and her mental game was over. The trip to Dr. Nowitz' office in *Bochum* would take about an hour and forty-five minutes, then she would return along nearly the same route to her office to begin her day late. Dr. Nowitz had helped her understand how important it was not to feel guilty about this diversion from her daily responsibilities. He assured her that if she did not take care of herself, the quality of care she gave to her patients would suffer. He couldn't yet know that there was a larger goal she would be unable to achieve if she weren't healthy and mentally strong when it counted, so she faithfully made the voyage to his office each week.

Modern trains bore only a superficial resemblance to the trains that she boarded as a child during the war. Still, the wail of the whistle awakened ghosts in her memory, people she would never see again, mothers with children torn from their embrace, husbands pulled from a wife's grasp, left sobbing on the platform. She was barely ten when the *Auswahlkommando*, the Nazi selection squads, began their campaign, before the concentration of Jews into camps began in earnest. It would take many months for the German people to accept this as normal, so people were hand-picked at first until someone put up some serious resistance. By provoking a response from an underprivileged class, the government could be seen as justified when it forcefully ramped up its transportation efforts.

The jolt of the train drew Freda from her unpleasant reverie and as the train gained speed, those memories seemed to float away behind her, like steam hovering in place over a frozen pond. With her medicine bag in her lap, she performed an exercise Dr. Nowitz had requested of her prior to their session. She imagined each of her patients in turn, well and whole again, mentally and physically. She tried to imagine the pride she might feel if...when...this outcome was realized. The exercise helped clarify the ultimate goal of her lifetime of work. She had studied psychological medicine at the University of Cologne and decided to open her practice in the *Medizinische Fakultät* at the university itself. She had access to work rooms near her patients on the ground floor, but the university administrators had given her an office space in a far corner of the basement, too far from her patients to be of much use during the day. Freda had heard whispers of various conversations, usually when she approached suddenly. Once, while rounding a corner in a hallway she overheard one of the interns remark, "I don't even know why we are bothering to treat these deviants," certainly referring to her patients. It then dawned on her why, no matter what she requested from hospital staff, resistance was always high. Clearly politics was involved in every decision.

Freda rapped lightly on the dark stained wooden door displaying *Dr. Wilhelm Nowitz, Doktor der Philosophie* engraved on a brass plaque at eye level. The doorknob clicked softly, worn smooth by decades of use. As the door began to open, it popped as it came loose from the years of tar and smoke that stained the door jam.

"Willkommen Frau Doktor," said Wilhelm without looking up.

The door creaked open under its own weight, set in motion by the older man as he turned his back to Freda, ambling back into the room. The smell of old pipe smoke that Freda detected in the hallway threatened to overwhelm her senses as undertones of cavendish, cherry, and rancid almond pressed into her nostrils. Ever since she had traded cigarettes for gin, the smell of tobacco smoke made her feel ill. She pressed her revulsion down and took a few steps inside, turning to gently close the door behind her.

Dr. Nowitz proceeded to the center of the dividing wall to the right of the room they had entered. A comfortable looking old leather chair like one might find in a family's living room sat next to a small table. A built-in bookshelf framed the chair displaying classic novels of great literature. Freda saw that Dr. Nowitz had been loading a pipe but he set it on its stand without lighting it before settling into the old leather chair. Freda realized that she was standing motionless holding her medicine bag for an awkwardly long time as she waited for him to invite her to sit. Once he was settled, he noticed her waiting and gestured for her to sit in a twin chair opposite his. The room was only slightly larger than her flat in Bochum and taking up most of the far wall was the classic chaise found in every psychiatrist's office. At its head was a goose-neck Tiffany lamp in the vineyard style with deep red grapes, dark green leaves, and ochre vines. At its foot was another small side table with freshly pressed handkerchiefs and a bottle of smelling salts with a tarnished brown label that must have been decades old. A small humidor, no doubt holding the finest cigars, sat to the rear of the table.

Freda moved to the chair to the left of the chaise and as she set her medicine bag on the floor to the side of the chair, she clearly heard the clink of glass on glass and froze with embarrassment, only for an instant, before being seated. She had only had a touch of gin this morning, being careful to keep the amount small enough as to be reasonably undetectable. Dr. Nowitz watched her, patient and expressionless, head tilted back so he could view her through the bottom half of his bifocals. Once seated, her eyes rose to meet his.

He lowered his head so he could peer over the top of his glasses, and realizing he would need his readers instead, placed his bifocals on the table next to the pipe. Feeling the urge to smoke, he realized something. He could tell by the faint odor of gin that she was also feeling a similar urge and by her sluggish manner he deduced that she had refrained for his sake. He could identify a high-functioning alcoholic easily, but it was no matter for today's session. After a slight hesitation, he picked up a set of turtle shell reading glasses from the table. He sat back, opening the glasses and placing them low on his nose. What he didn't notice was the feeling of relief Freda felt at seeing him resist the urge to smoke. In her current condition, the smell of the room was bad enough, but smelling a lit pipe would certainly be too much for her queasy stomach.

"How are you feeling this morning, *Frau Doktor?*" he addressed formally.

Freda was, at long last, becoming accustomed to her sessions with Dr. Nowitz and the initial trepidation she felt had begun to drop away. She had gone far too long without therapy after beginning her medical practice, but once she had finally heeded the advice of her peers, her emotional state had greatly improved. She found that the improvement spilled over to her patients, so these sessions were as much for them as for herself.

"I am feeling better, thank you, *Herr Doktor.*"

"When last we spoke, you had expressed some concerns about two of your patients. Would you like to continue?" he asked. From his side, between his leg and the arm of the leather chair, he drew out a notebook. The leather cover was soft and worn around the edges, stained in spots by his touch over the years and he held it as one would a precious heirloom. He drew his favourite pen from the breast pocket of his dark brown jacket, uncapped it, and prepared to write. Looking up at Freda, he indicated that she should continue.

"Actually, no, *Herr Doktor.* Your help with those matters is greatly appreciated, but if you do not mind, I would like to speak with you about something else that has been troubling me."

Wilhelm's forehead scrunched with intrigue as he peered over his readers at her.

He rested his pen on the notebook without releasing it and raised his head to look at her directly. It was a good thing to see some assertiveness on her part, the result of a genuine benefit from their sessions. When he first met Freda, she seemed naive. She had been trying to solve all her problems on her own as most inexperienced people do, but she was beginning to blossom...not just under his care, but as a practitioner and an independent woman.

When he seemed to be prepared, Freda continued, "*Herr Doktor*, I have lived very modestly since opening my practice, not because my practice is a poor one, quite the contrary, but I do this because I am spending my money on a mission."

"And where is this mission?" he asked.

She could tell that he had misunderstood her use of the word. "I do not mean the name given to traveling preachers of religion. I mean to say *Aufgabe*, that is, something I have given myself to accomplish."

"Ah. My apologies. May I ask you to explain this *Aufgabe?*" he asked patiently.

"As I am certain you are aware, there were many after the war who sought refuge from the consequences of their actions, fleeing Germany and taking shelter under false names in other countries." She felt anger rising in her chest and her face was beginning to flush. Taking a deep breath, she willed herself to maintain a calm demeanor as she explained. "I have been working with some sympathetic people who are compelled to bring these war criminals to justice; to answer for what they have done to so many who can no longer speak out against them. I find that it is very costly to pay someone's expenses so that they may help me discover these people, and this is where the bulk of my money is going."

He was momentarily stunned, not having expected this to come from her, but this sort of thing was not unheard of. He took a moment to remind himself that in this professional setting, it was not his place to pass any sort of judgment that might influence Freda, but instead to help her achieve a good quality of life, so he indicated that she should continue with the butt end of his pen and began to write as she spoke.

"I have been working with *Herr Krämer* who has been tracing the financial activities of someone I suspect was a Nazi doctor stationed at Auschwitz. This person, if it really is him, conducted horrible experiments on many thousands of people, killing most of them," Freda continued to explain about Dr. Horst Schumann and his relationship to the SS and the various hospitals and concentration camps where he did his ghastly work. As she spoke, Dr. Nowitz' eyes went wide. He stopped writing, set his pen down, and looked up at her in disbelief.

"You are working in a professional capacity with a current patient to bring a former Nazi to justice?" He was too overwhelmed to speak clearly and she did not feel that she should answer his question by repeating herself. "Horace Krämer, did you say?" Dr. Nowitz asked.

"Yes," Freda answered curtly, waiting for the flood of indignation that was certain to follow.

Freda had been treating Horace Krämer for nearly two years now, mostly for depression arising from his propensity to dress up in women's clothes and frequent the Red Light District. He had been pressed into service at his father's accounting firm and showed a great talent for the practice, but loathed it intensely. His appearance in women's clothing did not help the matter, but it was something he had been longing to do and finally done. There was little point in trying to convince him to avoid the activity, since it appeared to give him some kind of release or escape from his dreary life. One thing she had noticed right away was that, when he was talking about being Lolita or when he was acting as Lolita would act, his depression seemed to abate suddenly and completely. His alter ego was free and relatable in a way that the depressed Horace was not.

In their sessions, Freda learned a great deal about his accounting practice, since that was the aspect of his life he hated the most, but he also complained of being alone since he felt he had nothing to offer as a partner and his father would never accept his being in a relationship with a man. At first, she found herself feeling irritated when he droned on for session after session about how repressed he felt and how bored he was with the profession, but she was able to pay attention and as she allowed him to go on about it, she discovered something. He was searching for meaning in his life. Helping wealthy aristocrats accumulate more wealth was certainly not fulfilling to him, but he was prideful of his father's business so when he was given a task of some menial research or an investigatory project, he dug into it with a vengeance.

Freda had disclosed nothing of her correspondence with the Documentation Centre of the Association of Jewish Victims of the Nazi Regime which she was using to try to find information on war criminals that had escaped prosecution, but she decided after several months, to approach Horace with a proposal. She explained how each person left a money trail, something he knew all too well, but this money trail could be used to locate former Nazi criminals, politicians, and doctors. He was very interested, having been told as a child of the horrors of the war and how many family and family friends had fallen victim, either to the Nazis directly, or to the bombings and violence of the war itself. When she explained how someone with his skills could bring about good outcomes and gain justice for the deceased and the survivors, he seemed very interested. Freda did not want to press the matter, but the very next time they met, Horace brought with him a chart of lines connecting points. It was all very confusing so he explained it to her patiently. She was certainly out of her element, but soon she began to understand that he was showing her a map of financial relationships; routes of investigation which he could use to help her.

Wilhelm was at a loss for words. Being a mindful man, he was not about to berate Freda for complicating her relationship with one of her patients. However, it could be considered unethical to do what she had done. Freda waited patiently as he pondered, started to speak, then stopped, started again, stopped again. Finally, he asked a simple question. "Was the result of your actions worth the potential risks?"

It was Freda's turn to be stunned. She had fully expected to be the target of the elderly man's wrath, but he had surprised her. Once again, she had underestimated his wisdom and experience and she felt somewhat ashamed for her preconception.

Freda hesitated so Dr. Nowitz preempted her, saying "You have surprised me, not once, but twice in the same day. Please do not mistake me. I do not mind listening to whatever my clients have to say, but I have deep reservations with involving them in my personal activities outside our treatment relationship. Would you care to explain?"

"Thank you for that, *Herr Doktor*. I would like to explain. I, too, think it inadvisable to become involved in any way with a patient outside the treatment relationship, but in this case, I believed we would both benefit. Horace was looking for meaning and had a valuable expertise that he thought was being wasted. All he needed was an outlet for that expertise to improve his esteem. I was in possession of such an outlet and so I gave it to him with the understanding that we would exchange services in trade. I would provide for his treatment and he would help me with my investigations. We also agreed that we would keep those dealings separate from his treatment sessions so they would not interfere with giving him the mental health care he deserves. I must also say that his help with my investigations has been remarkable. He is very talented at what he does."

"And has this arrangement worked for you both?" Dr. Nowitz asked.

"I think it has been remarkably positive for both of us. Mr. Krämer has found such great meaning and motivation in this cause that it has augmented every aspect of our relationship. He has been so remarkably effective at providing me with an outlet for my efforts that I have benefited immensely from the relationship as well." The smile on Freda's face revealed her satisfaction with the whole arrangement, but she was understandably concerned about what Wilhelm might say. She waited for his reply but he went back to writing in his notebook, smiling.

"What is so funny?" she asked cautiously.

With a chuckle that shook his shoulders, he paused writing to look back up at her. "I am just pleased to see that you are broadening your horizons."

"I am sorry, but I don't see what you mean," Freda was a bit befuddled by his amusement.

"Would you say that your patient's quality of life has improved?" he asked.

"Yes."

"Would you say that your own quality of life has improved?" he followed.

"Yes."

"Is there any risk of you becoming romantically involved with a homosexual accountant who enjoys dressing in women's clothing?" He was beginning to smile again and worse, it was becoming infectious.

"Certainly not!" Freda couldn't help but smile at that question.

"Please list the negative consequences of this relationship," he asked as he attempted to force a look of seriousness onto his face.

Freda sat, fighting back a chuckle. She knew she had been cornered and could find no way out, so she gave a grudging smile she couldn't really keep to herself. He too was struggling to regain some seriousness and eventually succeeded.

"Freda, you are well trained, experienced enough to know when to protect yourself and your patients, careful enough to examine every aspect of a method before you attempt it, and have enough sense to accept a blessing when one comes to you. I do not think I can fault you for this, but I would ask one thing…that you keep the risks in mind."

"Thank you, Wilhelm," she said, looking up at him gratefully.

She had never called him by his first name before, but after this expression of kindness and understanding, it had escaped her lips unexpectedly. He recognized it too. He smiled and went back to his notes as she continued.

In their last session, Wilhelm had asked Freda to think about any cases which might be bothering her. His criteria were simple. Did she think about them too often away from her practice or spend an unusually long time researching their cases? Was she uncertain or troubled when dealing with them in person? Did she dread their sessions? In fact, there were several that fit his criteria, but she would not inflict all of them on the older man. They were, after all, in a professional setting under a time constraint, so she selected two cases that troubled her most.

Gerta was one such case. Dr. Freda had diagnosed Gerta with multiple personality disorder and schizophrenia. Often when one personality was dominant, he or she would hear the whispers of the other along with other distortions of thought that made her quite the complicated patient. Still, she seemed able to function in either state, so she was doing better than most people with her condition. She was a business owner in the hospitality industry, or what some would call the sex trade. Gerta, the female personality, was fun and carefree with enough cheer for a whole room. She was a brilliant business woman who owned the *Kabarett Seks*, the largest and most exotic cabaret in Cologne. At Dr. Freda's request, she had taught herself to keep copious notes all day as part of her treatment.

The male persona, Guy, however, was terribly unstable, but he understood that whenever he arose, he was to read Gerta's notes immediately and carry on. He knew it was in his best interest, but when Guy emerged, he seemed to antagonize everyone around him. Still, thanks to Dr. Freda's suggestion, the two personalities were able to communicate across their transitional barrier. Guy was definitely not the life of the party, but he could hold a conversation if not pressed for too many details. He treated people with indignation on his best days, and on his worst, no one wanted to be around him. Gerta's entourage could tell which personality was in ascendance at any given time, so there was always a safety net ready at a moment's notice.

Dr. Freda was concerned about the Guy persona having had several sessions with him when Gerta was suppressed. Guy always showed up on time because the appointment was written in Gerta's notes. Still, after so much time, Dr. Freda felt he wasn't improving and that he was on the verge of becoming violent at the prospect of always being trapped in a body without genitals he could not easily "go get laid" with. He was a salty, abrasive character and a terrible boss, as reported by the staff at Gerta's club. He threatened people wantonly and often without reason. He even threatened Dr. Freda with violence if she told Gerta about their conversations. Dr. Freda informed him that she was fully capable of defending herself. The look on his face told her that her message had been received loud and clear, leaving him to wonder exactly how formidable she might be, but it made no difference. His own frame was petite, not manly or strong. He thought of her as a witch doctor, helping add to the illusion of power she deliberately created in his mind.

Gerta had been called a hermaphrodite by people who didn't know the medical terminology, but the young woman had been born with deformed genitalia involving the internal organs as well as the external ones. For the purposes of her session with Dr. Nowitz, the details weren't necessary, as long as Wilhelm understood her reason for feeling anxious about the dual-personality patient.

Another of her cases involved a young person who had been reassigned as female in her early youth due to another birth defect in which the genitalia had not formed properly. For parents of modest means, there was only one real option. Assigning her female would be far less expensive and risky than trying to reconstruct the child as male and they wished to give the child a chance at a normal life. What they had not understood at the time was that the child's mind was male. As the child grew up and began to try to express male-oriented behaviour, both parents had pressured the child to adopt a female way of living. Over time, they had instilled a deep sense of shame and self-loathing in the child who, as a young adult finally feeling free to express himself as male, found himself ill-equipped to do so. When he realized that he would never father children, his condition had taken a suicidal turn and the androgynous boy had attempted suicide on several occasions.

Freda felt for the young man because he had no choice in what was done to him. He frequently expressed rage at being violated and blamed his parents, who in fact, loved him dearly and felt such guilt and pain at his angst that they had completely withdrawn from any attempts to help.

She and Wilhelm talked at length about how she should find ways to compartmentalize her feelings when dealing with difficult cases, not simply to shield her feelings, but so she could provide more objective and qualitative care for them. At the end of their session, she was grateful for the chance to see him alive and well again and they agreed to maintain their standing appointment for next week. He was not excessively old but it seemed his body was not holding up as it should at his age. She would have inquired further but it really was not her place to ask and she had little knowledge of geriatric phenomena.

Helga came around the corner too quickly again as one of the tenured doctors clucked at her, furrowing his brows and nodding in her direction. She straightened her posture, nodded at him as if she was doing nothing wrong, but kept up her fast pace. She had been working unsupervised for four hours and she wanted everything to be in perfect order when Dr. Freda arrived. As she rushed down the hallway at a barely restrained walking pace, the syringes and vials she carried on a small, shiny metal tray rolled and slid in place. A large insulated decanter of hot water helped to stabilize the tray somewhat, but holding it up for this long always made her arm sore. Her rubber-soled shoes were spotlessly white and chirped with each step. On mornings when Dr. Freda went to therapy, Helga was left alone with her patients... well not completely alone. The orderlies would come if she ever needed them and the doctors, interns, and students strode through the halls of the old teaching hospital on what seemed a never-ending schedule. The building in which she and Dr. Freda saw patients, and where their office was located, was one of the oldest on campus. The University of Cologne itself dated back to 1388 when the Romans ruled over what they now thought of as Germany.

As Helga proceeded down the steps to the basement level, the light grew dimmer and the space more confined. She knew that the likelihood of her running into someone down here would be remote because most of the rooms were stacked with boxes of musty papers. The odor of old documents seeped out from under the doors so that the basement did not smell like a hospital, but like an ancient library instead. She was amused that the medical administration had chosen the farthest-removed corner of the basement for the so-named Department of Sexual Identity Disorders which was staffed by only two, she and Dr. Freda. A single office space with two rooms, poor lighting, and no housekeeping service was a message to them that their activities should remain quiet and out of sight of the more respectable visitors to the hospital. On some days, when university patrons were to visit, Helga would find the lights turned out in the basement hallways, presumably to further remove the two of them from important sources of money for the university, lest they cause the university embarrassment.

Balancing the tray on one hand Helga shuffled through her keys, unlocked the overpainted door and put the keys back into her apron pocket. She should set the tray down, but the maneuver she was about to perform had become second nature to her. She grasped the door knob, turned it, then paused. With a sharp push the paint that always stuck the door shut gave way with just enough force to open but not enough to fling the door wide. The syringes and vials careened around the slick metal tray and Helga's heartbeat surged as she compensated for the jerky movement. In a moment, she regained control of the tray's contents and proceeded to open the door as if nothing had happened. Dr. Freda had come down the hall once just as Helga was performing this acrobatic movement and gently counseled her on what would happen if precious drugs were spilled or an expensive syringe broken. From then on when Dr. Freda was on duty, Helga had always glanced over her shoulder before she performed the trick.

In a singular swirl of movement, Helga flipped the light switch with one hand, slid the tray onto the counter with the other hand, and swung the door shut with her right foot, giving the door a sharp rap with the heel of her free hand forcing it to latch despite the thick paint that often caused it to stop just shy of a proper close. The office was small and brightly lit in stark contrast to the dim hallways of the hospital basement. Even though the entire basement had been filled with other departments' papers and medical records, one entire wall of Dr. Freda's office was filled with old manila folders sporting colorful tabs and dog-eared corners standing vertically on long white shelves resting on metal tracks in the floor. What appeared to be the handle of an old bank vault protruded from one end of the shelf so that when turned, the shelf moved away from the wall revealing another shelf behind it and a pathway between the two shelves just wide enough for a person to enter. Dr. Freda had repeatedly requested to have the adjacent room assigned to her department so they could move the records next door and have some extra office space, but her requests always went unanswered. It was Helga's duty to keep the files organized and tidy so that none of their precious office space was wasted. She took this responsibility seriously, not even letting Dr. Freda put files back herself, but insisting that they be left in the proper tray on the wall.

She picked up the decanter, opening the door to the inner office. This was Dr. Freda's private space where she kept both her desk and reference books as well as an old chaise, and a cart for medical instruments with a metal tray on top. The desk was turned sideways so that if one walked straight into the room to the far wall, they would pass between the front of the desk and the two chairs patients would sit in when they were not on the chaise. On the far side of the desk was a small end table with a delicate porcelain teapot. Helga had no idea where the design came from, but the curling blue vines against the craqueleur finish were very pretty. Helga didn't really see the value in holding on to old things, but it made Dr. Freda happy, so she wasn't about to disparage it. Still, bringing hot water down from the upstairs kitchen was tedious and made the balancing act that much more challenging.

Helga set the decanter on the edge of the large desk and removed a delicate tea cup and saucer from the shelf underneath the surface of the end table and set them on top carefully. Dr. Freda always appreciated it when Helga had tea ready for her. The doctor was due in at ten-thirty, so Helga took a small scoop of long-leaf oolong tea from a small silver box on the side table and placed it into the teapot then filled it with hot water, setting the lid to the side to wait for Dr. Freda's arrival.

As Helga went around the office, straightening papers into neat stacks and putting reference books back on the shelf, she was, as always, careful to leave certain items alone. She and Dr. Freda had developed an understanding that allowed Helga to keep the office in top condition while not impeding Dr. Freda's work. The first appointment wasn't until eleven so there would be a little time for her to relax before the patient arrived.

Helga went into the front room to retrieve Mr. Krämer's file and when she looked at the clock, she saw that it was nearly ten-thirty. She placed the file forward on Dr. Freda's desk, and turned the tea cup upright from its inverted position. She continued about her work putting on some gloves and pouring a small amount of cleaning solution onto a cloth from an upper shelf in one of the cabinets in the front room. When Dr. Freda entered, giving the door a sharp push to break the overpainted seal, Helga was nearly done sanitizing surfaces.

"Good morning, Dr. Freda," Helga's exuberant greeting was characteristic of her usual attitude, but today, Freda was feeling a bit shaky. "Good morning, Helga," she said as she passed through the front office to the back. She had overdone the gin a bit last night and then gone all morning with almost none, so when she saw that her teapot was steaming and her tea cup was ready the way she liked it, she smiled to herself. She set her medicine bag down beside the desk and placed the lid on the teapot so it wouldn't cool down any more than it already had. She wondered if Helga would ever get the concept of tea service, but how could she blame the girl? Tea service with gin before noon? She really had no room to complain.

Freda took the tea around the desk and sat down to enjoy it. As she held it to her nose to breathe in the juniper and oolong aromas, Helga peeked in to ask if she needed anything before her first appointment. There wasn't anything, so Helga closed the door gently to give her mentor some privacy. After her visit with Wilhelm, Freda felt deeply appreciative of those around her. Helga was one of those precious few who could take adversity and heartache and give back patience and understanding. It was certainly a blessing to have the young intern in her service. Remembering that she had been meaning to speak with Helga about her new volunteering schedule, she called to her.

"My dear?"

Helga's shadow darkened the frosted pane in the old wooden door and she answered without opening, "Yes, *Frau Doktor?*"

"Please come in."

Helga opened the door a crack, just enough to see inside and asked "Can I bring you something, doctor?"

"No, thank you. I'm fine. Please come in. I am interested to hear if you have made a decision about volunteering weekends at Wiesenhof yet."

"Yes, but to be honest, doctor, I haven't made my decision yet." Helga was obviously embarrassed at being asked, but Freda knew that this would be an excellent opportunity for the young woman.

"There is no need to make a decision right away. I think that if you decide to volunteer, as many young people do, it would be a good step in your career," Freda chided her, but not sincerely. "Would you at least go and visit with the staff over there? I would like you to meet a young woman there named Mila. She is a nurse working in the admissions offices. She is in about the same stage in her career as you, and I think the two of you could learn a lot from each other.

"I think I will do that this weekend. It would be good to have something to do other than study." Helga seemed intrigued by the recommendation and Freda also thought she might like to meet someone her own age in the profession.

Dr. Freda was feeling more herself after having some tea and she opened Horace's file as Helga rose to go to the other room. Only a few minutes after Helga had closed the door, Dr. Freda could hear Horace's voice through the glass. He and Helga exchanged some muffled words and Horace came through the door without knocking, as was his usual custom. Stopping short and looking down his long nose at Dr. Freda, he turned to close the door more quietly than usual before turning back to her.

Horace was a dapper man, always dressed in the finest suits with his hair perfectly styled, shoes shined, and his ladies' pocketbook at the ready. His day job as an accountant at his father's firm afforded him connections, prestige, and relationships, yet Horace, as a man, was unhappy and unfulfilled. Lolita, his transvestite persona, was campy, fun-loving, daring, and smart. She worked at Gerta's club doing the books for free in exchange for the privilege of performing there on a weekly basis. This was his element, though no one would call him glamorous with his unfortunate facial features. Makeup can't cover everything.

"*Verdammt!* You are hurting this morning!" he accused presumptively.

Dr. Freda rolled her eyes as she closed Horace's file and stood to welcome him in. When she reached to shake his hand, he came in further, taking a step up to a chair in front of her desk before grasping her hand and taking his chair.

"How have you been feeling, Mr. Krämer?" she asked as they both sat down.

"A lot better than you, I would imagine," he snarked. "With all the wonders of modern science you have to resort to gin? Disgraceful!" He chided her with sarcastic sincerity only giving a hint of a smile after the jab.

"I'm glad to see that your sarcasm is holding up well, even after our many attempts to break it down," she retorted half-heartedly. She knew she was no match for his wit and only joined the sarcastic banter because it was his way of showing affection.

He sat back, staring at her intensely, eyebrows raised, but with no indication of why until she gave him a shrug and an inquisitive look. "I told you I would bring you some clothes if you needed them," he professed. "You were wearing these the last time I saw you! I see I need to take care of my destitute doctor!"

She cocked her head and smiled with her lips pursed. She was not wearing the same clothes as the last time she saw him. This was just another attempt to get her to dress more provocatively. If she left it up to him, he would have her dressed in feathers and brightly colored makeup. His comments were a window into his true feelings, despite the sarcasm. He didn't banter like this with people he didn't trust and Dr. Freda appreciated that aspect of the man.

"Shall we get started?" Dr. Freda rose, inviting him to rest on the chaise with a palm up, fingers outstretched.

There was no room in the small office for an examination table since Dr. Freda's practice was nearly all psychotherapy. Along the wall opposite her desk was an old leather chaise so patients could be relaxed during their sessions. She turned out the overhead light leaving the goose-neck lamp on, casting dim yellow-green light upward. The leather chaise seemed in much better condition than it was, but it had been heavily worn over the years. It felt as soft as sheepskin now and didn't even creek when Horace reclined on it.

Being at the corner of the basement meant that there was no need to darken windows or deal with outside noise interrupting their peace and quiet. With the door closed and Helga working on patient files in the front room, it was nearly silent except for Horace's deep, slow breathing. Dr. Freda was well aware that the energy she transmitted into the room would affect the patient, so she also kept her breathing slow and regular, her voice soft and soothing.

"What do you see as you are climbing the stairs?" she asked Horace, whose eyes were closed in a deep meditative state.

"My father is upset. He is waving his arms and yelling."

"Can you see who he is upset with?" Dr. Freda asked in a low, calm voice.

"No. I can only see his head and shoulders," Horace replied.

"Climb a little further," Dr. Freda instructed.

"I don't want to," Horace resisted.

"You are invisible...no one can see you. This memory is distant and safe, seen through the veil of time. Take a few more steps and hear nothing but see what is to happen." Dr. Freda guided him in a slow, poetic cadence so as to maintain his hypnotic state.

As Horace ascended the basement steps a bit more, he could see the top of his *Mutter's* head. He recognized her golden hair pinned back the way she always wore it. He could see that his father was very animated, but the movements were slow, as if underwater. He could not hear what was being said, only muffled voices. He rose a little more so he could see her face. She was crying. She appeared to be pleading with *Pater*. Their motion slowed gradually as his *Pater* drew back a fist. When his elbow reached the apex of the blow, far behind his back, the motion slowed to a stop and all was still...almost. His *Mutter's* hair seemed to glow with its own light and though nothing else moved, her hair seemed to ebb and flow gently in the warm, misty light. She had drawn her hands up to cover her face as if she were afraid to see and as Horace reached the top of the landing, she turned slowly, hair flowing, to look directly at him, abject fear etched into her radiant features. Very slowly, she began to yell something at him and though he could not hear, he felt her command take hold of his soul as she tried to protect him... *"Lauf weg!"* ("Run away!"). Horace started awake, tears streaming down his face. Freda was standing next to him handing him a handkerchief.

"You always knew, didn't you?" Dr. Freda asked.

"I think I did, but I only remembered him hitting me when he was angry, never her."

As Horace sat up, taking a handkerchief from Freda, he swung his legs off the chaise and sat forward, staring down at his hands. Freda returned to her chair at the foot of the chaise, taking up her notepad and pen before sitting.

As she began to write she asked, "Do you remember if this was a common occurrence?"

Horace was still weeping, but his tears intensified as he answered, "Yes, I think all the time." He raised the kerchief to catch the tears as he went on. "I should have done something to protect her but I was always hiding until he found me. I should have been there for her."

"You each had your own way of handling a man who was too angry to control himself. Whether or not you think you *should* have done something differently, you *could* not have." She finished appending her notes and looked up at him. He was regaining his composure somewhat so she continued. "I will not tell you not to blame yourself because it appears you already do, but I will say this. Your mother loved you or she would not have tried to protect you...and if she loved you, she would want you to forgive yourself and live a happy life."

He nodded to himself and said "Yes, I believe she would. Thank you doctor."

Horace was still sporting the bruise on his left cheek that he got from a particularly unruly young man this past weekend. He wasn't the type of man to pick fights. He had a shorter build than most as well as a slight frame. His most noticeable feature was his large, Roman nose. His father had always joked, somewhat maliciously, that Horace must not have been his child because no one in his family had a nose like that. Actually, when Horace was young, just after the war, he attended a family reunion at which many of his extended family did, in fact, have more pronounced features like his, though none so obvious.

Since those days, Horace had come to understand what his mother had been saying about him being "special" with that being the reason his father was always so angry. Horace knew he was different when he was very young but he didn't understand how or why. He only knew that he liked the things that girls his age liked. He liked to play dress up and would create various characters from clothing in the basement waiting to be washed. He would play with boys and girls in the neighborhood equally and didn't understand why his father tried to limit his associations to boys only. He was very clean and orderly when most of the boys he knew were messy and dirty. It wasn't until his hormones began raging as a teenager that he noticed his desires were aimed in a different direction than most others his age. When he was with his male friends, they would be talking about this girl or that when all he wanted was to talk about this boy or that. At the same time he began to understand that he was different, he also began to try to hide the fact, but was never successful.

As a young man, his father dressed him in a suit, brought him into the accounting business, and insisted that he behave professionally and "...like he sees other men behave..." which Horace took to mean that he shouldn't behave like himself. Horace was very successful and as his knowledge of the intricacies of accounting, banking, and finance grew, so did his value to the company. As he became more skilled at hiding his undesirable behaviours, his father began to complain less and less until Horace noticed one day that his father had not berated him for weeks. Yet through all this, he felt unfulfilled. He was constantly unhappy, especially when clients would insist that "men should look out for each other" and would he "mind making this problem just go away?" When he took care of a good client's problems with some trickery of numbers, his father would congratulate him on a job well done and remark "I never thought you'd come around!" Horace hated every minute of helping wealthy men with no scruples cheat their way out of their obligations.

He came to Dr. Freda because he felt he was approaching a nervous breakdown and had no one he could turn to who would not then betray him to his father. He had no real friends, no sympathetic family, and no colleagues he trusted to hear how he really felt. Dr. Freda had been his counselor and confidant for over a year and when she had explained her proposal to him, he could not refuse. She offered him a way to help bring some measure of justice to the world instead of always being taken advantage of for the benefit of men who did not deserve it. They had thoroughly discussed the risks of complicating their relationship in this way and they both agreed that they would keep the two professional functions separate and distinct and so far it had not been a problem, but something was changing.

In their more frequent dealings, Dr. Freda had begun to open up to him in a more friendly tone and he had found himself doing the same. They had not become personal friends exactly, but had developed a mutual concern and a rapport that went beyond a professional relationship. Her feeling was that he had come to think of her as his sister, or maybe one of his entourage of working performers. The endearment wasn't unwelcome. In fact, Freda had grown quite fond of Horace recently and she enjoyed their time together, though it was always within a professional setting.

The proposal was this: Dr. Freda Dudek had been sending money to investigators and organizations around Germany and Europe in an effort to hunt down war criminals of the Third Reich. War criminals who had escaped the Nuremberg investigations and fled the country should be hunted down, but the resources of the groups to which she contributed were limited. Money wasn't that much of an issue. Neither was motivation. These groups had more volunteers than they could use. The problem was that information was lacking. As Dr. Freda described her extra-curricular activities, Horace began to show a deep interest until his eyes went wide with realization. Freda stopped her explanations and waited for the idea to mature in his mind. When he explained that everyone leaves a paper trail behind based on how they transfer and use money, Dr. Freda's eyes lit up. Here was a man with the banking and financial connections it would take to trace these criminals' activities, even from the other side of the globe!

It was then that they decided to dispense with Horace's payment for treatment and instead offer each other's services in trade. She would treat him and he would make inquiries for her, and whatever the outcome on either side, they would be even. In fact, as she began to teach Horace about her previous investigations, he began to form connections in his mind and she saw him begin to blossom. His treatment sessions went well. His outlook improved. His depression and despair abated. While she tried to make it a point never to become involved with a patient outside work, it warmed her heart to see him experience happiness and fulfillment in the services he provided for her.

Chapter 2

Helga's earliest memories weren't like the prodigies in her psychiatry classes saying that they could remember being infants. Her earliest memory was of being a little boy pulling his mother's favourite dress down from a hanger in her closet. Instead of just one coming down, several dresses, skirts, and blouses fell on him as he laughed and squealed. She could remember the way the various fabrics felt against her face as she dug her way out of the pile. The smell of her mother's perfume permeated everything in the closet. She also remembered the look of disapproval on her father's face when he found the boy playing dress-up in his mother's clothes.

As Heinrich grew up, there were occasionally times when he knew that he was different. Throughout grade school and high school, he was often singled out by one bully or another for his shocking red hair and freckles. During many of these pushing sessions, the boys would call him *die fee* (the fairy) or *abweichend vom Junge* (boy deviant or not really a boy), punching him hard on the arm as they passed. Once, in the eighth grade, Heinrich returned home from school with blood on his shirt, a deep cut on his lip, and bruises on his cheek and ear. Instead of consoling him or becoming angry at the perpetrators, his mother had placed the blame on him.

"You should be more careful not to incite them. If you watched how they behave and did the same, maybe they would be your friends instead of teasing you," was his mother's only attempt at comforting him, but somehow keeping quiet and trying to disappear never worked. Only a short time later he would once again be pushed into a locker or have his books knocked out of his hands in the hallway as the athletic boys passed.

Helga never felt she belonged anywhere until meeting Dr. Freda, but one day stood out in her mind as the worst day of her life. Heinrich had been sitting in the back row of his mathematics class ignoring several half-whispered insults, giggles, and rude comments when the professor had stopped the class to resolve the disruptions by saying that he was sure the young man would come to his senses before he embarrassed his parents too much. "You see, students, some children do not understand that it is their responsibility to support the family's reputation. Now that we have our homeland back from the Reich, mothers and fathers are trying to rebuild and children who do not do their part to help rebuild the family's reputation do not belong anywhere." All of this was said while the teacher stared directly at him.

When Heinrich had been accepted at *Universität zu Köln* (Cologne University) near the end of his senior high school year, he had hoped his parents would be happy for him. His grades had always been high, but he had never received any accolades for his hard work. Now, he had been accepted at a prestigious university just as his father had before him and they could only seem to express concern.

"You'll have to change your behaviour," reprimanded his father upon reading the acceptance letter.

"I won't be there to protect you," remarked his mother looking at Heinrich with an expression of hopelessness.

There were many occasions when Heinrich tried to explain to his mother how he felt. His father was a lost cause, caring only about his own image in the community and at his construction company, but Heinrich always held out hope that he could make his mother understand someday. It just never happened. She was never able to see past the labels that kept him isolated from other people, so when he went away to college, it really wasn't an emotional experience. It was just a move from a place where he didn't belong to another place where he didn't belong.

The shock came when he discovered that college aged students were just as horrible as grade school students. He had been looking forward to a respite from the ridicule, to acceptance into a more mature group. When he discovered that his expectations were far from the reality of college life and it became clear he would be shunned, perhaps his entire life, Heinrich began to lose touch with reality. He began to deliberately dress more effeminately, which would in turn bring on more intense ridicule. Though no one actually punched or pushed him as they did in grade school, the older students' hatred came across in more subtle ways. One day, when he returned to his dormitory after a particularly disappointing day in class, he found his window broken inward. It was only later that evening when he had finished cleaning up the broken glass that he saw the brick under the bureau. It had apparently slid under there when it had landed on the floor. When he pulled it out from its hiding place, he saw a pink triangle painted on its broad side with the Nazi swastika painted in black on the other side.

The next day had passed in half-heard echoes, reflections of anger and hatred, the clap of books shutting too loudly, dangerous whispers that cut through his skin. If he moved he would perish from the sharp threats around him, so he sat wide-eyed and frozen. A professor had dismissed the last class of the day after ridiculing him for not paying attention. Heinrich hardly responded, staring down at the books he hadn't opened all day. "Will you be leaving, young man?" asked the professor in a distant voice as if dreamed from yesterday's memories. "Are you going to say something?" He left in a huff, turning the lights out leaving Heinrich in the dark.

The next morning, Professor Hiedl had found him still in the same seat, still frozen, sweating and breathing in short gasps, sitting in his own urine. She had called for medical assistance and the orderlies who came to take him to the hospital had handled him roughly, hoisting him to his feet, taking his books from him. *Frau Hiedl* had come with him to the hospital where he was to remain pending further tests by the psychiatric staff.

Dr. Freda came into the clean observation room at the Wiesenhof Asylum where Heinrich was strapped down. Though his clothing had been replaced with the requisite hospital gown, Heinrich had not been covered with a sheet so his legs were exposed. Dr. Freda thought he must be cold so she went to the shelves in the far corner and retrieved a thick cotton sheet and white woven blanket from the lowest shelf. She gently covered Heinrich and sat facing her new patient for many long moments, observing. He had been diagnosed as a sexual deviant with psychopathic shock showing all the classic symptoms of a pedophilic rapist and sexual predator. His attending physician had suggested that he be confined indefinitely, but in that morning's staff meeting, Dr. Freda had assumed responsibility for him and had him transferred to her department.

As Dr. Freda sat beside Heinrich, she observed a person in torment, closed off, completely sealed away. The accounts of the professor from the night Heinrich arrived were useless. She knew the report had been written by a classic chauvinist but perhaps she could get some useful information from *Frau Hiedl* who had found Heinrich catatonic the previous morning. She would be coming to visit later today. For now, all Freda had to work with was the patient in front of her.

"They tell me you are Heinrich Wolf of Bitburg," recalled Dr. Freda. "Do you wish to tell me what has made you so distraught?" There was no reply. It was no use now. It was too soon and whatever pain had caused this catatonic state was still too fresh. When Heinrich turned his head away from Dr. Freda, she responded, "I understand. We need not have this discussion now. I want you to ask for me personally should you need anything. The hospital staff knows how to reach me at my home." She waited for any sign of acknowledgment, but none was forthcoming, so she continued, "I will come to see you in the morning." Rising to place her hand on Heinrich's leather-strapped wrist, she lowered her voice. "I can see that you are in great pain. I will help you if I can. If you want that help and you want to get better, please work with me tomorrow. In the meantime, I want you to rest, *Herr Heinrich*."

Chapter 3

As Dr. Freda walked up the steps to the Wiesenhof Asylum for her weekly rounds, she realized that she was underdressed for the day. A heavy woolen skirt and shawl were not enough layers for the walk from the train station and she felt chilled to the bone. This evening would not be pleasant. She would have to walk back to the train station at dusk while the temperature was falling. The gray mist of the day would certainly have settled into a chilling fog by then, but she did not keep any extra clothing or coats at the asylum. She would have to bear the uncomfortable return trip. Today was Wednesday, the day after a very productive visit to her therapist, Dr. Nowitz, and Freda was feeling confident and centered. The large, heavy door swung open with effort and she stepped into the warm lobby. Her headscarf dripped on the entryway rug as she removed it and shook it off before stuffing it into the outside pocket of her medicine bag. Her hair was only slightly damp, and with the way she always kept it pinned up it felt like a metal helmet. Cold water dripped down the back of her neck, tickling her, but she tried to ignore it as she approached Nurse Mila at the front desk. Mila was buried in her work, but she was an observant girl and looked up as Dr. Freda approached.

Face blooming with a smile, she said "Welcome, Dr. Freda! How have you been? Heinrich has been asking about you."

"I am well, but cold from the trip. How have you been?" Freda replied.

"Oh, no! I'm sorry. Let me bring you some hot tea while you visit with Heinrich. Would that be alright?" Mila offered.

"Why thank you, Mila. You're so kind." Freda had always enjoyed the young woman's friendly demeanor and the little acts of kindness she sprinkled around the asylum helped to brighten everyone's day. "I will go to visit him now."

After a couple prior visits, Dr. Freda had determined that Heinrich was not a suicide risk and ordered the restraints removed. Standard procedure always assumed the worst-case until disproved. That way, whether or not someone was a suicide risk was rendered irrelevant. They would not be able to harm themselves if they were restrained until an expert could make a determination. As she came down the hallway toward Heinrich's room, she saw that the door had been left ajar, which was not asylum custom. Keeping patients behind closed doors helped to reduce the stress they experienced during their treatment. The occasional outbursts from deranged patients, though posing no physical hazard due to the use of restraints, could pose a psychological hazard to those dealing with their own mental suffering. Before opening the door, she peered through the gap. Seeing Heinrich's covered feet on the bed, she pushed on the heavy, wooden door which swung open to reveal Heinrich sitting up on an inclined bed.

"Good morning, *Herr Heinrich*. How are you feeling today?"

"Restless...I guess," the young man answered in a quiet, squeaky voice. "I'm sorry. The nurses told me I should keep the door closed, but I just feel so cooped up...so isolated."

"That is a good sign. I am happy you are so much improved. Let us do something different today. Let us go for a walk in the courtyard."

Heinrich's face lit up like a child just finding out he was going to the zoo. He threw the covers off and stepped into his slippers as he reached for the robe thrown over the back of the nearby chair.

"Not so fast, young man. First, we should talk for a while."

Heinrich deflated onto the bed, sitting with his feet dangling, too short to reach the floor. He seemed such a waif of a boy that Dr. Freda wondered if he were properly nourished during his adolescence.

"I am glad to see they removed your restraints as I instructed. Do you feel resentful about being restrained?" she asked carefully.

"Nah. I understand. You didn't want me to off myself. I get it." Heinrich's manner of speaking was very much like that of a street urchin or the sloppy speech of today's college students.

"I do not want you to misunderstand. Anyone brought to us in a state such as you were must be treated as a worst case until we know more so that when the worst case actually does present itself, we don't lose someone who could have been saved if we had acted properly," she explained.

"I get it. I really do. Don't worry about it," he said, excusing the use of proper procedures.

Dr. Freda smiled as she mused, *Young people are so resilient. They can go through such devastating events and still accomplish great things.* She did not move to sit down. Instead, she stepped aside, gesturing to the door, and said, "Shall we go?"

Without replying, Heinrich hopped down from the bed and bounded out the door taking a jaunty turn toward the communal area that looked out into the courtyard. Dr. Freda followed at a calm walking pace and when she saw that Heinrich was pulling away, she cleared her throat to let him know how far behind him she was. He glanced back and immediately stopped his bouncing gait, stepping to the side to give her a spot beside him. As she caught up, she nodded and he followed at her side, slowing his pace to match the older woman's. Freda silently marveled at the energy level of young people. Only a few weeks before, Heinrich had been brought in catatonic and he had already regained the exuberance of youth.

"Dr. Merkel and Dr. Schmidt believe that you are well enough to be making decisions for yourself soon. Will you be going back home or do you want to resume your classes?" Dr. Freda asked.

Without pause Heinrich barked, "I'm not going home." Realizing that he had raised his voice, he lowered it adding, "There's no place for me there. I want to get back to campus and finish my degree so I can get out on my own and have a life."

"We all want to do that when we are young, but do you not think that it would be prudent to recover at home where your parents can look after you for a while?" Freda suggested.

"I don't need to recover. I need for people to listen. My parents have never listened and they never will."

As they reached the door leading outside, Freda withdrew her keyring, found the correct key, and looked around. Procedure required that she establish that there was no one within range of the door when she unlocked it, lest a patient dart out where they would be more difficult to subdue. Seeing that there was sufficient distance between them and the other patients, she turned the key and ushered Heinrich through before her. It was chilly outside but the high walls would shield them from the mist if they kept to the north side of the courtyard. She would allow no more than twenty minutes in the cool air before they would have to go back inside, but she wanted Heinrich to be in a less restricted environment for this next conversation.

Dr. Freda led the way to the right, hugging the inside wall of the courtyard where the air was relatively still and the mist was not falling. Heinrich followed behind and to her left as a young person showing deference to his elder should do, but this was not to be a conversation between elder and youngster. This was to be between mentor and mentee so she gestured for Heinrich to come up beside her as they walked.

"Dr. Merkel, Dr. Schmidt, and I believe that you are correct when you say that you are transsexual," Dr. Freda said bluntly, not sugar-coating the term. "We find no cause for diagnosing you otherwise."

"Well at least someone here is listening," Heinrich retorted, though without malice. It was clear that he had grown weary of being ignored by adults. "What can I do about it?"

"We don't live in the Dark Ages anymore, so you can choose what you want to do about it from the available options, whichever ones are practical in your case," she replied. "You are not deformed. Your hormone levels are right where they should be. You aren't suffering from any form of dementia that we can detect, and you aren't distraught or in an agitated state anymore. So it comes down to this. Who are you, Heinrich Wolf?"

At this, Heinrich stopped walking. Dr. Freda didn't realize he had stopped for a couple steps. Then she stopped and returned to him. He was looking down, wringing his hands. She came to stand facing him and, placing a finger under the effeminate young man's chin, she lifted his face to look at her. He was crying. Clinically, he was either upset by what she had said or about to release something he had been holding inside. She was certain it was the latter.

He made no attempt to wipe his tears, nor to remove her finger.

She cupped her hand and placed it on his cheek and said softly, "Young man, you can be anything you want to be."

He sniffed and looked into her eyes and said, "I just want to be me." After a long pause, he continued, "I want to feel like myself. I don't want to be a boy anymore."

"You are not a boy," Freda corrected. "You are a young woman *within* a young man's body. Is that what you mean?"

"Yes," he said meekly.

"Proper treatment requires a well thought out plan with the end result guiding that plan and the process flowing from it. If we are to help you become who you are, you must clearly communicate who you are," said Dr. Freda.

As she stood waiting for his response, his tears continued to flow freely, but it did not appear that he was becoming more upset. Quite the opposite. He drew his shoulders back. He stopped wringing his hands. He looked directly into her eyes with conviction and said, "I want to be a woman."

"Do you understand what that means?" she asked cautiously.

"I do," he answered confidently.

"Oh, do you?" she patronized. The time had come for a bitter dose of reality. "Are you aware that the suicide rate for transsexuals who have completed their transformations is higher than any group other than the elderly and infirm?"

Heinrich stood aghast. The tears stopped suddenly and his mouth dropped open. "I didn't know that," he answered, suddenly less certain of himself.

"It is the difference between *want* and *need*," she explained. "Those who need to change will be forever unhappy knowing the option is available but never taking it. Those who need the transformation will accept the results, whatever they are, and live their lives being at least closer to who they feel they are. Those who merely want to change will reach the end of their transformation or stop at some interim stage and realize that they cannot go back. Forced to live in a body that is farther from who they are, rather than nearer, they begin to see themselves as *mutilated* rather than *fixed*."

The look on his face told her he did understand. He was not crying anymore and he was not upset. If anything, he was curious and open to learning more, so she continued.

"Let me ask you. Do you want children?"

"Maybe someday, but I don't think so," he replied.

"You will never be able to be a mother and you could only be a father by saving your sperm before the procedures. Do you want to have a husband or wife?" The look of confusion on his face answered her question. "If you are to have a husband or a wife, this person must be able to accept you for who you have become and all the complications that come with clinical infertility as well as the baggage you will carry having grown up male. Such a person would be exceedingly rare and so you must also face the likelihood of being alone, forever."

Heinrich appeared far less certain than a minute ago. He looked off to the center of the courtyard and up to the gray sky as she watched him work through his thoughts. The tears he had shed dropped off his cheeks as he closed his eyes. Freda could sense that he felt the weight of the decision he now faced. This was one of the moments that gave her the most fulfillment...not giving patients difficult choices, but seeing them see their futures open wide before them.

Long moments later, he opened his eyes and turned to look up into her face. "Will you help me become a woman?"

Freda smiled warmly, something she rarely did. "I will help you in any way I can, but the first thing one must know about someone when meeting them is their name."

Chapter 4

Horace sat on a metal bench at the *Melatenfriedhof*, one of the most beautiful and peaceful cemeteries in Cologne. Just a short walk from the front gate, next to this bench, was a statue of the prophet Jesus kneeling down collecting a lamb that had become mired in brambles. This was his favourite statue. It sat upon a grand headstone with arches of black marble reaching around the grave toward the walkway to form a small court facing the Christian figure. To his right, a pathway grown high with manicured bushes and trees led into the shaded distance. All around him were testaments to great people and great families with rows of monuments of stone and concrete. Hearing footfalls, he looked up to see Freda heading toward him from the front entrance. Her long winter coat blew around her ankles as the wind swirled and tugged at her. The chill this afternoon wasn't as noticeable since the weather had been rather dry for a few days. He wore a heavy black London Fog overcoat with a Russian style fur hat. Freda had her usual plain, quilted hat that flapped down around her ears and neck.

As she approached, he rose with his arms outstretched. She met his embrace, but with elbows down making a conservative attempt at a hug while he put on a show. From this distance, only Horace's loud exclamations of greeting were audible, but their exchange might yield some other clues as to what these two were doing together.

A man was resting against a pillar at a grave site not far away, but nearly out of sight of the couple. He needed to observe the two without being observed himself, so he kept his head turned and the brim of his hat pulled down to hide the fact that he was not there to pay respects, but to watch the two of them.

This Horace Krämer was a boring *pisher*. A moderately well-off accountant working at his father's firm, going out in drag a few times a week, always going home alone, and digging into things that didn't concern him. This Dr. Freda Dudek, on the other hand, was far more interesting. She was a noted doctor of psychiatry specializing in treating sexual perversion but instead of helping her patients, she mutilated them, however they asked her to. Dr. Schumann wasn't that forthcoming with any reason why these two should be observed, but he had worked for the doctor when he was a young medical assistant and so he trusted the old man. He wouldn't have reached out if he didn't need help, but this assignment seemed like nothing more than detective work...not the kind of work he usually did.

After the war, it had been difficult for a medical assistant from Auschwitz to find work. He certainly couldn't use his profession as a reference and the economy of Germany and the surrounding countries had nearly collapsed forcing many to leave or take jobs they did not want. In his case, he had been lucky enough to find work as a strongarm. Each month he visited the businesses, mostly taverns and bars, in his jurisdiction, to collect protection money for his employer. In return, he would also watch those places that had paid and keep undesirables from moving in on them. He made decent money doing this and he seemed to have a natural talent, but something more pressing had drawn him to Cologne this winter.

Horace waited for Freda to take a seat beside him on the bench before he sat down. "Do you think you could find a less comfortable place to meet?" Freda attempted to pull her coat tighter together in the front, shivering.

"It is about Schumann. I've found some information you should know." He took a deep breath and sat back, settling in for a long story, but Freda stayed stiff-backed. She didn't enjoy being out in the cold like this and, though bundled up, she knew she would eventually catch a chill. "Our man in Frankfurt has found records of him at a hospital in Sudan."

"What is he doing in a hospital in Sudan? Is he ill?" Freda asked.

"Apparently, he showed up in Khartoum, Sudan without a passport but used his own name when trying to gain employment. He is now the director of a small local hospital that serves the local population." Horace chuckled sarcastically. "If they only knew what horrible things he has done."

The hot flash of anger that consumed Freda's face was unmistakable.

"The records we found show that after he fled Germany, he was recognized several times after using his own name. He moved from place to place until he showed up in Africa.

Freda's shivering subsided for a moment and she asked, "Who is he?"

"Jürgen? He is a small-time thug who roughs up Frankfurt club owners for protection money from time to time. I haven't been able to find out much more about him but he used to be a medical assistant when he was young. There's just nothing special about him, so why give him so much money?"

They sat musing for a while but neither of them could come up with anything other than wild speculation, so they moved on to other business.

"We can figure that out later. Now that we have found Schumann, what can we do to set him up for capture?" asked Freda. "If he's fled before, he will do it again and we might not be able to find him again after that."

Horace put his hand to his chin in a thoughtful gesture and sat still for several minutes. "Well, I think I could probably tie up his money for a few weeks with red flags, but that wouldn't be long-term, and as soon as he realized something was wrong with his money, he might go into hiding again. Could our man in Frankfurt go down to Sudan to make sure it's really him? Just how badly does a white man stick out down there?"

Ignoring his snide remark, she asked "Aren't you sure?"

"Not one hundred percent, no. Everything I can check from my end matches up and our guy says he has people who can pay him a visit, but he doesn't want to do anything without a plan. He says that's up to you since you're the one paying the bill."

It was Freda's turn to muse. She was glad Horace had chosen such a public place to give her this update. The last thing she wanted was to involve anyone she knew or worked with in this situation. How could they bring this Nazi criminal to justice from over six-thousand kilometres away? As she sat quietly, thinking to herself, formulating next steps for Horace and the hunters in Frankfurt, the man who had been paying his respects several plots away began to walk their direction. She wouldn't answer until he had passed. He was a handsome man of about fifty years old, short graying beard, and dark hair under a dark brown Fedora. His car coat was a similar shade of dark brown fur with oversized buttons, but not expensive. As he passed, he looked at them in turn, nodding and touching his brim in greeting before heading off down the overgrown side path. No doubt he was bracing against the brisk air while visiting his dearly departed.

"I will have to give this some thought. Please put together a plan to freeze every mark he has at a moment's notice. We may need it soon," she asked of Horace.

He agreed to the request with a nod and said, "My, my, quite the little spies, aren't we?" rhetorically.

Finals week for Helga was fast approaching and she knew she was behind on studying. Immediately after her finals was her second procedure with Dr. Harry Benjamin. He wouldn't actually be performing the procedure himself. He was getting up there in age, but he would be personally attending the surgery to make sure the younger doctors did everything he wanted. Helga was so happy that Dr. Freda and Dr. Benjamin had agreed to take her on as a patient. At first, she didn't think she had any way to pay them for the very expensive surgeries, but once Dr. Freda had taken a copy of her transcript to Dr. Benjamin and they had discussed her grades and her plans for the future, they had both agreed that she would work for Dr. Freda after graduation and while she was going through nursing school to pay off the debt. This would also give her a chance to have Dr. Freda as a mentor, not just a benefactor.

Since dispensing with the name Heinrich many months ago, Helga had been learning to dress and act as a young woman. On Dr. Freda's advice, she met Mila, an experienced nurse at the Wiesenhof Asylum, who had accepted her as Helga the moment they were introduced. Helga had not perfected her appearance or mannerisms and was certainly not yet passable as female. Instead, it was Mila's kindness and generous nature to accept people as they were. She was very short, barely up to Helga's chin, but her heart made her a formidable young woman. She took a compliment with grace and charm and took criticism with dignity and conviction. She also did not tolerate anyone denigrating themselves, as Helga discovered on several occasions. Mila had first come to the Wiesenhof as a little girl when her own mother began volunteering just after the war. When Mila's mother had heard that the facility was understaffed and having trouble giving proper care to its patients due to the shortage, she felt it was her civic duty to help. Not long after, she had decided on a nursing career and immediately after college, began taking classes, sometimes taking Mila with her to lectures. Dr. Freda had known Mila's mother and when the widow had passed away, Dr. Freda was one of the many people from the community who came to pay their respects. Mila's mother was loved by many, and missed by all who knew her. It came as no surprise that Mila would have the same generous heart as her mother and be called to serve the sick and the weak in the same way.

"I'm not going to let you ladle that negativity on yourself!" Mila said to Helga one afternoon when they were having a rough shift together. "You know what to do. Now do it and make a difference. You can curl up in a ball later, but not when you have people who depend on you!"

Helga's grades were outstanding this semester. She could probably have taken her exams now and done fairly well, but fairly well wasn't good enough. She was determined to repay Dr. Freda with more than just time. She wanted to show her how proud she was to be working with her and how appreciative she was of the interest the older woman had taken in her life.

Though she was just getting to know her way around, Dr. Freda let her volunteer in her office in the basement of the hospital at Cologne University. Helga could not understand why such a notable doctor should be tucked into a basement corner, but it wasn't her place to ask those sorts of questions just yet. This morning, Freda was running late returning from her visit with Dr. Nowitz. She had called just before leaving to let her know that their session had run long and to ask *Herr Krämer* if he would wait for her arrival. Helga was studying Dr. Freda's filing system when Horace threw the door open and stepped inside. Closing the door behind him, he didn't notice Helga until he took off his hat with a flourish.

Looking her up and down pretentiously, he remarked "Well who do we have here? The good doctor has certainly upgraded her office!"

Helga was not impressed. She never had any patience for pretentious people and Mr. Krämer just reeked of it.

"Aw, now, sweetie, don't be like that. You don't even know me yet," he cajoled as he sauntered across the small room toward Dr. Freda's closed door.

"Dr. Freda will be late returning from an appointment this morning. She asks that you wait for her here."

"Well that's it, then." Mr. Krämer drew off his coat with a swirl that a bullfighter would be proud of before tossing it over a utility cart stacked with manila folders. Placing one hand over the other in a royal manner, he sat on another stool behind where the door opened. Mr. Krämer was impeccably dressed in a black pin stripe suit, starched white shirt, wide black silk tie slightly askew, and black patent leather shoes with white accents. His red stockings stood out so badly that Helga couldn't help staring at them for several seconds as she watched the whole production in silence.

Mr. Krämer looked at her once he was settled and seeing her staring at his socks, he pursed his lips like Helga's mother used to do when she heard something she didn't like. "You look like you've never seen style before! Tell me, what is a sweet young thing like you doing in the good old doctor's office?"

"Dr. Freda isn't old."

"Excuse me?"

"Dr. Freda isn't old," Helga repeated.

"She's much older than you, but far younger than dirt, my dear," Horace quipped. Helga held his gaze and then turned back to her work without further remark.

"Now, there I've done it. I've made an enemy of my best friend's little protégé." He lamented, "What will I have to do to rectify my complete lack of social graces?"

She wasn't taking the bait. Horace pouted with an exaggerated sigh and pooched lips, but she didn't look up from her work. He would have to turn up the charm if he were to improve the situation.

"How long have you known our good doctor?" he asked, deadpan.

Helga answered without looking up from her work, "I've known her for a little more than a year and a half."

"That's so i-n-t-e-r-e-s-t-i-n-g!" Horace drew out the word to indicate that she was being anything but interesting.

At this, Helga looked up at Horace who waited for more from her. "She has been helping me with my studies and with my transition," she said, hoping to shock the older man.

Horace clutched imaginary pearls asking, "Are you a boy?" That was a mistake. He knew it the instant he said it. The look of hurt on her face brought back so many memories of the times he had been teased and bullied that his pretense dropped to the floor with a thud. "I'm sorry, honey. I didn't mean that."

Helga seemed on the verge of tears. Taking jibes from people her own age was common, something she was accustomed to, but someone as old as this man should know better. She turned back to her work.

"I really am sorry. I just don't watch what I say sometimes. It's a bad habit of mine...obviously."

Still nothing.

"Listen. Let me start over, my dear. My name is Horace Krämer, and I'm a flaming homosexual," he blurted. "I am dashing by day and *gorgeous* at night...and I *know* how to please a man!"

Helga couldn't help herself. She choked as she raised a hand to her mouth, turning her head to look at him askance.

"Our good doctor has been helping me deal with depression and anxiety about being a flaming homosexual for about as long as you have known her, but I don't recall ever meeting you before." This time, the hook was baited with sweeter treats and he dearly hoped she would bite.

She began to smile. She canted her head toward him modestly. "I'm pleased to meet you Mr. Krämer. Apparently she hasn't done such a good job with your social adaptation."

Horace was impressed with the little thing! Faced with a ferocious *lutscher*, she had the nerve to take a stab at him. "Apparently not, but she seems to be doing a great job with you!" he complimented sarcastically.

She contained a giggle and smiled. "So why *are* you here, Mr. Krämer? You obviously don't have a problem with anxiety, so what is it?"

"No, if I'm being truthful, I make fun of people so they can't see how anxious I am. See? That's her therapy talking. She really is one of the best if *I* can come off sounding classy," he offered. "So how far along are you?"

Chapter 5

On days when her class load was light, Helga helped Dr. Freda. She showed up bright and early this morning to find the front office door unlocked, the lights on, and Dr. Freda asleep in her chair, leaned over the letter she had been writing. The ink was smeared and the smell of gin was strong throughout the small room. As she slowly placed the bottle of gin back into the drawer so as not to disturb Dr. Freda, her inebriated mentor opened her eyes. With a sluggish turn of her head, Dr. Freda looked at Helga and laid her head back down on the desk.

"Is it morning?" she asked with a cheek pressed between her teeth.

"It is six in the morning, doctor," Helga answered.

"What day is it?" Dr. Freda asked with lips drooping to the side.

"Why didn't you know? It's tomorrow!" joked Helga.

All Dr. Freda could manage was a weak smile. As she sat up wiping her face to catch any drool that might have escaped during the night, she looked at Helga's back as she left the room. Promptly, the nurse returned with a tray containing a glass of water, a biscuit, and some hot tea. *How long had this girl been in the office without waking me?* Freda thought.

"I was thinking about what you said the other day, about volunteering, and I think it would be a wonderful thing to help people at the asylum," Helga said in such a cheerful manner that Freda thought she might be sick. No, she *was* going to be sick. She turned in her swivel chair and dragged the dustbin under her as she leaned forward with her elbows on her knees, waiting for a relief that never came.

Helga took the opportunity to waylay the doctor. "You said that if I gave it proper thought, I should plan out my future and take action to bring about those plans. I have done just that." She laid a single sheet of paper on the corner of the desk near Freda's sagging head.

Temporarily buoyed by Helga's assertion, she tried in vain to focus her eyes on the paper without moving around too much. The foreshortened view appeared to be a timeline of events. She saw the words *classes, summer vacation, recovery, recovery, classes, graduation* and others laid out in a logical manner. She knew what she was looking at, but just now, it was too much to ask of her mind to digest it all.

Chapter 6

It was just days after her third procedure and Helga was feeling much better. She removed her stock and cleaned it, carefully and slowly reinserting it to maintain the internal cavity the doctors had created. This would be her morning routine for a long time, so she didn't really think of it as work. It was progress toward an ultimate goal. Dr. Freda had helped connect her with one of the best gender reassignment surgeons available and had even offered to sponsor the girl to pay for the procedure.

Dr. Harry Benjamin was her consulting physician during her transition which included hormone supplements and the surgeries which he directed but could not perform, given his advanced age. She had come to cherish him as a mentor and accomplished doctor of gender reassignment. Though he had been effectively exiled to New York when his ocean liner had been caught by the Americans in international waters during the war, he made trips to his homeland and other locations throughout Europe each year. He was such an admirable man. At eighty-five years old, he was quick-witted and smart, able to hold rousing debates with doctors a fraction of his age and occasionally trounce them when one made a mistake of accepted psychology or medical physics. In the last few months, he had taken ill and had been writing to her and her physicians from New York, but she hoped she could see him again before he retired.

She prepared for her day volunteering in the Wiesenhof Asylum. One could say she was blissful after the most recent procedure, despite the physical discomfort. The first procedure had made her question everything, just as Dr. Benjamin and Dr. Freda said it would. She was in so much pain! All day, she had to keep herself from pressing on the incisions. If she were to heal properly, she would have to alternate between packing ice bags between her legs and letting the area warm back up to body temperature. Applying the ice was painful. Once the area cooled down, the pain was greatly reduced, but almost as soon as the ice was removed and warmth returned, the throbbing pain was back. She wept almost constantly for days after the surgery from the constant pain. She even mourned the loss of her *unneeded bits*. As Michelangelo said, "The sculpture is already complete within the marble block, before I start my work. It is already there, I just have to chisel away the superfluous material." This was a quote she came back to many times as her transformation progressed. It gave her some relief to know that even a great artist knew that he was only playing a part in the grand scheme.

As she stepped out of the claw foot tub, continuing to dry herself off, she saw her image in the floor-length mirror across the water closet of her tiny apartment. She turned sideways to the mirror, noticing the curvy shape her body had begun to take on. Her hips had begun to fill out as the hormone treatments started working. Dr. Freda had explained to her that some things would change and others would not. Her voice would never rise from where it had been, but her breasts had begun to grow and her behind had begun to fill out as well. Her nipples were still painful and hard as the tissues developed. This happened to both boys and girls in early adolescence, but boy's nipples stopped developing after a month or two. Girls' nipples and breasts continued to develop for a long time and some of these changes were happening faster in her because the synthetic hormones were more potent than those produced by the ovaries she would never have.

She turned to face the mirror and convinced herself to drop the towel. The scars were still red and the recovery was far from over, but she forced herself to look at her body as a work in progress...and she felt happy. She had been deeply afraid that she would see herself and be appalled by what she had done. From what she knew of psychology, if she saw herself as mutilated, she would know that she had made the wrong choice, but as she stood before the mirror, she felt no remorse, no grief at the loss of her *Little Heinrich*. She felt as if something foreign had been removed, like a growth or a tumor.

She allowed the thought of children to rise in her mind. As she rolled the idea around, she discovered that, yes, she regretted having to give up ever having her own children, but she also realized that it was a longing to carry a child, not father a child, that she felt. It really didn't matter if she was Heinrich or Helga, neither would ever carry a child so that was a longing that would never be fulfilled. If she ever met a man who wanted children, he would have to be open to the idea of adoption or the relationship probably would not work out.

Rather than feel an aversion to touching herself, she felt a curiosity. It was not sexual desire, though she did have those urges and would have to learn new ways to deal with them. Instead, it was wonder at the craftsmanship; interest in the procedures that yielded this result. She also experienced fear. When she stood like this in front of a man, would he want her or would he only be thinking of her as a boy missing some parts? She noticed her mind wanting to go down that dark path but she surmised that every woman probably has a similar fear. Will he want me when he sees me naked? Will he accept me for who I am, flaws and all?

A smile crossed her face when she remembered her grandmother's wizened old face near hers, whispering, "Every woman has a secret or two that no one will ever know." Her memories of the grand old woman were always fond and as she allowed those memories to fill her mind now. She thought that Gran would smile if she were here. She remembered another time years later when Gran was in her bed, penned in by a railing to prevent her from falling out of bed again. Heinrich climbed up on the rocking chair beside the bed to get a better look at her. He must have been about five years old. Gran was restless, coming in and out of episodes of senility, but this day she had some of her wits. As she turned to see the young boy reaching from the rocker putting a hand on the railing and she turned to place her bony hand on his. Her skin felt warm, thin, and loose against his. She looked at his shocking red hair and freckles for a moment before saying "Well, now, you are the *special* one, aren't you!" It had been years since she had come to realize that Gran was referring to Heinrich's effeminate behaviour. Now, looking at her reflection, she said aloud "Yes, Gran. I *am* the special one."

Chapter 7

In his short, young life, Albert had never felt such pain. At night, he huddled with his two friends and they protected each other. Since the surgeries, they really had no need to worry about other prisoners preying on them because the doctors and soldiers had warned the other children to leave them alone or they would be beaten. The doctors were not interested in the welfare of their subjects but they were interested in keeping their experimental subjects in good condition. The boys knew they were little more than dogs to these men, but as long as they kept clean, didn't get infected, and didn't die, the doctors' interest would continue. Otherwise, they would die, be put down, or worse, have more drastic experiments done to them. They huddled on the cold mat, all three of them, heads together, clutching each other for comfort and warmth. Now and then, one would let out a whimper but if it was too loud, one of the other boys would clasp a hand over their mouth and help them hold it in. One of the boys, Gabriel, was in a particularly bad way. The opening where he urinated now was not healing very well and constantly weeped pinkish fluid. They were all worried that this might be the end of him. When he urinated, he winced with intense pain. The others could see the anguish on his face. As the long, painful days and cold nights passed, he finally began to heal along with his friends, Albert and Lukas.

Every day, the Nazi doctors would take them back to the room where they had been mutilated to see how their work was healing and to have Hugo Jaeger, one of Hitler's personal photographers, take pictures of the place where their genitals used to be. All of the boys knew about Hitler from the propaganda on the radio and from their parents' discussions about what was happening to their homeland. The boys didn't really understand why the adults were so fearful, but now they understood that people could do horrible things to each other. That is not to say they understood why. Friends, neighbors, and playmates would not play with them before they were arrested, or speak to them on the street for fear they might be seen by one of the soldiers.

One morning when things had started getting bad, Albert's mother had told him that if he were to see a Nazi soldier or one of the Nazi youth, he was to keep his eyes down and walk on the opposite side of the street or turn down another street to avoid passing them at all. Albert could see the fear and panic in his mother's eyes, so he did as she asked without question until the night the soldiers came to take them. He hadn't seen his mother or father since they were separated at the gate and there were rumors passed around the camp that they had all been killed or sent away.

Occasionally, elsewhere in the camp, the boys could hear yelling, sometimes followed by gunshots. This usually meant that one of the prisoners hadn't followed instructions quickly enough and had been executed on the spot by one of the soldiers. They had no patience and treated everyone in the camp with hatred and disdain, spitting on them as they passed or kicking them if they were in the way.

It was common to see someone being beaten and the soldiers would laugh and chide the victim as they did so. Either the victim would get up and keep living after the soldiers left or they would be dragged away and thrown on the back of a cart, destined for a mass grave. Albert knew that the limp ones were either still alive or had just passed, but it didn't matter to the soldiers or the doctors.

The boys were inseparable. If they were given a crust of bread, they would split it evenly three ways, even though they were all starving. They had more food than most because of their status as pet projects, but it wasn't nearly enough and as the boys wasted away slowly, they began to understand that this would be their life now. None of them had realized that being hungry could be so painful and as their bellies bloated from malnutrition, they began to accept that they would probably die. They concentrated on staying out of trouble and healing, until one day, they realized that none of them were in pain from the surgeries anymore. Healing had not been easy, but they would all survive. The boys knew this was not necessarily a blessing. Now that they were healed, it would soon be time for more experiments. The Germans didn't really care how much suffering their subjects went through as long as they got the results they wanted.

So they continued, for weeks it seemed, when one day the soldiers came through pushing nearly everyone toward a gate at the far side of the camp where a corral had been assembled from barbed wire and stakes. Then the gate would periodically be opened and a group would be forced through with shouts and threats and at least ten from each group would be shot in the head in front of the others so everyone would know what would happen to them if they resisted. The three boys were terrified that they would be forced to go with one of the groups, but after a few hundred had been gathered and passed through the gate, they realized that it was only adults who were being taken. Men who had been spared because they could work in the camp were being taken somewhere else, but no one knew where. The doctors made it clear that their subjects were to remain in the barracks until all the others had left, so they would not get caught up in the throng of emaciated prisoners shuffling toward the exit.

Albert didn't find out until much later that this was a death march. The Russians were moving through Krakow occupying the city and would soon arrive at Auschwitz and the Nazis wanted to be certain that there was as little as possible remaining to liberate. At the time, he remembered hearing rapid gunfire off in the distance and the soldiers were rushing around, loading trucks with equipment and guns, and leaving in a hurry. Most of the doctors left, but most of the nurses stayed behind hoping to be treated humanely by The Red Army as it took possession of the camp.

The fighting grew closer and more violent with explosions and dirt raining down on the metal roof of the barracks as the prisoners huddled together inside. The nurses stood over various groups in a valiant effort to shield them from harm. One of the prisoners was struck by a bullet that came through the wall taking away most of the flesh of his neck. The wound fountained blood as he leapt to his feet and instinctively stumbled toward a nurse trying to hold in the blood. With each step, his progress became more erratic until he fell on his face with a crunching thud that broke open his skull killing him instantly. He didn't even twitch. He just lay there, eyes open, until the gurgling from his neck stopped.

Gabriel, Albert, and Lukas closed their eyes, gripping each other tightly, hoping that somehow if a bullet came for them, they could shield each other, each whispering the same prayer: that Yahweh would take them and spare their friends. At some point, it seemed that the fighting was moving away and they could hear new people in the camp. The nurses all raised their hands while huddling with their various groups and as different soldiers came into the barracks, Albert recognized the language they were speaking.

"Das müssen die Russen sein," ("These must be the Russians,") Albert told the other boys.

The soldiers demanded something of the nurses who were still huddling with their hands raised, but no one could understand what they were saying. The nurses were taken roughly by the arms and, with their hands tied behind their backs, began to plead and cry to the Russian soldiers. At least it seemed as if the new soldiers were not going to shoot them dead, which is what the Nazis would have done without hesitation. The nurses worked themselves into such hysteria that the Russian soldiers began to consult with each other about what to do with them. Finally, one soldier left the barracks and came back with a man who appeared to be their superior. He walked in, confident and erect with authority. The nurses fell silent, knowing that this was their judge and could be their executioner. He said something in Russian and the nurses were set upon, each by one soldier. They began to wail with their last ounce of strength until they realized that the soldiers were only checking for weapons. Then as each examination was completed, they were untied as they stood there, speechless.

The commandant pointed at each of the nurses in turn and gestured to them saying, "Иди со мной." ("Come with me."). None of them understood what they were saying but the gesture and the tone of his voice made his meaning clear. They were likely to be spared. On their way out, one of the nurses, Marie Stromberger, Albert remembered, stopped in front of the commandant facing him calmly and asked what would be done with the children left behind using a sweeping gesture to include the entire room. He knew she would not understand him, but he placed a hand on her shoulder saying, "О них позаботятся." ("They will be cared for.") She hesitated, looking into his eyes and finally decided she would have to trust the prisoners with this man.

The children were taken along with everyone left in the camp to the center of the open area. Numbering just over two thousand people, this was only a fraction of the people who were here before the Nazis left. They were counted, questioned, and sorted into groups based on what language they spoke. The prisoners began to console each other, hold each other, and weep together. Some groups invited other smaller groups to join them but the Russian soldiers kept them apart and no one argued. They understood that the Russians were there to liberate them and they wouldn't do anything to irritate their emancipators.

One by one, each group was led by someone speaking their own language, out of the gate that the other prisoners had been forced through. They walked slowly, still weeping, their prayers going out for the nearly seven thousand people who had been taken away by the Nazis. They had all known that the Nazis were not taking them to care for them. They had been taken to keep them out of the hands of The Red

Army. Albert learned later that they had been marched to death, very few of them surviving, and many of those that did survive were executed.

Albert's group was not the largest. Only thirty-five German-speaking people remained in the small group. The boys saw *Frau Stromberger* coming back through the gate, walking to their group. She began explaining what was about to happen, reassuring the group that their medical needs would now be looked after. Albert remembered her telling them that The Red Cross had set up a hospital on site and that they were bringing in food, medicine, and doctors to treat them. When it came time for them to move, Gabriel, Albert, and Lukas gripped each other's hands so tightly their fingers hurt, but none of them would release their grip.

At the St. Lazarus Hospital, The Red Cross brought in many doctors, nurses, and paramedics. They certainly did not have enough beds for everyone, though they brought as many cots as they could fit into the hospital. For this reason, no one argued when the boys wanted to remain together, but the doctors and nurses needed to treat them despite their fear of being separated. Several times, when they were being bathed, the nurse or paramedic cleaning them, upon seeing their condition, would dissolve into tears and leave the room and another would take their place. Albert thought these adults should be able to handle more than he could, but he would eventually come to understand, the degree to which he had been desensitized by his experiences.

Across Europe, orphanages and schools became processing facilities where children would go after their medical needs had been addressed to be matched and placed with families willing to open their homes to these children. If an old school had been abandoned, it was brought into service as an adoption center to serve alongside the others. Whether nuns at an orphanage, or volunteers at a repurposed school, everyone understood that these children had been through things no one should suffer and there would certainly be psychological problems. Psychotic breaks were common as was unruly behaviour and acting out, but most of the children were quiet and withdrawn.

One morning, the three boys were informed that they would be sent to an old abandoned school outside London which had been converted to a humanitarian center that saw to orphans' medical needs and tried to place them into good homes. The boys had only one hour to ready themselves, but since they had few belongings, this wasn't a problem. Many of the children were being taken there. To Gabriel, Albert, and Lukas it was a whirlwind of confusion and uncertainty and they clung to each other, never letting each other out of their sight. The doctors and nurses understood and granted the boys their attachment without question. On the day the nurses came to take them, one of the nurses unknowingly attempted to separate the boys. She found it impossible to do so without using force. Later at the school, the administrators who were in charge of placement had several conversations about the three. They knew it would be nearly impossible to place all three boys together and doing so would probably enable the boys to become hopelessly dependent on each other. Day after day, the three boys were counseled on the importance of going to live with caring families and that they would be able to reunite at a later time.

Gabriel was placed first, but when the father became impatient with the boy's attachment to the others, he took Gabriel roughly by the arm and compelled him to leave the other two boys behind. Albert and Lukas knew things wouldn't go well for Gabriel, but they contained their objections as best they could, crying in each other's arms. On the way out, Gabriel's adoptive father told the woman at the front desk that they should be vigilant with *those two*, meaning Albert and Lukas. The volunteers shushed the rude comments and ushered the man out with his family, plus one.

Albert was placed next. One morning, one of the nuns came with an administrator to tell him about his new family. The Rabinowitz family had been lucky enough to find their house intact when they returned after fleeing the Nazi takeover before the war began. Ernst had retired from service as a rabbi and took a wife, Lena, and they had two daughters, Selma and Etta. They appeared to be a happy family with a good standard of living and a respectable home life. When the Rabinowitz' heard of so many children being moved by train from the hospitals to the schools and orphanages, they wanted to help. Adopting one of the children was their duty and so they were on their way to take Albert. They would be arriving the next morning.

That night, Albert held his friend as Lukas cried silently. Albert knew that Lukas would be alone and gave him constant reassurances that one day they would meet again. When Lukas was finally exhausted, he drifted off to sleep. Then Albert began to cry, for every minute that passed was one less they would have together, but he didn't have the heart to wake Lukas.

The next morning, the volunteers woke the boys early. The Rabinowitz' were due at eight o'clock and Albert should be awake, bathed, and ready to go with them before they arrived. As the two boys prepared for the day, they hardly looked at each other, having said their goodbyes the previous night. They were taken into the front lobby where they waited, each with a counselor sitting beside them in case some encouragement was needed to separate them. Today, though, they weren't holding hands as was their custom. The two women shared a few glances, giving each other questioning looks, clearly confused by the boys' sudden change in behaviour. What they didn't know was that the boys had made a pact the night before to behave like the adults and they were putting great effort into suppressing the urge to reach for each other.

As they waited, they heard a car pull up to the front. Through the windows, they could see two figures approaching. Though it was after sunrise, the day was dark and gloomy and when the two figures entered, they were dripping water on the entryway carpet. An older man with salt and pepper hair folded a large black umbrella and placed it in a tall urn to the side of the door as the woman lifted her veil to reveal a kind, careworn face. They apparently did not see the counselors and boys seated to the side and approached the information desk to ask questions. The woman there pointed at the boys and, not knowing which of them was Albert, their eyes played back and forth between the two boys as they approached with an overly-restrained gate. When they were close, they stopped, hands folded, and the woman seated next to Albert nodded toward him to indicate that he was their new charge. Both laid their eyes on him and smiled.

"Wie geht es dir heute, Albert?" ("How are you feeling today, Albert?") the woman asked in a voice saturated with kindness. Albert did not answer.

Ernst asked, *"Haben sie Dir viel über uns erzählt?"* ("Have they told you much about us?") Albert still did not answer.

The counselor next to Albert leaned down to him and whispered, *"Sie sind hierher gereist, um Dir zu helfen, Albert. Bitte sei nett zu ihnen."* ("They have traveled here to help you, Albert. Please be kind to them.") so Albert simply said, *"Danke Ihnen, Herr und Frau."* ("Thank you, sir and madam.")

Chapter 8

Many months passed and Albert was finally beginning to open up a little. Lena began to relax around him and the sisters had begun to tease him as they had each other before he came to live with them. Being from a faith of very conservative values in a well-off family, Albert was given his own room in the back of the house with his own lavatory. He was expected to wash his own clothes and the family had a washing machine which worked with a handle which turned a crank that rotated an agitator inside. It was much easier than the way Albert's mother had washed clothes with a washboard in the family's only sink. His current situation made it easy to hide his deformity since there was no chance anyone would walk in while he was relieving himself or cleaning himself.

Even before the adoption, Ernst had been made aware of the mutilation Albert had suffered and he had accepted that the boy would have unusually private medical needs. Occasionally, as Albert grew, a specialist would have to make surgical modifications to the mutilated area so that things would continue to function properly. If, for example, his urethra did not close flat after urination, if scar tissue had held it open, he would be prone to bladder infections and possibly suffer more scarring. Ernst and Albert had agreed early on to keep these doctor visits between them. There was no reason for Lena or the girls to know. The only time the subject came up was just before his bar mitzvah. Ernst sat the boy down before his coming-of-age ceremony and asked if he had any questions about how to care for himself, how to start a family, or how to stay pure in the eyes of Yahweh. The situation was so uncomfortable for them both that the conversation ended without much exchange.

Almost seven years had passed, yet he still felt like a stranger. They had done everything that a normal family should do together. They went to the synagogue, they observed the holy days, they studied the Torah. Selma and Etta, his two sisters, had accepted him into the family as if he were their own brother. Selma, the elder sister, was always offering her advice in a protective way while Etta, the younger, more whimsical sister, was always coming to her brother for advice. Ernst was a rabbi in the *Fasanenstraße* Synagogue in Berlin which had survived largely undamaged during the war. After the war, he helped repair the structure, originally built in 1912, with his own hands despite being significantly older than most of the other volunteers.

Lena was the matriarch of the family. While she deferred to her husband in most matters, her strength and loving touch were unmistakable. She loved and nurtured Albert as if he were her own son. Albert did not develop rapidly in his youth. When other boys grew big and strong, he remained slight. Instead of going through the typical adolescent growth spurt with a cracking voice and clumsy manner, Albert grew slowly and gradually. She was probably the only one in the family to notice this, but she said nothing, accepting him and protecting him as best she could. He was often teased and bullied by the other children at school; not just the boys, but also the girls. The children were probably unaware that they were being cruel, but she could see it in his eyes on days when he would come home and go directly to his room. He would do his homework without resistance, but sometimes, when she listened at the door, she could hear him crying softly and wished she could wrap him in her arms. She never did this because she had brothers of her own. She knew that Albert would only be more embarrassed if she intruded, so she kept her distance even though it silently broke her heart.

He was lucky to have been adopted by such a loving family, but sometimes he didn't feel so lucky. Even after so many years, Albert still missed his friends, but Ernst and Lena had discouraged him, in earlier years, from seeking them out. Now that so much time had passed, he found that the volunteer organizations running the adoption centers had not kept good records and his requests for information about his friends usually went unanswered. One morning, a letter came from the administrator at the orphanage giving the location and new family name of a young man, but upon writing to this person, Albert was sad to discover that, though he had been liberated from the same camp, he knew nothing of the boys Albert described in his letter. With each attempt, the pain deepened until he eventually stopped writing to the administrators and went on with his life.

To Ernst's great delight, Albert was accepted into college where he studied mathematics, the sciences, art, and philosophy. Albert was not optimistic about going, knowing that he would continue to be taunted by young men much larger and stronger than he. Unfortunately, he was correct. He bore constant invasions of his privacy when he was feeling down. The students were not yet adults and they could not resist the opportunity to ask invasive questions when he would rather be left alone. One of his counselors diagnosed him with *a depressive disposition* and recommended that Albert be exempted from social activities, but this would mean giving up one of his few passions, soccer, so Albert refused. Albert might have been small, but he was quick and agile. Albert was a respected player because he combined his innate talent for the game with his study of famous players and their historic plays. The soccer field was one of the few places where he could forget the worries of life, classes, and childhood.

Albert also excelled in philosophy which Ernst thought made him a perfect candidate for the Budapest Seminary, his alma mater. The beautiful old seminary had been converted to a prison in the early 1930's when the Nazis seized power, a deliberate affront to the Jewish community. A great weight was lifted from Ernst's heart when the seminary reopened soon after the war, having been converted back to a place of knowledge and worship.

What Ernst didn't know was that Albert excelled in philosophy because it was an escape from the way the world really was. Pure ideals never worked in the real world, but if they could, they would make everything predictable and measurable. His intensive study of philosophy allowed Albert to imagine a fantasy in which people treated each other with respect and kindness and horrible people were eliminated from the equation. When Albert received his acceptance letter from the Budapest Seminary for admission to the Rabbinical Studies program, he was happy that it made Ernst so happy. He was looking forward to playing soccer again having already received an invitation from their athletics department to try out. For two months, Ernst would pat the young man on the back and tell him how proud he was and that he would bring pride to the family. He would retell the story of Albert receiving his acceptance letter to anyone who stayed still long enough to hear it. Of course, Lena was just as proud, but her praise of Albert was much more subdued. She could see that the news didn't thrill him the way it did Ernst, so she would only tell Albert that she was proud of him in a hushed voice, laying an approving hand on his shoulder. Occasionally she would ask what his plans were after the seminary, but she never pressed the issue when Albert couldn't answer.

On the morning Albert was to leave for the Budapest Seminary in Hungary, he reviewed his list to ensure he hadn't forgotten anything. He didn't have many personal belongings...probably the result of having everything taken from him when he was separated from his parents. He would have to leave his soccer ball behind, but they would have many at the athletics department. He had packed all his clothes, the shoes he would need, and the school supplies that he could save money on by bringing them with him: paper, pencils, and such. One thing he must not forget was his copy of *The Brothers Karamazov* which was a gift from Lena. Lena had overheard him telling Selma that his mother had read to him from that book when he was younger, so Lena gave him his own paperback copy for his bar mitzvah. What his new family never knew was that, between the pages of the book she gave him, he kept his most cherished photograph; that of him with his two best friends in Auschwitz.

His copy of *The Brothers Karamazov* was the one gift he had that tied his two families together and, in his mind, made Lena seem more like a second mother to him. He had read it so many times that the edges were beginning to soften like well-worn fabric, but he didn't want to replace it. When he was ready, he headed for the train station with Etta, Ernst, and Lena standing on the stoop holding each other. They couldn't help remembering how it felt when Selma left home to study at the convent and they were feeling the same things they would feel if their real son had been leaving.

Albert settled into seminary life, having his father as an excellent example and source of information on how to behave, whom to seek out, and what not to do. Months passed and his studies were going very well, though he did have to take some precautions to keep his deformity secret. He was always careful to use the stalls when he went to the lavatory. He avoided courtship and other social rituals, and he was always certain to be fully-dressed whenever possible. Nevertheless, one day, in the locker room after a late-afternoon soccer game, Albert was standing in front of his open locker wearing a bath towel around his waist. He had so far been successful at hiding his deformity, but one of the other young men who often took special delight in tormenting him, snatched his towel before Albert could grab it and he was left standing there naked. All of the boisterous congratulations and bragging stopped abruptly and Albert knew as he covered himself quickly with a spare towel from the locker, that it was too late. Albert was in such shock that he just stood there holding the towel in front of himself, stunned and silent. Because everyone was looking at him, he couldn't do his normal trick of waiting until no one was looking, face the locker, and pull the towel around himself so no one would suspect anything, so he stood motionless.

None of the young men said anything to him directly, but as the shock wore off, the whispering started. They gradually went about their business, talking about him all the while, some giving him looks of derision, others too embarrassed to look in his direction at all. Eventually, the room emptied and it was safe for him to finish changing in solitude, but he found that he couldn't move. It wasn't that he was frozen with fear or anything like that. He simply had no will to move, or cover himself, or go to class, or anything. Confirming his worst fears, the coach came into the locker room, apparently looking for him. Finding him standing there, Albert looked up at him. The coach couldn't help himself. He looked down, directly between Albert's legs, even though he could not have seen anything through the towel Albert was still holding, then back up at Albert's eyes with a horrified expression. There was no mistake. The secret he had kept for more than half his life was out.

Albert was escorted to the truck after having been dressed by the paramedics. He had been standing in the locker room, unmoving, for over an hour when the coach decided that he wasn't coming to his senses. Rather than try to deal with Albert himself, he called the *Szent Rókus Kórház* (St. Roch Hospital) asking for them to take Albert for an evaluation. When the paramedics arrived, they found Albert exactly as the coach had, so taking care to dress the young man, they of course saw what the soccer team had seen. Being medical professionals, they had heard of such deformities and knew of their origin but it still came as a minor shock to them as well. Nevertheless, they slowly and gently escorted him to the truck since it appeared that he could walk just fine. They were no more successful in getting any kind of response from him, but finding his pupils responding correctly and smelling no alcohol on his breath, they decided he should walk with a paramedic on each side just in case his motor control was impaired.

When they arrived at *Szent Rókus Kórház*, Albert was a little more coherent. The two-hundred-year-old structure was in a nearby town in Hungary so they hadn't traveled far, though he was unable to judge how long it had really been. The paramedic that stayed in the back of the truck with him had tried to engage him in conversation, but all Albert could remember about the trip were echoes of someone talking as if in the distance, underwater, unintelligible. They led him up the steps to the small hospital and he was eventually situated in a room with doctors coming to ask him questions every half hour or so. They did not perform a physical examination beyond vital functions because they thought that might worsen the trauma. Ultimately, the head nurse came to inform him that he would be staying at least overnight for observation. The nurse left some books and a newspaper. She was a kind, older woman who had been at the hospital for decades and she said she would be nearby if he needed anything. She recommended that he get some rest and they would try to talk again the next morning. She set her reading glasses down so she could lean on the side table as she placed a hand aside Albert's face and gently kissed him on the forehead.

Albert wasn't in any immediate danger and wasn't suffering any progressive condition like organ failure, so there was no need to wake him for tests during the night. She would make sure he was left in solitude to collect his thoughts, but she asked him to think about what might have led to his being admitted to the hospital. Apparently, little information about the incident had been passed to the hospital. She sat for a while in silence giving Albert the opportunity to speak, but he only lay staring at the ceiling with unfocused eyes. She checked one last time to make sure his pupils were responsive, but since he wouldn't follow directions she could not tell if his eyes were tracking together. Because the state had come on suddenly yet he had no drooping of the face, lips, or eyelids, they were able to rule out stroke, as well as Wernicke syndrome, and Myasthenia gravis which comes on gradually with a range of other complications. She eventually realized she wasn't going to make any progress today, so she hung his chart on the door and went about her evening rounds.

In Albert's mind, so many thoughts were competing for his attention that he just could not focus on any of them. He never told anyone about his dreams. His mother's face, crying but forcing a smile...the pain of the soldier's crushing strength as he was grabbed by the arms and pulled away from her...the pain of healing where the doctors had cut him, taken his manhood, everyone knowing that he was an abomination against Yahweh, every friend lost at once, shamed and shunned, the embarrassment his father would feel when this got back to him, being thrown out, losing another family, breaking his promise to find his two friends from the concentration camp. What if they had died and he hadn't even bothered trying to look for them for years? The wailing cut off with a shot through the head, hundreds of times, sometimes lined up in the frozen mud, shot, thrown into a pile to freeze solid, frozen blood icicles, frozen vomit and dripping urine as a body relaxed in death, steaming fresh bodies atop a frozen pile, the steam slowing and eventually stopping, incinerators smoking, his own retching, fat dripping, catching fire, would the dreams ever stop? Would this secret ever be forgotten? Never, no more friends or family, never any peace, always nightmares.

Albert began to wake from his stupor. He wasn't sure exactly where he was or how he got here, but he knew that he was tired...so tired! He couldn't go to sleep or the dreams would just begin again as they always did. The memories persisted just behind his vision like a shadow in a poorly lit room. He looked around for something to stop the pain and weariness. There was a pair of reading glasses on the nightstand sitting atop a newspaper and some books. They looked like the cheap turtle shell type with thin lenses. He immediately knew how the glasses could help him stop suffering and end the hopelessness. There really wasn't anything left to lose, so he took the glasses and snapped the frames with a quick twist. One of the lenses popped out and landed in his lap. He dropped the glasses and picked up the lens. He had only one spare lens if this didn't go as he hoped, so he was careful to hold the lens symmetrically with both hands and both thumbs in the center of the concave side of the lens. With a quick levering motion, he pulled on the opposite sides of the lens while pressing his thumbs into the center and the lens snapped cleanly in half. The edges came out nice and sharp from the clean break. Even the points at the perimeter of the lens halves were perfect.

He only hesitated for a moment because he knew it would hurt, but nothing compared to the pain he felt every day keeping his secrets and memories hidden from everyone else. This pain would be quick and then it would be over. He knew that it wasn't necessary to cut his throat from ear to ear as in horror stories. It was only necessary to open the left and right common carotid artery with a two inch incision about one inch down. Then he would still be able to breathe and wouldn't choke on the blood. After that, he would still have time to open the accessory cephalic veins in both wrists with a lengthwise incision between the radius and ulna on each side.

He was acutely aware of the medical application of what he was about to do, and reviewing it in clinical terms somehow made it comforting. Specific actions would lead to specific results. It was really unfortunate that nothing in life could be as predictable. He clenched his teeth and pressed his lips together so as not to make a sound and he felt both sides of his neck to precisely locate the arteries. He would probably have only a minute or two until he fell asleep from the blood loss. He located the perfect spot on both wrists and noted where the tendons were so he could slip the glass between them.

He guided the glass to the right spot on his neck with his fingertips and with his other hand, made the incisions, first the right, then the left. Surprisingly, it didn't seem to hurt as much as he thought it would, but it did make him see stars instantly. Then the left wrist, trade hands, now the right. He could feel the blood coursing down both sides of his chest in warm streams, thick, smelling of iron. His wrists flowed very well, though it seemed he had cut one of the tendons in his right wrist while using his left hand. That wouldn't matter in a few minutes.

He took a deep breath and relaxed, laying his head back on the raised pillows. He was remarkably sedate, long before the blood loss would have done anything and he realized that for the first time since the camps, his future was entirely predictable. Since he had lain back, the streams had begun to flow backward around his neck. He closed his eyes, breathing deeply, enjoying the feeling of resolution and certainty. While the incisions did hurt a bit, he had done a good job for having no real medical experience and now they were beginning to tingle rather than sting. In fact, his nose and teeth were tingling as well and through his closed eyelids he began to see swirling flashes of blue, yellow, and lots of red with flecks of white that would flash bright and fade in a few seconds.

He had always been aware of the things he had seen...the bodies, the suffering, the frozen mud and barbed wire...but now, he noticed it was more difficult to see them. They seemed to be receding into the distance. The awful cold of the barracks, the soldiers that killed and raped the helpless without remorse, the frozen mixture of blood and mud, was almost too far away to see anymore. The faces of his two friends in the camp were darker now, as if a cloud of smoke rose between them as they backed away. His breathing was slowing and he wondered why the smoke didn't make him cough. He actually didn't need to breathe as much anymore so he relaxed into the sensation, relishing the soothing darkness washing over him. He was not upset that he couldn't take the memories of his mother and friends with him if it meant he could leave behind all the other nightmarish memories. He could hear someone speaking, off in the distance, a muffled voice unintelligible coming toward him. He felt a dull pressure on his cheek that made his teeth click together.

He heard his mother whispering *"Albie? Albie? Wo sind Sie?"* ("Albie? Albie? Where are you?")

"Ich komme, Mutter..." ("I am coming, Mother...") he whispered back to her.

Chapter 9

Jürgen Żądło climbed the steps to the old Wiesenhof Asylum. The day was bitterly cold, yet the bright blue sky and brilliant sunshine was enjoyable. His heavy fur carcoat helped keep out the sting of the dry air. The weather had been beautiful for days and everyone seemed in a good mood because of it, but the constant freezing wind had Jürgen wishing Frankfurt were closer so he could go home. Instead, he had to stay here, in Cologne, through each phase of his work. Today, he had an interview at one of the oldest asylums for mental patients in Germany. The Wiesenhof had been converted to what the Reich called a "euthanasia facility" during the war which made it a target for the British bombers. The British had always been "bleeding hearts" as far as he was concerned.

British intelligence operatives in the town had infiltrated the asylum in coordination with other teams across Germany because Winston Churchill wanted a clearer picture of what was happening. A big debate had been brewing in England about whether or not asylums in Germany should be bombed. At first, the people and the government leaders had found the prospect abhorrent, but on closer examination of the situation, Churchill made his decision to bomb not just the Wiesenhof, but every asylum throughout Germany. What the public did not know, but Churchill, Parliament, and the House of Commons did, was that every patient in every facility had already been killed and that new patients were being routed to those facilities through the vast machine that the Reich had become. Churchill unilaterally decided that not one more person should be put to death because they were mentally disabled, distressed, or otherwise indignified. At thirty-four years old, he had been an ambitious little *wichser* (wanker), creating the Royal Naval Air Service as a branch of the Royal Navy in 1913 as an answer to the times. When the Blitz began, Churchill resolved to "extract a pound of flesh" from the Reich along with crushing operations that were being used to exterminate the unclean and ill-bred. Jürgen still felt disgust toward the British who seemed to *want* the drain on resources and morality that the mentally ill represented.

The Wiesenhof Asylum was not one of the most prominent facilities of its type under Nazi control, but it was putting people to death as part of the war machine, so the British felt it had to be shut down. It was just chance that the structure had only been partly destroyed, but it was enough to shut the *Tötungsanstalt Wiesenhof* (Wiesenhof Euthanasia Facility) down. The structure itself was later saved by architects who felt a duty to preserve it. The structure had been rebuilt and restored to its original grand appearance, but in doing so, the architects had left little of the original structure standing. As one approached the front entrance, a visitor could see a bronze plaque that told the story of how the facility was resurrected over some older looking stones that were part of the original structure.

Jürgen pulled on the heavy, overly-tall doors and walked into a lobby flooded with sunlight. The high front arch of the building, made almost entirely of glass, might have seemed like a good idea to the architects but they did not have to work in the place. The nurses at the front counter squinted and shielded their eyes, obviously annoyed by the sunlight streaming in and reflecting off the floor, giving them a double dose of glare. As he approached the young nurse at the front desk, he positioned himself so that his shadow blocked the sun in her face. She immediately relaxed, sighed, and thanked him. He affected a pleasing smile he knew would disarm her.

"Ich bin hier, um Herrn Kraus zu sehen." ("I am here to see Mr. Kraus.") he stated.

"Herr Żądło. Bitte folgen Sie mir," ("Mr. Żądło. Please follow me,") she said with a smile. As she rose from her chair and turned to lead him down the hall, he thought *If everyone here is as trusting as her, I could ask for the lead surgeon position and probably get it.* The truth was, that ever since the war he had been frequently disgusted by how little people cared about who was around them. People were far too complacent, letting all types of low-bred people work in their employ or be friends with their children. In his world, it was obvious that the moral degradation of society was like a disease that ignorant liberals seemed to enjoy catching. Still, since they were back in control, it was necessary to fit in and act like them, regardless of how contaminated it made him feel.

As they came to the office of Mr. Kraus, Director of Personnel at the asylum, nurse Mila left him and returned to the lobby. He rapped on the door with his class ring and the man inside immediately responded with an invitation to come in. As Jürgen opened the door, he affected a warm smile of greeting and reached out to shake the man's hand. Over the next half hour, they reviewed the extent of his medical training, who he studied under, and where he had practiced, all of which was fabricated. The training and experience itself were true, but no one would hire him if they knew that he worked for the Nazis. The truth was that hundreds of doctors, medical assistants, and nurses had discovered that, regardless of their political views, they were lumped in with the Nazis whenever someone found out where they had worked. This made it very difficult for honest, hard-working people to find jobs after the war, so they all lied. They had no choice because the backlash of prejudice was now working against them instead of for them. It was all terribly unfair, but no one could escape being prejudiced by their surroundings. It was a fact of life everywhere.

He was to return in a week's time to begin his shifts at 8 o'clock each morning, taking every other Sunday off. He explained that he had no problem with the extensive schedule. They discussed the risks of being over fifty and doing orderly work; that he should take extra precautions to protect his back so as not to be injured when lifting patients. Actually, the long hours would give him ample time to observe. When filling out the application, he entered the name Günther Schuhmacher, from Frankfurt where he would return on his days off. Since home was only two hours away by train, it shouldn't cause him any hardship and he expressed his gratitude for the opportunity.

Chapter 10

Helga Wolf entered her name into the log at the admitting desk and as she did so, nurse Mila said "We have a new one for you today."

As Helga picked up the clipboard with her daily assignments she noted the new name and indications on the top sheet. *Albert Novak, suicide, high risk, restraint required.* She thanked Mila and as she walked down the hall to her orderlies' station, she continued reading. Albert Novak had suffered a nervous breakdown, and was transported to the St. Roch Hospital where he attempted suicide. Her heart ached for the man before she had even met him.

When she came down the long corridor toward the psychiatric ward rooms, she could hear the occasional despondent cries of delusional patients. She volunteered on weekends at the urging of Dr. Freda who thought that, as part of her transition, it would be good to help people who were much worse off than she was. As a nurse, she was always driven to help people and as she became involved with the patients and got to know them, she realized how much good it could do, both for her and the patients. She could get involved in their lives as a volunteer in a way that their attending nurses could not. Her job was not to rush around preparing and dispensing medications, changing pillows, and obeying doctors. Instead, as a volunteer, her job was to identify those ways in which a patient could be helped by conversation and human interaction and then to do exactly that, without any of the time constraints that hampered the paid nurses. She was free to spend the time however she felt best and it wouldn't hurt the asylum's budget. She felt a deep sense of gratitude toward this institution after they had helped her recover. This was where she met Dr. Freda and without that meeting, she might still be trapped in a body that wasn't her own.

Her normally jaunty gate was more tame as she came to Albert's room. She approached the door, slowing and listening to see if there were any commotion. She took the clipboard out of the tray on the wall beside Albert's door and read over the medications, the doses, and the attending physician's notes. If what she read were accurate, today would be a day of sitting in silence. Based on his weight and the doses prescribed, there was little chance the man was awake. She replaced the chart and slowly turned the doorknob. As she cracked the door and began to enter, the ripe smell of cold urine permeated her nostrils. She backed away from the door, exhaled through her nose, and took a deep breath through her mouth, holding it. She opened the door and walked in, all the while letting the breath out through her nose as slowly as she could. Dr. Freda had taught her this trick to use whenever she was working with certain chemicals like chloroform or smelling salts so as not to be overcome by them.

Albert Novak was strapped down in the same way that she had been after her mental episode. He looked so frail and thin. At first, she thought they might have recorded the wrong age on his chart. The man before her looked to be in his late sixties judging by his frame, but his head was turned away from the door. When she realized she was running out of breath, she left the room, took another deep breath and reentered. She would need to work quickly, but not to exert herself more than necessary. The breathing method she was using was notorious for making people light headed and causing hyperventilation once they left the offending environment. She came around the foot of the bed so she could see Albert's face more clearly. Now this was a surprise. He wasn't an old man. He was just very thin. On closer inspection, the unconscious man was quite handsome with a smooth chin and delicate features. As she came closer to that side of the bed, she saw that his bedclothes were wet and yellow.

"First things first," she thought. She went to the closet in the corner of the room and drew out a clean set of bedclothes and gown. She left the room and went to find an orderly to help her. Returning with an orderly named Günther, a bald man in his early fifties with a salt-and-pepper beard, they proceeded to freshen Albert's bed. Loosening his straps so that his wrists were still bound, but there was a greater range of movement, they turned him to his side, gathered the wet sheets up against him, and Günther held him on his side as Helga cleaned the rubber-coated canvas mattress on that side. She gathered the new fitted sheet around the two corners so that it was tight on her side and most of the fabric was gathered close to but not touching the wet fabric up against Albert's back. As the orderly rolled Albert's flaccid body onto the clean sheet, Helga took control of his body so Günther could pull the wet sheet away, clean the exposed mattress, and then pull the clean sheet taught, catching the corners into the fitted sheet corners. Part of the standard procedure for changing soiled bed clothes was to wipe down the patient and change the gown.

She had been sure to retrieve several washcloths when she was out finding Günther, so she turned to the table to get one while he was removing Albert's gown. She heard him gasp and turned to see Günther staring down at Albert's missing manhood. The orderly seemed frozen in place as if he hadn't seen anything like this before. In actuality, his mind was racing. This type of surgery was not common, even in the Nazi camps, but he knew it well. He looked at Albert and realization caused the blood to drain from his face. "Let's just finish what we are here to do, alright?" Helga suggested firmly. Günther nodded and tried to act naive as he regained his composure. *Well, he doesn't have much of a future here if something like that phases him,* she thought. The truth was, though, it phased her too.

As Günther gathered the soiled sheets and gown for washing, Helga thanked him and he nodded to her with a smile. Günther had already removed the slack from Albert's restraints so he was once again immobilized but Helga felt no fear. A man so heavily sedated and frail couldn't possibly pose a danger to her, or himself for that matter, yet under the padded leather straps around his wrists and also visible on his neck, she could see the sutures, holding the fresh wounds closed. The one on his neck still wept and she moved to dab at it with a clean cloth, feeling a bit uncomfortable about leaning in so close to an unconscious man. As she did so, Albert's eyes opened, though he didn't look up at her. His sudden awakening startled her but she remained composed and continued to care for his wound.

"Albert, my name is Helga. I will be visiting with you for a while."

Albert made no sound. He did not move. He did not even blink. He just stared through her at the wall. She was not used to such a quiet room, being the naturally boisterous type, so she continued talking.

"I understand that you tried to take your own life. I'm not here to judge you; just to take care of you if I can." As she walked around the bed, she drew the only chair in the room up to the side as Albert continued to face the wall. "I see that you are missing something," she blundered. Stopping herself, she lowered her head. "I'm sorry. I shouldn't have said that. People tell me I talk too much, but that's how mine looked just a couple surgeries ago."

Helga bowed her head in contemplation. The memory of the pain she had gone through was still fresh in her mind, but when reliving it, she was not resentful or despondent. Instead, she was appreciative and grateful. The pain was just something that she had chosen to go through, but it was something she knew Albert was *forced* to go through. She hoped to forge a connection with him, but he wasn't talking so, for now, it would have to be all her.

"A friend and colleague introduced me to a specialist named Dr. Harry Benjamin. He is the foremost gender reassignment surgeon in the world right now. Someday, I hope I can help as many people as he has. He helped me understand why I felt the way I did. He didn't just treat me like a piece of meat. He treated me as a whole person and he is helping me become the person I am on the inside."

She looked up and saw that Albert had turned his head to look at her. Her heart panged with pity for this man. Even looking directly into his eyes, there didn't seem to be much there. His eyes were unfocused, pupils dilated.

"Why?" Albert whispered.

Helga did her best not to appear excited by the voluntary response. "It is me. It is who I am. My doctors are helping me be who I am," she stammered. She was used to being questioned about her transition. It was part of the required psychological evaluation before her procedures began.

"Not me," he whispered, closing his eyes and turning his head to face the ceiling.

"Yes. I read that," she confirmed. "What they did to you must have been awful." Helga did not want to patronize him, so they sat in silence for the remainder of the afternoon. She spent the time trying to absorb his pain as if she were a sponge, or a martyr who could absolve whatever he was blaming himself for, since that was often the root of suicide. After a few hours in silence, Helga decided to do a little investigating. Once Albert had fallen asleep, she quietly rose, left the room, and went to Mila in the front lobby.

"Mila, did Albert come in with any personal effects?" Helga asked from behind Mila's back.

Startled, Mila turned and seeing that it was Helga, calmly answered, "There was a paperback book brought in with him. We put his clothes and shoes in storage with the book in the personal effects room."

"May I see them?" Helga asked.

"Certainly, but you'll have to view them in the office and leave them there since we can't get permission from him to remove them while he is sedated," Mila cautioned.

"Thanks, Mila. Would you mind?" Helga asked as she gestured behind her toward the offices.

"Not at all," Mila said as she looked at the other nurse manning the desk.

The two nurses exchanged a glance and responsibility was passed between them without a word. Mila rose and led Helga down the long hallway to the back offices.

"Can you tell me any more about him, Mila?" Helga inquired.

"The Suicidal Rabbi? Sure," Mila started to answer.

"Excuse me? The Suicidal Rabbi?" Helga interrupted.

"Sorry. That's not very nice, I know, but that's what everyone started calling him when we found out who he was. There was a professor at the seminary who came to see him the day after he was admitted. I think that's how it started." Mila seemed embarrassed by the admission, so she fell silent.

At the first door marked *Büro* (Office) they entered a long room lined with file cabinets on the far side and desks positioned along the front wall and down the middle of the room so as to maximize the utility of the space. In the far corner was the room where personal effects and valuables were kept. Crossing the room and coming to the desk nearest the door, Mila picked up the clipboard sitting on the corner of the last desk and handed it to Helga to fill out. Mila counter-signed and said, "Let me know if you need anything."

Helga nodded and Mila left her alone in the office. Helga was a little surprised that there wasn't better security. The door wasn't even locked when she turned the knob and walked in. The smaller room was lined with shelves from floor to ceiling and on each shelf, the support posts formed slots, into which wooden bins were placed. Names were written on paper tags on each bin, so she started on her left and worked her way around the room. There didn't seem to be any kind of order to the names on the bins, so she examined each one until she found the name Albert Novak on a bin at floor level near the middle of the far wall. She slid the bin out of its slot and carried it to the wooden table in the middle of the room. The table was large enough to lay out a large number of items, but Albert's box was not full. A towel, pants, shirt, undergarments, a pair of shoes, pencils, notepad, shin guards; Albert must be a soccer player; and a paperback book.

As she laid each item on the table, she noticed that the copy of *The Brothers Karamazov* felt more bulky than it should have. Turning the book to look at the page edges, she saw that the book's binding did not seem right. It felt as if something were stuffed between the pages. She opened to the front cover, reading the inscription. The book must have been given as a gift since the note was a heartfelt birthday wish. The book was well-used and the page corners had been worn round and smooth. She turned the book binding-edge-down and let it fall open in the middle. As the pages slowly relaxed open, she saw that an old photograph was inside. Its edges were curled and the pages bore two yellowed squares, one in front and one behind, where the photograph rested indicating that it must have been there for years. She took the photograph by the top and bottom edges so she would be certain not to leave her fingerprints on it and turned it so she could see.

The image brought tears to her eyes. It was of three naked youths. At first, she thought they might be girls, but seeing the scars she was all too familiar with, she realized they were three boys. Where their sex organs should be, were instead incisions closed with what appeared to be catgut sutures. She had read about the Nazis performing sterilization experiments on prisoners. Dr. Mengele especially preferred twins so that he could observe the effects of X-ray radiation on one twin while measuring the changes against the other twin. The picture held her fixated. As she stared at the three boys, she tried to estimate their age. Based on bone structure, lack of any body hair, and the small lower jaws, she estimated about ten years old, but given their state of emaciation, she could only guess. The surface of the picture was cracked in places, the emulsion peeling off at the corners, so she handled it with great care. The boys had obviously been ordered to smile. Their lips were pulled tight, but she didn't see any smile in their eyes. It appeared to be a medical photograph, not a candid one, because the boys were lined up against a gray wall, either concrete or canvas, she couldn't tell because the photograph wasn't taken in sharp enough focus. The boy's collar bones, ribs, and elbows seemed to protrude as if their skin were dried leather stretched too tight. Their bellies were not terribly distended, so their emaciation must have either been recent or they were receiving some nutrients from their captors, just not enough to live on.

On the back of the picture, written in pencil nearly worn away, were three names...Gabriel, Albert, and Lukas. Helga's mouth fell open. As she stared wide-eyed, she turned the picture around, trying to pick out which one was Albert. Could it really be the Albert she had just sat with? Slowly, she began to recognize some of the features of the boy in the center. At least twenty years has passed between the boy in the photograph and the man in the room up the hall, but some features persisted. The distance between the eyes always stays relative to the location of the cheekbones, which stood out so much in this picture she had trouble imagining them with flesh. The shape of the eyes was the same. The picture was black and white but she could tell that the darkness of the eyes matched, so they must be brown but there was no way to match the hue of Albert's eyes with a black and white photograph. Then she saw it. The two front teeth were offset in a particular way that exactly matched the way Albert's two front teeth were offset. This could not be a coincidence. The boy in the middle was Albert.

Chapter 11

Helga fairly skipped down the corridor, she was in such a bubbly mood this day. She hadn't been able to visit with Albert last weekend because she had an exam coming up. Her final procedure had gone exactly as expected, the pain was gone, and she was only using her stock each evening when she slept. She had been very careful to keep as clean as possible and all of the sutures had been removed. Though there was some evidence of minor scarring, which was expected, she only noticed it when she looked closely.

Helga had come to terms with her childhood abuse and how it affected her identity as a young woman when she began caring for Albert's physical wounds. She was often unnerved by the man's continued silence. The room was so quiet she felt uneasy unless she talked...so she talked. Other people probably thought she talked too much, but for Helga, it was just the right amount. Given no choice but to listen, Albert slowly began to open up, just a phrase now and then, and Helga could hear echoes of her own pain in his voice. She was convinced that Dr. Freda could help him; that she might be the only one who would be willing to help him. With her typical stubbornness, Helga had insisted that Dr. Freda come to see him to evaluate his mental state. The doctors had been keeping him so heavily sedated that he slept nearly 20 hours each day. She thought they must have classified him as a lost cause, not worth their time to treat, but Helga was convinced that he could get better and rejoin society.

As she entered Albert's room, she found him sitting upright in his bed. One of the nurses had raised the head of the bed to support him and he was drawing with his right hand on some watercolor paper affixed to a board with tape. His left hand was still constrained against the side rail and there wasn't enough slack in his right hand to reach either his face or the other hand. The orderlies had been careful to arrange the strap attachment far enough under the bed and through the railing so that Albert could not reach it even if he knew where it was.

As she drew closer, she turned her head to view the paper from his perspective. "It's beautiful," she remarked, looking at him with admiration. "Who is it?"

"My mother," he replied with a wistful sigh.

"She died in the war, didn't she?"

"When we were brought to Auschwitz and the children were separated from their families, this is how I think she looked."

"But that must have been a traumatic time for you both. In this, she is smiling." Helga's statement was a confused query.

"It was, but this is how I remember her then," Albert replied.

"It's beautiful," she repeated. She looked him in the eye with resolution. "I want your permission to bring someone to see you."

"I prefer not to have any more visitors." He resumed working with the black pastel and she noticed that it was down to a barely useful nub.

She took a fresh pastel from the side table and handed it to him, taking the nub in the other hand. "This would not be an ordinary visitor. This would be my friend and mentor, Dr. Freda Dudek."

"Another psychiatrist. Don't you think I've seen enough of them?"

"Apparently not. You're still here, aren't you?" She meant it to come out as a joke, but it fell flat and the cheery grin drained from her face. "You need someone who can help you, but also someone who knows more about your sort of problems than the textbook doctors you have been seeing."

"I'd prefer not," he reiterated.

"Oh, I see. You think I'm giving you a choice," she jabbed. He actually did smile a bit at that, so she continued. "Dr. Freda is the resident head of the Department of Sexual Disorders within the Department of Psychology and Behavioural Disorders at Cologne University Hospital. She's my friend and she's helped me a lot. I think she can help you too."

"I'm not going through any sort of transition like you," he answered cautiously.

"That's not why I'm suggesting seeing her. My transition was only the last step... something that made me more like who I knew I would become. I mean, if you wanted to do something like that later, that would be up to you, but for now, I just want to help you get your head on straight." As soon as she said it, she knew she had been insensitive and shot him an apologetic glance.

"Let's say I agree. What would she know about being a man?" he probed.

"I think you're a good *person*. She's a good person too. What would be the harm in one good person helping another?" She crossed her arms, watching him, waiting for more resistance. To her surprise, he simply nodded before turning away. "I have to get on with my rounds, but I will arrange for the two of you to meet."

"Will you come with her?" he asked.

"If you want me to, yes," she answered simply.

When Helga brought Dr. Freda Dudek to see Albert, he had recently recovered from the physical effects of his suicide attempt at St. Roch Hospital. The doctor avoided referring to this incident as an "attempt" because if he had not been accidentally discovered, he surely would have died. Psychologically speaking, Albert had killed himself. This had a radically different effect on his mental state than the dramatic event she referred to as a "suicide attempt" in which a situation is concocted, not to lead to death but to lead to attention and sympathy. In Albert's mind, the deed was done. He had no right to be alive or to enjoy any of the pleasures of this world...and he was definitely not seeking attention. During her investigations she had found an old photograph between the pages of a book in his belongings. Freda remembered being frozen, stunned to stillness for many long minutes. When surreptitiously questioned about the crumbling old photograph, Helga said that she had seen it in the personal effects room but couldn't understand why anyone would carry such a horrible memory with them, even if it were out of sight.

Helga had been summoned to the front desk to meet Dr. Freda this morning. As she rounded the turn at the back of the wing, she could see Dr. Freda waiting in the distance at the front desk. She resisted the urge to rush down the hall to meet her. Today was the day that Helga would introduce Dr. Freda to Albert. The asylum staff had been unusually resistant to the idea of someone from another hospital working with their suicide patient, but Helga pressed the fact that Albert's mutilation could be at the root of his issues and Dr. Freda was one of the most qualified people in Germany to make that determination. Ultimately, she and the attending physician agreed it would be in Albert's best interest if Dr. Freda took over the case.

As Helga approached the front, she passed through a spot where the sun coming in the high glass entryway met the reflection of sunlight off the polished floor and she put up her arm to shield her face until she got closer. When she was close enough to converse without raising her voice, she greeted the doctor with a smile.

"Good morning, Dr. Freda. You look all bundled up. Is it still that cold outside?" Helga asked. When she had arrived just after sunrise this morning, it had been bitterly cold with a biting wind.

"It has actually started to warm up a bit. I trust your morning is going well," Dr. Freda replied.

"Very well, actually. Albert's medications have worn off and he is lucid enough to meet with you...whenever you are ready. Would you like me to take your coat?" Helga reached to help Dr. Freda remove her heavy coat, but Dr. Freda declined.

"Thank you but it is still a bit chilly in here for me. I'll keep it for now. Let us go somewhere you can brief me about Albert before I meet him."

"Certainly, Doctor. Let's go to the lounge and have some tea. That should help warm you." Helga led the way, but Dr. Freda had been working at the Wiesenhof Asylum for many years and knew her way around. Before suggesting that Helga volunteer here, Dr. Freda had been asked to help the resident doctors with several cases involving "sexual deviants" as they were called. Dr. Freda hated such crude uses of vernacular terms in a medical setting, seeing them as uneducated and socially insensitive.

As they walked back the way Helga had come, Dr. Freda could not help but notice Albert Novak's room as they passed. There would be plenty of time to meet him today. She had her other cases covered by colleagues anytime she met with a patient for the first time. She never knew what she would find on that first meeting. Sometimes first meetings were highly productive and worth spending all day on. Other times first meetings might yield no immediate progress, but with every encounter, there was at least some accumulation of knowledge, so no meeting was a total waste of time.

They came to the double doors that led into the adjacent wing and just through those doors was the door to the lounge on the right. They entered and Helga gestured for Dr. Freda to take a seat while she went to the counter to prepare some tea. On cold days, the asylum kept a carafe of near-boiling water ready at all times. It helped take the edge off the cold when doctors and nurses could not wear coats indoors. It wasn't that the facility was run cheaply, but it was nearly impossible to keep a place so large with forty foot ceilings and a four-story lobby properly heated in the winter. Today, they were lucky. One of the reasons the lobby's windows had not been covered was the sun's light warming the marble floors. This helped to reduce heating costs and helped to circulate that heat more effectively.

Dr. Freda took her coat off and draped it over the back of a chair before sitting. It was good to see Helga feeling at home in a professional setting other than just her office at the hospital on the Cologne University campus.

A moment after Dr. Freda sat, nurse Mila poked her head through the lounge door and asked, "Would you mind if I join you?"

"Not at all, Mila. Please, come and sit next to me," Dr. Freda invited.

"Would you like some tea as well?" asked nurse Helga.

"Oh, yes. Thank you," Mila replied, and took a seat next to Dr. Freda, folding her hands in her lap in a posture of reverence.

Nurse Helga brought them their tea, and all three women lifted their cups to breathe in the first steamy vapors of the orange-flavored black tea. All at once, they sighed with relaxation. Each of them knew how stressful medical work could be and how important it was to take advantage of each rare opportunity to unwind and destress. A few sips and Dr. Freda was ready to talk. The two younger nurses, who were always completely comfortable around each other when they were alone, displayed some apprehension in Dr. Freda's company. She tried to put them at ease by not questioning them, but they had to start somewhere.

"You two know much more about Albert's case than I do at this point. Can you tell me about him? I have read the profile that the doctors wrote up. I'm not asking about that. I'm asking what you know that isn't in those reports."

Helga and Mila looked up at each other over their cups and it appeared Helga deferred to the more experienced Mila, so Mila began tentatively.

"Well, when he was brought into the facility, he was naked. The paramedics had covered him with a sheet and it was a very cold day, but he wasn't shivering. I checked his temperature from the admission records and he wasn't in hypothermia yet, so he should have been shaking like a leaf. His eyes were...somewhere else. He was unresponsive, but not completely. His reflexes were there, but not as strong as they should have been. The Patellar reflex was suppressed. That must have been due to his lower body temperature, but it wasn't so low that we were worried. He was nearly catatonic for over twelve hours, so we knew that the state wasn't the result of classic intoxication and he didn't smell like he had ingested anything like alcohol, opiates, or morphine."

"Yes. I have read all that. What I would really like to know is what you think of the man," Dr. Freda encouraged Mila to continue.

"I like him. He seems nice."

"Well that's not very scientific," joked Helga and all three women smiled.

"That is alright. Actually what I am asking of you two is your non-scientific observations. This information can often be more useful than a doctor's records," Dr. Freda assured. "Please do continue, Mila."

"I think he is very sad and he doesn't talk much at all, but when I am in the room with him, I get the feeling he is a good man," Mila added.

Helga, feeling a boost from Mila's disclosure, said "I have spent a lot of time with him. He doesn't talk much. The doctors here keep him heavily sedated most of the time, so he sleeps too much. I think if he had the chance to talk with someone, and if he were awake enough to participate, that he might get better."

"What can you tell me about the picture in his book?" Dr. Freda asked Helga.

"What picture?" asked Mila, interrupting.

"He has a book with an old picture between the pages. It's in his personal effects bin," Helga answered Mila. Turning to Dr. Freda, she continued, "Honestly, I haven't brought it up with him. It is so disturbing, I think it should be left to a doctor, not a nurse, to bring up."

"That was a wise choice, young lady." Dr. Freda smiled at Helga, a generous helping of pride coloring her grin and Helga positively beamed before her humility caught up with her and she lowered her gaze in deference.

"Do either of you think he is a danger to others, or just to himself?" Dr. Freda asked, bluntly.

Talking over each other, both young women answered "Oh, no! Not at all!"

Helga had the most experience with Albert so she took the lead. "He wants to die, but I don't think he would harm anyone else."

"One thing to remember, ladies, it is always possible to harm others without intending to." Dr. Freda gave them a serious look, first Helga, then Mila, to emphasize this important point. "When doctors take the *Hippocratic Oath*, we understand that doing harm may come from inaction as well as action." That perspective seemed to bring the conversation to an end, so Dr. Freda concluded, "Let us go see our patient."

Meeting with Albert for the first time reminded Freda so much of her early years. She was very lucky to have such academically inclined parents. Throughout her young life they taught her to take a dispassionate view of events and behaviours when making decisions, but what Freda remembered most was the love and support. They never passed up an opportunity to let their feelings show. It was quite a different experience than many of her friends who were in dysfunctional or even abusive relationships.

Both of her parents held degrees from the finest European universities. They taught at the best colleges in Germany and graduated many students with honours, the product of their mentorship. When it was time for Freda to go to college, she was accepted by nearly every university she applied to. It was still a difficult choice, because none of them had any courses in advanced sexual psychology. Her parents had always been open and clinical when talking to her about the topic and when Freda discovered that there was indeed a neglected segment of the population who were not being treated by experts, she turned her passions toward that void. She wanted to make a difference like every doctor does...to improve the quality of life for their patients, and above all to *do no harm*.

"Good morning, *Herr Novak*. How are you feeling today?" Freda knew Albert was moderately sedated but she wanted to see if he was still in crisis.

Albert tried to raise his head, but he was still very weak from the blood loss he suffered. His thought processes were certainly still impaired but he should regain much of that function as time passed. He turned to look at her and she could see the haze in his eyes as if he were in a dreamland.

"Who..." He began to ask something but abandoned the effort and closed his eyes again.

"My name is Dr. Freda Dudek," Freda said, raising her voice so he could understand her through the drugs.

The sound of her speaking seemed to startle him and he opened his eyes again. She saw that he was putting a lot of effort into remaining conscious so this would have to be a short discussion. They would have more time together in the coming days. "How are you feeling, Mr. Novak?" she asked loudly.

In slurred but still intelligible speech, he answered, "Oh. I'm fine. Just tired." He began to fade away again, but a question seemed to gnaw at him and he squinted in confusion. "Who are you?"

"I am going to be your specialist for a while." She proceeded slowly, giving his mind time to process the information, though he probably would not remember a single word. "I will be taking care of you now."

"Are you the one Helga told me about?" Albert seemed intrigued and raised his eyebrows momentarily before the energy drained out of his inquiry.

"Yes. Helga told me about you too. She thinks we would work well together." Albert was falling unconscious again and appeared to already be spent. She rose and patted him on the arm. "I will come and see you again when you have had some rest." She rose to leave the room when she heard Albert trying to say something in a low whisper.

"Please don't be mad at me..." He trailed off to sleep.

Jürgen read down the sign-in sheet in front of the personal effects room. He had seen Dr. Dudek and nurse Wolf come in a couple weeks ago, but he had not been able to investigate until there was a gap in the schedule. He was looking for some indication of why she was using Mr. Krämer's firm to make financial inquiries about his old friend and mentor at Auschwitz, Dr. Schumann. A few days ago, he had gone to his home in Frankfurt to find an anonymous post from the doctor. Using the code they had worked out, the letter read like an update about family, but actually it gave new information about his location. He had relocated to Khartoum, Sudan after most recently serving as doctor aboard a Russian submarine. Jürgen was instructed to dispose of the woman, meaning Dr. Dudek, as quickly as possible, but he was to take no action until he had an explanation of her interest.

As he casually scanned the sheets on the clipboard outside the personal effects room, he saw her name entered several times, but he noticed a pattern. The days she had signed in were all Saturdays. This must mean that her primary practice was not at the Wiesenhof, but somewhere else. If she had signed any items out, she would be required to put the item's new location on the list or, if an item was taken and returned, she would have to write down the purpose for borrowing it.

"Dr. Wilhelm Nowitz, therapeutic consultation, out on Saturday the 5th, in on Saturday the 12th" was written in Dr. Dudek's hand in the middle of the third page. Dr. Wilhelm Nowitz...now who was that and why would she take a book and picture to him? Jürgen would have to write to his mentor about this detail. In any case, Albert Novak would be one of the few people surviving that could identify Dr. Schumann, so certainly he would have to be eliminated, but he would still have to figure out why Dr. Dudek was the one making inquiries and how she might be connected to Albert. He wrote the name down on a slip of paper and tucked it into his pocket just as he saw nurse Wolf coming through the door behind him.

"Good morning, Günther. Can I help you find something?" Helga asked the older man.

"No, thank you. I'm still trying to familiarize myself with this new place. It is very different from where I used to work," he covered.

"I'm curious. Where did you used to work?" she asked with genuine curiosity.

Die Arschloch! (Asshole!) he thought, but he looked up and smiled saying, "It was a very long time ago. I was a medical assistant in a high security hospital. Pardon me, please. I have to go clean up *Frau Masche's* room." He folded the pages back down on the clipboard and set it on the counter. Picking up the stack of sheets and pillow cases, he left Helga in the room alone.

It was late morning, nearly three months since he was hired. The sun was high. Most of the patients and faculty were having lunch, but a few were still ambling about. Jürgen had completed his to-do list over thirty minutes ago, but he had one more task to accomplish. One that was not on the list. He had passed by Albert Novak's door several times in the last half hour, but there was always someone in the hallway or talking nearby. Tomorrow, he would be going home for his Sunday off so he could collect some tools and write some letters. One of them, to Dr. Schumann in Khartoum telling him about Albert's sudden passing. He knew the doctor would be pleased to read that.

The hallway was empty as he walked toward the front desk. There was always a break in visiting hours to allow time for lunch, so no one was at the front desk. As he approached Albert's door on the opposite wall, looking both ways to see if anyone might observe him, then crossed the width of the hallway and took down Albert's wall chart. A quick review of the medications and timing of the last dose indicated that this man should be unresponsive for a few hours. He slowly replaced the chart so as not to make any sound and as he took hold of the door knob, he looked both ways down the hall to see if anyone was coming. There was no one so he turned the knob slowly. The door didn't fit perfectly, so when the latch released, there was a loud clack that echoed down the hall. He froze just long enough to make certain no one had heard it, then he pushed the door open quickly and quietly. The low creak the hinges made was unavoidable, so it was best to get it over with. As he entered the room, he saw the patient was still, so he turned and shut the door. To avoid the loud noise that happened when he opened it, he put his weight against the door before slowly releasing the door knob. This time, the latch engaged silently.

It was bright outside, but the curtains were drawn, so there was just enough light to confirm Albert's identity, but not enough to wake him. The patient was covered, but not strapped down like so many others. Dr. Dudek had changed his status to allow him some freedom of movement, but kept him heavily medicated. Jürgen stepped slowly around the foot of the bed being careful not to let his rubber-soled shoes squeak against the floor.

Albert Novak had been one of the special cases under his care while he and Dr. Horst Schumann were stationed at Auschwitz. When he discovered Dr. Dudek and then found Albert Novak in the same place, he knew it was not a coincidence. There must be some connection. Albert, along with two other boys, were emasculated, completely castrated, as part of an experimental procedure to determine if they could change the developmental direction of Jewish boys toward being female. If they were successful, this would have been one more tool the Reich could use to insulate themselves from future contamination by Jewish scum. If procreation were no longer possible, then reproduction would cease. This would provide a suitable method to help along the extinction of the race. When Jürgen had investigated Albert's belongings he had discovered a photograph he knew well. Hitler had personally instructed Hugo Jaeger to create a visual record of their experiments to compliment the written record. Their work would be watched closely and he wanted thorough documentation. Written on the back of the photograph was the name "Albert"...the same as the patient's name, so he was certain this was the same person.

As he stepped closer to the patient, his heart began to pound in his chest. Albert seemed helpless enough to be taken easily. His breathing was slow and regular indicating that he was indeed sedated. The medications should also make him too weak to struggle much while Jürgen did what he needed to do. It was imperative that no one ever be able to identify him, so this should work out just fine. So many things were racing through his mind. How did the boy survive? They had surrendered Auschwitz when The Red Army advanced, so how long did it take him to heal? Did he know what ever became of the other two boys? He was so distracted that he actually startled when Albert's eyes popped open.

Albert turned his head upward groggily to look at the visitor. An expression of abject fear and recognition flooded his face and he took a deep breath as if he were about to call out. Jürgen slapped one hand over Albert's eyes and another over his mouth and nose, forcefully turning Albert's head to face straight up and as Albert began to struggle, unable to breathe, Jürgen heard someone talking in the hallway just outside the door. He roughly applied more pressure, but Albert was so weak he could hardly resist even modest pressure. As Albert began to weaken further, more voices could be heard through the door. Damn! He hadn't been quick enough and now he might have been found out.

As Albert relaxed in his grip, the door knob turned while simultaneously someone knocked on the door. He recognized the mop of red hair coming through the door as Helga's...one of the people he knew could identify him. As Albert went limp, he released his grip and darted around the bed, shoving Helga out of his way against the wall, knocking the wind out of her. It happened so fast that she didn't even have a chance to scream. As he ran out into the hallway, he collided with Dr. Schmidt who had been coming up behind Helga when she opened the door. Dr. Schmidt lost his balance, landing hard on one hip and Jürgen lost his footing.

"Günther! What are you doing?" he roared. Jürgen went down on one knee, sliding, trying not to fall. When he regained his balance, he rose in a crouch then turned toward the front door and bolted.

As Dr. Schmidt got to his feet, orderlies began to arrive. Seeing Jürgen running toward the lobby, they turned their attention to those who had been hurt in the incident. An old woman who had been ambling down the hall, was crying out in pain on the floor. One of the orderlies came to her side and encouraged her to try to remain still until a doctor could get there. This was probably a broken hip by the way she clutched her leg. Most of the people involved were just stunned, but Helga had regained her wits quickly and was busy checking Albert's vital signs.

"I need a doctor!" She yelled at the top of her voice.

"I'm here," Dr. Schmidt said as he entered the room, favoring his bruised hip, and came up behind the nurse.

Helga was switching from Albert's neck where the scars were to his wrist, checking for a pulse. Dr. Schmidt pulled Albert's eyes open, watching the pupils contract in the light.

"Pupils responsive, but not tracking," he said aloud.

One of the orderlies leaned through the door and barked, "What do you need?"

"Bring me an oxygen bottle, nasal cannula, ten milligrams morphine in a sixteen gauge!" There wasn't any time to lose. He placed his hand over Albert's mouth, pinching his nose and providing just a slight resistance to the air flow so he could see how strongly the unconscious man was breathing. As soon as he applied resistance, the airflow stopped, even though the breathing movements continued, indicating that he was breathing autonomically. This was not a good sign. Dr. Schmidt pinched Albert's nose hard, took a deep breath, sealed his mouth around Albert's, and blew hard.

"Heart rate forty-two!" barked Helga.

"Well at least he's still got one," said Dr. Scmidt, gratefully. "Keep monitoring."

The orderly who had asked for instructions returned, and moved around Dr. Schmidt to the head of the bed. He set an oxygen bottle down and tore open a sterile package containing the tubing. He connected it to the bottle's regulator and moved to place the cannula around each of Albert's ears so the tube would be positioned under his nose. He approached Albert's head with the tubing, but before executing the motion, he paused.

"Go," Dr. Schmidt barked as he released his grip on Albert's nose and stepped out of the way.

The orderly had the cannula on Albert and the regulator open and flowing in less than a second. Placing a hand over Albert's mouth so he would have no choice but to breathe in the pure oxygen through his nose, they waited. Nothing changed for what seemed like a long time. Then they saw fog appear and vanish in the cannula. He was breathing the oxygen now. A few more breaths and Dr. Schmidt took his hand away from Albert's mouth.

"Just wait," said Dr. Schmidt. "Just wait."

Nothing happened. At least fifteen seconds had passed when Helga became impatient, moving up to begin breathing for Albert.

"Not yet." Dr. Schmidt gave her a calming look. "He will be alright."

A few seconds later, Albert began to choke and sputter. His eyes began to flutter. It was almost like watching a drowning victim come back to life.

"You OK?" the orderly asked Dr. Schmidt, waiting for more instructions.

"Got it," Dr. Schmidt answered. "Find the attending." The orderly stepped out of the room to see if he could find Dr. Freda.

"Well done, Helga. Well done," Dr. Schmidt congratulated the young nurse. Helga seemed embarrassed by the compliment, but accepted it gracefully with a nod. "Now let's find out what is going on!" Dr. Schmidt said, looking directly into Helga's eyes. "You stay here and let me know the minute anything changes."

He turned to look at Albert thinking *You are one lucky man.*

Dr. Freda climbed the steps to the landing in front of the Wiesenhof Asylum. She was running a few minutes late today, which was unusual for her. She actually felt a pang of guilt at not being the completely reliable and punctual mentor she should be, but she knew Helga wouldn't say a single word about it.

Just as she reached for the door with her free hand, it flew open. The door handle smacked the backs of her fingers pressing them painfully into her palm. A blur of motion was all she saw as someone in a white coat and scrubs pushed her out of the way, knocking the medicine bag out of her hand and sending her toppling sideways. She heard the muffled crunch of glass breaking and knew her gin bottle had been a casualty of the fall. As she fell, she rolled over toward the assailant receding into the distance. At first, all she could see was the back of a man's head and a white coat fluttering in the wind as he headed down the path, but about halfway to the street the man turned to look back, presumably to see if he was being followed. It was just then that Freda, lying on her side, had a flash of recognition. It was Günther, the orderly, but something more pressed at her mind. She felt she knew him from a long time before but could not place the feeling at any specific time in her life. In an instant, he turned away and headed across the street and through the park.

As she sat up, she noticed the liquid leaking out of her bag and detected the odor of rubbing alcohol mixed with juniper and grain alcohol. She sat and placed her hands on her knees thinking this was not going to be a good day.

The door opened again, more slowly this time, and Mila looked down at her asking "Are you alright, doctor? He didn't hurt you, did he?"

As Dr. Freda maneuvered to get up, Mila came out onto the landing and offered both hands to her, shifting her weight back while helping Freda up.

"I think I am whole," Freda said, brushing the folds of her skirt down, "but who was that? What happened?"

Just as the door finished closing, she heard shouting inside that sounded like Dr. Schmidt, Helga, and a couple other voices. Mila and Freda looked at each other and back at the door. As Mila reached for the door handle, Dr. Freda picked up her dribbling medicine bag, hoping that Mila didn't recognize the odor. They rushed inside to a chaotic scene and as they reached the front desk she handed the bag to Mila saying "Wrap this in a towel and don't open it. I don't know what broke and it might not be safe to breathe. Can you keep it to the side of the desk until I come back?"

Mila didn't speak, but nodded vigorously and snatched the bag from Dr. Freda, stepping behind the front desk as Freda headed down the hall. Only ten feet past the front desk, she noticed that the commotion was centered around Albert's open door. As she stepped around an old woman who had fallen and an orderly who was holding her down as she howled in pain, Dr. Freda reached Albert's door and stepped inside. Helga looked up with a frightful expression on her face. Dr. Schmidt was between the door and Albert, so Dr. Freda couldn't see much, but he turned when he saw Helga looking. Recognizing Dr. Freda, he swung out of her way. As she entered, he began rattling off the patient's current status and vital signs. Dr. Freda stepped to Albert's bedside between the doctor and nurse as Dr. Schmidt finished relaying the information. Realizing that Albert was no longer in physical danger, she breathed a sigh of relief saying "Just how many lives *do* you have, Mr. Novak?"

Chapter 12

It had been several weeks since the attempt on Albert's life and he seemed to be recovering well. Freda was looking forward to today's session. For the first couple weeks, she had kept him under heavy sedation so that his emotional responses would not overwhelm him, but sedation could often be inhibitory to progress. One of the philosophies that she believed was a truism, meaning that it is true with everyone, everywhere, was that a person is an accumulation of memories. Remove a memory and who that person is changes as a result. Her work involved creating new memories as a person worked through their trauma, but doing so in such a way that the new memories created a new person. If treatment were successful, the new person still harbored the preexisting trauma, but the new memories of treatment provided a filter that lessened the damage the trauma created each time it was remembered. Too much sedation and patients would not remember enough of their sessions to contribute to their recovery. Too little sedation and patients might become despondent during a session rendering the session unproductive. Her goal with each of her patients was to help them build that filter and teach them how to maintain it so that they could become a productive member of society again.

As she walked to the Wiesenhof Asylum from the train station, Freda felt the warm sun on her face and smelled the jasmine from a nearby garden wafting past her. The bitterly cold winter had given way to spring and today was just perfect. Blue skies, cool breeze, birds singing, and children playing on the asylum grounds while parents visited patients inside, all conspired to lift her mood. She had even been drinking a bit less in the evenings, surely a benefit of the success she was having with Albert's case.

Dr. Freda had been corresponding frequently with Albert's parents, asking them to be patient and not to visit too soon. It wasn't simply that she did not want them to be upset by Albert's appearance, but in her opinion Albert's mental state was not stable enough to deal with emotional visitors. As the weeks progressed and Lena's letters became more insistent, Dr. Freda decided that it might be a good idea for Albert to begin writing to his parents and to begin keeping a journal for himself. She had asked to be allowed to read the first few letters and he had granted her that. Usually, she sat with him while he wrote, taking the pencil and letter from him, promising to post it immediately.

As Albert began opening up in his journal and their sessions began to show improvement, Dr. Freda decided that he should be granted the freedom to write whenever the inspiration struck him. She found a pad of lined stationary with plenty of sheets, matching envelopes, and stamps which she left with him along with a fancy pen, all bundled as a gift. Seeing the smile on his face when he received the writing materials warmed her heart and she felt sure that he would make significant improvements over the next few weeks. Maybe he would even be well enough to receive a visit from his parents soon.

As Freda approached the bottom step, she gathered her heavy woolen skirt with one hand so she wouldn't trip and holding her medicine bag in front to help her balance, climbed to the top landing. Dropping her gathered skirt, she walked briskly to the tall, heavy doors and entered. The sun beaming through the glass had made the lobby delightfully warm, but she knew that by this afternoon, it would be uncomfortably stuffy inside. On a beautiful day like this, they would probably open many of the doors and windows to allow the fresh air in. That would be good for the patients.

Mila was at the front desk and when she looked up, her face beamed with happiness. Freda had become quite fond of Mila and appreciated the way the young woman took Helga under her wing. Though nearly the same age, Mila was turning out to be a good mentor and friend to Helga. She seemed to enjoy sharing her experience and was quite tolerant of mistakes as long as someone was giving their best effort.

"Good morning, Mila, my dear. How have you been?" Dr. Freda asked.

"Very well, thank you. It's so good to see you again, doctor. You're not scheduled to see Albert until later today. Is the schedule incorrect?" the young woman asked.

"I thought I would drop in to see how he is doing. Maybe we could spend some time outside. The weather is perfect for some time in the courtyard, isn't it?"

"Yes, it's such a beautiful day today!" Mila rose as Dr. Freda signed in and gave a little curtsy before sitting back down. The doctor knew her way around and didn't need her guidance this morning.

Dr. Freda stepped around the desk to the left and cheerfully marched down the hall toward Albert's room. As she reached the door, she took her customary deep, calming breath before turning the knob. It was definitely going to be a good day.

The first thing that struck her was the silence. She couldn't see the head of Albert's bed unless the door was fully opened. He usually sat up as soon as anyone entered, but this time his feet didn't move. As the door swung wide with a creak, she saw him lying very still, blood soaking the sheets and oozing into a puddle on the floor in a stream, a strong odor of iron in the air. Despite her years of training and experience, Freda stood in shock, unmoving.

"Verdammit." ("Damn.")

Albert was sitting up on his own in the tidy hospital bed, clean white sheets tucked in neatly around his wiry legs, the truly uncomfortable gown gathered above his rump and the knots were pressing into his back wherever the ties were. Even though he was covered, he still felt naked in these hospital garments. His IV had been removed and the back of his hand where it had pierced the skin was blue and yellow and ached terribly. The tape the strange nurse had used to bandage the wounds on his wrists had made his skin peel off and nurse Helga had complained about uncaring colleagues the entire time she spent delicately removing it and replacing it with ointment and a dry wrap which she then taped around his hand so the glue was never in contact with his skin. He knew she was just trying to make him feel better, make him feel cared for, but he had become used to being treated like a piece of meat. Helga had then brought in some broth, milk, and rolls for him to eat. He found it a bit unnerving but he understood why she sat through his entire meal observing each bite with interest. It had been many days since he had eaten and the movement of his fingers made his wrists ache painfully. When he had finished, Helga had taken the enameled metal cups and plate from him and helped him clean his chin since he could not close his hands firmly around a napkin yet.

It had been over a week since his last visit from Dr. Freda, though he had seen her several times stealing a glance at him through the open door or when he was being led down the hall to the courtyard by one of the hulking orderlies. Today would be his first formal visit with her since the incident and he was not looking forward to the encounter. He was certain she was feeling betrayed and he had no idea how he would explain his actions to her. She had been decreasing his medications over the past few weeks so that his sessions with her would be more productive but as he had become more collected, more sorted out, he had also become more despondent. Dr. Freda had explained that as he became more able to express his feelings they would have less of an impact on him and yet the more lucid he became, the worse it got.

As he waited patiently, he could hear voices in the hall. Occasionally he thought he could hear nurse Helga and Dr. Freda talking but they didn't come in so he spent the time thinking about how to explain his actions. As the bright white of the midday sun waned to afternoon yellow, he began to wonder if she would follow through with today's visit. His room had been conspicuously cleaned of any writing or drawing materials and he could hardly blame them. He finally resolved to re-read one of the books she had brought to him from the personal effects he had left at the seminary. He climbed out of bed letting the cotton gown fall down and checking it to make certain it had covered him just in case someone were to enter. The floor was cold at this time of year but it felt good to touch something other than the rough fabric of the hospital bed. He crossed the room to the small closet which was missing its door pull. He stuck his finger through the hole left by the fixture's removal and pulled the door open. Standing up on the balls of his feet to reach the upper shelf, he rummaged until he felt the one he wanted. He had read it so many times he knew *The Brothers Karamazov* by touch.

Just then the door to his room opened and Dr. Freda entered. Albert was caught off guard and he turned to cover himself, since the back of the gown was surely gaping open. He fumbled the book and lost his grip on it. As it thudded to the floor, an old picture fell from between its pages face-up, floating several inches away on a cushion of air until it came to rest facing Dr. Freda.

She showed no embarrassment, either at Albert's indecency or at the picture. She knew he would not be able to pick it up, so she bent down and picked up both the book and then the picture. Studying the picture carefully, she waited for Albert to get situated back in bed. He clumsily maneuvered around her being sure to keep his flaps closed behind him with one hand. Not having much success, he kept his back to her as he made his way to the bed, sat, and covered himself with the sheet. Reclining now, but elevated, he gestured to her to sit in the sole chair beside the bed. She did so with a very stiff posture and without repositioning the chair so they might speak face to face. The tension was palpable but she did not let it last.

"I would appreciate knowing the reasoning behind your most recent attempt. Were I not to have come when I did, you would not have survived. Clearly that is what you wanted, but you seem better today. Help me understand that," Dr. Freda said in a flat, analytical tone. She was obviously angry, no matter how well she tried to cover it with professional demeanor. She had done so much for him, given him so much of herself, and he had discarded that as if it were nothing. Albert sat for a very long time looking at his folded hands but she made no attempt to fill the silence. She was generous in that way, but she also expected a response. As he composed his thoughts, she sat watching him in the soft afternoon light.

Albert began, "When I was taken with my parents to the trains, the soldiers let us stay together, but when we arrived at the camp and the families were crowded through the gates, we could see that children were being separated from their parents ahead. I was very young, I think eight or nine, and it became clear that we would not be allowed to remain together. If I had been older, they would have made me stay with them, but when my mother realized what was happening, she began to panic. As we drew to the front, the fear of the people around us grew." As he went on, his shoulders began to tremble. His lips began to pinch. Clearly the memory was burned into his mind, but Dr. Freda saw something else. He was afraid, not of something that happened then, but of something that was about to happen. A confession.

"When we were finally separated and I was put in the barracks with the other boys, some of the boys would be taken every day by doctors who would come into the rooms and select which of us they wanted. Those boys would be taken the next day and usually not seen again, but sometimes a few would return. They had been... cut by the doctors. Even though I was very young, I knew what a grown man should look like and how babies were made but these boys had been..."

"The medical term is *emasculated*...removing all reproductive organs," Dr. Freda interrupted.

He was unphased by the brutally clinical description. "Yes. I was selected along with two friends I had made in the camp. We were very close, like brothers."

"Yes. You have mentioned them to me," she confirmed.

Albert was clearly lost in a terrible memory.

"Then how did you come to be in this picture with your two friends, also altered as they were?" she asked.

"The doctors were notorious for conducting whatever experiments they wanted. Often, if they found a set of twins they would experiment on only one so they could observe the effects more objectively, but they were often indiscriminate. If they thought you would survive long enough to study, they took you. A soldier came to our barracks one day, picked me up by the arms, and took me to a room where he held me down on a table. They took all three of us. I did not struggle when they took my clothes. From the table, I could see my two friends with doctors leaning over them...cutting them."

"I am sorry, Dr. Freda, I am, but when I sat down to draw as you suggested, these were the only images I could remember." He trailed off again. He was becoming calmer, so Dr. Freda finished the thought for him. "You used the pen that I gave you to try to kill yourself again."

"Yes," Albert said in a soft voice, ashamed of what he had done.

Dr. Freda looked up into Wilhelm's probing eyes allowing the memory of the exchange to linger for a while. "I did not know what to tell him. We have called the authorities but the man who attacked him got away and I gave him the instruments he used to try to kill himself. I left Albert sitting in his room after our last session and I think I may have made things worse. He seems to be in a worse state now than when I first met him!" She was becoming rather frustrated with herself.

"It seems to me that you have a choice," said Dr. Nowitz. "You either treat him as a textbook case, of which you have seen many, or you try to give the man a purpose he can possess for himself." He mused for a moment and resumed, "Are you prepared to tell him your secrets? To give him something of yourself you do not share with other patients?"

"How do you mean, *Doktor*?"

"He will make no family of his own but that does not mean he cannot have a family," Wilhelm explained. "Family is not only the flesh and blood offspring we create. Family is also the people we care for, the ones who give purpose to our lives. Are you prepared to let your family have another member?"

"But I have told you that I have no family, *Doktor*," Freda said, wondering why Dr. Nowitz wouldn't remember something so important.

Wilhelm leaned forward with a creased brow and a questioning look on his face. He smiled giving the impression of a kind and gentle father figure. "So certain of that, are you? And I assumed you were trying to be objective." He shrugged with his palms lifted slightly. "My mistake. You see? Even in our profession, we do not always know what is before our eyes."

"I need to tell you something, *Herr Novak*," Dr. Freda said with trepidation clearly etched on her face.

"I am sorry I did that to you," Albert preempted.

"Actually, that is what I was going to say to you," Dr. Freda added, prompting a look of confusion on Albert's face. "When last we spoke, I must admit my...having a feeling of you....*enttäuschung*?" she looked at Albert needing help with the word.

He looked down at his hands in his lap and provided a word for her. "Disappointment."

"Yes. That is it. I became angry that you had used my trust to again try to take your own life, even after telling me what I wanted to hear, that you were making progress."

She was not displaying any anger now. Instead, she was showing resolution and confidence. She sat upright in the room's only chair facing Albert who was sitting on the bed. As always, the room was immaculately clean and devoid of any fixtures or cords. She brought no writing instruments with her. She would be writing all her notes immediately after their session while her memory was fresh. Albert was in a plain cotton short sleeved shirt and white cotton elastic pants with blue pinstripes of the type issued to all the long-term male patients of the Behavioural Disorders ward. These gowns were specially made to tear easily and the hook that held the pants closed was made of wood instead of metal. It did not keep the fly closed while sitting, so Albert was careful to keep himself covered with his hands, though he couldn't help but recognize the futility. He had flung his sheets off and sat up respectfully when she had asked permission to enter, as a child would when being rightfully scolded. The early morning sun streamed in through the window making every point in the room glow brightly with cheerful light. It was a cheer neither of them could take part in just now.

"*Herr Novak*," she addressed him formally, "what would you like to explain to me?"

There was so much going through Albert's head. He felt so guilty for what he had done, but how could he make her understand? He was already dead. If he told her about the man that had almost killed him, she would certainly not believe him, but he was certain it was the man from the camp. Even if she did believe him, he did not know where the man was now and he would certainly come to kill him if anyone found out that he had told her. She could see that he was struggling, trying to sort out his thoughts, so she sat patiently waiting. She knew there was no benefit to impatience, so she relaxed into her chair in an imitation of how Dr. Nowitz had appeared relaxed when she was the one who was nervous. She placed her hands on her knees, fingers splayed open, elbows and shoulders relaxed, and waited.

He appeared to be at an impasse in his thoughts, so she prompted, "You have told me of the benefits of ending your life. Is that what you wanted to accomplish this time?"

"Not exactly," he replied. He realized that she had turned his thoughts in the right direction, so he continued, allowing them to flow out. "When that man tried to suffocate me, I recognized him. I knew him a long time ago." Albert waited for the intensity of the memory to fade so he could speak. His heart was pounding in his chest as he relived not only the attack, but also the memory from his childhood. "He was the medical assistant to Dr. Horst Schumann, the man who did this to me," he said, gesturing with both palms up, angled toward his groin.

Dr. Freda was displaying the utmost confidence toward Albert, but inside, she was fearful that this new twist in his psyche would yield some as yet unpredicted result that could make the situation worse, but she held her fears in a tight bundle inside her chest. "Let me ask you something, *Herr Novak*. Why did you not weep when you first suicided? You must have known that the action would hurt those who loved you."

"I was not thinking about that at the time. I was in shock and feeling too much pain. I did not realize it at the time, but I was only thinking about myself," he answered, almost with a touch of pride that he would do so well as to recognize such a thing. "I am not feeling that way now," he countered. "This morning, I feel ashamed as I speak with you, so I am clearly able to think of the way others feel. I recognize that I have disappointed you and probably my family."

"I am glad to see that you did not damage your intelligence with your last suicide," she chided.

"I am confused, Dr. Freda. Why do you not say suicide *attempt* instead of suicide?" he asked.

"Because in both cases, you performed the act flawlessly. It was only by chance that you were saved each time." She conjectured out loud, "You, *Herr Novak*, should be dead. Yet you live through the actions of others who want to save you." Pausing for a heartbeat, she added, "Now why would people put in such extraordinary effort to save your life when you did not care enough to keep it?"

He was aghast. His mouth dropped open. This woman was being brutal to someone who was suicidal and trying to apologize to her?

She didn't wait for his answer. "It is for one reason and one reason only, *Herr Novak*. It is precisely because you deserve to live. I know it. The other doctors know it. Helga and your parents know it. The question is, how do you not know it?" She could see he was dumbfounded, so she decided to go a little farther. "Albert," she said with a softer, more compassionate voice, "do you know that all psychotherapists have their own psychotherapists?"

"No. I did not know that. Why would you?" He was intrigued by the admission.

"It is not because we are all crazy, though sometimes I wonder about myself," she said jokingly. "It is because we all need someone to help us accept and understand that we all make mistakes, like my mistake with you." He was clearly not understanding her meaning, so she continued. "I have an advanced degree with many years of experience. I have studied with some of the greatest minds in the field and yet I was so stupid as to allow a patient to have the means to kill themselves."

He was beginning to understand. He began to giggle to himself. He couldn't help it. He had been ready to bear whatever shame or blame she wished to heap on him and instead, she was helping him to lighten his own burden.

"*Herr Novak*, I apologize for my mistake," she said with sincerity as she leaned forward, placing a hand on his and looking into his eyes.

As he looked up to meet her eyes, he lost control. He began to sob and laugh at the same time. Tears streamed down his face. He was so overcome that he drooled on his lap. She quickly maneuvered her hand out of the way of the hanging slobber, and then she began to laugh. As the laughter and tears blended and he lost the ability to communicate, she stood and held his head to her chest, ignoring the drool she got on her apron and the sweat she got on her hands from his hair. She placed her cheek on top of his head as he released the guilt and shame he had been feeling for so long.

"Albert," she said in a soft, motherly tone, "You will take responsibility for your actions and honour those that love you."

He could only nod in the affirmative.

"I am one of those that love you," she added cautiously. His sobbing began to abate as a new confusion set in. She released his head and stepped back to look him in the eyes. "I see a man I would like to get to know and I see a man who would rather kill himself than get to know me and that makes me very sad."

The sadness began to swell in his face again, about to draw him back down into sobs when she took him by the face with both hands, gently.

"Don't take that chance away from me," she sincerely requested.

Chapter 13

Even sitting in his favourite cafe in the shade with a dusty breeze blowing, was unbearably hot. The dust seemed to swirl and float in the air, each grain that touched him sticking to his sweaty skin wherever it was exposed. Horst Schumann's favourite cafe was a tiny porch in front of a two-story mud structure with dry wooden posts holding up a type of thatched pagoda that looked as if it would fall on him at any moment. Khartoum, Sudan had not improved significantly in the last couple decades. The local savages still lived in squalor and foreigners were still treated with hatred and violence, but the Aryan races, the British who had colonized, the Germans, and other groups like the occasional Italian, Swede, or Norse, were treated like royalty. Of course they were. They rightfully held nearly all of the money in the country and were the only source of class and decorum.

After the war, as The Red Army marched through Auschwitz, he and Jürgen Żądło, his medical assistant, were forced to flee. Jürgen was young and of little note, so it was easy for him to disappear into nearby Hungary under an assumed name until the Allies could be overthrown by the rightful heirs of the Reich, the Aryan races. Unfortunately, that never happened and the German people had been kept under the reign of the Allies who carved Germany into blocks for each country to plunder. The economy had remained in shambles until recently. Horst didn't have the luxury of anonymity since he was one of the most famous and prestigious reproductive research doctors in the Reich. He had spent the better part of his career looking for the most effective and economical way to sterilize the Jews so the race would go extinct, but now it didn't appear that this would be accomplished in his lifetime.

When practicing in Auschwitz, he had the blessing and power of the Reich and Adolph Hitler himself to conduct well-documented experiments, but when the Allies moved in, his team was not able to take all the records with them. Much of their research had fallen into the hands of the Allies who then proved what hypocrites they were by using the research they called unethical in their own medical practices, but this time on willing subjects like those with gender disorders. Instead of calling them what they were, deranged perverts, they made up medical sounding terms like transsexual. If it were up to him, they would all be put down. Why would any society accept and even encourage this sort of rotting from within? It was just beyond his way of thinking.

After some coffee, he picked up the letter he had received the day before. It had taken longer this time because of all the upheaval going on in the local government but also because Jürgen was less than competent and not very good at medicine either. The network of operatives that kept the Nazi political party alive had to be very careful when transporting letters and goods around the globe. Though they had the assistance of many powerful groups like the Vatican and many of the ruling parties throughout Africa and South America, some places were still risky like America and Europe. It was a constant worry that Jürgen might write something stupid that could be intercepted by the Allies as it made its way out of Europe.

DEAR UNCLE,

I WAS ABLE TO PAY AN EXTENDED VISIT TO MY MOTHER, YOUR DEAR SISTER, RECENTLY. SHE IS DOING WELL BUT IS UNHAPPY ABOUT THE FAMILY MATTERS WE DISCUSSED. WE HAVE NOT COME TO AN AGREEMENT YET ABOUT WHAT WE SHOULD DO WITH THE FAMILY PROPERTIES, BUT ONE FORTUITOUS COINCIDENCE WILL ENTERTAIN YOU GREATLY. IF YOU RECALL THE FAMILY PICTURE YOU SHOWED ME ALL THOSE YEARS AGO, I HAVE LOCATED ONE OF THE THREE LONG-LOST SONS THAT USED TO GO CAMPING TOGETHER. ALBIE WAS VERY HAPPY TO SEE ME, BUT UNFORTUNATELY, I WAS NOT ABLE TO STAY VERY LONG AND WE DID NOT GET TO SETTLE THINGS BETWEEN US. PLEASE LET ME KNOW IF I SHOULD PURSUE THIS FURTHER. HE WOULD VERY MUCH LIKE TO HEAR FROM YOU TOO.

MAMA FREDA IS SO HAPPY TO KNOW THAT YOU ARE LOOKING OUT FOR HER, BUT SHE WOULD ALSO LIKE TO KNOW WHAT TO DO ABOUT THE FAMILY PROPERTIES, SINCE SHE HAS LITTLE EXPERIENCE IN SUCH MATTERS. HOPEFULLY, WITH YOUR WISDOM, SHE WILL COME TO FIND A NEW PATH.

YOURS ALWAYS,

J

Even in his fifties, the man was nearly as useless as he was in his twenties. At least he had discovered something Horst had not anticipated. One of the three boys they had been experimenting on toward the end of his tenure at Auschwitz was now located and, though Jürgen had attempted to eliminate him, he was unsuccessful and may have been identified. He had also confirmed that this woman, Dr. Freda Dudek, was indeed using financial records to locate him, so that question was now answered. What he did not know yet was why. Horst would have to deal with Jürgen eventually, but that could wait until he either made another serious mistake or outlived his usefulness. The problem now was how to find out more about this Dr. Dudek. He would write back to Jürgen later, but the letter would have to be carefully formulated to transmit the necessary information re-coded into a family letter. Since Jürgen had been forced to return to Frankfurt after his failed attempt to kill Albert, they would have a little time to regroup, but he was starting to wonder if funding Jürgen's activities in Cologne was a mistake. Perhaps he should have chosen someone else.

He folded the blue postal tissue gently and stuffed it into his breast pocket before leaving money for the cafe owner and his wife. As the cafe owner saw Horst leaving, he beckoned to his wife to go collect the money before a street urchin could steal it and as she rushed to the rickety table, she bowed and put her hands together in an overly-grateful, nearly prostrate degree of thanks. *Dogs were the same in any part of the world,* he thought. He always left a little extra money so he would be well treated, but these people weren't capable of the advanced thinking that were a prerequisite of social graces. He brushed off some of the dust that had accumulated on his pants while he sat and joined the throng of people moving toward the market. As he walked, he was careful to keep a hand in the pocket where his money was. This had the advantage of making it impossible for a pickpocket to put their hand in unnoticed, but it also indicated *to* a pickpocket where his money was located, so most of his money was in a money belt worn under his pants at his waist. One had to think like this in a society of thieving scavengers. Just in case, he also kept his Nazi-issued Walther PPK in a holster strapped around his shoulder under his coat. It was small enough to go unnoticed and was easily accessible, resting just under his ribs tight against his side.

As he walked toward the hospital, he formulated his response. Certainly, Jürgen would be waiting for specific instructions, not knowing what action would yield the greatest return at the lowest risk. If he had any intelligence at all, he would have already figured this out for himself, taken action, and reported the results. It was probably a good thing that he had not. After all, how can an orderly in a mental asylum fail to kill a helpless patient? The foolishness was remarkable! The next step would have to either answer the question of who Dr. Dudek was or result in her death, which would be unfortunate if they did not discover who else was involved in tracking him. In any case, he would have to be more careful when moving money around and Jürgen would not be able to receive any more funds through official channels.

Late in the evening on Thursday, the door to the bar swung open too hard and the bells clattered as the heavy door bounced off the adjacent wall. *Frau Guten* tapped her husband on the arm when he failed to look up from serving a customer and when he saw Jürgen followed by two other suited thugs, he cursed under his breath as he affected a broad smile.

"Willkommen Freunde!" ("Welcome, my friends!") he said as he stepped around the side of the bar.

Arms outstretched, he approached Jürgen who merely sat at an empty table and struck a match to light the cigarette. As Jürgen looked up sidelong at the mark, he leered and the bar owner dropped his arms from the aborted greeting.

"What can I bring to you good men?" he asked, hoping to gain a little favor before discussing the money situation.

Jürgen said, "A stout." As he looked back down at the table, dismissing the older man, his two apprentices remained standing.

They were both physically larger than Jürgen, but neither of them had the mental fortitude to gain, and keep, the loyalty of their marks. This would be a learning experience for both of them. He did not acknowledge either of them and expected them to remain standing. This was an indication to the entire establishment that he was there to conduct business and the few customers who were talking at a table in the far corner of the bar downed their beers and gathered their coats, heading for the door. As the owner returned with the stout beer, he knew it would not be a pleasant visit.

He set the stout down in front of Jürgen. Suddenly, Jürgen snatched his wrist and held it flat against the table. This put the man in a very uncomfortable position, especially due to his age. Bending over and not being able to stand or move, his back began to ache almost immediately, but he stayed still as Jürgen took up the stout with the other hand and downed half of it in one gulp. He set the glass down on the table and the old man thought he would say something to move the situation along, but he just sat there holding his wrist in place against the table as the ache in his back continued to mount.

"Your payment is late," Jürgen said, not moving or looking up.

"Yes. I am very sorry about that, but this week has been even worse than last week. I have last week's payment for you but not all of this week's yet. By Saturday afternoon, I should have the rest."

Jürgen stayed very still for a long while. The bar owner, and his wife behind the bar who was listening but trying to look as if she were not, stood perfectly still... waiting. Jürgen then turned, throwing one leg over the bench so he could face the old man. Loosening his grip on the man's wrist, he allowed his hand to slide down so that his palm was cradling the bar owner's palm. As he did so, he placed his other hand on top of the other man's hand so that his hand was between both of Jürgen's hands. He then began to contract his grip, very gradually, as he spoke.

"You know how understanding I am with you and your wife and I am only too happy to be so." His manner was that of a haughty society brat. "I want to take care of you both and make certain you can have a prosperous business here." Jürgen's grip ran out of room at this point and the pressure on the man's fingers and knuckles began to increase. "You have my word that I will continue to keep you safe and make sure you always have a place to do business."

As the man's restraint began to waiver, a grimace appeared on his face, deepening the lines around his eyes and drawing his lips tight. His wife, watching intently from across the room, set the glass and cloth she was using down and put her hands flat on the bar. Jürgen's grip continued to build pressure and one of the man's knuckles popped. Neither of his henchmen moved at all, but stared straight ahead.

"I want you to know that my boss is very sympathetic and he has asked me to give you some extra time, but we know how expensive it is to provide protection for the community and we don't want his faith in you to waiver, now do we?"

Through gritted teeth, the old man forced, "No, sir."

"I'm so glad to hear you say that." The pressure ceased building, but Jürgen did not release it. "It is out of my way to come back here tomorrow so I will take what you have ready for me today and we can leave the rest for next week, but I don't want to have to explain to my boss why you were late again, so we'll just keep this between us. Would that be a good thing?"

The pain was getting to the old man and he answered too quickly, "Yes, yes."

Jürgen released the pressure, but not all at once. He very gradually relaxed his grip making the man wait for him to decide when to let go. Finally, Jürgen patted the back of the old man's hand as one might console the elderly and looked into his eyes. "I'm so glad we agree."

Warily, the old man retracted his hand and gestured for his wife with a too-fast wave. She immediately took up a paper bundle from under the bar and stepped quickly around the bar to stand behind her husband, handing him the bundle. He extended the bundle toward Jürgen, but the strongarm did not take it. As the man stood with the bundle extended, Jürgen took up his glass, downed the rest of the beer, and moved to set the mug down. Instead of resting the glass on the table, he drove the mug down so hard against the table that it exploded into shards leaving the glass handle still in his grasp. He set the glass handle down gently as pieces of glass scattered, some falling off the table. Without looking up, he tapped with a flat palm against the table before withdrawing his hand. The old man set the *Deutsche Mark Bündel* down where Jürgen had tapped and one of his henchmen reached for it, tucking it into his front coat pocket.

"I look forward to seeing you next week," said Jürgen, rising and straightening his coat. Touching the brim of his hat, he nodded and the two younger men turned to exist before Jürgen.

The old woman came up behind her husband and cupped his aching hand in her own, resting her forehead against his shoulder while he patted her arm.

Dear Nephew,

I was so glad to read that you and your mother were getting along so well after so many years apart. The whole family is interested to see what she will choose to do with the family's properties, but they would like me to suggest that she dispense with the properties in favor of something more short-term like cash. I suggest speaking with her therapist, who is certainly nearby, to see where her mind sits on the matter and then helping her to decide to end ownership of the properties.

We are all so astonished to learn that you found one of her longlost sons! It is amazing that you should find him after so many years and we would be very interested to know his plans for the immediate future. Please let us know if he has any plans for his education or if he would rather go into something more rural like tilling the land. He should make this decision soon because life is too short to leave things unfinished.

Please let me know if you have any news for the rest of the family, especially if your mother would like to come for a visit so we might help her plan that. Please take care of yourself, nephew.

Best Regards

H

Jürgen sat in his modest room in Frankfurt, holding the blue postal tissue under a dim electric light. He hadn't spent much time in this place for the past several months, spending six days each week in Cologne. He sat back and thought about the language of the letter feeling stupid for not realizing what the doctor had understood easily. Every therapist had their own therapist. That was a truism of the medical industry because of the difficult and sometimes heartbreaking work they did. Dr. Dudek would have a therapist within a reasonable travel distance of where she worked...the teaching hospital on the grounds of the University of Cologne, not far from where he observed Horace Krämer and her talking. A therapist would only see patients on workdays, so there would probably be one day each week when Dr. Dudek was late for work or left early. If he found out where she went on that day, he would have all weekend to get in and study her therapist's notes. Depending on what he found he would make the decision of whether or not to try to finish the job on Albert, but Dr. Schumann had made his wishes clear in the letter. Dr. Dudek was to die after he learned all he could about her and before she had a chance to go much farther with her cohorts looking for Dr. Schumann.

"*Guten Morgen meine Liebe!*" ("Good morning, my dear!") Wilhelm said cheerfully as he opened the door for Freda.

"Good morning, Wilhelm," Freda greeted her old friend as she followed him into his office.

She had almost become used to the heavy odor of pipe smoke and tar residue that permeated the leather chairs, but not quite. He was always gracious enough to refrain from smoking when they were indoors, but today they had decided to take their session outdoors, so as she stood patiently, he finished tamping fresh tobacco into his pipe and putting in the pocket of his dark brown cardigan. He took up his overcoat and scarf, both heavily worn over the years, and turned to Freda.

Freda was also bundled up in preparation for a lengthy walk in the park today. It had been sunny all week, but today the clouds had moved in and darkened the sky. Luckily, the wind had died down so her legs wouldn't get so chilled. She had chosen a long woolen skirt and three layers of coat, shawl, and overcoat thinking that if she grew too warm, she could remove a layer or two. She had her hair covered with a plain, lightweight cashmere scarf and she had opted for dark shoes and thick stockings today. She set her medicine bag down with several clinks of glass containers settling against each other and turned to lead the way outside. As he followed her into the hallway, she paused for him to lock the door.

Just outside the heavy doors to the old office building, Wilhelm gathered the lapels of his overcoat to block out the cold breeze. The way the wind whipped around the corners of the structure, there was often a small whirlwind of leaves moving across the back landing. As they waited for one to pass, Freda also gathered the front of her overcoat together. The whirlwind spent its energy and drifted aside, so Wilhelm walked to the edge of the first step and offered his hand to Freda. She accepted by placing her hand on his for support as they descended the steps. The gravel walkway from the back of the office building to the park was a short walk, but the path wound its way around the pond coming closer in some spots and moving away from the water in others. Spaced randomly around the meandering walkway were benches and the occasional picnic table. On many, the black paint had weathered and exposed rust from underneath, but the public workers would be around to paint them again when the weather improved this spring.

They walked toward the water and when they reached the spot where the path diverged left and right, he gestured for her to precede him to the left. She nodded and walked along the edge of the gravel. The grass had been mostly dead all winter but with the warming weather, she could see some patches of green here and there. As he fell into step beside her, they breathed in the smells of impending spring and watched the waterfowl cruising around the pond's edges.

"I need to talk with you about something that has happened at the asylum," Freda began, uncertainty coloring her voice.

Wilhelm had been sensing the hesitation since he first saw her, but he would let her get to it on her own, as was his common practice. "I do hope you are well," he said with genuine concern.

"Yes. I am fine. Just a little bruised. There was an attack on Albert Novak by someone who worked at the Wiesenhof Asylum."

He had been expecting something upsetting, but this made him stop in his tracks. She stopped after a couple steps and turned to face him. He took both of her hands in his saying, "My friend, are you in danger?"

"I am not certain. I don't believe that I was the target, but Albert has suffered a serious setback in his treatment as a result of the attack. The asylum has tightened security and is monitoring him continuously, but just when he was beginning to rebuild his sense of stability, he was attacked in the place where he should have been safe." She took her hands back and turned to continue walking and as he joined her, she continued. "I am telling you for two reasons. If I am somehow connected to this person, you might also be in danger. I want you to take precautions to keep yourself from harm if this should be the case."

He nodded. "Certainly, and thank you for being so considerate."

"Albert has been making such wonderful progress. It may be difficult for him to see it from inside his particular psychosis, but from the outside, I see it." As she went on, she glanced at Wilhelm to gauge his reaction. His face betrayed his curiosity, so she continued. "Since his adoptive parents are still living, I have written to them and asked that they come visit with Albert."

He thought for a moment and nodded affirmatively saying, "That would probably be a good thing for him at this stage."

"I am very hopeful that they will be able to come and see him soon so they can help him come to terms with what he has been through. I think he would trust the point of view of family members over mine. I mean, I think he trusts me, but, well, you know what I mean," she added.

"I do indeed. He may well come to trust you implicitly, but family always outranks you." He looked up into her eyes as they walked and shrugged away the cold. "So far, it sounds like a good plan of action."

"I have described some of the situation to the Rabinowitz' but I will meet with them when they arrive to ensure they are well-informed. Albert has been writing to them, but I want to make sure they have a clinical view before seeing him. I do not wish to cause them emotional stress, but if I am to help Albert recover, he will need others to ground him."

Wilhelm didn't respond verbally, but slowed his pace, looking up at the sky through the new growth in the trees. He took a deep breath and let it out as she slowed and returned to his side. She could tell he was weighing many conflicting paths of advice so she joined him in his appreciation of the crisp air, breathing deeply, and waiting.

"I believe that Albert's quality of life is worth significant investment, as do you, and I think that you have already decided to do your best to help him. Has he agreed to meet with them?" he asked.

"I informed him and he did not object," she answered without opening her eyes. "I am going to take that as a 'yes'." As she spoke the conviction, she bobbed her head to the side slightly.

He looked at her askance. "I see." A smirk traced its way across his lips. "I think this is a good thing...in my professional opinion." He grasped his lapels, tugging them taut and lifting up on the balls of his feet in a bob like an expert salesman.

"Please go on." He gestured ahead so they might continue walking and she obliged. As they walked, they approached one of the benches around the pond. He diverted toward it and sat with Freda moving to sit at his side.

Freda continued their discussion. "Albert's situation is unusual in that he was deliberately violated in the camps. He cannot disregard the event as someone who is castrated by infection or by accident, for example. He is also prevented from seeking justice while he is in his current state, so he may be unable to find a suitable outlet for his grief."

"Yes. I can see how that could be so," he added, nodding for her to continue.

"I want to find out what you think about another idea, which may or may not bear fruit," she asked in a requesting tone.

"Please. Continue," he invited.

"The procedures performed on Albert were not common and though finding survivors may be unlikely, I would like your opinion on locating others who have suffered the way he has suffered," she asked.

"You mean to find others who survived castration experiments and bring these people together?" His tone was dubious as was the look on his face.

"That is exactly what I hope to do," she replied. "Understand that I would also perform a psychological evaluation of each respondent to determine if meeting them would help or hurt Albert's mental state."

He relaxed, feeling a little chided and realizing that he had allowed his own doubt to show on his face without realizing it. "When no risk is taken, the likelihood of progress is low indeed."

"Thank you, Wilhelm." She took a deep breath, looking out over the water. Admiring the view, she said, "I appreciate your counsel."

Chapter 14

The 1952 cream-colored Pontiac Chieftain pulled up the circular drive to the Wiesenhof Asylum. The sky was gray. The wind was cold and biting. The mist saturated everything. Lena Rabinowitz opened the door and stepped into the drive. The breeze was erratic, swirling her long woolen coat around her ankles. Ernst stepped out of the back seat behind her. Both were bundled for the weather in proper visitation attire. His hat was fresh and new, bought for the occasion, but the rain was making it droop. Her coarse veil glistened like a spider web in the icy mist. As they climbed the slushy gray steps, Ernst hoped his wife was not uncomfortable. This last gasp of winter had turned the early spring gray again, killing the flowers that had emerged too soon and burying the tufts of tender grass in dirty sleet. Lena had forgotten her gloves and her hands were certainly chilly but nothing would deter them today, so they pressed on against the wind.

He could tell this place was making his wife nervous. Both of them had experiences during the occupation that left them with sour memories, but being in this place, where so many of their family, friends, and colleagues had been treated, must be weighing on her mind. Ernst could feel his wife needing him, drawing strength from him, hurting. He would make this happen. He would see this through. He would be there for her no matter what became of their son. Ever since Ernst had adopted Albert into the family, he had known that Albert belonged. His daughters had accepted the boy immediately and treated him better than most sisters treat younger brothers. Where had he gone wrong with the boy? Ernst knew things were different with Albert early on but he never thought it would come to this. In his day, if you had a problem you dealt with it and no one else knew, but so many had succumbed to the stresses of poverty, persecution, and starvation that his way of thinking might not have a place in this new world.

Lena certainly had not wanted to come to this place but there were many such places throughout Germany where phantoms of memory lingered. Years before, when Lena's sister had passed away, she had been in this very same institution. As Lena watched, dementia extracted is price slowly and painfully...relentlessly. The visits, family members, weeping, consoling, arguing...she caught her breath and pressed the memories down. Ernst probably never knew how often she drew on his strength. She appreciated that. He was not simply proud, he was kind. A nod here, a squeeze of the hand there, never in sight of anyone but reassuring nonetheless, he was there, strong.

Opening the slow-swinging door to the spacious lobby, they brushed off the mist and debris. The soft woolen rug at the entryway could have been one of the pieces taken from some wealthy household during the occupation. It looked out-of-place here, with dark colors and fading around the edges, though the surrounding lobby was bright and clean. The space was large enough to be a cathedral with a very high ceiling making the two of them feel small and insignificant. As Lena started across the open space, her steps rang against the walls echoing out of time with her husband's. As they approached the receptionist desk a nurse looked up. She was fresh-faced, without makeup, and nearly expressionless save for an almost imperceptible smile.

"Good afternoon. And you are?" queried the nurse in a flat tone.

"Mr. and Mrs. Ernst Rabinowitz," he stated matter of factly.

"We would like to see our son," Lena interjected, suddenly falling silent as she realized her overstep. She knew that she had spoken out of turn but her son was here, somewhere, needing her. It was impossible to remain entirely calm.

"Dr. Freda has been expecting you," the nurse said impatiently, but without irritation. In fact, they were to be the only two visitors of the day and she was relieved to be able to get back to her patients.

"Please wait here," she instructed with a nod.

The nurse rose from her station and turned. As she receded down an adjacent hallway to her right, her footfalls echoed loudly into the lobby. After a few moments, a squeak, a turn, and a loud clack. Ernst and Lena both started at the unexpected sound but remained composed, patiently waiting as instructed. Some muffled voices, the distant door opened again shutting more quietly this time but instead of one set of footfalls there were two. The nurse's calm, regular steps were accompanied by another pair, impatient, squeaking, rushing. A few moments later a red-haired, red-faced youth came around the corner, hand extended.

"I'm so glad you're here! How was your trip? I am Helga," volunteered this new nurse, grasping his hand with a vigorous shake. "Lena, I'm so glad you could come. Albert has been doing so much better lately since we told him you would visit," she said reaching energetically for Lena's hand. "I'll take you to Dr. Freda."

Without further invitation the young woman turned and walked down the hall. Clearly, she expected them to follow so they did so at a modest pace. After several strides, the exuberant youth slowed her gate to match theirs. She hadn't even turned to check their progress. Obviously she was quite a bit more practiced than her age would suggest. Ernst and Lena both had the same thought. *My, how these young people adapt so!* Each of Lena's steps echoed with memory. She recalled the powder green wainscoting and the shine on the floor. The walls were the classic enamel white one would see in any hospital. Gurneys freshly made with white cotton sheets and pillows occupied some of the empty spaces between the heavy wooden doors that lined the long hallway. Only the frames at each doorway showed signs of wear, having the paint chipped off at the level of the gurney rails.

Helga stopped at a door two-thirds of the way down the hall and waited for them patiently. Ernst noticed how calm and still she was despite her energetic gate. As they approached, she opened the door for them and nodded inside. He had forgotten to remove his hat so he removed it before entering. Lena saw his *faux pas* and smiled ever-so-slightly. The room seemed empty. White walls, wooden desks, but no one here. Suddenly, a woman appeared through another doorway.

"I'm so glad to meet you both," Dr. Freda beamed, handshake at the ready. "How was your trip? Are you well?"

"I don't understand. I thought we were coming to meet my son."

"You are, you are. I just want to talk with you before we meet him so you understand what is going on."

"Warum? Was ist los?" ("Why? What is going on?") Ernst did not intend it to come out so impatiently.

"Nothing is wrong. You know that your son has been in treatment and we are going to talk about that treatment before you see him so that you will understand what you see and so you do not do anything that might make him worse," she said with an even, studied tone. Dr. Freda had the stoic expression that only comes from seeing people suffer and Ernst felt for her. For someone to deliberately put themselves through pain to help others had always been a quality he admired. *Now I can relax,* Ernst thought. He was an excellent judge of character and had been so all his life. This woman cared. Dr. Freda appeared to Ernst to be an even-minded woman of approximately his son's age. While it was true that in his time it was uncommon to permit oneself to be treated by a female doctor, times were different, times were changing. Regardless of his trepidations, his son had benefited from her intervention and so he respected her stewardship.

The conversation lasted barely a half hour but in that time Ernst and Lena learned more than they wished. Their son had made two attempts at suicide following a nervous breakdown at the Budapest Rabbinical Seminary. "How could this happen?" "It doesn't matter" "...but, men of faith?" "Men of faith are just men..." "If you are ready to go see him I think we can visit for a while. He should be waking up soon." Another hallway, another turn, footsteps echoed louder all the way. "Albert is in here. You may visit for one hour and then he must rest," Dr. Freda said as she held the door open. Husband and wife stood motionless before entering slowly, not looking up. Dr. Freda came in behind them and softly closed the door.

The room was clean, smelling of antiseptic. The entire room was white from floor to ceiling. In a sole bed between two windows lay a young man, emaciated, head pulled back and face mildly contorted in distant pain. He was sleeping but not peacefully. As Lena looked up slowly, she drew forward toward the resting man. As she approached, her heart raced. She felt her face flush. She had been told that it was important to remain calm so she took a deep breath and grasped her son's hand for the first time in nearly two years. They had wanted so much to visit him before now, but each time they questioned the doctors caring for him, they were told that "Now was not a good time," and "It would be best for Albert if they waited." She laid her hand on his. His hand was cold, twitching as if in a dream, and as thin as his grandmother's hands had been at her end. Lena squeezed back tears and examined the sleeping form. It was Albert.

She bent to his ear and whispered *"Liebling, Mutter ist hier."* ("Darling, mother is here.")

Albert immediately awoke with a start turning to look directly into her face, disbelieving, then doubting, almost knowing.

"Meine Mutter?" ("Mother?") Albert said questioningly. "Are you here?"

"Denkst Du ich würde ohne Deinen Vater kommen?" ("Do you think I would come without your father?")

"Nein, mutter." ("No, mother.")

As Albert's grogginess cleared, he began to see distress in his mother's eyes. It had been nearly two years since she had seen him and when she and Ernst had entered, she had initially thought Dr. Freda had brought them to the wrong room. He was so thin and looked so much older than he should.

Lip trembling, she raised her hand to her mouth as the lines around her eyes deepened with the realization that her son must have been far more ill than she knew. His letters had been infrequent, but at least he kept in touch. He had told them about being in the hospital and about the suicide attempt which they already knew about from hospital officials but she had assumed that the report was exaggerated. Albie's letters hadn't included anything about him losing so much weight or the scars she could now see plainly on his neck. Her breath caught in her throat as she tried desperately to control herself. They were there to help Albie if they could, but how could they keep his real condition from her like this?

Albert was awake but he doubted that his eyes were seeing clearly. Dr. Freda had suggested many medications that she said would help him. He liked the fact that she didn't simply tell him what to do or force treatment on him. She explained it to him as if they were working together to solve a problem and she always made him feel as if it were his decision to take the medicines. He had agreed but after taking the medication for several days, or could it be weeks, he had realized that the pills did not stop the dreams. When he was on the highest doses of medications, he would awaken remembering nothing but feel drunk and nauseous most of the day. He knew this was not good for his body as it made him not want to eat but the good doctor convinced him it was necessary and he trusted her. For Albert, this only meant that he worried more. He was not the type to let things go easily and so the medication had not resolved the problem. It was merely delaying the fact that he would have to deal with events in his own time. As he and Dr. Freda had agreed, he was taking fewer medications and going to counseling sessions so he had been sleeping less and remembering more. He was fearful that he would end up back in the situation that put him under Dr. Freda's care. He was always afraid that the memories would come rising back up to swallow him.

Recently, he had begun to awaken with an echo in his mind, almost like the echo of someone in a large room crying out, just after they have been silenced. He remembered a beam of dingy green-gray sunlight angling down, illuminating motes of dust in the air and landing on dried black liquid on an uneven concrete floor. He thought there might be tall men and metal tables about head high in the room but the memory faded too quickly to be sure. This was a distant, terrifying memory, but the memories of what happened in the Rabbinical Seminary were always clear in his mind. He still couldn't get past the betrayal of faith that he experienced. The jeers and pinches of his classmates bruised far deeper than his skin. He relived each slight, each insult constantly, like a ghost image behind his vision, just behind his eyes. Sometimes he could almost see the communal shower room behind his waking sight where the boys were all bigger, stronger, and endowed in a way he would never be.

Albert realized that he was daydreaming again and quickly shut away his feelings. Clearing his eyes, he gazed at her still disbelieving. She was here. She was real. The expression on her face made it clear that she had watched the painful memories play across his face over the last few moments. She was holding one hand to her mouth and with the other, she held his. Her skin was warm. When she closed her hand around his thin wrist, he reached to place his hand on the back of hers. She looked down and saw a terrible scar on his wrist. She brought her hand down from her mouth, her trembling lip visible now. Gently but insistently turning his hand over, she stared at the tattoo on his arm. Some of the numbers had been divided and when rejoined, the blurry black figures no longer lined up. They were only slightly offset, but she knew then that this image would be burned into her memory until her last day on Earth.

The tears that had been welling up in her eyes now obscured her vision but she made no attempt to wipe them away. She stood next to Albie, her son, drowning in a flood of emotions as the occasional tear fell to land on the white sheets. Ernst took a step up behind her and placed his hand on the back of her shoulder, hoping he could steady her.

Albert became aware of the Rabbi looking around Lena's shoulder, smiling down at him, one hand on his mother's shoulder.

"Mein Sohn." ("My son.")

"Vater." ("Father.")

"Was ist los?" ("What is going on?")

Albert was overwhelmed with memory and emotion. He couldn't help himself. He wanted to be strong for them, to show them how grown he was, but he descended into tears just as he had when he was young and had skinned his knee. As his shoulders began to shake with silent sobs, his mother squeezed his hand and stroked his hair. Many moments passed in silence as he struggled to regain control of his emotions.

"Entspann Dich, mein Sohn. Kümmern wir uns nicht drum." ("Relax, my son. Let us have none of that.")

Albert could feel their strength reinforcing his own as they patiently waited for him to compose himself. They could not possibly understand what he had been through even though he knew Dr. Freda had explained the sequence of events to them. It was time for him to confess his past and accept his parents' judgment.

"Was ist los?" Ernst repeated imploringly.

"I am an offense to you and Yahweh. I have turned my back on my life and my family," Albert whispered shamefully.

"We are aware that you tried to suicide and we are thankful that you did not succeed. Yahweh may yet forgive you if you turn away from these ways of disgrace, son," Lena assured.

"I fear He will not forgive the thoughts I have had," Albert retorted.

"*Mein Sohn*, we have all fallen into despair at sometime or another. Many of those who perished in the war did so by their own hand because they could not bear the fear of what would happen to them if they fell into the hands of the Reich. They chose a path away from Yahweh into darkness. War does this to people," Ernst explained. "The important thing is that you are alive and that you realize the insult of your actions. You must vow never to repeat them."

"You know that I love you, father, but you do not understand," Albert replied hoping that his words would not be taken as disrespect for his father.

Albert's skin flushed cold as he realized what he was about to do. He weakly began to work his way into an upright position so that he could see his parents more easily. Tears continued to well up in his eyes and run down his sunken cheeks but he made no attempt to dry his face. He was resolute. Dr. Freda had allowed his medications to be reduced over the past few weeks so that he could be reasonably coherent for this confession, but she had promised that she would keep his secret and let him be the one to tell his parents. Albert began to tremble.

Ernst turned to face Lena more directly. "We have *geheimnis* (a secret) to tell you."

Lena's expression changed from one of empathy to one of fear and surprise. What could her husband have to say to her that she did not already know? She turned to look into Albert's face where his expression of sheepish guilt confirmed. Her husband and son whom she had adopted and loved as her own had kept something important from her. It seemed that she had a choice. Either to get upset now or remain calm until she learned what the secret was and then decide how to handle it. She took a deep, calming breath looking at both of their guilty faces in turn. Then, she leaned forward placing her hand on each of theirs to acknowledge that they had her undivided attention. Then she sat back, folded her hands, and waited for her world to change.

When Albie was young, just after the war, he was extremely depressed and quiet. Who wouldn't be? Ernst and Lena had both known that he was rescued from Auschwitz, Block Ten, where horrible doctors like Horst Schumann tortured and mutilated Jews, homosexuals, and the homeless who had been rounded up. They had both read about the horrible things done to people and knew that Albie would have been treated very badly. He was lucky to be alive. They had been told that of the many thousands of prisoners in his block, only thirty-five German-speaking Jews remained. They knew about the two friends that he had become attached to. Naturally, they were not in a financial position to adopt all three, but they had promised to help him find them at some future date. Unfortunately, that date had never come.

Theirs was a conservative, but not entirely repressed, Jewish household and they did what they felt was appropriate to help him recover and build a new life for himself. Nevertheless, Ernst would periodically take Albie out for a day in the city and when they would return, they would not discuss what had transpired. Lena did not press either of them, thinking it to be a matter between father and son, but she found it odd that neither of them would talk about any of these trips or what happened on those days.

Ernst traveled to the adoption center just outside Krakow one day before the adoption after asking Lena to join him the next day. At the time, she thought this a completely normal thing, though in reality she had no idea how this process was supposed to work. She was following his lead and doing her part to help a young survivor. That was enough for her. What she did not know at the time was that Ernst had been summoned by the adoption center to submit to an evaluation and interrogation. When he arrived at the center, he was greeted by an ancient specimen of a nurse, he could not remember her name, who took him into a room where he filled out many forms, answering the same questions as he had previously, but puzzling over new ones as well. Did they have any criminal insanity in their family? Had they any experience with sexual deviants? Was their marriage traditional or more progressive? Would he choose to communicate openly or handle Albert's special medical needs himself?

Medical needs?...Lena wondered and glanced up at Albert then at Ernst realizing that those trips to the city were part of the secret.

The trips into the city were necessary to see the only doctor for kilometres who could deal with Albert's problems. As he grew he would periodically experience discomfort or even intense pain from the buildup of scar tissue, stitches that pulled out, and bladder infections which were one thing he would deal with all his life. The doctors at Auschwitz were only experimenting. They were not motivated to preserve the quality of life for people they fully intended to kill after their usefulness as medical subjects came to an end. If the procedures had been done in the free world the result would have been much more acceptable.

What would be acceptable? Bladder infections? Isn't that a female problem? Lena's mind raced no matter how she tried to calm herself.

When Ernst finished explaining where they had gone and what they had done on the days they would never talk about, Albert tried to edit the details down to a level he thought she would find acceptable. He told them about how Gabriel had been the one to suffer most, taking so much longer to heal than he and Lukas. The doctors that took their manhood had no regard for the welfare of their patients and the quality of their work was abhorrent. That was why he needed the occasional doctor visit with someone who would keep things private. His father had put himself and his family's reputation at risk to help his son and he was so grateful for that.

Albert finished talking. The room grew quiet. For a long minute, the only sounds were the squeaks of shoes and clack of door latches in the hall. Lena's shoulders hung low. She hadn't moved since they started. Ernst's head had been bowed with his hat in his hands while he told his side of the secret and listened carefully to Albert. Now, he too was sitting motionless, preparing for her to pass judgment.

Albert's secret was known and there was no way to take it back. Would the woman who had become his mother rise and leave him to his own end? After such a story, he was exhausted and wanted to rest but he remained upright. Tears had dried on his face leaving salty streaks and dampening the front of his gown but he made no attempt to clean himself. He barely breathed.

Lena took a short breath and sighed with a catch. She thought it might have been her first breath in a half-hour. She was afraid to move, to break the silence that had fallen over them like a frost. She opened her eyes, still looking at her lap and realized that tears hung from her eyes, trembling, distorting her vision. As she raised her head slowly, she blinked and the bloated tears finally fell to join many others scattered across the backs of her hands folded in her lap.

"Mein Frau," ("My wife,") Ernst began, but she did not respond immediately.

"Wir sprechen uns später." ("We will speak later.") She gave him an ominous glance and he withdrew.

Ernst knew when Lena was angry or upset and the slight tremble in her voice gave him enough pause to remain silent. He was, of course, the man of the household, but a man knows when to keep quiet.

Lena turned to Dr. Freda with a stern expression. "You could not have told me about this...about how sick he was?" There was unmistakable anger in Lena's voice that stung everyone in the room.

Dr. Freda had been standing in the corner throughout the encounter and only now realized that her professional demeanor had crumbled some time ago. Tears threatened to reveal her weakness but she dared not move. On visitation days she made herself forgo some of her daily gin and now she was feeling the effects. Her feet ached. Her back ached. She felt unsteady after standing still for almost an hour. She knew Lena's question was rhetorical and did not warrant an answer.

Lena stood slowly, uncertainly, hands still folded, but she remained where she was. She appeared to Albert to be trembling. He thought he would faint from fear as he waited for her to respond. She would turn and leave, he was certain. The silence had lasted too long. Slowly, Lena turned to her husband who also stood, straightening his lapels. Irresistible tears began to rise in Albert's eyes even though he thought he was past crying anymore. It was over. He had lost his manhood, his sanity, his faith, and now he had lost his parents. Lena took Ernst's right hand in her left and turned to Albert, taking a cautious step toward the bedside. She laid her right hand on his hand at his side and curled her fingers around his. She was definitely trembling.

Lena's mind was racing. From the time they had adopted young Albie, she had never known any of what had happened to him in the camps, beyond what she assumed happened to all prisoners. She knew that prisoners were starved. Certainly, Albie was very slim but since his treatment by The Red Cross in London included feeding him, he wasn't starving when they adopted him. She had never imagined that such horrible things could be done to one person by another. Ernst would surely say that it was their duty to forgive these men, but to Lena, this seemed impossible just now. Despite her normally quiet and stoic demeanor, she felt a true sense of ill will for the men that had hurt her son.

"Why was I not told any of this before now?" Lena asked and suddenly realized that her voice was raised. She took a deep breath. No one answered. She looked at Ernst for an answer but he lowered his gaze to the floor. She looked at Albert but he lowered his gaze to his lap. She looked over her shoulder at Dr. Freda whose gaze was already lowered. At this moment, she realized that she was about to erupt, so she took a deep breath and attempted to calm herself. She repeated several breaths while everyone in the room remained silent.

As she reigned in her emotions, the ill will she felt toward the Nazi party for what they had done to her family, to her relatives, to her son, swelled to a deeper hatred than she had ever felt before. Killing innocent people was bad enough, but these wretched men had tortured and mutilated defenseless children. If there was a single one of them left alive, she wished they would be struck down. Then she realized that many others had...have...the same wish. She continued to control her breathing. Ernst and Albert both felt her trembling subside.

Albert looked up to discover that she was looking directly into his eyes. She smiled and the love that radiated from her was more than Albert could bear. Her eyes at once contained both judgment and sympathy. As the scene became more emotional and tearful, Dr. Freda quietly took the door handle behind her back, opened the door, and slipped out of the room to find Helga standing across the hallway. Dr. Freda wiped tears from her cheeks and smiled at Helga's imploring stare. As relief washed over Helga's face, she crossed the space to stand directly in front of Freda. Taking Freda's hands in her own, she nodded her approval with a smile. Dr. Freda had accomplished what many other doctors had failed to do. Not only had she reached Albert, but she had helped him regain his ties to family and possibly given him a reason to live.

Ernst looked down at Albert who had stopped crying. Lena had pulled a handkerchief from her pocket and done her best to dry his tears. He must admit. She had once again amazed him. She was far stronger than he, though he wasn't a man prone to tears.

As he examined Albert, he regretted what he must say next. "*Sohn*, I am happy you were not successful in taking your own life. You and I both know what it means to lose your soul, so why would you do such a thing?"

Albert took a long time to compose his thoughts, even though he had thought about this answer for weeks. "I was certain I had no future other than pain and suffering. Why would anyone go through that?"

"Because you were meant to," answered Ernst.

"I just wanted to rest...for the memories and the pain to stop," Albert admitted.

"It was the pain and the memories that were creating who you needed to be for what comes in the future. If you end that, you make the decision for Yahweh." Ernst felt he did not need to clarify further. His son knew his mind and his stance on the issue. He became a man more than half his lifetime ago and would ultimately choose his own path but he had to say one more thing. "This was no coincidence that twice you have failed to kill yourself and more than that, someone else has failed to kill you. Everything that you have gone through has been the will of Yahweh. For some reason, He is not ready to let you go so easily, so He surrounds you with the right people at the right times."

Albert accepted the lesson without argument or resistance. He already knew that he was weak, but he had not considered that he might need to be stronger for some future purpose. He had also come to think that perhaps the medications were not going to be a good idea if they took away his ability to defend himself. His father's advice was the teachings he had grown up with, but he did not understand what it was like to be emasculated and to carry the memories of death and horror that Albert dreamed nearly every night.

As Ernst and Lena comforted their son, the sunlight grew dimmer and the sky outside grew grayer. They had stayed too long and surely the doctor was waiting for them outside. She had told them one hour and they had been here for nearly two, so they hugged, wished each other well, and collected their coats. Ernst held his coat over one arm and the crown of his hat nestled in his elbow. With the other hand, he opened the door for his wife. She turned one last time to smile, bestowing one last dose of love before leaving. Nurse Helga and Dr. Freda waited for them on the opposite side of the hall and the doctor gestured back down the hall to the room where they had talked before seeing Albert.

After the door closed, the silence seemed to absorb Albert. His ears rang with it, enhanced by the medicines wearing off. He sat thinking and as the memory of his mother's loving eyes melded with his birth mother's eyes, he began to weep silently. He knew he must find a way to get better and go on, but he hardly knew where to start.

Helga opened the office door for the three older people, Dr. Freda nodded at her, indicating that they would need some privacy, so she closed the door behind them and resolved to get caught up on her chores. As she went about her business delivering pillows and comforting patients, she felt a constant nagging curiosity about what they were discussing. At times she found it difficult to focus, but Dr. Freda would fill her in later if she felt it necessary.

As Helga and Albert sat in the warming sunshine of a springtime day, the courtyard was alive with the buzzes and clicks of bees sampling every fresh flower they could find. Grasshoppers sprung from place to place. The grass was a lush green, thanks to their groundskeeper. After several sessions, Dr. Freda had concluded that if Albert was ever to be trusted again, now would be a good time to start. Helga leaned toward him with a sigh, and turning her face down from the sunshine, she focused on the stationary in his lap. He had been scribbling for quite some time and she had tried to leave him alone to write, but her chattiness got the better of her.

"Who are you writing to?" she asked.

Albert paused writing, took a deep breath, and looked up with his eyes closed to let the sun warm his face. "I am writing to my parents."

"Have they written back to you recently?" she wondered aloud.

"Not my adoptive parents, my birth parents," he clarified.

"You mean the ones who..." the question died on her lips.

"The dead ones," he said quietly, almost whispering. "I have been thinking that they would want to know how my life has gone, the good people I have met, and about my new parents and sisters."

Helga sat quietly looking at the sunshine on Albert's closed eyelids, wondering if this was a painful topic for him, but seeing no sign of anguish, she asked, "What are you telling them?"

Albert said, "I told them I wasn't ready."

"What for?" Helga asked as she reclined into the grass on her elbows.

"To join them," Albert said. "I don't think they would want me to leave too soon."

Feeling a bit snarky, Helga said, "You'll join them soon enough. There is no need to speed up the process." She knew that was an insensitive thing to say to a suicide patient in recovery, but she was feeling more comfortable with Albert and he was progressing quite well. She didn't look to see his reaction, but continued warming her face with her eyes closed breathing in the fresh scents of flowers and earth. She could hear Albert's breathing, soft and deep. He hadn't taken offense and this was a good sign. Though he was far from well, she felt good about being his friend, which is not something one feels good about if someone is about to kill themself.

Chapter 15

Gabriel had only been told that someone would be coming to take him to a new home. Over the past few days he had been heartbroken, crying himself to sleep, missing Albert and Lukas. Though they had promised the adults, the nuns and nurses, that they would be grownups, none of them could contain their tears when it came time for each of them to be taken away. He wasn't a baby. He didn't cry all the time, but this was so difficult to bear. Efforts had been made to find his parents after the liberation of Auschwitz, but the Reich's killing operations and record keeping had been meticulous and when his parents' names were found in the ledgers, he finally knew that they were dead. When the nun had come to tell him what they had found, she didn't even have to say a single word. Her face was an open book to Gabriel and for the first time since he and his parents were separated at the Auschwitz gate, he knew they were gone.

One morning, the nuns woke him up earlier than the other children. Trying not to disturb those sleeping around the room, they whispered that he should rise and come with them. He should bring his clothes and toothbrush. They escorted him to the communal bathing room and waited patiently for him to dress. Miss Ana, who had spent many an evening holding him as he cried, fixed his collar and straightened his pant leg. As she knelt, she looked up at his hair, avoiding his eyes, and brushed a curl from his forehead with her fingernails. Gabriel saw a tear falling slowly down one cheek and the smile on her face was forced. Her lips were tight and her chin wrinkled as she breathed in controlled gasps. He could feel a kind of pain emanating from her and he wondered why, with all of the children she had seen pass through this facility, she would be feeling this way with him. He raised a palm and placed it against her cheek, wiping the tear away and wishing he could absorb her pain. She finally looked into his eyes and, placing her hand over his, closed her eyes and said a small prayer for his future happiness.

Jakob and Charlotte Arslock were a Polish couple living in East Germany on a farm outside the village of *Tauche*. Gabriel knew right away that things were not going to go well when Jakob had taken him roughly by the hand and dragged him out of the lobby of the orphanage. The man's grip transmitted angry disappointment without saying a single word and when his wife, Charlotte, reached to hold the door open for Jakob, her sleeves lifted for a second and Gabriel saw what he thought could be bruises.

When Jakob ordered him into the back seat of their rust-colored Volkswagen 1500, the look of judgmental disdain was palpable, washing over Gabriel like a dirty blast of sand. He had always been very intuitive about people and could usually tell friend from foe on the very first glance. When he was young, his mother had frequently remarked about his keen senses while his father remained indifferent, but Jakob was blatantly hostile. The minute they pulled out of the driveway, he wished he could go back. The drive to their farm was long, dusty, and uncomfortably quiet.

Charlotte did not look at Gabriel in the back seat, facing forward and saying nothing the entire time. When they turned from the main road onto a hilly, bumpy country road, Jakob continued driving at the same speed without seeming to care that the dry rivulets and uneven ruts in this road bounced the car's passengers around in an uncomfortable and tiring way. Gabriel tried to hold himself in a proper upright position, imitating Charlotte's rigid posture, but the constantly changing forces on his body made it impossible. He couldn't see, but Charlotte must be propping herself very firmly against the seat to hold so still as the car lurched this way and that.

As they turned up the dirt drive to an old farmhouse in need of much attention, Gabriel could hear a dog barking, getting closer. A horse whinnied not far away, and birds sang in the trees. Chickens clucked and suddenly panicked, scattering with a ruckus. Gabriel saw a blur of brown feathers streak the corner of his view through Charlotte's passenger window and Gabriel couldn't understand how they had not hit the bird. It was so close. Jakob skidded the car to a stop, flung the shift lever up, and opened the car door almost in the same motion leaving Gabriel and Charlotte in the car. Charlotte opened her door, unlatched her seat belt, and without turning around, asked Gabriel to come inside. As Gabriel opened the door, a slobbering oaf of a hound accosted him, assessing him with a snarf and a taste. In an instant of hesitant uncertainty, the two sized each other up and decided...friend. Seconds later, Gabriel was slicked over with the dog's slobbery affection. Charlotte called to him and he pushed the dog bodily out of the way as it continued to try to climb on him and lick him.

Just then, Jakob belted out a command *"Komm her!"* ("Come here!") and the dog turned away, head hung low, shoulders dropping suddenly as if in fear but the wag of the tail irrepressible, if subdued. Gabriel felt a pang of sympathy for the dog, sensing all the pain that must have led to that reaction. *No dog reacts like this unless it has been beaten for many years,* he thought. He stood, closed the car door, which didn't latch, but instead bounced up and down when it should have closed. He took the door by the handle and pushed it shut firmly and this time it did latch. He turned toward the cottage and saw Charlotte beckoning him to walk faster. He caught up to her and she escorted him to the steps, putting a hand on his shoulder and pressing him to go first. The squeeze of her hand on his shoulder passed into him a message of warning and a wish for things to go well. As he reached the three concrete steps leading up to the front door, he noticed that the steps and landing were cracked unevenly and tilted to the right corner so that if water fell on it, it would run through the uneven separation against the house. The structure was suspended on piers with a lattice skirt that must have been painted when it was first installed, but now only some flecks of paint remained as the wood aged and rotted away. As he adjusted to the tilted landing and opened the screen door, he saw Jakob inside, opening the cupboard and taking down a brown stout bottle with a lever cap, which he opened and drank immediately.

Putting the bottle down, but not letting it go, he looked over his shoulder at Gabriel saying, "So what happened to you?"

Gabriel could not tell what the man was referring to, since he had been through so much...being arrested, going to Auschwitz, losing his parents, being raped and repeatedly tortured, operated on, mutilated, rescued, moved to London and back, losing his two best friends, and being adopted. He thought it might be a good idea to give a response that would both answer the man's question and garner some kind of sympathy from him, if there was an ounce of sympathy left in the man.

Gabriel answered in a soft voice, "My parents were killed."

"WHAT? Can't hear you!" Jakob interrupted.

"MY PARENTS WERE KILLED IN THE CAMPS," Gabriel answered with his voice raised loud, but not yelling.

"That's better." Jakob's reply was a lesson disguised as a compliment. "Well, I'm very sorry for what happened to your parents, but we all have someone that isn't around anymore." He looked down at the bottle and lowered his tone. "There's nothing you can do about that," he stared listlessly at the opening of the bottle. A few moments passed before he looked back at Gabriel.

Der Scheißkerl (This piece of shit) was his responsibility now. *Scheiße* (Shit). They could have least gotten him a boy instead of this *Lutscher* (sissy)! He would be saddled with this pansy boy for years, but there were people he needed to impress who wouldn't treat him as well if he didn't do something *humanitarian*. In a small community, he had to be careful or this *Lutscher* would make him look like a fool.

Throughout Germany, those with the means to adopt children were expected to do so. One day, at the Orthodox Roman Catholic Church in town, the priest had given a rousing homily after the Bible readings. He talked about the horrible things the Reich had done, about how children were born innocent, about how every parishioner was a child of God and needed to care for those in need. When Charlotte brought the news home to Jakob, he knew what was coming next, but he could see no way out of it. The priest all but ordered everyone without children to adopt all the children they could support. *Well, maybe this wouldn't be so bad,* he began to think to himself. It had been very hard on him, running the farm all by himself. He always thought Charlotte was worth less than a pissant when it came to real chores. Maybe if he adopted a young boy, he could get some work done. The boy would be earning his keep, so it wouldn't be so bad.

In fact, Charlotte cooked every meal, cleaned the entire house, tilled, planted, weeded, and harvested the garden, washed the clothes, and helped out with chores on the farm.

"They told me you would need some medical fixing sometimes," he stated bluntly.

"They told me that too," Gabriel responded with his voice deliberately at the raised level, holding the man's gaze.

"We all have to pull our weight here. Got that? If chicks die, we get no eggs. If the goats die, we get no meat. If the horse can't pull, we get not vegetables. Got it?"

"Yes, sir." Gabriel didn't feel the words, but he knew he must say them to avoid causing unnecessary grief.

Jakob stared at Gabriel as if stunned. Maybe he expected to hear something more defiant? He lifted the bottle using the mouth as a pointer toward the boy. *"Genau."* ("Exactly.") He just now noticed that the bottle was empty and set it aside to reach for another. It had been almost a whole day without a drink. He knew that he needed to do the *right thing* or his neighbors, or worse, his sister, would think he wasn't doing his part and cut off the money, so he swallowed his pride and did what he had to do. This bastard would be the price and he needed to pay it, but *Verdammit!* this wasn't fair.

Gabriel could feel the hate and rage radiating from Jakob. Gabriel was frozen...not from fear, but from knowing that a misstep could lead to a beating. Maybe a beating wouldn't come on the first day, but he felt it would happen soon; perhaps a few days from now. At that moment, he knew what his future would be like in this place.

His sister, Miss Mina Arslock, knew what Jakob thought of her but she didn't care. Jakob had been completely irresponsible his whole life. When her father was running the farm and expected Jakob to do his duty and work hard to help support his family, more often than not, the boy would be found sleeping in some hiding place or playing nonsense games. A few times, he had been caught terrorizing the animals, which her father explained would have consequences. Stressed chickens laid fewer eggs and wouldn't hatch chicks; stressed goats would be more prone to disease; and so on. When Jakob had been caught having carnal relations with Charlotte, a homely girl in the village, their father forced the young man to marry her under threat of disownment. While Mina had gone to university and made something of her life as a business woman, Jakob had only done just enough to get by. The farm had the potential to generate income beyond what his family consumed, but he simply did not have the motivation to try, so when it came time to help the children rescued from the concentration camps, Miss Mina knew she would have to act. Her father had put the whole of his estate in her name, so she used her leverage to get Jakob to do his patriotic duty.

Dear Jakob,

I know you are as heartbroken as I am at the plight of the orphaned children of Germany. I am certain that you will want to do your part to help these poor souls find their way in the world. I want to continue helping you with expenses and upkeep of our parents' farm, but I must insist that you take on at least one child so they might have a chance at a good future.

Please let me know when you have done this so I may release the funds to you.

Miss Mina Arslock

Chapter 16

Gabriel had been working on the farm for a couple years and had actually started making some progress, though it was agonizingly slow. He was small and did not seem to be growing like other boys his age. He was averse to getting his hands dirty and splinters or scrapes seemed to disable him for extended periods of time. He wasn't very good at the things Jakob was trying to teach him about running and maintaining a farm. This led to frequent eruptions of yelling and hitting in which Jakob's frustration would overflow, often spilling onto Charlotte. Gabriel felt bad about these times, so he tried his best, but was clearly not suited to farming.

Shortly after moving in, Jakob had started showing Gabriel some of the basic carpentry and animal husbandry skills his father had shown him when he was young. Jakob remembered the constant badgering his father subjected him to when he was alive. Nothing was ever right. Nothing was ever good enough. Nothing was ever done the way Jakob's father would do it, and everything turned into lesson after lesson. After a while, Jakob realized that if he were going to be hounded about everything he did, whether it was good or not, why bother with the effort? Everyone else in the family thought the man could do no wrong, but they never saw how often the old man would beat Jakob. He was careful to do that sort of thing out in the barn away from others and after a while, Jakob became numb and just bore the beatings. This made his father even more abusive, but since no one ever saw what he did, everyone thought he was a good man.

Gabriel had recently replaced most of the fence rails that had been chewed by the goats so he would have something to nail the pickets back into. It had been backbreaking work and he had gotten countless splinters from the effort, but it had made Gabriel stronger and given him a way to take his mind off Jakob's constant demands. He hated this place. The only redeeming thing about this whole situation was Charlotte. She was kind to him and tried to shield him from Jakob as much as she could. She reminded him of The Red Cross nurses and the nuns who saw such terrible hardship day after day and still found a way to remain dedicated.

It was early Saturday morning and Gabriel stooped to collect some eggs that had been laid in the chickens' secret hiding place rather than the nest boxes. His bruised side ached with a dull pain. He was probably nursing a cracked rib, but there was nothing he could do about that right now. He had more than a full day's work to get done before sundown and he couldn't slow down or he would receive another beating for *being lazy*. One of the hens had gone broody and stopped laying so the number of eggs he collected each day was fewer than it should be. If he didn't collect the right number of eggs, that would also be his fault even though it was the chickens' job to lay eggs, not his. Gabriel had been reading thanks to Charlotte's frequent trips into town. She brought books on farming and farm animals home for him to read, but Jakob was never to find out.

Gabriel learned that when hens went broody, they plucked out their own breast feathers, stopped laying, and began to defend other hens' eggs, sitting on them to try to hatch them. He had found that a broody hen could be broken of this behaviour if he took the hay out of their nest boxes so there was no insulation. If the eggs grew cold, the broody behaviour would eventually stop and the hen would go back to laying eggs. He also began collecting eggs three times each day so there would be nothing for the broody hen to sit on. Today, the deep reddish brown hen was snuggled into one of the nest boxes, no doubt trying to incubate unfertilized eggs again, and when Gabriel put his hand under her, she pecked his arm hard enough to draw blood. He jerked his hand back and, feeling the rage building inside, grabbed the broody hen by the neck and pulled her roughly out of the nest box, tossing her to the ground to run away flapping and squawking. He stood still for a moment, looking at the two eggs that were under her thinking about what he had just done. She was only trying to keep the eggs safe and warm but he had reacted with violence and hatred.

He despised what was happening to him in this place, on this farm, under Jakob's heel. He set the egg basket outside the pen where he could retrieve them after mucking the goat stalls. As he went about his work, one of the peahens that roamed the yard outside the stalls and pens found the basket and began pecking one of the eggs until it broke. The peahen hungrily gobbled down the contents and broke another. One of the other peahens saw the treasure and rushed to join in, breaking eggs and gorging on their contents. When Gabriel came out of the stalls carrying the muck bucket and shovel and saw what was happening, he ran to the gate. Setting the shovel and bucket down, he yelled at the peahens who were oblivious to anything but their newfound feast. Gabriel kicked them away and retrieved the basket to find that they had broken every single egg.

In the commotion, Jakob had apparently stirred. Gabriel had left him drunk at the kitchen table early that morning. Charlotte had started cooking before the sun rose and Jakob had come from the back bedroom slurring curses at being awakened, but the smell of cooking sausage and eggs had distracted him so he sat down to eat. A few bites in, he laid his head down next to his plate and began to snore as Charlotte and Gabriel stared at him. Gabriel hoped he would remain that way for at least a few hours so he could get some work done, but when Jakob stumbled out of the back door to see Gabriel holding the egg basket, dripping albumen and yolk onto the dirt, he began to turn red and stomp toward Gabriel breathing heavily and tottering this way and that as his drunkenness gave way to fury and Gabriel knew there would be no more chores today.

The next day was Sunday. The hymn ended in the customary echoing crescendo from the little pipe organ in the corner of the church and the dissonant voices fell silent. Gabriel tried to keep tears from welling up in his eyes again. Jakob had been careless in his beating yesterday and hit Gabriel in the same place he had the day before. Gabriel didn't think the rib was broken, but it was certainly cracked deeper than it had been and every breath caused stabbing pain. Still, he knew that if Jakob found out he hadn't sung every hymn, said every prayer, and smiled throughout the Mass, he would be beaten again. So he smiled, he nodded, he stood, sat, knelt on cue with each ritual of the liturgy. He shook hands when the ritual offering of peace demanded it. He winced when a parishioner took his hand and gave it a vigorous shake, not intending to do any harm. He was just being aggressively friendly, so Gabriel did his best to contain his reaction to the pain.

By the end of the hour-long service Gabriel was sweating profusely. Charlotte had seen his distress but was under the same obligation to put on a good show as Gabriel was, so she reassured him by placing her arm around him gently. His jacket was beginning to show signs of dampness under the arms and down the back. It was a warm day and the church was not air conditioned, but it wasn't hot enough to make anyone else perspire. He knew it was from the pain but he kept up the facade of being happy and faithful. After the ceremony, as the people filed out of the church, each person shook hands with the priest who stood in the center of the landing outside the double doors, so the people would stream around him on both sides. The priest took Gabriel's hand without looking down as he tried to keep up with the stream of faithful, but noticing the sweaty palm, he stopped and looked down. Gabriel couldn't walk away unless the priest let go, so he stopped and looked up into the priest's eyes.

He thought this would be the perfect opportunity to make a plea to the priest and be taken away from Jakob's abusive household, but Charlotte would certainly bear the brunt of Jakob's wrath if he did that. When the priest saw his sweat-soaked face and hair, he asked "Son, are you feeling alright?"

Charlotte's eyes grew wide, and she shot a pleading look at Gabriel. When Gabriel looked past the priest at Charlotte, it was clear that she knew a beating would follow if he didn't give the priest a good excuse, so Gabriel turned back to the priest and said "Yes, Father. I think I am just a bit under the weather today."

The priest placed his hand on Gabriel's sweaty hair, made the sign of the cross on his forehead with the side of his thumb, closed his eyes as he faced the sky, and prayed "Almighty Father, bless this child and send your Holy Spirit down to watch over him and make him well again."

Gabriel thought *too late for that, Father,* but thanked the priest as he released the boy from the prolonged handshake. Charlotte's look of panic began to fade and she reached for Gabriel's hand, nodding her approval at a deception well done.

Gabriel's eyes popped open from a deep sleep. Someone was watching him. This far from town, moonless nights were pitch-black so he could see nothing but the faintest starlight through the sheer window drapes. As he turned toward the door, he saw Jakob's form standing in the darkened doorway.

In a low voice, Jakob said, "You di' guh tuhday." His words were barely intelligible through the drunken slurring.

Gabriel remained silent and unmoving, wishing there were something he could say to avoid what was coming.

"I'm sorry fur hittin' ya, but you gotta understan' how hard it is tuh…"

Jakob trailed off, either from an alcohol swoon or from not having anything to say after that. It didn't matter. Gabriel had heard all the excuses Jakob could make up, all the apologies that meant nothing. Not for the first time, he wished Jakob would drop dead right then and there before he could do what he was about to do. He wished it would be the most painful death, Jakob writhing in agony, but awake so Gabriel could climb out of bed and stand over him, look into his eyes, and watch the life drain from him.

Jakob took a couple steps toward the bed. He stank of urine and old sweat mixed with that cheesy smell Jakob got when he didn't clean himself properly. Gabriel's chores this Sunday were apparently not finished but he was so tired. He was tired of the hard labor. He was tired of watching Charlotte being beaten into submission. He was tired of the hatred and vitriol that always spewed from Jakob's mouth whenever he spoke. He never seemed to get a break from Jakob's sexual needs and every Saturday night since a few weeks after he had come to live with them, Jakob had forced himself on Gabriel. Finally, Gabriel began to accept that this was his duty and obliged without a struggle.

As Jakob approached, Gabriel knew what was expected of him and what the consequences would be if he did not satisfy. Jakob lowered his pants as Gabriel slid off the bed to sit on the floor and as Gabriel reached up to pull Jakob's pants down further, he noticed that they were wet. Jakob often pissed himself when he was blackout drunk. As he stepped closer so Gabriel could service him, the stink almost made the boy vomit...and he hadn't even started yet. In this much of a drunken state, it would take forever to make Jakob ejaculate. As he forced himself into the boy's mouth, Gabriel began to move his head in the way that Jakob had taught him. While he worked, he tried to distract himself with thoughts of the animals he liked caring for, his dear friends from the camp, the way food tasted after starving behind wire fences for over a year. It just wasn't working. He couldn't block out the memories of the surgery, the bleeding, the pain, the beatings and the forced starvation when he didn't get his chores done or when Jakob went soft before he could finish. Gabriel was beaten whether he did everything right or nothing right and his hope for a brighter future continued to fade with each passing year.

A deep rage began to build in Gabriel's mind as Jakob began to curse. The drunk was starting to go limp and Gabriel knew that he was about to be beaten for not satisfying him. The hatred welled up in Gabriel's heart. As he cursed Gabriel for not trying hard enough, Jakob slapped the side of his head so hard it made his ear ring. With no way out of a beating, Gabriel began to think of a way to escape this place and then, it just happened. Gabriel bit down...hard, tasting blood and hearing his teeth crush the soft tissue between them. Gabriel felt the soft tissue and sinew separate and when he released his bite, Jakob jerked backward, sucking in a deep breath and teetering on his heels for a moment before he fell hard against the wall and slid to the floor holding his crotch. He checked to make sure his member was still attached. He lifted his hand in the darkness trying to see the blood that covered it. With the other hand, he could tell that his penis was only attached by some loose skin and he descended into whimpering anguish. Gabriel stood over him and spat blood onto Jakob.

"I'M GOIN' TUH KILL YUH!" Jakob wailed in barely discernible words.

"Then DO IT you fucking BASTARD!" Gabriel screamed in a high-pitched voice.

Jakob struggled to stand, but the best he could manage was to roll onto his side, still clutching himself and sucking air through his teeth. "I brought you into this house when you had nothing! ...when no one wanted you! ...and THIS is how you repay me?!"

The hallway light came on and Charlotte pushed the door open to see Gabriel standing over Jakob. Without even a second's pause, she entered the room, grabbed a pile of clothes from the floor at the bedside, seized Gabriel's hand and rushed for the door dragging Gabriel behind.

"Go down the road to the Andersen's house," she whispered so as not to let Jakob know where Gabriel would be. She shoved the clothes into his hands and pushed him toward the door. She opened the door with one hand and with the other, attempted to usher Gabriel out, but he didn't move. "What will you do?" he pleaded with sympathetic panic in his eyes.

"If he's lucky, I might let him live," she said with a tone Gabriel thought might be deadly seriousness. "Now you take care of yourself and don't dally!" she insisted as she shoved him toward the screen door. He opened the latch just in time to avoid being pushed through the screen when Jakob let out a howl from Gabriel's bedroom. The boy stopped just outside the screen door and let it slam shut. Charlotte attempted to give him a reassuring smile as she closed the door, but it didn't fool him for an instant. She was afraid.

Gabriel ran. When he got to the end of the dirt drive to the road, he heard Jakob yell from the house "Don't you *ever* come back here or I'll *kill you!*" So Gabriel continued running in bare feet and worn britches down the road toward the Andersen's farm. By the time he got there he was spent, walking slowly, and smarting from the blisters on his feet. As he approached the small country house, the dog began barking. The lights came on and a shadow appeared in the open door. He could hear Anna Andersen's voice saying "That's the Arslock boy!" before scampering down the steps. She walked quickly toward him, her husband John following. Coming to a stop before him with her husband one step behind, Gabriel also stopped. She looked into his face, and Gabriel began to cry. She came around to his side, putting her arm around him, walking him toward the house as he began to sob. Two shorter shadows appeared in the doorway backlit by the entryway lights.

"Go get some hot water started and tell the boys to go back to bed right now," Anna instructed John in a measured urgency, walking slowly with Gabriel, letting him set the pace, steadying him as best she could. John turned and walked quickly toward the house. There was some commotion, raised voices, and then the boys' shadows were no longer visible.

Chapter 17

Gabriel sat on some newspapers in the cold alley taking a break from the day's tricks. He had been bounced from household to household until he just didn't want to impose on anyone else, so he walked all the way to Berlin, over 50 kilometres from where he was. From there, he used his last *Deutsche Mark* to buy a train ticket to Cologne, near the Red Light District, where he knew he could make money doing what he had done for Jakob for the last couple years. At least this time, he would have some choice in the matter.

A few days later, when he was all but starving, he met two girls who were also working the streets. Ada and Lina were both much older than he but they said they would keep an eye on him while he slept. He couldn't sleep. It was cold and wet today, though it hadn't rained since yesterday and the small room they all shared was too far from here to walk to just now. The cold soaked through to his bones. Today, he wasn't even sure where his next meal would come from. He wasn't making enough money lately, but his situation was certainly better than the treatment he would get at the farm. He was a short, lanky boy, somewhat effeminate, and the doctors said he would never grow into a man...at least that was what Jakob kept telling him, usually while he had his dick in Gabriel's mouth.

It was at times like these when he had to remind himself how much worse life was in the concentration camp. When he was only ten, he and his parents had been taken from their home in Stuttgart, forced aboard a train packed with other families, and taken to Auschwitz. He remembered the look on his mother's face as she made him promise to be strong. Approaching the gate to the camp, he was shoved to one side while his parents were forced to the other. His parents had probably died within hours. As the Nazis collected Jews from all over Germany, Poland, and Austria, the ones who were of child-bearing years like his mother, were taken directly to the gas chambers as were the men who were too old to be worked to death and those who put up any sort of resistance.

He thought of Albert and Lukas, how they all slept sometimes, huddled on the dirt floor for warmth, all of them in shock, fighting for any scrap of food that was tossed to them. He imagined they looked to the well-fed soldiers like mindless chickens squabbling. One day, the three of them had been selected by one of the doctors to be taken away for medical experiments. So very few of the boys ever returned and the ones that did return were usually disfigured in the most awful ways. That night, he huddled with his two closest friends, two boys he had met on his first day in the camp. They comforted each other when they felt sad or missed their parents. They defended each other when bigger, stronger boys would try to take something from them like a moldy crust of bread. After they had been drugged and experimented on, they were reunited, naked and still bleeding from what the doctors had done to them. They each had been...cut away...by the doctors who were experimenting. The doctors had made it clear that if they wished to receive extra food they should keep themselves clean and come when called.

Gabriel was disgusted, with himself, with the tricks, even the ones who paid well, with the Nazi doctors, with the girls who worked the streets with him. At least they had the proper equipment for the job. He had to offer his behind when propositioned, which didn't usually go so well. Ada and Lina promised tonight would be different. They were collecting on some debts owed them by other street walkers and they were going to help him *be a girl* so he could feed himself. No doubt they saw him as one of their own since he didn't have any boy parts to worry them. It was revolting, all of it.

That night in their one room apartment just outside the Red Light District, after Ada had dressed him and Lina had adjusted an adult's wig to fit his smaller head, they both worked on cleaning him up, applying makeup, and teaching him how to walk and act. At this age, no one expected the sultry movements of a grown woman. He doubted any of these men cared, but he *did* want to eat. The girls called him Gabby, which he didn't object to so he adopted the name whenever he was dressed up. In one night on the streets as a girl he made more than he ever made in a week as a boy. He just had to be careful to cover where his parts should be and continue offering his behind saying that he was having his period, which would never be true. The scars the doctors left behind were beginning to hurt after a few years and he knew that it would only get worse if he didn't get the medical procedures the orphanage doctors told him he would need.

The Nazi doctor, Schumann, had not cared to do high quality work. He was only interested in his own sterilization experiment's outcome and did not think of the young Gabriel's future. As he had grown, scars had formed on the outside and adhesions had formed on the inside. Gabriel didn't really understand the terms the doctors used, but now he understood why it would be a problem. As he was growing, the scars and adhesions shrank, pulling on whatever they were attached to. A couple weeks ago, he had felt a sharp pain between his legs as he climbed off his cot. Ada and Lina had come to him when he yelped in pain, but he didn't want to worry them, so he acted as if everything was alright. He knew it wasn't. The pain was intense and when he was alone, he examined the empty space between his legs and found that one of the scars had ripped where the normal skin and the scar met. It looked like a zipper of torn skin and wept blood and clear liquid that crystalized when it dried.

For days he tried to hide his pain, but Ada and Lina could tell that he was hurting. It was almost time for the two girls to update their health and registration status with the police so they could continue working in the sex trade, but Gabriel was too young to do this work legally. They had found him homeless, hungry, and alone and had tried their best to help him, but they could barely afford to feed and clothe themselves. There was no way they could support another, so they had helped Gabriel make money without getting caught by the police. Sometimes they pointed customers in his direction. Sometimes they worked as lookouts.

It was only one day later, when Gabriel began to run a fever and spent the night writhing in pain, that the girls knew that they must take action. The clinic they went to for their health card and sex trade license wasn't far away and Dr. Johan Weber was a sympathetic old man who seemed to genuinely care about their well-being.

The two girls left Gabriel in their shared apartment since he was clearly too ill to work and went about their day walking the streets serving customers. They decided to end the day early so they would have time to get to the clinic before it closed, so they went home to retrieve Gabriel and take him to the clinic. The clinic was run as a satellite of a nearby hospital and provided all sorts of medical care to the people in and around the Red Light District. The waiting room always held a diverse mix of the elderly, sex trade workers, and locals who could not afford to go a proper hospital. Dr. Weber was a kind man that often helped out members of the community whenever he was able and he knew many of the local officials, police, and sex trade workers. He had no wish to see anyone caught up in the legal system and the police did not want to book anyone if they weren't causing any disruption, so it became an unspoken pact between the police and the clinic, that anyone who was practicing with an expired health card could be brought to the clinic where they could be checked and have their card renewed rather than making the police take time out of their day to book someone at the station. It was an amicable solution for everyone involved and had persisted for many years, to the benefit of the community.

Gabriel was in even worse shape than when they had left him this morning, so they helped their younger roommate get up, clean himself, and the three started walking toward the clinic late that afternoon. Gabriel had to stop and rest, shivering in the cool breeze despite being properly bundled up for cold weather. Ada and Lina waited with him whenever he needed to stop and once he had rested for a few minutes, each would take him up by an arm and support his weight while they continued toward the clinic.

When they arrived, the nurse didn't need to be told that something was wrong with Gabriel. She could see that he was in distress by his sweating, pallid color, and lethargy. The clinic was always busy since it was the only one within several blocks' distance, but she put him down for a walk-in at six o'clock, just before the clinic closed. The girls were examined by a nurse who pronounced them well and renewed their health status cards. Then they sat on either side of Gabriel, determined to wait with him to make sure he was taken care of.

Dr. Weber was walking from examination room to examination room as the nurses kept the queue full. He didn't particularly like working in the clinic for such long hours, but he was pleased that he could help so many people. It was not that he supported the sex trade, but if people were going to make money, they should be healthy and safe while doing it. He drew great satisfaction from the occasional case where he was able to help get someone out of an abusive situation or help them find a way off the street and into a more permanent living arrangement.

At one point, he looked into the waiting room and saw three prostitutes he recognized. Nearly every morning, on his way to the clinic, he had seen these three on nearby street corners, trying to pick up tricks. German law was very strict and street walking was strongly discouraged, but the few brothels in town were not enough to satisfy the demand, so some of that business spilled into the streets. The police kept a close watch, frequently stopping prostitutes to ask for their health card and trade license. After WWII, Germany had decided to decriminalize prostitution. The Nazis had put prostitutes in concentration camps, seeing them as the dregs of society, but the reformed government of West Berlin and most of Germany allowed women and men the freedom to exchange sex for money as long as they followed certain patterns of acceptable behaviour.

Two of these three prostitutes looked pretty enough, but one of them was small, too thin, and could perhaps be underage. At first glance, the smaller one was either having a drug problem or was very sick.

When it was time for his examination, Ada and Lina helped him up, but were not allowed to go with him into the examination room, so the nurse supported Gabriel by one arm while he made his way to the examination room and left, closing the door behind her. He didn't have to wait long since there were no more appointments that day and when Dr. Weber knocked on the door, he came in right away reading a chart as he entered and quickly shut the door.

Turning with the clipboard in hand, he looked up from it to Gabriel saying, "I understand you are not feeling well," but when he took in Gabriel's appearance, he realized that was a moot question. Gabriel hadn't even answered because he was in the middle of a shivering episode. Dr. Weber set the clipboard down on a table against the wall and put on a pair of disposable latex gloves. He asked Gabriel to remove his shirt but Gabriel was so cold he did not want to do it, so Dr. Weber maneuvered a thermometer under Gabriel's arm. He didn't want the boy's chattering teeth to break the mercury-filled glass bulb. As he waited for the thermometer to get a reading, he used his stethoscope to listen to Gabriel's heart and lungs. His heart rate was high, but his lungs were clear and when he withdrew the thermometer, he read 40.2°C which was approaching the level of heat stroke. He insisted that Gabriel remove his clothing immediately and opened the door to ask a nurse to join them. When the nurse came to the door, he asked her to retrieve a couple bottles of rubbing alcohol and come in when she returned.

Closing the door again, he turned to Gabriel and explained. "You definitely have an infection." As Gabriel began to explain while taking off his pants, Dr. Weber shushed him, so he stripped without warning the doctor about what he would...or wouldn't find. When he laid his clothes on a bench against the wall and turned to face the man, Dr. Weber's expression was one of disbelief. "Please sit back on the table," he asked Gabriel. As the boy hopped up onto the table in a seated position, Dr. Weber pulled the slide-out extension under the boy's legs, prompting him to lift them and then rest them on the extension. Gabriel reclined, but could not control the shivering now that he was naked.

Dr. Weber was at a loss for words. Though Gabriel was beyond perceiving anything from him, being in the throes of another bout of shivering, the man had trouble controlling his emotions. His heart ached at what he was seeing. He had read the Nazi accounts of this unique form of sterilization experiment, but he had discounted them as fantasy. Yet, here was evidence that these atrocities had indeed taken place. He did not realize how long he sat staring at Gabriel lying on the table shivering, but when he came to his senses, he realized he was tearing up. *Dear God,* he thought. *How can men do such horrible things to each other?* Blinking tears from his eyes, he saw something he hadn't noticed before. The boy, previously dressed in girls' clothes, had a tattoo in now-blurry numbers on his forearm.

Dr. Weber, hearing a knock at the door, came to his senses and sat on a swivel stool as he called for the nurse to enter. She did so, carrying two bottles, one in her left hand and the other cradled in her arm leaving her right arm free to close the door. As she turned from the door to Gabriel, she froze, staring at where his genitals should be.

Dr. Weber did not have any patience for embarrassment or emotional reactions from his staff since they were not here to judge their patients, so he encouraged her with a curt, "Come on in, please. I want you to bring his temperature down with some towels and alcohol." Seeing the nurse's hesitation, he said, "*Now,* please." The professional firmness from her employer jolted her out of her stupor and she got to work. She pulled two thin cloths out of a drawer under the table against the wall, draped them over Gabriel's shivering form, and began to pour just enough alcohol over them to saturate the fabric. As the alcohol began to evaporate, Gabriel began to shiver harder and moan as the heat was sucked out of him. He ached all over.

Dr. Weber asked, "When were your sexual organs removed?" as he drew up close to examine the area through his bifocals.

Through clenched teeth, Gabriel said, "Auschwitz, 1944."

"Clearly this was done by a sloppy physician and it doesn't look as if you have had any cleanup done since then, " Dr. Weber asserted. Gabriel confirmed with a stiff, shaking nod. "It appears you have kept the wound bandaged, have you, son?" he asked without really expecting an answer. He reached to draw out another cloth from where the nurse had found them and reached for the alcohol bottle she was holding. She handed it to him and he saturated the still-folded cloth. Handing the bottle back to the nurse, he advised Gabriel, "This is going to hurt. Try to remain still," and he went to work carefully cleaning between Gabriel's legs. There was a significant amount of dried blood plasma on the surface, and when Dr. Weber pressed on the soft tissue anterior and superior of the tear, a small amount of puss flowed from a small open wound. Scooping this with the cloth, folding it inside, and wiping the wound with a clean side of the cloth, he tried to ignore Gabriel's pained reactions. He turned to drop the cloth into a bin to the side of the supply table and drew out surgical tape and gauze, then began dressing the area.

"Are you allergic to penicillin?" he asked.

"Not that I know of," Gabriel responded, actually feeling a bit better...until the nurse poured more alcohol on the drying cloth draping his chest, arms, and torso.

"I'm going to give you an injection of a penicillin derivative. You should be feeling better in twelve to twenty-four hours, but I don't want you resting alone. Your two companions just got a health certification...I assume for sex work?" The statement was really a question.

"Yes," Gabriel answered without embellishment.

"Nurse, will you be able to stay in my apartment with him overnight?" The look he gave her indicated that this was less of a question and more of an instruction.

"Yes, doctor," she replied with a nod.

"Very good." He closed the matter without even discussing it with the boy, though Gabriel didn't have any objection. He was too exhausted to say much of anything.

"I'm going to send your friends home then. They can come back to pick you up at close of business tomorrow...*if* you are responding to the antibiotic. Good?" He never gave Gabriel the chance to answer before he was out the door and headed for the waiting room.

Gabriel could hear muffled discussions among Ada, Lina, and the doctor. His voice sounded much more sympathetic and soothing when he was talking with them, but when he came back into the examination room, he instructed the nurse, "Please wait for me outside." Without a word, the nurse left the room shutting the door behind her. "Son," he said to Gabriel, "you've had a very close call." As he drew the thermometer out of his pocket again, cleaning it with more alcohol and gauze, he aimed it at Gabriel's mouth. Gabriel turned his head to the side where Dr. Weber was sitting and opened for him, the chattering teeth beginning to fade, more from exhaustion than from anything else. Dr. Weber must have thought it would be alright to use his mouth this time since the shivering had gone down.

"Your temperature was dangerously high and you might be feeling a little groggy just now." Gabriel nodded slowly as he realized that he was experiencing exactly that. As the doctor spoke, he wheeled himself to the supply table and opened a lower cabinet under the metal table which contained rows of glass vials. Taking one out and setting it beside a syringe already on the table, he set about drawing the dose while talking to his patient.

"I have an apartment just a few doors down that I use when I have to stay close by. I want you to stay there with my nurse, tonight. She will come back to the clinic in the morning, but you are to remain in bed until she comes back for you. Understand?" As he looked toward Gabriel, he tilted his chin down so he could see over his bifocals. Gabriel nodded and he seemed satisfied, so he turned away, finishing whatever he was doing. Turning back to Gabriel, he had a long needle on a syringe full of yellowish liquid pointed upward. As he approached with the syringe in one hand and dripping gauze in the other, Gabriel could feel the good intentions and genuine concern emanating from the man. He had a practiced hand, and while the shot did hurt his arm, it was hardly painful, at least on Gabriel's scale. Dr. Weber seemed impressed as he administered the injection. The boy didn't flinch or move at all other than the twitching that was still apparent from the fever.

He asked Gabriel to get dressed as he left the room and after some time, he and the nurse came to retrieve him, changed into their street clothes and coats. The office had been empty for a while and as they escorted Gabriel out to the street, they were careful to ensure that his weight was supported. They could also tell that he was becoming a bit delirious and probably wouldn't remember much from this point on. They walked a few doors down where a doorman opened an old wooden door as they approached. "John, this young man will be recovering in my apartment tonight. Please make sure he doesn't leave unescorted."

"Certainly, sir." The doorman closed the door as they entered and crossed the small lobby to open the elevator for them, pressing the only button waist-high on the dark wood wall. The brass doors opened and the three stepped in with some difficulty. Getting off on the second floor, they turned left down the dark hallway and he handed a key to nurse Ilsa, who left Gabriel leaning on the doctor as she opened the door. They entered a well-appointed room with a queen sized bed, night stands, armoire, and vanity. A few velvet-upholstered chairs lined up against one wall made it seem less like living quarters and more like an extension of his office. They put Gabriel to bed and as he drifted off to sleep, he could hear them discussing the evening meal, he would pay for whatever she ordered and the doorman would retrieve it for her.

Ilsa awakened him from time to time, checking his temperature and offering him broth and bread, of which he ate very little before nodding off to sleep again. It wasn't until the next afternoon when he was fully awake and starting to feel much better. He was so weak, he had to prop himself up with pillows just to sit upright, but there was nothing to do here but look out the window. He wasn't even sure where he was, but he did remember something about a nurse taking care of him and a doctor being kind to him. This must be the doctor's place, but it didn't make sense. Why would a doctor have such a small apartment?

About half-past-five, there came a knock at the door, but before he could answer, the lock turned and in came Nurse Ilsa. Seeing Gabriel propped up she paused saying, "Well, you look *much* better!" She came in and closed the door behind her. "Collect your things and bundle up. It's time to head back to the clinic. Do you think you can walk?"

Gabriel thought he could so they prepared for the short trip. As Ilsa locked the door behind them and they walked down the hallway, it all seemed new to Gabriel. His memory of the trip here was very cloudy. He thanked the doorman who seemed glad that Gabriel was feeling better and they walked only a few doors down the street to the clinic. When they entered, the nurse behind the desk saw them and rushed off to alert the doctor. Nurse Ilsa took them straight from the front door, through the waiting room, to the examination rooms in the back and into an empty one saying, "Get undressed and lie down. Dr. Weber will be in shortly." She slid the leg extension on the examination table and turned to leave the room, taking off her coat to reveal her nurse's uniform underneath.

Gabriel lay on the table naked for about fifteen minutes before he became impatient. He gathered the thin cotton sheet from the table, wrapped himself, and went to listen at the door. He had already lost one day of work. He couldn't really afford to lose another. He could hear people talking and moving around outside the room and he didn't want to be intrusive, so he turned to go back to the examination table when someone knocked on the door. Dr. Weber entered without invitation again and saw Gabriel returning to the table.

"I'm sorry to keep you waiting, young man," Dr. Weber said. "It seems we have a bit of a problem."

"What do you mean? I'm feeling much better." Gabriel's look of confusion told the doctor that he didn't understand the issue.

"Have a seat, son." He gestured to the table and Gabriel hopped up to listen. Dr. Weber pulled the wheeled swivel stool up between his legs and sat down in a practiced motion. "The problem is this. You have an infection in your groin. I know you don't have anything down there that would make this a sexual contagion, but the regulations don't make an exception for your case." Admitting ignorance with a glance at the floor, he continued, "I had to check because I've not come across this before." Looking back up at Gabriel, he continued. "The situation is this. First, you are underage and not eligible for the required health certification and police registration for sex trade work. Also, your scars have not been properly cared for since the original procedure. There has been some damage because of how much you have grown since then…and…I'm afraid it isn't going to get better with just one shot." Gabriel was staring blankly, still not understanding, so Dr. Weber continued.

"No doctor can legally give you a health certificate until you are older and are healed and that's going to take a long time, I'm afraid."

Gabriel's mouth dropped open. "You're telling me that I'm going to starve."

"I see I've underestimated you. You connected the dots just fine. Yes. You won't be allowed to work legally in your trade and if you try to work illegally, no brothel will permit you and no customer would have you." He sat, waiting for the news to sink in. He didn't want to burden the boy with too much bad news all at once.

Gabriel looked into the doctor's eyes and said, "There is more you're not telling me."

"My goodness!" Dr. Weber exclaimed. "You are a bright one, aren't you?" He wasn't expecting an answer, but Gabriel was. "Very well. I am required to report your infection and its location on your body to the proper authorities. I'm sorry, but that's the law. If you are even seen on the street without a health certificate, you'll be picked up immediately."

A look of resolve came over Gabriel and he hopped down from the table, beginning to collect his clothes without a word.

"Where are you going?" Dr. Weber asked.

"Home," Gabriel answered as he dressed.

"You're going home?"

"Yes. My flatmates and I are a team. We help each other," Gabriel said, proudly.

"Are they going to feed you for a couple months while you go into hiding?" Dr. Weber waited for Gabriel's response, but Gabriel only froze, thinking.

Dr. Weber answered his own question. "I didn't think so. I've been at this clinic for a long time and seen similar situations before...I don't mean with your..." he gestured down low on Gabriel adding, "...well, you know what I mean."

Gabriel stopped dressing and sat down on the bench against the wall where his clothes had been. Leaning to rest his forearms on his knees, he clasped his hands in deep thought.

"I'm sorry, my boy. I'm not trying to make your life miserable. I've been out here for many years and I want to help. If you can make me *one* promise, I will help you."

Gabriel looked up at the doctor's face with skepticism coloring his features. "What is it?" Gabriel asked sourly.

"Only that when the opportunity presents itself to help someone else in the future, that you do so just because you can," Dr. Weber said with a profound kindness.

"Pay it forward?" Gabriel asked with sarcasm.

"That's it. That's all I ask." Dr. Weber looked at Gabriel and waited for the boy's response.

As Gabriel opened up to the doctor, he began to sense things he hadn't noticed before. The man was blatantly genuine. He couldn't sense even a trace of pretense from the man. There was also loneliness, but the kind that is permanent, long-lasting, as if someone he loved had passed away. He also sensed a willingness to accept a refusal, so the old doctor couldn't be invested in Gabriel's decision yet.

"Fine," Gabriel said, sitting back upright. "I'll do that. So how can you help me?"

"You'll need treatment which I can make sure you get, so you'll have to come into the clinic at least once each week for that, but I am not running a charity...well, I am, but there are costs involved. I want you to help around the clinic while you're being treated."

"What about food?" Gabriel interrupted.

"*And* living quarters," Dr. Weber added to Gabriel's interruption. "You will come to stay with me at my house."

"You mean that apartment?" Gabriel asked with incredulity.

"No. My late wife and I used to stay there when she would join me for events. I still keep it so I can come to town for the symphony or the theatre and not have to make the trip all the way home afterward." Dr. Weber sat musing for a moment, recalling the fun he had when he and his wife were together.

As Gabriel watched the emotions play out across the old man's face, he could see that he was an honest man, a caring and good man. He felt bad about his own tone of voice and about being so skeptical. "I would really appreciate that," he interrupted the doctor's reverie, "and thank you. I just need to tell the girls where I am going so they don't worry."

"Please write them a note so they will see it in your own hand and leave it with the front desk. They will be free to send notes to you in the same way." Dr. Weber rose from his stool, took a step toward Gabriel, and placed his hand on the boy's shoulder. "Let's get the rest of your treatments scheduled. Right now, it's time for another shot."

As the chauffeur drove Gabriel and Dr. Johan Weber out of town, the doctor peppered Gabriel with questions about his past. Occasionally, the chauffeur would look up at the rear-view mirror with eyes wide in shock, but Gabriel didn't care. Johan had turned out to be someone he could actually talk with and share with. Johan was also open to answering Gabriel's questions too, which was a rare trait to find in an old person, he thought. Older people always seemed to be off in their own comfortable world. Maybe it was because Johan was still in medical practice, seeing people suffering and giving of himself and his time to heal them and make their lives better.

Gabriel had been working at the clinic every day and staying in the doctor's apartment at night, but the solitude got lonely, so he would often go find Ada and Lina on the street during his breaks and talk with them about how they were doing, ask if they were getting good business, and so on, but Gabriel sensed something coming between them. He was giving them money to pay the weekly rent to keep his place at the apartment they shared, but there was a barrier going up. Certainly, they were jealous that someone would so selflessly be taking care of Gabriel. Why couldn't they find someone to take care of them? The growing distance seemed unavoidable. Of course, who would turn down an advantage when it presented itself, so they couldn't outright blame Gabriel, but the emotional toll was still there.

"So, what happened to your wife?" Gabriel asked rather bluntly.

The pain that flowed from Johan filled the car with a palpable silence and Gabriel thought he had overstepped, but Johan took a deep breath and began to explain. "Amelie Koch Weber was her name. She was a sweet young woman, always giving of herself and deeply sensitive to the needs of others. We met when I was much younger, but to her, I was still an old man. When she was to have our first born, there was a complication and she miscarried. A year later, it happened again, so we began to investigate. I took her to one of my colleagues who specializes in reproductive medicine. He tried for months to identify the problem and we discovered that her excessive bleeding and cramps were not due to a *strong reproductive tendency* as her mother had put it. It was a condition called Adenomyosis. Do you know what that means?"

Gabriel shook his head *no* but appreciated that Johan respected him enough to ask.

"Adenomyosis is what we call it when the lining of the uterus that is supposed to come out every month, instead grows into the muscular layer of the uterus so that not all of it comes out. As this tissue builds up, the uterus enlarges causing cramping, excessive bleeding and, in her case, had already led to uterine cancer. By the time we found it, it was too late." Johan looked down to his hands as if the account had taken all of his energy and Gabriel placed his hand on Johan's in a sympathetic gesture.

Johan placed his other hand on Gabriel's and looked up at him with a smile saying, "I'm alright. It was a long time ago and she is resting peacefully now."

Johan's health had been in decline for quite some time. His long hours at the clinic were not helping his condition, but he could not bring himself to retire and pass the clinic along to someone else while he was able to work. Gabriel tried to draw more detail out of him, but he changed the subject, so he did not press further. He would learn more when he was ready to tell him.

Chapter 18

While living in the large house, Johan had his butler and housemaid see to Gabriel's every need. Meals were lavish and far more than the two of them could eat and Gabriel assumed that the two staff that ran the small estate ate the leftovers. He was uncomfortable eating at such a large table, so Johan invited him to sit by his side rather than at the opposite end of the table.

"My wife hated that too," Dr. Weber said with a chuckle.

In the short time they had spent together so far, they had learned a lot about each other. They had many common interests, but when Johan asked Gabriel if he had ever been to the symphony, Gabriel acted as if that were something he would never do.

"A bunch of old people sitting in the dark listening to someone play music for two hours? No thanks!" but when he saw Johan's reaction, he adjusted his attitude. "Well, *maybe*, but I don't know if I would like it."

"Would you like to go as Gabby?" Johan asked.

The question gave Gabriel pause. Since the infection and the day he spent in Johan's apartment in town near the Red Light District, he had not dressed as a girl, specifically. He had worn the clothes he had brought with him, which was a jumble, but given the choice, he answered, "I would rather go as Gabby, but I don't have what I would need." He meant the things that any normal fourteen year old girl would expect to be seen in, but this was not a small decision. Simply putting on a dress was good enough for the street, but he wouldn't dare go to a high-society event so poorly dressed. As Gabriel and Johan talked, Johan served as a sounding board, giving advice, listening to Gabriel's concerns, and recounting his experiences with people he had met or known who lived as men dressed as women. A few of the stories left them both roaring with laughter, and after hours of discussion Johan looked Gabriel in the eyes.

"Thank you, young man." Johan's face was sincere in a way that Gabriel had not seen before.

"What for?" Gabriel asked.

"For laughing with me...for giving me a *reason* to laugh again." Johan looked up and leaned back in his chair, remembering the times he laughed with Amelie, before the illness took her. "You've made me feel young again, son...err...uhm...young lady," he harrumphed and sat up straight, putting on an air of aristocratic superiority which made Gabriel burst into laughter again.

"Let's do it, then!" exclaimed Johan and beckoned the butler to his side. He leaned in, whispering to the butler. The butler whispered back, objecting to something. Johan made another suggestion and they apparently worked something out.

The butler stood and said, "Very good, sir." Before Gabriel could ask what it was, the butler turned and retreated, apparently with tasks to do.

With a clap of his hands Johan pronounced, "This is going to be fun!" but he left

Gabriel in the dark about what he meant, dancing around the boy's questions and diverting the conversation. Gabriel finally surrendered and they enjoyed the rest of their meal, talking about various plays and performances that Johan and Amelie enjoyed most. Gabriel felt a little left out of the old man's reminiscing, but he saw how happy it made Johan to be walking down memory lane, so he let the scene play out until they were both tired and ready for bed.

Each day, Gabriel was dressed and ready for work at the clinic before Dr. Weber came downstairs, but today Johan took him by the shoulders at the bottom of the grand staircase saying, "Not today, my dear Gabby! Someone is coming to meet with you. Please try to be nice to her, won't you?" The look of curiosity on Gabriel's face set the doctor to laughing and he answered by saying, "Don't worry. It's going to be fun!" He toddled out the door of the waiting car and the chauffeur drove him away, leaving a trail of blue smoke behind.

Suddenly, it was quiet. This was the first time Gabriel had been left in the house all alone, well not completely alone. The butler and housemaid were always there, retreating at night to their living quarters downstairs in the rear of the house, but they were very resistant to interacting with him whenever he tried. When he turned to go back upstairs, he noticed the butler at the top of the stairs. Gabriel ascended to the top level and faced the butler who obviously had something to tell him.

"Master Köhler, please prepare to receive a guest in your quarters at ten-thirty." With a bow, the butler headed down the stairs to see about his duties and Gabriel could see that the housemaid was already dusting the great hall.

With his head cocked to one side, Gabriel tried to guess who could possibly be coming to see him, so he went to his quarters to pass the time reading. At ten o'clock, through his closed door, he could hear commotion at the front door, then some heavy things being wheeled around on the marble floors downstairs. He was dying of curiosity, but he didn't want to seem like a child, sneaking out of his room to peer over the banister. Adults didn't do that. Nevertheless, the next half hour sitting on the side of his bed was torture. Then, at precisely ten-thirty, the butler's distinct knock came at the door. Gabriel leapt to his feet, but then restrained himself taking a respectable amount of time to cross the room.

He opened the door and the butler announced that a Ms. Mazel was here to see him. As the butler stepped aside, Gabriel wasn't sure what to expect. What he saw was a woman around fifty years old in a blue dress. Her corset was so tight, that her loose skin piled on top of it in a vain attempt at cleavage...deeply wrinkled cleavage. She stood for a moment, with her head turned to the side as if posing for a beauty portrait before slowly and gracefully turning her head to look directly at Gabriel. All three stood still for a long moment before Ms. Mazel finally spoke up.

"It is customary for one lady to invite another in when introduced," stated the overdressed old woman.

Gabriel shook his head, "My apologies, Ms. Mazel. Please do come in." He imitated the sweeping gesture he had seen used by the butler and stepped out of the doorway. Ms. Mazel did not enter immediately, and Gabriel thought he might have done something wrong. She took her time, examined the entryway, and walked ever so slowly into the room, taking it all in. She glided by the low bureau with a standing vanity mirror and gracefully stroked the surface with her once-elegant white gloves which were now looking a bit worn. She examined her fingertips approvingly. She rounded the corner of the room and drew the sheers open on the tall window letting the sunlight brighten the room. She turned to face Gabriel, letting the window sheers slide effortlessly off her open hand to billow back into place. Her movements were deliberate, yet natural.

She moved toward Gabriel who noticed that his discomfort was growing. He was feeling very intimidated by this woman and he began to fidget in place. When she stood before him, she raised one hand to waist level with the palm up, resting the downturned palm of her other hand in the first. The movement was so graceful that Gabriel immediately wished he could move like her. She thanked the butler without actually addressing him saying only, "Thank you," and nodding in his direction while maintaining eye contact with Gabriel. He knew a teacher when he met one. He stood waiting for her to speak as the door slowly closed and latched.

"Miss Gabriella Köhler, I presume?"

"Yes, ma'am," Gabriel stuttered as he answered.

"Miss Gabriella, please call me Ms. Mazel," the woman requested.

"Yes, Ms. Mazel," Gabriel obliged nervously.

"Dr. Weber has asked me to teach you; to help you become a young lady. Is this what you want?" she asked. Her voice was measured and serious.

Gabriel could only nod vigorously in the affirmative.

"Then we will go about this systematically. First, we will select some clothing from what I have brought with me. I believe I have a good selection in your size," she said, stepping back one pace to look him up and down. Continuing in her slightly raspy voice, she said, "If we need to, we will have some pieces made to fit your exact measurements. Then you will learn the proper use of utensils, glassware, and china. I will subscribe you to several magazines and I will order several books. You are to study them and be prepared for testing on their contents." She stopped talking because Gabriel's face had taken on a confused expression. "I know this is a lot to take in, but we are going to be working together for a long time. I must ask that you focus at all times. I will also be conducting your home schooling on an approved curriculum. You will submit to testing regularly and must keep pace with the other students who go to schoolhouses."

She turned away from Gabriel and moved toward the box of light on the floor projected through the window. As she stepped through the box of light at her feet toward the window, the beam striking her body rose higher until she turned just as the light illuminated her auburn hair from above. Her posture was flawless and her speech sounded so proper.

"Do I have your attention?" she asked in a matronly yet playful tone.

"Yes, Ms. Mazel." Gabriel nodded and stood up straighter, figuring that her posture was meant to be a model for him to follow.

She watched him straighten up and arch his back, imitating her. "That's very good, Miss Gabriella. I'm impressed," she said with an approving raising of the chin and subtle nod.

She looked down at the tattoo on Gabriel's forearm and approached him to examine it further. She reached to lift his forearm so she could see it more clearly. Her hand wrapped all the way around Gabriel's thin arm and she rubbed her thumb across the blurry numbers with her gloved hand. She looked into Gabriel's eyes saying softly, "They never go away, do they?" With a sympathetic smile, she let his arm go saying, "Please come with me."

She stepped around him to the door, opened it, and nodded outside indicating that he should go through. Once in the hallway, she gently closed and latched the door and then preceded him toward the grand staircase. When she reached the bottom of the stairs, she turned right and they went into the sitting room which had been converted to a dressing room. Racks of hanging clothes and stacks of folded clothes along with rectangular boxes and round boxes and several very long tube-like boxes crowded the room. The sheers had been drawn, letting sunlight in, but blocking the view of the forested property outside. In the middle of the room was a circular pedestal less than a metre in diameter. As they came into the room, Gabriel was startled by a young man hiding behind the door, who swiftly closed and latched it behind him. He had a measuring tape hanging around his neck and a pin cushion that looked like a padded tomato on an elastic band around one wrist. His pinstripe vest and pants framed a crisp white shirt and long black tie.

They started by helping Gabriel up to the pedestal and the man started taking measurements while Ms. Mazel stood back and began to walk around him, scrutinizing. She introduced the young man as Hörs and began to describe what they were there to do.

At one point, Hörs reached up between Gabriel's legs without so much as a warning, placed the tape measure against his leg, read the measurement, and moved on to the outside of the leg. Gabriel was stunned and suddenly feeling very vulnerable. He had never had someone do that before, but then he had never had his measurements taken either. As Hörs finished his maneuvers, Ms. Mazel came up to Gabriel. Reaching to take his hands, she became serious again.

"My dear, it's time for an uncomfortable topic. Regardless of whether or not you choose to develop your own breasts later, you need them now. Most girls have started growing by your age and so we will be showing you how to create the illusion. You will need to adjust larger as you grow." She stepped to the side and picked up a silver bag, reached inside, and pulled out a bra made of white silk. The inside of each cup had been filled with something and then sewn over with more white silk.

Hörs helped Gabriel disrobe, balancing him when he needed to lean. As the last piece besides his underwear came off, she handed the bra to her helper who held it up as he guided Gabriel into it. He didn't know why he should be smiling so broadly, but Gabriel couldn't stop. Ms. Mazel stepped around Gabriel's side where he couldn't see her and returned with a beautiful gown of silk and lace in a seafoam green shade that Gabriel loved.

They applied light makeup and fit a styled wig on his small head. As they laid the dress around the pedestal, they indicated he should step into the center. Once the dress surrounded his two-inch green velvet shoes, Hörs and Ms. Mazel began to lift the dress up around Gabriel's body. It was a little loose-fitting and, though it barely had a bodice, Gabriel had nothing to fill it out with. Hörs went to work on the dozens of buttons up the back, while Ms. Mazel worked out the folds and draped the fabric as if she were designing a flower arrangement, stepping back to critique, then swooping back in to adjust until all was just right. Hörs draped an emerald pendant around Gabriel's neck, fastening it in the back before reaching for a small box containing a lace hat with small brim.

Hörs came around to face Gabriel and, conferring with Ms. Mazel, they whispered and gestured from a couple metres away before coming to a conclusion.

"Would you like to see?" asked Ms. Mazel with a satisfied smile.

Gabriel nodded, so Hörs went to the far side of the room where an oval mirror was draped with pink fabric. He wheeled the mirror closer to face Gabriel and aligned the mirror without taking the cloth away. As if building suspense, he paused and then drew the cloth away with a flourish, tossing it over his arm and walking around behind Gabriel.

Gabriel wasn't sure what he was seeing in the mirror. It looked like someone else entirely. She was pretty with a lovely figure for a young lady. She looked like she was ready for a social function, but the way she moved was definitely all Gabriel.

Ms. Mazel stepped into Gabriel's view just to the side of the mirror so he could see himself standing next to her. "Stand up straighter. When you move, do so slowly and pay attention to how you move. Don't worry about how you move just now. We will be making adjustments. By the time we are done, you will be ready to go to social functions with Dr. Weber, but we will be far from finished."

For the next half hour, Ms. Mazel gave her ever more subtle instructions, walking around her and back into view. It was often confusing, but she was patient, yet firm. As Gabriel began to master the positioning and movements she was showing him, she began to give fewer instructions until finally, she hadn't spoken for several minutes. Her animated semicircular pacing grew less frequent until she came to rest beside the mirror again. She held a criticizing forward lean for another minute, then relaxed into a more normal, upright posture.

"There you are, Miss Gabriella Köhler. I'm so very glad to meet you." Ms. Mazel stepped toward Gabriel and reached to shake her hand.

Measurements had been taken, several order forms filled out, and boxes had been stacked to be left behind. The rest would be delivered in a week's time. As they were finishing up and Gabby was about to broach the uncomfortable topic of the cost, there was a commotion in the great hall. Johan must be arriving home from work. His raised voice boomed and echoed and drew closer to the door which flew open. In stepped Johan. Ms. Mazel came to his side behind Gabby whose back was to the door. She extended a hand and Hörs stood at attention.

"Gabriel?" Johan asked tentatively.

"Dr. Johan Weber, may I introduce Miss *Gabriella* Köhler." Ms. Mazel stepped just into Gabby's field of view, gesturing for her to turn toward the door.

As Gabby turned, she saw Johan. His face showed an instant of questioning, then began to light up as he smiled wider and wider. "Oh my, Miss Köhler. You look quite pretty."

She was at least a half metre over everyone's heads since she was still standing on the pedestal, but she turned as gracefully as she could and extended a hand, palm down to him so he could help her down. Taking her hand, Johan steadied Gabby as she stepped to the floor and looked up into his face.

Without breaking eye contact with Gabby, he congratulated, "Ms. Mazel, you have quite outdone yourself!"

"Why thank you, Dr. Weber. It has been a great pleasure to work with Miss Köhler. We have been getting along famously." Ms. Mazel was obviously layering on the sweetness for her customer, but she did it in such a way as to make everyone in the room feel encouraged. "I have several pieces on order which should be delivered early next week. There is the matter of the bill..."

Johan was still holding Gabby's hand between his two, marveling at her work, when he said to Ms. Mazel, "My dear, I would like you to double the amount and keep the remainder as a bonus." He released Gabby's hand and faced Ms. Mazel.

Ms. Mazel was completely unphased by the man's generosity, though Gabby knew they must be talking about a huge amount of money. "Thank you, Dr. Weber. It is always a pleasure to serve you." Ms. Mazel turned to Gabby saying, "Please expect the magazines and books to arrive soon. I will look forward to discussing them with you. Shall we meet again next Tuesday? Your wardrobe should be here by then."

"Yes, thank you, Ms. Mazel," Gabby said and curtsied the way her new mentor had shown her earlier.

Hörs began collecting the unneeded clothing, racks, and boxes and moved them to the car as the three began discussing upcoming events. Gabby had not begun studying yet and felt a little left out of the conversation, but she smiled and participated as best she could. Ms. Mazel and Johan talked about plays Gabby had never heard of and composers she had never listened to until Hörs was done packing. Gabby felt like an observer instead of a participant. Hörs indicated his readiness by approaching the group, bowing, and thanking them for their time.

"I believe we must go," said Ms. Mazel. She took Gabby's hand from Dr. Weber saying "I am so glad to have met you, Miss Gabriella."

"Please, call me Gabby."

"I will do that, Gabby." Stepping back, she bid them both a good evening and set off to the waiting car.

Over the next four years, as Ms. Mazel taught Gabby about life, current events, history, philosophy, economics, and language, Gabby's view of the world expanded. She began to engage Johan in discussions which he surely found sophomoric at first, but which he enjoyed nonetheless. Gabby had little formal schooling, so Ms. Mazel made certain to include a remedial curriculum along with her other lessons until Gabby could hold robust debates with grace and poise.

Since Gabby was committed to improving herself and would not be working, Johan decided that she should have an allowance, which Gabby dutifully saved each month. Johan always took care of any costs associated with the household, clothing, and such, but Gabby enjoyed the feeling of independence she got from going into town on her own to visit the cosmetics salons, picking out this new shade or that new lipstick. She was always responsible with her spending and began to accumulate a respectable sum in her bank account.

Johan and Gabby spent many evenings walking in the garden and talking about his work, how passionate he was about helping others, about the fears he held that the newest generation would not live up to its potential. Gabby appreciated his views and provided compelling ideas about how the future might unfold, both in Germany and throughout the continent.

Johan talked so much about taking his late wife to the symphony and the theatre that Gabby began to think she might have judged them too harshly. One evening during an impassioned description of a musical piece that he had thoroughly enjoyed and which had brought him to tears, she turned to him and asked if he wouldn't mind taking her someday.

"My dear, I didn't think you liked the symphony!" His tone was both surprised and apologetic.

"I didn't think that I would, but after hearing you describe it, I think I might be mistaken. Would you mind?" Gabby's change of heart brought a glowing smile to Johan's face. She could tell it warmed his heart and that made her smile too.

Her first symphony was a nerve-wracking experience. She had never seen so many people pressed in so tightly. When the auditorium went dark, she was enraptured by the discipline of the musicians marching out to take their places row by row. By the end of the performance, Gabby was unable to control the tears streaming down her cheeks. She thought that making such an unladylike scene would be frowned upon, but Johan found it endearing and held her hand until the tears subsided. It had been a long time since Gabby felt genuine love from anyone as she did from Johan.

They spent many a weekend going to garden parties, museums, musical and theatrical productions, and all the while they jousted in rousing debates. They both loved a good argument, but never fought. She was always so attuned to his passions and he to hers that they could often complete each other's sentences.

Gabby began to take on more and more responsibility for social functions and entertainment, helping to lighten the burden on Johan. He was still traveling to the clinic each and every weekday, but as time went on, his workdays became shorter and shorter. Sometimes, if he worked too long, he didn't have the strength to return home, so he would spend the night in his apartment. She had asked him if everything was alright and he always answered that it was, but she sensed something was draining him more and more recently.

Still, he was always up for a good party and Gabby kept their social calendars full. They were becoming quite the social butterflies and Johan would insist on thanking her after each event, saying that he had not had as much fun for a long while before she came into his life. He introduced her to many of his friends, and she made friends of her own, getting to know the wives of the various manors between Cologne and Bohn.

Chapter 19

Gabby's homeschooling was not easy. She had lost so much time because of the war and the time on the farm that she was several grades behind the other children her age, so she started studying younger children's books and worked hard until she began to catch up. She practiced her movements, read about current events in the newspapers, and scoured every page of every magazine that Ms. Mazel sent and still she wanted more. Johan had not asked her to work in the clinic since she had agreed to schooling, but occasionally, Gabby would go to the clinic to help out, leaving with him in the morning and returning in the evening, then catching up on her studies the next day.

As months passed, Gabby began to gain confidence enough to join the other young people who attended some of the high-society functions. She went once to a lecture Johan was giving at the University of Cologne and she was impressed that he was so important. At the reception, Johan introduced her to some of the sons and daughters of a few prominent families who attended the lecture.

On an evening in the winter of 1951, nearly four years later, Johan invited her to a particular social function. He wanted to take her to a party thrown by his close friend and colleague Dr. Anton Gorski, a widower and prominent gender reassignment surgeon with a huge estate near Bohn.

Gabby had grown into a vibrant, beautiful young woman of eighteen when she had decided to start taking hormone therapy so that her body would develop more feminine features. Johan had insisted that this was a serious move with risks and he made certain that Gabby was well informed when she made the decision. Secretly, Johan was so proud of his young protégé. She had become like a granddaughter to him filling a void in his life.

Before the event, he took her to the fashion district in Cologne where rows of posh boutiques offered gowns and expensive jewelry like Gabby had never seen. Johan introduced her to the attendants and Gabriella allowed them to show her around the shops.

"Miss Gabriella Köhler, please come this way," a beautiful attendant said as she turned with a flowing grace and poise and went toward a rack at the back of one shop.

As Gabriella followed her, she tried to imitate the woman's gait. Her imitation was coming close to a perfect match when the woman stopped and turned, waiting for her to catch up. Gabby immediately dropped the imitation, not wanting to offend the woman, but she gave no sign that she had noticed. Looking over her shoulder at Johan, Gabby saw that he had a smirk on his face and when their eyes met, he turned his eyes to the floor with a chuckle. The attendant looked up and down Gabby's figure and, coming to a decision, brought down a beautiful gown of flowing white silk with delicate lace embroidery and hand-sewn pearls that covered one shoulder and plunged to the hip on the opposite side. Some pearls hung from short filaments making it appear that the dress had cast them off, but they never fell to the floor.

As the clerk held the gown up to Gabby's form, she remarked "I do so wish I had your figure. I could never wear something like this, but you, my dear? This dress was made for you." Gabby asked how much the dress cost but the clerk brushed off the question saying, "I don't think you'll have to worry about that."

They visited cosmetics shops and shoe boutiques, and by the end of the afternoon, Johan was smiling broadly and Gabby was laughing and twirling with bags and boxes being carried off by Johan's chauffeur who followed them with the car as they walked from store to store.

That evening, Johan asked his housemaid to go to Gabby's quarters to do her hair and help her dress. Gabby was becoming quite the makeup artist so she didn't need any help, but the girl did give her some tips on gala makeup versus the usual evening makeup. The end result was stunning. As Miss Gabriella Köhler stood before the oval mirror in the bedroom, the housemaid brought her a fur stole of the most beautiful gray fox. Draping it over Gabby's shoulders, the girl stepped to the mirror tipping the oval slowly up and down so that Gabriella might have a full view of herself. What she saw in the mirror was a beautiful woman. There was no trace of the angry boy, Gabriel.

The door opened and the chauffeur stepped in to announce that he was ready to take them to the gala saying, "Dr. Weber wishes for you to join him in the car."

The housemaid helped Gabby lift her dress on the left, attaching the fabric to her wrist by means of a hook on a pearl bracelet and a crocheted loop extending from about the calf on the dress so that it floated up when she raised her wrist, allowing her to manage stairs more easily. This left her other hand free to take a man's arm, hold a cocktail, or for dancing.

Gabby joined Johan and the chauffeur climbed into the driver's seat. They drove through the forested country roads toward Bohn. Johan had explained that Anton's manor was not far away, since most of the wealthy doctors, government officials, and old money lived in sprawling estates like the ones they drove past. The memory of that first drive to the Arslock's farm pressed at her mind, but Gabby refused to let it in, instead taking in the scenery as the sun went down. The cold night air caused condensation to form at the tops of the windows and as they sat, Gabby placed her hand on the back of Johan's hand. Looking at her hand on his, he patted the back of her hand with his other hand, as a grandfather might. He looked up to watch the road approaching before them, and she did the same, leaving her hand on his as they traveled.

They pulled up to a vine-covered wrought iron gate and Gabby could see headlights farther into the property. As they drove down the winding driveway, the manor house came into view. It was completely lit as if it sat in a beam of sunshine coming up from below. Cars were waiting in line to disgorge passengers at the steps as drivers took empty cars around the circular drive and behind the manor house to wait out the evening. When it was their turn, Johan handed the coachman his card and climbed, with difficulty, out of the car. Gabby's door swung open and a young man in double-breasted white tails and black slacks offered his hand. Johan waited for her as the car pulled away and she closed the space between them, slipping her arm under his. They climbed the stairs between two rows of servants standing at attention. Gabby could see the coachman hand Johan's card to the butler who kept the guests' cards in careful order. As he announced each guest, they paused for recognition and then entered the manor.

"Dr. Johan Weber and Miss Gabriella Köhler!" The butler's voice was loud and clear with a practiced flourish as they entered the huge, stately ballroom.

"Don't look up," Johan whispered to Gabby with his head tilted toward hers. She hadn't realized she was doing it, so she quickly brought her chin level. "My dear, these women will chew you up without a second thought. Have some fun with it."

Gabby's nervousness faded quickly with the first glass of champagne. When it was only half empty, it was snatched from her hand by an attentive waiter and replaced with a fresh one. The elegant and precise movements of the staff left her in awe. As she surveyed the clutches of women and men grouping together, breaking apart, and milling about, she noticed some of the women eyeing her up and down and whispering, until one of them suddenly gained a look of resolve, lowered her drink, and walked straight toward Gabby. Thanks to Ms. Mazel's teachings, Gabby noticed that the woman's stride could use some polish and her face displayed her intent too obviously...mischief. Gabby began to feel nervous about the upcoming encounter. Nearly everything about her look and manner was flawless, but because she had not had any cosmetic surgery there were a few masculine traits that she could not hide from those who were observant.

She stood waiting for the woman to approach. Ms. Mazel had taught her to face any social challenge with resolve and to maintain poise no matter what happened or how embarrassed she might feel.

"My dear, you look fabulous!" the woman exclaimed in mock astonishment.

"You are so kind, Miss..." Gabby baited.

"Mrs. Hannah Meyer. I am so glad to meet someone new Miss..." Hannah baited as well.

"Miss Gabriella Köhler."

"Miss Köhler, I don't mean to complain but it is always the same people at these parties. It's so rare to find an unpolished gem among the crowd." Mrs. Meyer had just tossed an insult at Gabby and stood before her, anticipating her response with glee.

"Why thank you Mrs. Meyer. How kind of you to say so." Gabby placed a hand gently on the woman's raised hand, the one holding the champagne glass. Ms. Mazel had taught her that this would paralyze any woman for fear of being made to spill at a party. "I was concerned that I wouldn't encounter anyone as gracious as you. It's so encouraging to know that the *established* families are still around." Gabby curtsied slightly and affected a subtle smile as she removed her hand and watched the glee drain from the woman's face. Inside, she relished being able to call someone *old* with style. She was preparing herself for the next exchange when Johan interrupted.

"Hannah, are you behaving yourself?" Johan chided sending the woman into a predictable giggle, hair flip, and dismissive pat on his arm. Johan wasn't falling for it, so he decided to take control. Looking from Hannah to Gabby, he said, "My dear, there is someone I must introduce you to." He took her free arm under his, leaving Mrs. Meyer to retreat to her group. Gabby smiled gracefully toward the clutch of women as each of them affected a contented smile and nodded. Did Gabby sense a measure of respect in their eyes?

They came to a door in the far corner of the grand ballroom which opened into a brightly lit sitting room filled with people. As they pressed through, the crowd parted when they saw her. The men bowed as they backed away and the women curtsied slightly. A path opened before them leading to three well-dressed older gentlemen standing in a tight group at the far side of the sitting room near tall windows through which the dark of the night yielded to the interior lights cast against the forest of trees.

Johan and Gabriella approached the group and when they arrived, all three men looked up expectantly. "May I present Miss Gabriella Köhler? This is Dr. Harry Benjamin," Johan said, gesturing to the man on the left. "This is Dr. Anton Gorski," he continued, gesturing to the man in the middle. "And this is Dr. Jonathan Brigham." Gabby curtsied as all three of them tipped their glasses to her.

"Great God Almighty!" remarked Dr. Gorski. "You look stunning this evening, Miss Köhler!"

"Miss Köhler, if you would please excuse me, I saw someone I must go harass," Johan said and he disengaged from her arm, leaving her with the three men to fend for herself.

As Johan retreated, Gabby suddenly felt completely exposed. "Gentlemen, please pardon me. I certainly did not mean to intrude." Gabby began to retreat as well when Dr. Gorski reached out and took her hand saying, "Miss Köhler, it would make me very happy if you would stay and talk with me...us," he shook his head as he corrected himself.

In a staged whisper, Dr. Benjamin leaned between Anton and Gabby saying to Dr. Brigham, "I do believe he means to dump us."

Gabby's breath caught in her throat and Anton's eyes went wide, then all four suddenly lost themselves in a hearty laugh that brought tears to their eyes.

"Young lady," crowed Dr. Benjamin, "you must stay and keep us entertained! I insist!"

It was the first time Gabby felt welcome in someone else's home, other than Johan's, and she enjoyed the feeling immensely. The four of them talked and laughed the hour away discussing current events and their respective practices. Gabby was fascinated at how each man saw their effect on the world. They all collaborated on various types of cosmetic and reconstructive surgeries. Their techniques were very advanced and had become highly desired among movie stars and the ultra-wealthy in Europe and America, but their real passions lay in gender reassignment methodology. Dr. Benjamin had pioneered the earliest procedures when he was a young man and had written several texts on the subject. Dr. Gorski had studied all of Dr. Benjamin's work and the two had begun to develop newer, more advanced procedures that lowered the risk to the patient and improved the results and recovery times. Dr. Brigham had joined the other two only a few years ago, but his work with antibiotics and micro-sutures had shown them ways to almost eliminate the scarring that was, until then, an unfortunate side-effect of their work.

Gabby found all this fascinating and none of the men ever talked down to her or asked if she understood. They treated her as they would any colleague, and she appreciated the way they respected her intelligence. At one point, she asked if they had ever considered using the micro-suture technique on the inside as a way to avoid the large adhesions that formed as a result of this type of surgery. All three men stood flabbergasted that she would ask such an insightful question.

"Actually, no, Miss Köhler, but that's a very good question! You see, the time that it takes to use micro-sutures would leave the body cavity exposed too long as well as make the surgery longer, increasing the risk for the patient, so we use standard sutures on the inside and micro-sutures on the outside," answered Dr. Brigham.

Over an hour later, Johan returned laughing and coughing and spilling his cocktail as he walked toward them. "My good man," addressing Dr. Gorski, "I have had the most rousing good time positively thrashing young Mr. Grayson. I thank you for the opportunity to put that young whippersnapper in his place a time or two!" Johan grasped Anton's hand and shook it vigorously enough to spill his cocktail again.

Gabby turned to Johan saying, "I should join you and meet the other guests."

"Quite right, my dear. Quite right." Johan raised his elbow for Gabby to take when Anton spoke up.

"I very much hope that we might spend some more time together...very soon, Miss Köhler. I have thoroughly enjoyed this evening, thanks to you," Anton said with a dreamy look in his eyes.

"You see, Jonathan," Harry blurted, "we're just window dressing next to Miss Gabriella here." That brought the two men to laughing again, but Anton kept a straight face looking directly into Gabby's eyes. As she took Johan's arm, she maintained eye contact with Anton until she had almost completely turned away.

Gabby turned to Johan, leaning in so she would be heard over the din. "I'm so sorry, Johan. I didn't mean to stay away for so long."

"My dear, you have nothing to apologize for. He's quite the catch, and he's a widower. You should get to know him better." Johan kept walking as if he thought nothing of her confession, but she tugged on his arm and when he stopped to look at her, he saw a question in her eyes. "My dear, you are quite the catch too. I think you young people should go and get to know each other." The question in her eyes deepened and her lips parted but she said nothing. "I won't be offended if you want to go back to him. He seemed quite smitten with you as well," Johan said. Seeing the desire in her eyes, he resolved to make her decision for her so she didn't have to. "I must insist that you go back to him at once and see what flourishes." He released her from his arm and the look of unconditional love on his face removed her doubts. He turned unsteadily and tottered off through the crowd leaving Gabby alone in the crowded room.

Suddenly she felt a hand on her elbow from behind. It startled her and she jerked to see who it was. Harry backed away with his hands raised saying "My apologies, miss. I didn't mean to startle you."

"Not at all, Dr. Benjamin," she replied. "I had such a lovely time with you and Jonathan...and Anton." She didn't realize it, but Harry noticed that she smiled more broadly after she said Anton's name.

"I have come to make a request on behalf of Dr. Gorski," he stated, officially. "He wishes you to come back and continue the conversation at your earliest convenience."

Gabby studied his face. He wasn't joking. Dr. Benjamin was quite serious and being very careful to steady himself against the liquor. She sensed no insincerity or deception from him, only a genuine request, so she followed him back to the sitting room where Dr. Gorski and Dr. Brigham were still talking. When Anton looked up and saw Harry with Gabby in tow, he lit up and a warm smile of gratitude spread across his face. He had been leaning with an ear toward Dr. Brigham, but as they approached he stood erect and faced Gabby directly. Jonathan, sensing the shift in Anton's attitude, also turned toward Gabby and smiled.

"I do hope I am not intruding, gentlemen," Gabby said as she rejoined the group.

"Not at all, Miss Köhler." Anton clearly wanted to continue speaking, but Gabby held an index finger up to interrupt.

"Now, if we are to continue, I must insist that you call me Gabby."

"Of course, Miss Gabby," Anton replied only to garner another demerit as Gabby interrupted again.

"Just Gabby, if you please." As she lowered her finger, everyone in the group could see that she took great pleasure in exercising power over Anton.

Gabby had never told anyone about the technicalities of her condition. The closest she ever got was to say that she didn't have "the proper parts" anymore, but there was something so relaxing in Anton's manner. He never reacted negatively to the topic. Most people who Gabby thought might be able to accept it, were not. She could see tiny micro-expressions of disgust flash across people's faces so she always ended the conversation saying that she was uncomfortable talking about it, when in fact, it was they who were uncomfortable with the details. Not Anton. His face displayed intrigue, curiosity, and interest. He never interrupted her while she was unpacking her emotions, and better still, he answered her questions openly and honestly without reservation.

He had two sons by a previous wife whom he loved very much. His wife had fallen ill during childbirth and never fully recovered from one complication after the next. Once the boys had been born, they discovered that she was lucky to have carried them to term at all because the placenta had partially detached early enough in the pregnancy for the lesion to have healed. When she passed away, he threw himself into his work and now spent long hours nearly every day in his medical practice. He had become one of the most important and talented gender reassignment surgeons in all of Europe, which is how he met Dr. Harry Benjamin. While it was Dr. Benjamin who had pioneered the procedure in the early 1900's, his passenger ship had been caught in open water during the war and he was forced to either exile to America or be taken as a prisoner of war. Upon reading about the encounter in the *Telegraf*, Anton worried about the fate of his friend for weeks until he received a letter from Harry letting him know that he had made his way back to America. During the war, most of Anton's patients had been very careful to hide their transitions, but since the war, Harry and Anton consulted across the ocean, Harry working in America and Anton working in Germany, to help those who needed surgery.

Over the past few years, he had grown very lonely and, to make matters worse, had developed hypertensive impotence, so he had not been with any woman in years. While he could relieve himself, the act was neither masculine, nor satisfying. As the evening progressed, and the ruckus began to fade, the two hardly noticed until Johan's chauffeur entered the nearly vacant sitting room to inquire if Miss Gabriella would like to come back to town now or should he return in the morning. Gabby was having such a wonderful time, but she didn't want to impose on Anton any more this evening, so she rose, said her goodbyes, and joined Johan at the car.

Gabby went on about Anton during the whole trip back to the estate and Johan could tell she was completely enamored. "Then I insist you must visit him often and get to know the man," was his response.

Gabby felt that it wouldn't be appropriate, that Johan had given her so much, but Johan insisted that she must follow her heart while she was young enough to do so. Her guilt was misplaced and he would demonstrate his goodwill by having the car pick her up the following evening. He happened to know that Anton would be home by sundown and had no plans for the evening. He would send word first thing in the morning that he was to expect her shortly after sundown.

Gabby attempted to refuse, but without success. The entire time she resisted, Johan could see the happiness blooming on her face and that gave him a sense of satisfaction as well. Word came the next morning that Miss Gabriella should expect to dine with Dr. Gorski at half past six and that her return to Johan's house would be arranged by Dr. Gorski. When she received the note, written in his own hand, she squealed with delight and held the paper to her smiling lips. She inhaled hoping to detect his scent, but all she could smell was the acrid paper, the smell of the ink, and the aroma of the house she had visited.

That evening, the housemaid helped her get into one of the gowns purchased for her. Flawless hair, subtle evening makeup, a pearl encrusted clutch bag, and a pendant with a single large teardrop pearl completed the ensemble and she was escorted to the car by Johan's chauffeur. All during the trip to the Gorski estate, she wished he would drive faster, but she attempted to relax and hold her impatience in check.

The dinner for two was a glorious spread with the servants and the butler making sure that everything went perfectly. The food was delicious and the waiter served a specialty cocktail taken from the mid-1800's with each course. As they sipped, Anton told her about the history behind each cocktail, who had invented it, and where it was popular. Tarragon in a vodka cocktail from the Bolshevik Revolution and a delicious Rosemary Gimlet were her favourites of the evening. After dinner, they took their champagne out to the back patio where she saw votive candles lining a path off into the forest that covered most of the property. She wondered why the lights were there so he suggested they go find out. As they walked into the woods along the glowing path, they talked about their pasts and what they would like for the future.

Anton was nearly twenty years' her senior and he couldn't offer her the affections of a young man. He was resigned to that, but he could offer her something she dearly wanted. To become a woman. He would perform the procedures she would need to complete her transition. Gabby was dumbfounded. She knew how much this type of procedure would cost and though she had saved most of the money Johan had given her, she didn't have nearly enough to cover the surgeries. He insisted that the only cost would be her continued presence, her openness, and her honesty. She would become the lady of the house and eventually his wife. She would take her place by his side and seek affection discreetly whenever she needed it, but not let anyone else into her heart. She would help him become more of a society man, since that was not one of his strengths.

As they came over a rise in the path, there was a small clearing which opened to them, surrounded with votives and lit from above by a chandelier of candles hanging from a tree. Servants were waiting there with cold water to refresh them and cucumber sorbet to cleanse their palates. As they sat talking, the bright full moon passed overhead, casting blue beams through the trees that amplified the orange light of the candles making the entire clearing glow with a dreamy light. As the moon fell and the sky began to take on a touch of orange, they realized that it must be early morning. The candles had mostly burned down and they could both see that the waiters were getting tired.

"I've had a guest room prepared for you and Johan was kind enough to have some of your belongings delivered." Anton laid his hand on hers with a request in his eyes.

Why that sneaky devil, she thought of Johan. She knew this could not be a sexual advance from what she had learned earlier in the evening, so she felt no threat to her...*chastity*...though she knew that word didn't really apply.

The next morning, very early, Anton had asked the cook to prepare places for the children at the dining room table, which was apparently unusual given the cook's puzzled expression. The portly old woman with graying red hair did not argue, but Anton could see the disapproval in her eyes. When Gabby came down for breakfast and saw two extra settings, she asked Anton who would be joining them. She was so delighted to finally be formally introduced to the boys.

Jonas, ten years old, and Elias, eight, were Anton's two children with his late wife. They were the most well-behaved children Gabby had ever met, but it was clear from the moment she saw them she would have to earn their trust. She sensed their sullen attitude but did not blame them. She had no right to expect their courtesy so soon.

"Now, boys, don't be rude. Introduce yourselves properly," Anton insisted.

They rose, introduced themselves, and sat without ceremony and still without looking at her. Anton sighed in frustration, but Gabby smiled, and shook her head slightly to indicate that it was alright. They had a quiet breakfast and the boys were off to school, the chauffeur, Mr. Bauer, ushering them off to the car. The boys wished that their father could spend more time with them, but nearly every night he was doing challenging and important work.

One morning seven months later, as Gabby awoke, she realized that she had not seen Johan for several days. This wasn't particularly alarming since it was sometimes his practice to stay at the apartment in town when the number of patients coming to the clinic was excessive. Rising early and preparing for the day, there came a knock on her door. She lifted her pink silk kimono from the back of the chair and wrapped herself before answering. It was Anton.

"My goodness, I didn't expect you here." She was embarrassed by the state of her room, not yet having a chance to let her housemaid clean up, and did not want to let him in, but when he didn't answer and didn't make eye contact with her, she knew something was wrong. She opened the door, stepping aside, saying "Please come in, Anton. What is wrong?"

"May we sit?" he asked with his hat in his hands, not bothering to take his coat off. Gabby noticed that the butler hadn't taken it at the front door and was nowhere in sight.

"Please," she said, waving toward the small table and chairs in the corner.

Anton crossed the room and stood next to the chair, waiting. Gabby shut the door and came in behind him. Touching his arm gently as she passed, she sat in the chair against the wall. Then he sat in the opposite chair facing the window and finally looked up at her sullenly, then stared out the window for a moment.

"I wanted to tell you in person," he said.

"What is wrong, Anton?" she asked as she leaned forward, placing her hand open on the table inviting him to take it. He remained seated and leaned forward to place his elbows on his knees, looking down.

"Johan passed away last night," he said with a sigh. "It happened while he was sleeping in his apartment and appears to have been peaceful. I just didn't want you to find out from someone else."

She sat back, withdrawing the offered hand. The news wasn't surprising given his recently declining health and Gabby thought that perhaps this was why he had been spending the evenings at his apartment more frequently. They sat in silence and reverence for several long minutes before she asked, "Have you made any arrangements?"

"Since Johan had no family, he chose a lawyer to execute his will. We may be called on to attend a meeting," Anton answered.

"Oh my." Gabby felt tears welling up in her eyes. As one fell upon her cheek, she sat up straight, resolved, and looked at Anton who sensed the change and looked up at her. "When is the service scheduled?"

"Johan made no provision for a service." Anton seemed disappointed by that but Gabby was determined to honour the man properly.

"Then we will take care of it," she asserted.

Anton smiled through his grief and nodded. He hadn't expected her to be so strong but realized that he had underestimated her. "I will put together a guest list since I knew most of his friends. Would you like to handle the formalities?"

"Should we have the services here?" she asked.

"This house won't be big enough for all those who will want to attend," he said.

She nodded reverently asking, "May we have them at your manor? I think the clearing you took me to would be the perfect setting. We could say goodbye surrounded by nature. What do you think?"

"I think he would like that. Thank you for doing this." He and Gabby sat for a long while.

Gabby and Anton spent the morning talking about how best to pay their respects to Johan. His kindness and generosity had affected so many they felt overwhelmed by the responsibility. After a few hours, Anton left for Cologne to meet with Johan's lawyer and Gabby set about the task of arranging a memorial for the man who had changed the direction of her life.

When Anton first met Gabby, he was so enamored with her that he had offered to complete her transition, if she wished. Gabby was concerned about the cost and the trouble, but Anton would hear none of it. He and Dr. Benjamin planned out how the procedures would go and consulted as the months progressed. It was Dr. Benjamin's habit to visit Europe three times each year and when Gabby saw him, she always threw her arms around him.

Between procedures, Gabby continued to educate herself and to practice living as a woman. The walk, the grace, and the dignity were very difficult for her, but she worked at it every minute of every day and her progress so delighted Anton that he would laugh and tease her whenever she forgot herself and reverted to walking like a boy. The two spent much of their time together, but Gabby missed him dearly during the day. He was so dedicated to his work and had such a passion for helping those unhappy with their bodies, that she rarely saw him during the day. Her evenings would often be spent alone too.

The day finally came when her procedures were complete and only the occasional maintenance procedure would be required, when he asked her to marry him. She had been concerned that once he was finished with his "project" he would lose interest, but quite the opposite happened. When they lay together, he often whispered how he wished he could please her as a man would, but his own doctors had told him this was a thing of the past. They had tried medications to treat his hypertension, but he had not responded well to the treatment and so his impotence was likely to be permanent.

Mr. Anton Gorski and Mrs. Gabriella Gorski were presented to the posh gathering of socialites in the immaculately manicured garden behind the manor house between Bohn and Cologne, where Anton had lived his whole life.

Her womanhood was perfect. There wasn't a scar visible, not a curve out of place, not a bit of discomfort. She knew she was fortunate to have the most talented doctors do the work, but there was something else. She felt content. Unfortunately, her husband showered her with material pleasures, but not physical ones. Granted, she would never experience the sensations that a woman would feel. There had been too much damage done in the medical experiment for that, but emotionally, she felt fully feminine. She was tall, with long flowing dirty-blonde hair and a perfect figure.

She wore only the finest designer outfits and dutifully attended every function and party on her husband's arm, but there was something missing from this life. There was never the rush of excitement, never the thrill of intrigue.

Gabby was just getting used to her new *position*. Anton was a sweetheart, but he didn't seem to be able to avoid making her feel like an employee now and then. Ulva came in without knocking or saying anything. She ran the place, being the housemaid of the late Mrs. Gorski, and Gabby knew they would become friends.

During Gabby's education with Ms. Mazel, the astute woman had noticed something odd. Gabby did not seem to be able to tell the difference between certain colors. She had surreptitiously tested Gabby, asking questions about various pictures in the magazines they discussed. She determined that Gabby had a type of colorblindness that prevented her from seeing yellows and blues properly. To Gabby, they appeared as shades of gray. To someone in high society, mismatched colors would be fodder for gossip, so she set about helping Gabby develop methods to avoid public faux pas by creating a journal of fabric swatches and labels. Whenever she had clothes made in colors that were difficult to identify, she would have the seamstress add a swatch to the journal with a description of what the color was and what it would match well with.

At first, Gabby was hesitant to share the journal with Ulva thinking that she might look down on her for the flaw, but Ulva took the journal, read it thoroughly, and even helped Gabby add to it when new clothes arrived from town. She laid Gabby's clothes out for her every morning, but rather than simply take over the duty of dressing Gabby, she went one step further. Ulva marked the pages in the journal that corresponded to the clothing she laid out and also laid out makeup that would complement the clothing.

Ulva had been Gabby's personal housemaid since moving in, long before her procedures were completed, and Ulva had been Gabby's source of strength through many trials. When she was in pain, Ulva would bring her cool towels to soothe the incisions. When she was uncertain, Ulva would give her subtle signs to let her know what was expected of her. Ulva was a wealth of information about all of the socialites and professionals in town. It seemed she knew everything there was to know about Anton's friends, colleagues, and all the wives. She helped Gabby understand who would be lifelong enemies and who had the potential to be won over. Once, when Ulva was ill and unable to serve, Gabby insisted on taking care of her, bringing her soup and bread prepared by the cook and making sure she was comfortable. Ulva protested the entire time, but Gabby would hear none of it.

Gabby sometimes felt like an outsider. Tonight, she stood on the landing in front of the manor house observing the workers in the garden. Frau Bürste had run the estate for over thirty years and whatever she recommended was incontrovertible as far as Gabby was concerned. Anton completely deferred to Gabby and she, in turn, deferred to Ulva and Frau Bürste. They were both much older than she, but Gabby had grown to trust them, so enamored was she with these women and their decades of experience. They often commented on how refreshing it was to be appreciated by someone so young. In truth, it was Gabby who was the beneficiary since their loyalty deepened whenever Gabby demonstrated her appreciation and grace.

One Sunday morning, Gabby rose with the sun and took her morning tea on the balcony. The warmth of the sun on her face felt delightful, but soon it would be time to get the day started. She turned, allowing the flowing silk of her nightgown to trail behind her as she stepped through the French doors into her boudoir. Picking up the delicate brass bell from her nightstand, she rang for her breakfast. After a few moments, Ulva opened the door for one of the housemaids, stepping inside and holding the door wide so the young girl could bring through an oversized tray. As she awkwardly maneuvered the tray through the door sideways and struggled to turn it after entering, Gabby could see a trace of disapproval on the older woman's face and wished she would go easy on the girl, but she said nothing.

Gabby crossed the room as the two women left in silence. Just before backing out, Ulva asked, "Will there be anything special for you this morning?"

Gabby looked at the garments hanging just outside the dressing room and said, "No, thank you."

"Very good, my lady." Ulva preferred the formal address, even though Gabby had made it clear she would accept a less-formal manner. She pulled the door quietly closed leaving Gabby alone to prepare for the day.

After some coffee and a light meal, Gabby began her morning regimen, starting with a bath that she could hear being drawn in the walk-through lavatory while she was having breakfast. The enormous expanse of marble, wood and plaster was appointed with an oversized claw-foot tub which the servants were filling with hot water mounded high with pearly bubbles. As she slipped into the bath, she felt the warmth penetrate through her, relaxing her every care away. As she soaked, she could hear the manor coming to life. Voices downstairs issuing orders echoed softly throughout the upper rooms. She heard her bedroom door open and a tray being set on the corner table. She had received letters which she would read before dressing.

It had taken her a while to get used to putting on makeup, but she and Ulva had worked out a system in which Ulva selected the clothes, accessories, makeup and jewelry the night before based on the plans for the next day, but Gabby would dress herself. Every morning, there was a slip of paper next to her makeup palette indicating which squares would be appropriate for the day. Ulva came to work on her hair while she applied foundations and powders.

Satisfied with her hair and makeup, wrapped in a thick terry cloth robe, Gabby went to the bedroom. Sitting in the deep, leather Queen Ann chair aside the corner table, she took up the letters, one by one, reading about the family's business, relatives keeping in touch, and social invitations. Upon reaching the bottom of the stack, she drew out the newspaper. Each morning, she had the early edition of the *Telegraf* from Berlin brought to her so she could keep up to date on the affairs of the day. As she read, the dappled sunlight streamed in through the open door. At this time of year, the old oak trees straddling the manor helped to keep the rooms cool. The birds sang in the branches just above the balcony making spring mornings bright and musical.

Several pages into the paper, she came across an advertisement placed by a Dr. Freda Dudek in Cologne. Reading the ad, she was dumbfounded. Her eyes went wide and her heart began to race. It had been many years since she had thought about her two friends in the concentration camp, and regret had always colored those memories, but now she might have a chance to keep the promise she had made to them nearly three decades ago: to find them someday.

Her thoughts raced in pace with her heartbeat. She certainly would not want the secrets of her past to become common knowledge. Granted, Anton knew everything there was to know about her, but the high-society wives would relish the opportunity to drag anyone through the mud just for the chance at feeling important. They could seriously damage one's reputation if not properly managed.

Public Notice: Subjects Of Auschwitz Experiments

If you survived a unique sterilization experiment in early 1944, conducted exclusively by Horst Schumann in Auschwitz, Block 10, please contact Dr. Freda Dudek at the Medizinische Fakultät, Cologne University, Joseph-Stelzmann-Straße 20, 50931 Köln, Germany. Only three boys were involved in the experiment. If you were one of the boys, please reply. Your help is sorely needed by one of the other boys, now grown.

My Dear Dr. Dudek,

    My name is Gabriella Gorski, formerly Gabriel Köhler, and J was one of three boys experimented on by Dr. Schumann in Auschwitz, Block 10 in 1944. Since it is quite possible that you might receive unsubstantiated claims to your advertisement, J will give you a piece of information that you may check. Of the three boys who were experimented on to remove testicles, penis, and scrotum completely, J am the one who took the longest to heal. Either of the other two boys, named Albert or Lukas, will know this and be able to verify my identity.

    J understand that you are a reputable psychotherapist and there will certainly be a vetting process and discussions before J meet your patient, but J look forward to the event with great anticipation. J do, however, have one request. J would appreciate your confidence in keeping the matter between us and closely held as a private affair. My husband is Dr. Anton Gorski, a surgeon of some note, and J would want to avoid any unnecessary controversy.

    Yours Truly,
    Gabriella Gorski

"Hallo, Medizinische Fakultät, Dr. Dudek speaking."
"Hello, Dr. Dudek. This is Gabriella Gorski. I trust you are well."

"Mrs. Gorski! It is so good to hear your voice. I received your letter yesterday. Please let me assure you that our conversations will be treated confidentially since they relate to patient treatment." Freda began scribbling on the blank page.

"Thank you, doctor. I want to do anything I can to help. I just don't want to cause any unnecessary controversy for my husband." The woman still sounded apprehensive, but that would pass with some encouragement.

"I assure you, we will keep your involvement confidential." Dr. Freda kept her voice level to help Mrs. Gorski begin to trust her.

"Please tell me, doctor, whom are you treating?" Gabriella asked, holding her breath to steady herself for the answer.

"Albert Novak is under my care at present."

"Oh, my. I thought I would never see him again," Gabriella whispered.

Dr. Freda did not want to leave the woman to worry, so she added, "He is alive and reasonably well, but I believe his mental state could be improved by reuniting with someone from his past who has been through similar circumstances."

Gabriella regained her composure. "Anything I can do to help, I will. Please tell me when I can come to visit."

"Are you available to come to the Wiesenhof Asylum on Saturday, May the thirteenth at ten am?" Dr. Freda asked as she wrote the date down.

"Yes, of course, doctor."

"I will see you then, Mrs. Gorski. Please come early and leave plenty of time for a lengthy visit if the situation should warrant." Dr. Freda waited for confirmation before drawing a box around the date.

"It seems you are quite energetic today, *Doktor*," Dr. Nowitz remarked with interest in his voice. "Something has you...*aufgeregt*." He thought for a moment and translated "...excited."

"*Ja, Herr Doktor,*" replied Freda. "I have received a reply from Gabriella Gorski. She will travel to visit Albert in a week's time." Freda lowered her eyes to her lap where she noticed she had begun wringing her hands. She stopped moving and attempted to affect a relaxed but stoic posture.

Dr. Nowitz regarded her for a long time before speaking. "This reply seems a positive one, my dear. Her visit is sure to help Albert's recovery."

Freda looked up and smiled sardonically. "I am very hopeful that this will be the result, though it may be painful for Albert."

"May I ask why you feel this way?" he asked.

"I have told you already about the three boys who were mutilated by the Nazi doctor Horst Schumann. Albert Novak was one of these boys, and he has identified as male continuously since the war. Gabriella Gorski has answered an advertisement that I placed in the *Telegraf* on the first of May. She happens to still be in Germany and wrote to me the very same day the ad was printed. She is one of the other two boys. Since the war, she has lived a very different life than Albert has. She has identified as female since running away from an abusive foster home at about fourteen. She has a good home now and is quite wealthy, enough to have the foremost gender reassignment surgeon, Dr. Harry Benjamin, oversee her procedures from America and to have her husband, a preeminent gender reassignment surgeon, perform the procedures here in Germany. She has not only agreed to meet Albert, but also wants to help his recovery." Freda took some time to weigh her next words carefully. "I am optimistic that meeting her will improve his prospects for recovery."

Freda sat perfectly still for long moments, contemplating. She had been feeling a bit guilty ever since the suicide attempt under her care had tarnished not only her self confidence but also her reputation as an effective psychiatrist and physician. She knew that the process of recovery rarely went as smoothly as one would hope and that the best outcomes are often preceded by times of turmoil. Freda took a deep breath and let it out slowly. She felt a great responsibility for every one of her patients, but Albert more than any other.

"I hope that this meeting helps both Albert *and* yourself." Dr. Nowitz' reply was unexpected and Freda's face held a puzzled look, so he continued, "Your self-worth is still very much the result of your investment in your patients because you are a good person." He paused and sighed adding, "Professional detachment is not always a possibility, my friend."

Chapter 20

"Maria! Maria! *Herkommen!*" ("Maria! Maria! Come here!") Hugo sat reading the local paper but when he came across an ad from the *Medizinische Fakultät* in Cologne he bolted upright in his chair, eyes wide.

Maria leaned through the door to the sitting room with a look of curiosity on her face, but when she saw him staring wide-eyed at something in the paper, she brought the cup and dish towel with her to see what had him so excited.

"Look here!" he said, pointing to one of the many advertisements populating the page.

She tilted her head up so she could read through the bottom of her bifocals and, finding his finger, read the blurry type. When she finished reading, she stood up and looked at him, also wide-eyed. Her mouth hung open and they stood stunned for a long minute.

"*Glaubst du, das könnte er sein?*" ("Do you think it could be him?") he asked in amazement.

"*Kann kein anderer sein,*" ("It could be none other,") she confirmed. A look of concern crept onto her face. "What do you think could be wrong with him?" she asked Hugo.

"We must find out." The resolve in his voice made it clear that this was not going to be a topic for debate, only planning.

It had been nearly three decades since Hugo had given one of the boys a copy of a photograph he had taken. While it was not common to associate with prisoners of Auschwitz, Hugo had been assigned to capture as much of Dr. Horst Schumann's work as possible. Adolf Hitler himself had ordered complete photographic and written documentation of Dr. Schumann's activities so that if his experiments went as predicted, they could be replicated across the world's occupied countries, hopefully leading to the extinction of the Jewish race. The photo he gave to one of the boys was of three of them, naked, just after healing from the procedure. He wanted them to have some evidence of what was done to them, under the pretense of giving "the wretched dogs" a memento of the experience. He remembered that they were still alive when it was announced that The Red Army was advancing on Auschwitz. He was given no choice but to leave ahead of the last wave of Nazi guards, but he had been forced to leave Maria behind.

Before they parted, they arranged to meet six months later in Nuremberg to rekindle their affair, but just then, Hugo was in danger of the Allies treating him as one of the soldiers and taking him as a prisoner of war. If that happened, they might never see each other again, so he had to get away. They both knew that it was unlikely for nurses to be treated the same as soldiers even if they were sympathizers because the nature of their mission was humanitarian. In fact, many of the nurses who cared for patients in the camps volunteered for service immediately after they were liberated and worked side by side with The Red Cross to help ease the suffering of the survivors.

Hugo carried many of his photographs in a leather case when fleeing Germany after the war ended in 1945 and at one point, he had been stopped by some American officers. They had no idea who he was but he had been terrified that he would be prosecuted simply for having photographs of Adolph Hitler, Horst Schumann, and so many high-ranking officials in the Nazi Party in his possession, but when the officers saw the bottle of cognac he was also carrying, they became blind to the stacks of photographs and instead, spent the evening toasting and sharing stories with Hugo. He was so rattled by the experience that he hid the photographs in metal cans and buried them, later digging them up and selling them to Time magazine in 1965. The resulting mixture of fame and hatred had driven him and Maria into hiding.

Maria stayed with the three boys to protect them during the liberation. She and the other nurses refused to leave with the Nazi guards fearing that the Russians would simply execute the remaining prisoners since that would be the easiest solution. By remaining, they knew they were possibly giving up their lives, but that is what nurses did. They lived in the service of others. Maria remembered huddling with the three boys when someone nearby was shot through the neck by a stray bullet coming through the barrack wall. She remembered standing up to the Russian commander who had turned out to be quite a reasonable man who had promised their safety, helping The Red Cross to process and care for the medical needs of the prisoners.

Six months after the war, after being deposed in Nuremberg as part of the Nazi hunting efforts of the new government, she traveled to *Bürgermeistergarten*, a picturesque park near the old part of Nuremberg. When they were both stationed at Auschwitz, she had become enamored with him, and he with her. Though they could not display any sign of their affections, their attraction was obvious to anyone who cared to see. That spark reignited the moment they saw each other and they had committed to spend the rest of their lives together. They married as soon as time allowed.

Awash with distant memories, they came out of their reverie, each with the same decision. They must help if they were able. Maria looked down at Hugo and he looked up at her. In each other's eyes, they saw their shared decision.

"Will you write to her or shall I?" Maria asked.

"I will start right now. Finish what you are doing and come help me," he instructed.

Maria resumed her task of drying dishes and since they had been unattended for a while, she had to pay special attention to some spots that had dried on the glassware. As she worked, she could hear Hugo in the other room preparing stationary, copying the address from the newspaper, and putting it aside. Once she finished putting the dishes back in their proper places, she joined him in the sitting room. Pulling a chair to his side, she looked over his shoulder while he continued writing. He had asked for her assistance, but he knew her mind and was composing exactly what she would have written if their positions were reversed.

Dear Dr. Dudek,

My name is Hugo Jaeger, and I am writing for myself and Maria Stromberger. We were surprised to read your advertisement in this morning's edition of the Telegraf and hope that we might be able to help. As you are probably aware, I was one of Hitler's personal photographers, but what you might not know is that I was ordered to keep a visual record of all experiments conducted by Dr. Horst Schumann in Auschwitz which included three boys. I tried to be their friend and confidant to the extent that I could be in a Nazi camp. Maria was their nurse. She helped with their recovery after the surgeries were performed. These three boys were very dear to us and Maria protected them during the liberation of Auschwitz. She continued to care for them when they were transferred to The Red Cross facility but lost contact with them when they were taken to London for further treatment and processing.

I took a photograph that you might find useful if you are the one treating these three boys. It is possible that one of them might still have a copy. The photograph is of the three boys, quite emaciated, taken just after they healed. They were unclothed and you can see that their sexual organs had been removed.

We would both very much like to visit and pay our respects. Would you please write back? It will be a long trip for us, but we would like to visit with you and the boys at your earliest convenience. Please include a date and time for our arrival in late June if this meets with your approval.

Warmest regards,
Hugo Jaeger & Maria Stromberger

Maria left nursing a few years after the war ended, but she could never get rid of the memories. She became interested in the post-war efforts to bring Nazi war criminals to justice and continued documenting articles and hearsay until she was asked to testify in 1947 in the Nuremberg trial of Rudolf Höss. During the trial, she explained how she would occasionally be asked by Höss to help with his experiments by caring for survivors of the procedures he would carry out. She learned that Höss was the one responsible for keeping the frequent Typhoid outbreaks from becoming an epidemic.

One day, Maria arrived at Auschwitz, went through the normal security clearance routine, and realized as she made her way to her assigned barracks, that there seemed to be far fewer prisoners than the previous day. She said nothing, going about her business of checking on patients of the experimental ward until she saw Höss heading across the camp's open ground. She rushed to catch up with him and when she asked what had happened, he said that he had remedied a Typhoid outbreak.

She was dumbstruck and stopped in her tracks. When Höss turned to see her standing in the mud, she only said, "Thank you, Commandant." Then she turned to return to her barracks. She realized that instead of treating the lice that spread the disease, he had gassed and incinerated the people carrying the lice. The rest of her day passed in a fog of disbelief and disjointed awareness. She was so horrified that she was numb for several days, remembering prisoners she had come to know, letting them steal an extra bit of food or giving them an excuse to rest for an extra minute or two as she stood guard.

It astonished her that even after the war, there were pro-Nazi sympathizers who would accost her or threaten her for telling what she knew. Reconnecting with Hugo around that time brought a ray of sunshine back into her life.

Chapter 21

Jürgen sat at a small wooden table outside Mia's Cafe on a quiet street in Frankfurt in early May. He was chuckling to himself with a copy of the morning's *Telegraf* open on the table before him. He was amazed by the arrogance of this Dr. Dudek. She had just disclosed to the whole world that Albert Novak was not the only person she was interested in. He had been considering when would be the right time to go back to Cologne to eliminate the doctor and now he was glad he had not acted too soon. She had just sounded the dinner bell and if there were any other people who could identify Dr. Schumann, she had just called them all to the same place.

Dr. Dudek had solved the problem of tracking down everyone who could identify Dr. Schumann, but one problem remained. He had been seen when he was interrupted putting an end to Albert's misery, and not only had he failed at doing that, he had not gotten away before at least a dozen people had seen his face. He would need to change his appearance.

For the last few weeks, he had his two protégés watching Dr. Dudek and they had located the office where she went for therapy every Tuesday. Dr. Wilhelm Nowitz had an office a short train ride from her office at the *Medizinische Fakultät* at Cologne University. Jürgen made plans to be there this Saturday night just before midnight. The building would be empty, according to his two thugs. The last occupant went home at seven o'clock on Saturday evening so he should have plenty of time alone with Dr. Nowitz' notes...and Dr. Freda Dudek's confessions. Then he would find out who else she had been talking to so he could decide if he needed to eliminate them as well.

The trip from Frankfurt to Cologne Central Station took a little longer than usual. Jürgen stepped off of the last car onto the platform. Looking around, he noted how few people were about this time of the evening. He still had another ninety minutes until his next train took him to the Bochum station, just a couple blocks from Dr. Nowitz' office on Ostring. As he walked from one side of the platform to the other, he saw that the train to Bochum was still disembarking, so he found a bench and sat for a while watching the passengers. While he waited, he unfolded his copy of the *Telegraf* and resumed reading an article about the upcoming summer Olympic Games to be held in Munich in August and September. Apparently there was some reason for concern since there had been decades of tension between the Palestinians and Israelis and several threats had been made among the competitors. The journalist seemed to think that this was nothing more than politics and distraction from a historic event, but Jürgen knew how deep the hatred between the groups ran. He was sure there would be blood shed at these games.

In 1936, Jürgen was a bright-eyed member of Hitler's Youth, an organization that sought to educate people about the purity of the Aryan race and how to foster progress toward a planet dominated by one people under Hitler's rule. He could not understand how this race was not all interested in preserving its heritage. It baffled him that they would advocate for the rights of other races and even interbreed with those other races to create mongrel offspring. It was his interest in this aspect of the Nazi party's message that drew him to medicine. He remembered those early days, being taken under Dr. Schumann's wing, learning the principles behind the methodology of purification.

The bell sounded for passengers to begin boarding and Jürgen looked up to see the platform almost empty. Today was Saturday and this late in the evening, nearly everyone wanted to be home with their families, but he had something much more important to take care of. He folded his paper and rose to board the train, heading to the last car. He was always one to plan for the worst. In his line of work, the better the scheme, the better the chance of survival. Sitting in the back gave him the best chance of survival if the train derailed or struck something. The front cars were the most likely to be damaged, killing their occupants. As the train began to move, each car lurched forward and then began to accelerate. As they pulled out of the station, he unfolded his paper while most other people looked out at the beautiful landscape that emerged from the Central Station walls. The sun was setting over the trees and the warm orange glow filled the cabin, but Jürgen didn't see any of this beauty. He sat reading even though he was already having difficulty in the low light. He was getting older and his vision wasn't as acute as it used to be.

The announcement came that they would be stopping at the Bochum Ostring station shortly. Jürgen didn't look up, but mentally acknowledged the notice by folding his paper. He was a fast reader and was nearly finished reading the entire paper in the three hours since he had left Frankfurt. As he sat, listlessly looking toward the front of the car, he reviewed his plans. He would surveil the building for a while, enter and take the stairs to the doctor's floor. He was very good with locks, so getting through the door should not be a problem. Once inside, he would be careful not to touch anything with his bare hands and would move nothing that he didn't have to. When he left, he would lock the door and return to the train station. He would have nearly two hours until the next train, which should be plenty of time unless the doctor's notes were difficult to read. If possible, he would avoid taking the doctor's notes since that would be noticed early on Monday morning when the doctor had his first session.

The train pulled into the Ostring Station causing Jürgen to squint as the train came into the brightly lit building from the dark of night. Nothing outside had been visible for the last hour and a sleepy dullness had settled over the train's occupants who stirred to life, sitting up and anticipating the next leg of their individual journeys. He sat unmoving until the train came to a stop. There was no point in being emotional or anticipating anything. It only showed how mindless people were and how much energy they wasted. Once the last person ahead of him stood, he collected his paper and rose, calmly heading for the door. Stepping down into the station, he noted the slight chill in the air. The weather lately was unpredictable as spring gave way to summer.

Walking to the street corner outside the station, all was dark except for a small cone of light under each light post. He could tell he was in a smaller town just by the lighting. In Frankfurt or Cologne, the entire city would be well lit by street lamps and cars well into the night, but Bochum was a smaller town with less need for extensive lighting. This would work in his favor. He put his hands in his pockets, tucking the paper under one arm, then proceeded toward *Ostring 30* across the street, he observed that there did not appear to be anyone around. A few passengers crossed the street behind him but then turned this way or that, heading for their destinations. He went straight down the walkway to the large pond behind the office building. It was a shorter structure, less than ten floors, and only one window was lit, but it was not on the floor he was going to. He walked along the path around the left of the pond and found a bench a few dozen paces away where he sat, seeming to admire the pond, which was black at night. The streetlamps in the distance reflected off the water and shimmered with the occasional ripple traversing the pond. Most of the waterfowl were sleeping, but occasionally one would dunk its head to catch something, sending a ring of waves out that propagated to the far end of the pond before dying in the grass and reeds.

There was no one around. Bochum was quiet. A police siren off in the distance indicated someone was having a bad night, but where he was there seemed to be no activity. He stood up from the bench and walked toward the back side of the structure. Up a few steps, then on to the leaf-strewn landing, he walked around the side of the building along a walkway tilted slightly away from the building and washed over at the joints by mud which had flowed over the concrete and dried. There was no apparent wearing away of these patches indicating that the path was rarely used. He did not walk across the front of the building, but instead went across the street where he could observe the offices from the front door of the Bochum Planetarium. Seeing nothing out of place and still no activity, he walked back across the street and around the other side to the back of the building and to the door. The landing was poorly lit by a two-bulb fixture. The bulb nearest the building had gone out, leaving the door in darkness.

He looked at the lock on the door and recognized it as an older model. This would be easy to pick, but as he reached in his breast pocket, he looked more closely at the space between the doors. There was no bolt. He put his tool pouch back and put a gloved hand on the handle and pulled gently. The door was not locked, so he opened it just wide enough to slip inside and held the door as it closed, making certain it was silent. When the door came to rest, he proceeded to the stairs down the dark hallway. He climbed several flights and came out cautiously onto the appropriate floor. Opening the door and holding it by the knob until it too closed silently, he released the door knob and the door gave out a loud clack as the bolt engaged. He froze with his hand inches from the knob, ready to retreat if anyone came to investigate. There was no one.

He turned to face the hallway and saw no lights under any doors. The floor appeared to be deserted and the one light bulb in the center of the hallway was insufficient to light the entire hall, so the two ends of the hallway, one where he stood, were in darkness. He stood silently listening. Hearing nothing, he walked down the hall reading the name plates until he came to a plaque reading *Dr. Wilhelm*

Nowitz, Doktor der Philosophie at eye level. It was old and tarnished as was the doorknob. Just to see if any effort would be needed, he gave the knob a try. At least the doctor was smart enough to lock his own door even though the outer door was not secured.

He drew out his leather tool kit, selected the proper sizes and picked the lock easily. He turned the knob and pushed the door slightly ajar, holding it open with the toe of his shoe while he replaced his tools. He put his gloved hands on the face of the door and pushed it open slowly. It appeared the door would continue swinging under its own weight, so he prevented it from doing so and eased the door shut behind him. He stepped quietly into the dark room. The odor of old pipe tobacco was thick in the air, so he drew out his lighter and struck it to life. He knew that no one would notice the smell of lighter fluid buried under the odors of tar and cavendish. He walked slowly down the short hallway into the main meeting space with two leather chairs and that long kind of chair you lie down on. All this therapy was something high-minded people did to make themselves feel better about doing nothing that really mattered.

To the right, he could see the doctor's desk. Holding the lighter in one hand, he flicked the lamp on with the other, then flipped the cover closed to extinguish the lighter. He held it to his lips and blew on it to cool it down before he slipped it into his hip pocket. He began to familiarize himself with the stacks of papers spread across the doctor's desk. Holding each stack down with one hand, he lifted the corners of various papers. Invoices signed and noted paid, lists, a few diagrams...he would lift them just enough to read, then let them fall exactly where they had been before removing the hand holding them down. This way, no one would ever know he had been there. He opened the center drawer which contained clips, pens, some small note pads, and other miscellaneous bits that had accumulated over the years, but no notebook. Leaving the center drawer ajar unlocked the other drawers. This old-style desk allowed the user to lock all of the drawers with a single key turn by a mechanism that engaged a lock on all the drawers when the center drawer, with the keyhole, was pushed closed. Now that the side drawers were unlocked, he tried the top-right, no luck, middle-right, no luck. When he opened the largest drawer on the right, the one at the bottom, a well-worn leather-bound notebook sat on top of a stack of similar notebooks. He picked up the notebook and set it on the desk opening to the inside front cover. In pencil, he read the inscription *Dr. Freda Dudek, 1959 to 19___*, lacking a final date. He opened to the first page and began reading. He skimmed the pages, not finding what he was looking for, so he began turning several pages at once as he progressed through the sessions. When he came to the current year, he slowed down. As he skimmed, he saw the name *Dr. Horst Schumann* and turned back to it. He read carefully and as he did so, his eyebrows scrunched together. *Nazi hunting group...sending money...Horace Krämer...accounting firm belonging to his father...Gabriella Gorski...estate outside Cologne...Albert Novak... patient Wiesenhof Asylum...Ernst and Lena Rabinowitz...coming next week...Mrs. Gorski coming to see Albert...*this was exactly what he had come for. He continued reading, keeping track of the time.

When he finished, he carefully placed the notebook back in exactly the same position it had been before, closed the drawers, latched the top drawer, and flicked off the lamp since he could retrace his steps in the dark. He stood up, eyes wide but temporarily blind. He felt his way around the desk and headed for the hallway, one hand out to catch the corner of the hallway where he knew it would be. Suddenly, he felt his coat brush something on the corner of the desk and the sound of papers fluttering to the floor made him freeze.

"Verdammte scheiße!" he blurted in a forced whisper. He raged at himself for letting this happen. As he turned to reach for the desk lamp, the papers crunched beneath his feet. He found the lamp and flicked the switch. He stooped and collected the papers. There were at least twenty and he had no way of knowing exactly where they were before they fell, so he collected them into a stack and spread the stack a bit on the desk, trying to make it look like the others, but the damage had already been done.

It was Monday morning when Dr. Freda opened the door to her office to find Helga sitting at a stool near the entrance, holding the phone to her ear. She had heard the phone ring once from down the hallway but she was too far away to have reached it in time.

Helga turned to face Dr. Freda saying, "She just came in Dr. Nowitz. Please wait a moment." Addressing Dr. Freda, Helga's voice was thick with worry. "You might want to take this in your office." Helga held the receiver over the phone's cradle, waiting for Dr. Freda to pick it up in her office.

Confused at why Dr. Nowitz would be calling so early, and why Helga looked so worried, Freda said nothing, but opened the inner door to her office, closing it behind her as she headed for the desk. The light coming through the frosted window gave ample light to see, and once she was seated, she took up the receiver and turned on the desk lamp. Sitting down, she said "Good morning, Wilhelm. How are you today?"

"Good morning, Freda," he replied. Such a familiar tone was out of character for him, so she knew something was wrong. "I need to make you aware of something." He took a deep breath and Freda could hear him letting it out slowly in the relaxation technique they often used. "Someone broke into my office sometime over the weekend."

Freda was stunned and sat silently before coming to her senses. "Are you alright, Wilhelm? You were not there, were you?"

"No, no. The police are on the way here now," he said, reassuringly. "I try to avoid working on the weekends. When I came to my desk a few minutes ago, I could see that papers had been moved and some appeared to have been stepped on, as if they had fallen on the floor. As you are aware, my mess has method. I know where every paper belongs and I arrange things in my own particular way. It does not appear that anything is missing, but my papers were moved."

"I am so glad you are alright," Freda sighed with relief.

"There is one other thing," he continued. "Whoever broke in read my notes. The notebook was moved but still in the same place." He waited for a response from Freda, but none was forthcoming. After a long silence, he added, "You remember the things we have talked about over the last few years, do you not?"

Freda's mind was racing. They had discussed so many things. Then she began to realize his meaning. She had discussed her treatments and specific patients with him. One of those patients was Albert. The man who tried to kill Albert must be the same person who broke into Wilhelm's office. Surely he was aware of this and hoping she would make the connection. "*Herr Doktor,* I think we should discuss this in person."

"I have already cleared my schedule for the day. Let me come to you. It would be a good thing for me to see where you work."

Freda had a full day of counseling scheduled and could not leave, so she agreed. "Please come to see me as soon as you can." Her tone was urgent and concerned.

"Very good. I will see you about ten-thirty?" he asked.

"*Ja, Herr Doktor,*" she confirmed and he disconnected the call.

Freda's mind was still racing. She had many suspicions but most seemed far-fetched. She knew that Albert was one of the boys from the Auschwitz group and Gabriella was another. Freda had been looking for the doctor that mutilated Albert and Gabby using Horace's accounting firm to trace financial transactions, but something didn't make sense. If Freda were helping someone to hunt down the Nazi doctor, why was she not the target of the attack? Why Albert? Unless the Nazi was just trying to clean up after himself. Her eyes went wide with a new realization. If someone were coming to kill Dr. Schumann's patients, they would certainly kill the person who exposed them. Horace would also be in danger. They had discussed several of her other patients like Gerta (and Guy), Ida, and even Helga would all be in Dr. Nowitz' notes. They must all be warned.

Albert had been having serious problems since the attempt on his life. He would not sleep without heavy sedation, but he was afraid to take the sedatives because they were the reason he was defenseless when attacked. Even under heavy sedation, his sleep was fitful and he reported constant nightmares of being buried, which stemmed from a subconscious fear of being smothered. It was an awful setback for him, but his room was now guarded with a nurse's station being set in the hallway to protect not just him, but all of the patients. The asylum was also researching all new hires before bringing them on and would extend that research to their existing staff as soon as time permitted. Independently, the police were conducting an investigation but they had made it clear they would not be sharing any information with the asylum's administrators.

Gabriella would be coming for a visit in just a couple days so she could warn her then, just as a precaution. Helga could be told now and Gerta would be coming in for her session later this morning. Horace should be told immediately since he was involved in the financial research being used to hunt down Dr. Schumann.

"Helga?" Dr. Freda called.

Helga's shadow darkened the window just before she opened the door and stuck her head through. "Yes, doctor?"

"Helga, come in please," Freda said, gesturing to the chair in front of the desk.

With a look of concerned curiosity, Helga came in, shut the door and sat, gathering her apron in front of her. She waited for Dr. Freda to speak.

A look of genuine concern spread across Dr. Freda's face followed immediately by a smile of affection and appreciation.

"Am I being sacked?" Helga asked, bluntly.

Freda's face fell and she said cautiously, "No. Nothing like that." Helga's tension subsided and her look of curiosity grew stronger. "I have something to tell you. You know that I see a therapist. Most therapists do."

"Of course, doctor. It's only natural," Helga confirmed.

Dr. Freda nodded in affirmation. "The notes taken during sessions are valuable when something needs to be diagnosed, but for therapy they are kept strictly confidential." She paused for effect, but the connection with Dr. Nowitz' call did not seem to have been apparent to Helga so she continued. "Someone broke into Dr. Nowitz' office over the weekend and read his notes. They did not take anything. They seem to have only been interested in information."

"Dr. Nowitz started to tell me about the break in when you arrived," Helga said.

"Albert was attacked recently. You and I were both there." Dr. Freda sat waiting for the girl to catch up, but it didn't seem to be happening. She would have to explain more clearly. "Since I discuss my patients with Dr. Nowitz, don't you think that it is a bit coincidental that Albert was attacked by someone who went to the trouble to get a job at the Wiesenhof Asylum?"

Helga's eyes suddenly went wide. "Did you talk with him about me?" she asked in alarm.

"Yes I did," Dr. Freda replied. They both sat for a moment to let the realization sink in.

"Do you think he will be coming for us too?" Helga asked with fear building in her voice.

"I do not know for certain why Albert was attacked and I have no idea why someone would want to harm you, but I must urge caution. I do not want you coming down here without an escort. Understand?"

Helga nodded.

"When you are here, you are to keep the door locked until just before patients' appointments. Anyone else will knock when they see the light is on. Ask who they are before letting anyone in. Do not stay late and do not leave without an escort. You can call the front desk so they can send someone for you. Do you understand?"

Helga nodded vehemently.

"What about you?" Helga asked, real concern for her mentor apparent in her quavering voice.

"I will take precautions. I would *also* like you to keep me apprised of your movements. Leave me a note when you step out or call me if you are running late."

"I will," Helga assured.

"Dr. Nowitz is coming at ten-thirty today. That is when Gerta or Guy will be coming, correct?" Dr. Freda asked.

"Yes. I believe so," Helga confirmed.

"I would like you to call Mr. Krämer and see if he can come at the same time. Please tell him that it is urgent." Dr. Freda dismissed Helga to go about her work while she prepared for her first patient.

Chapter 22

Gabby spent the entire weekend directing the setup and breakdown of the memorial for Johan, attended mostly by colleagues of Anton and Dr. Benjamin. She absolutely adored Harry and during his infrequent visits to Germany, she and Anton liked to make certain he enjoyed himself and received the attention he deserved. They each had the chance to say their goodbyes and the eulogies were touching and heartfelt. Johan meant so much to so many people. After the services, as guests traded stories of how Johan had worked tirelessly to improve the lives of others, Gabby, Harry, Jonathan, and Anton spent time away from the others, getting reacquainted and catching up on recent events.

She was exhausted, but more than that, she was feeling the need for companionship. With all the arrangements to be made, it had been nearly two weeks since she had been to the *Kabarett Seks* in Cologne's Red Light District. She was always given the red carpet treatment there and she enjoyed seeing her dear friends Gerta and Lolita. It had been several minutes since she had rung the bell and she was beginning to feel impatient when Ulva opened the door to her boudoir.

A few paces in, she stopped and asked "What can I do for you?"

At least she has stopped calling me my lady, Gabby thought as she looked up from her stationary desk. "I want to go into town this evening. Would you please lay out something appropriate for cocktails at a small gathering?"

Ulva nodded. "I'll have Mr. Bauer prepare to take you," she said.

"No. Have him report to me instead," Gabby instructed.

"Very good, my lad..." Ulva cut herself off, waiting for a reprimand, but Gabby just looked up past her brows at Ulva and smiled impishly. With a sigh and an appreciative grin, Ulva turned to leave the room.

Five minutes later, the chauffeur came into the study and stood at attention without speaking. Gabby was standing in the window admiring the gloaming light outside as the sun sank behind the old oak and pine trees, casting their shadows across the manor. She heard him come in but did not respond immediately. Slowly, she took a deep breath letting her chest rise and exhaled as she turned with a flourish. Ben had been her chauffeur for years and the man was a beauty to behold. His posture was flawless. His jaw was square and his cheeks were rosy and set high. His skin was smooth as cream and his piercing blue eyes were so bright that no one could resist staring into them. His shoulders were broad and muscular and his arms looked so strong he might be able to lift and carry her without any effort at all. Many nights she dreamed of exploring his impressive body, but one did not fraternize with the help. It got complicated too easily. Still, she enjoyed the power she had over him, not from her position as lady of the house but, as a woman. She glided gracefully toward him and stood only slightly too close before him, looking up as he struggled to keep looking forward. She could smell him this close and she relished his unique scent.

"I'm going into town this evening, alone," she said. She stepped around him, moving to the chair at his left. She sat in a sultry pose and crossed her legs so that the slit in her gown revealed her long legs. "I will be taking the Bentley, so please have it ready for me by seven."

"You won't be wanting me to drive you?" he asked, turning to face her. His eyes immediately fell on the exposed skin of her legs and he caught himself, raising his chin to look over her head again.

Gabby smiled a wicked grin. She enjoyed teasing men and this young thing was no exception. She liked him. He was far more controlled around her than most other men. He was able to resist her alluring figure and maintain a respectful posture when most men would be rutting by now. Unfortunately, her husband, Anton, rarely looked at her that way anymore. He was always exhausted from work and preoccupied with the social unrest that still racked the country. He rarely even noticed when she wasn't home, so when she needed some attention and satisfaction, she would go to the cabaret in town to find and bed some handsome young buck. Soldiers were always the best lovers because she would likely never see them again and their military duties kept them pent up for long periods of time. To keep things simple, she mostly sought out married men. That way, there would be no chance of breaking her arrangement with Anton and married men were not eager to publicize their own indiscretions. She enjoyed gaining a man's release, often against his will. Lost in rapturous thought, she sat for a long moment before answering Ben.

"I think I'll be going alone tonight," she confirmed politely. "Please have the car ready by seven."

"Yes, my lady," he acknowledged. He turned rigidly and marched out of the room, the whole time Gabby's eyes examined his behind. His tight, round behind. She definitely needed to get out for a night.

She rose and went to her dressing room where everything was laid out for her. Ulva was ready and waiting to make her the most glamorous woman in town and as she dressed, she took care to smooth every wrinkle, tuck every fold. The result was perfection and she knew no man would be able to resist her tonight.

The sun had set and the gas lanterns had all been lit. The black Bentley T1 was running and waiting for her as she emerged onto the front landing. Ben couldn't help himself. She was so beautiful. He smiled a big grin which he struggled to reign in as she descended the steps and approached him. As she drew close, heading for the driver's seat, she reached up and brushed a finger along his jaw line saying, "You kids behave yourselves while Mama's away."

It was mid-morning the next day when Jürgen pulled up to the Gorski estate just outside of Cologne in his aqua BMW 2000 Touring M40. The wrought iron entry gate was old and grown over with ivy. The call box appeared to be newly installed since it looked out of place mounted onto the old brick pillar. He pressed the call button and a muffled electronic voice responded. He explained that he had an appointment to meet with Mrs. Gorski and he was admitted with a whir of motors and creaking of the gate. The grounds were impeccably manicured with hardly any leaves on the pristine grass. The trees were well trimmed with no dead branches and the drive was perfectly level with no ruts. *These people must have a lot of money!* he thought. From the public road, he couldn't even see the main house, but as he drove into the estate, he could see a smaller structure off to one side; probably for servants. The manor house gradually came into view as he rounded a hedge row. It had the luxurious feeling of old money and would certainly have more than ten bedrooms. He had never actually visited a place like this, but he needed to find out how much Gabriella knew about Dr. Dudek's work. It could be that the only connection was finding one of the three boys experimented on all those years ago, but once he took care of Dr. Dudek, there would probably be no way to find out without using force. He knew from Dr. Nowitz' notes that Gabriella was going to visit Albert soon, so he may have only this one chance to get to her before she could grow suspicious.

As he pulled around the fountain in the front circular drive, a coachman came out to meet him while another servant went inside, presumably to alert the rest of the household. As the coachman walked closer, he reached for the handle and opened the door for Jürgen. He wasn't used to being treated like this, but he would enjoy it while he could. He had a convincing badge ready and flashed it to the coachman, quickly putting it away so he could not get a good look.

"I'm here to see Mrs. Gabriella Gorski," he told the coachman who closed the door behind him. Jürgen took the keys making it clear that he did not want his car moved from this spot.

"Very good, sir." The coachman, having no further duties here, headed back toward the house at a quick pace, while Jürgen followed behind at a slow walk.

There was no reason to appear impatient or in a hurry. That would only serve to raise Gabriella's suspicions. Instead, he would act as calm and collected as he could while he probed her for information. As he climbed the steps to the front landing, the other servant returned. Standing in the center of the landing, he waited for Jürgen to advance before saying in a haughty tone, "Mrs. Gorski will receive you in the sitting room. Please follow me." He turned and marched in through the front entrance which was now being held open by two servants. *Just how many servants does this woman need?* he thought. As he entered, he refused the offer to take his hat, instead taking it off and holding it inverted in one hand. He saw the butler motioning to him across the large open entryway and he set off in that direction, looking around, marveling at the opulence. He looked up the grand staircases on both sides as he passed between them and once through, followed the butler to a door on the left of the main room. It was bigger than any ballroom he had seen in any hotel and could probably fit his childhood house inside a couple times with room to spare. The butler stood to the side of the door where Gabriella must be, so Jürgen went through and stood just inside the door. The butler closed the door behind him, startling him, but he kept his reaction contained.

The woman seated on the wave-shaped couch was stunningly beautiful. Her gown draped across the red velvet upholstery with a flowing elegance that was quite alluring. The sun falling on her golden hair made her glow with warmth. The pink silk gown she wore hugged her body above the hips and draped all the way to the floor. As she rose, she breathed deeply, giving her breasts an extra fullness as she stood. When she exhaled, her cleavage deepened and he realized he was looking directly at her chest. He looked up into her eyes to find a smirk on her face. She knew exactly what she was doing.

"Mrs. Gorski?" he tested.

"Yes mister..."

"Mason, ma'am. Mason Jackson," he replied to her query.

"Please, Mr. Jackson, call me Gabby." She approached with a smooth gait, presenting her hand for him to kiss.

Instead of kissing her hand as she indicated by the positioning of her fingers, he took her hand and shook it a bit roughly. "A pleasure to meet you. You have a beautiful home. Would you mind if I ask you a few questions?" he asked, gesturing her back to her seat with the brim of his hat while he sat in a nearby leather Queen Ann chair.

Gabby retreated, but before sitting, she turned in such a way that, with a little help, the flowing silk spread away from her as she sunk to the cushion. The billowing fabric deflated, perfectly draping the couch and her thighs, which he realized he was staring at. He looked up into her eyes again and saw that she had been watching where he was looking. She must be doing this on purpose. He resolved to keep his eyes on hers.

"I understand you are an investigator?" she inquired. "May I see your credentials?"

"Certainly," he replied. As he drew out his folded leather badge wallet, he said, "I am checking some background information about a potential client. I think you are aware of Dr. Freda Dudek."

"Why, yes. I recently answered an advertisement she placed in the *Telegraf* in Berlin. It seems she was looking for someone. Do you know anything about that?" she asked.

"I'm sorry. There is very little I can tell you, but I would like to thank you in advance for your cooperation," he recited, trying to affect an officially-scripted tone of voice. "Can you tell me the name of the patient she was referring to in the paper?"

"Well, no. I haven't actually met her yet, but we had a nice conversation the other day," Gabby lied. She already knew about Albert, but something wasn't right. It had only been a few days since she had seen the ad and a day since she had talked with Dr. Dudek about Albert. She hadn't expected someone else to be so interested as to come to her at her home. At this point, she couldn't put her finger on what was bothering her, so she decided to play this investigator's game to see where it would lead.

"I see. What do you think she might need from you?" he asked, pretending to be using a memorized set of questions.

"Unfortunately, I won't know until I visit with her next week." In actuality, her appointment with Dr. Dudek was the very next day. "What do you think she could want from me? I mean, I'm no psychotherapist, so I can't imagine I would be able to help."

"I'm not at liberty to say. I'm sorry. Do you know anything about the concentration camps?" he asked.

Gabby put on a heartbroken facade. "I read about them years ago. It must have been awful." She looked away as if she were an emotional woman trying to regain control when in reality, she was beginning to sense an innate resentment for this man. She could tell beyond any doubt that he was not only lying but posed an imminent danger to her. She would have to keep up the demure lady-of-the-house act until she could figure out what this impostor wanted.

"I am sorry to have bothered you," he feigned. He stood and walked to an old oak desk behind the couch where Gabby sat. He set his hat down and bent to pick up a pencil. Writing on the bottom edge of a pad of paper, he said, "I'm going to leave my number with you. If you would be so kind as to call when you have more information you could share with me, I would be very grateful."

Rubbish! He wouldn't be grateful, she thought. He seems like he could kill me if the notion struck him. "Why, certainly, Mr. Jackson. I will be sure to do just that." She smiled and rose gracefully and when he turned, she saw the way the light reflected off his smooth face. With a shock of realization, she knew who the man was. When she was young and starving in Auschwitz, the doctor that mutilated her and took away any chance she had of growing into a man, had a medical assistant. Then, the man was in his early twenties, but certain things did not change that much with age. The bone structure, the shape of the eyes, the way he leaned over...she was certain of it! If she hadn't been so practiced at controlling her facial expressions, she would be staring wide-eyed at him just now. When he looked up at her, she felt a rush of panic, but held her hand out to him again. This time, he took it and kissed the back of her hand.

"Well I had best be going, Mrs. Gorski. Thank you for your time." He placed the hat on his head and walked for the door. Just as he neared, the coachman opened the door and stood aside. *The servant had good ears,* he thought. He looked back at Gabby one last time before touching the brim of his hat with a nod and walking for the front door.

Gabby had been genuinely rattled by Mr. Jackson's visit and she was certain that was *not* his name. A war criminal who had helped the Nazi doctors had been in her house sitting a few feet from her. Obviously the man wasn't too bright because he had left a number he could be reached at. She knew he could have killed her if she had let down her guard. This was something Dr. Freda needed to know about right away.

Freda was in a hurry today, so she answered the telephone call before she was ready to take notes. *"Guten Morgen, Medizinische Fakultät,* Dr. Dudek speaking." She wrote the date 12 May 1961.

"Doctor, this is Gabriella Gorski."

"Well, *hallo Frau Gorski!* Are you looking forward to your visit tomorrow?" Freda was pleased Gabby was calling to confirm.

"Yes, very much so, but I have some disturbing news we should discuss before I come." Gabby's voice was rushed and Freda thought she could detect panic.

"Disturbing? How so?" Freda asked.

"I have just been visited by a man I believe to be the medical assistant who helped Dr. Schumann perform the surgeries on us. He was posing as an investigator asking questions about you." Gabby waited, through the long silence on the line.

"What did you tell him?" Dr. Freda asked calmly.

"I acted as if I knew nothing. I don't think he recognized me but I am certain it was the same man from Auschwitz." Gabby was trying to calm herself, but having little success.

"In that case, let us discuss this in person when you arrive. Please come at least two hours earlier than the time we scheduled and say no more on this call."

"Yes, doctor. I will see you then." Gabby felt odd about hanging up on someone without the social niceties, but she knew Dr. Freda was right to be cautious.

Chapter 23

"I'm lying on a tablecloth. There are white and red checkered boxes. I feel the warmth of sunlight on my arms and my legs and I am squinting. The light is very bright. There is green grass beyond the tablecloth. There are white clouds and the sky is blue. I can see trees when I turn my head. There is someone sitting next to me." Gerta's breathing was soft and slow in the darkened room. The pinpoints of light projected by the meditation lamp made the walls and ceiling seem to disappear revealing a night sky of stars.

This was one of Dr. Freda's main methods for facilitating clear memory recall. Hypnosis for this purpose was not some magician's trick. By definition, it was creating the right environment and stimuli to allow memories to rise from the flotsam of human thought. The problem with the hypnosis method is that the environment is not always under your control. Hypnosis could probably not be performed if there were voices or office noises on the other side of a wall. She was never worried about Helga in the front room. She was absolutely silent during hypnosis sessions.

In a melodic, breathy voice Dr. Freda asked, "Who is there with you?"

"Her dress is covered with roses and leaves. It is my mother's favourite dress. She is leaning back on her elbows with her eyes closed. The wind is making her hair move a little. I can smell her perfume." Her eyes still closed, Gerta began to smile at the childhood memory.

"Is there anyone else there with you?" asked Dr. Freda as she tried to keep the sound of her pen on the notepad from disturbing the ambiance.

"I...I think there is. I can't see him clearly." A grimace began to form on Gerta's face.

"That's alright. Just describe what you see," Dr. Freda guided.

"There is a shadow lying next to me on the tablecloth. It looks like smoke and I can see my mother through it. He is lying between me and my mother, but she is right next to me. There is no room for anyone between us." As she began to strain to recall the memory, Dr. Freda could tell she was losing her focus.

"Don't worry about that. There is a smoky shape between you. Do you know who the shadow is?" Dr. Freda asked.

"No, but I know he belongs here. He is always here," Gerta responded with a disquieting tremble in her voice.

"He has always been with you, but he is safe. He has never harmed you. He protects you. Does he want to say anything to you?" Dr. Freda was intrigued by Gerta's description of Guy as a definite shape in this session. In past sessions, his emergence was only a feeling of something coming...something about to happen. Why would he appear this time as a smoky shape?

"He is coming closer. He is trying to say something but I can't hear him. He looks like he is trying to tell me...." Gerta trailed off, struggling to hold onto the memory. "He looks like he is screaming, but I can't see his face. I can't see anything but smoke, so why do I think he is screaming?"

"Don't worry about that right now. He protects you, but he wants to tell you something. Relax and listen."

"He is getting louder, but I can't hear what he is saying." Gabby was straining now as fear crept into her voice. "He is so loud but I can't hear him! Why can't I hear him?"

As the shape began to consume the space between her and her mother, she looked up where his face should be, but only wisps of darkness were there, swirling, transparent. She could still see her mother's distorted form through him as he sent more and more power toward her. He was trying so hard to make her hear him, but there was no mouth or eyes, or anything. There wasn't even an outline. He was just smoke, shifting and reforming before her. She turned her head to look away from him, but he was on the other side too. The tablecloth under where he lay was pressed down as if he had weight, but the smoky shape ebbed and flowed in and out, darker, lighter, so close to her. He leaned toward her which made her freeze with mounting terror. He was so close, she could feel his breath on her face, but there was no sound except the breeze...and...something else. He was trying so hard to tell her something and a sound began to build on the wind. In the air near her face, a voice began to vibrate. She could feel it prickling her nose and her ears. The voice continued to build until it was painful, but still there was only the slightest sound. As his strength grew, he became darker, less transparent, like smoke thickening in a burning room. The intensity of the memory continued to build until the girl began to hear something like words that suddenly overwhelmed her in a wave of pressure.

Gerta was crying into her hands. Her chest shuddered like a child when they have been distraught for too long. She clenched her eyes shut, afraid to see. Tears soaked her fingers and palms as she held her hands tight over her eyes, nose and mouth, staunching her own breathing. As the air rushed between her fingers, she began to hear a voice she recognized. It was a woman, but not her mother. The voice was distant, blurry like the smoky figure. As the voice grew louder, it also grew clearer.

"Gerta, you are in Dr. Freda's office. You are safe. Gerta, you are in Dr. Freda's office. You are safe." Dr. Freda continued to repeat the recall phrase and when it appeared that Gerta was regaining control, she very gently placed her hand high on Gerta's back, exerting almost no pressure. Just a pat or two should help ground Gerta again.

"I'm sorry," Gerta apologized as she began to sniffle. Dr. Freda had a handkerchief ready and suspended it before Gerta. When she opened her eyes, she took the handkerchief.

"There is nothing to be sorry about. That was an excellent attempt, Gerta. I'm very proud of you. You are getting stronger with each try," Dr. Freda said soothingly. She never patronized either Gerta or Guy, but when Gerta was in this condition, her mental state was fragile. She would need time to regain her emotional fortitude before they began to analyze what she had just experienced.

Dr. Freda had diagnosed Gerta with multiple personality disorder and schizophrenia. Often when one personality or the other was dominant, he or she would hear the whispers of the other along with distortions of thought that made her quite the complicated patient. Still, she seemed able to function in either state, so she was doing better than most people with similar conditions. There were several things that made Gerta's case unique.

Gerta sometimes demonstrated two profoundly different personality states. Each of these states would have access to its own complete set of memories, but perceived through the emotional filter of that personality. Dr. Freda moved from beside the chaise to her desk and set Gerta's file down to take a sip of tea and to recall past sessions with the young woman as she recovered. Her case had been referred to her department because it involved "sexual deviance" as the administration put it, in addition to other mental disorders not related to gender. Since Dr. Freda was trained in both, she was clearly the best person to handle such a case.

At their last session, the more masculine personality, Guy, was dominant and was his typical abrasive self. He was aware of his physical condition and had long ago accepted that the feminine personality was carefree and happy with her uniqueness, but he was not. In cases of schizophrenia, the risk of suicide is high because perceptions become gradually more distorted over time and though schizophrenia is not the same as multiple personality disorder, Gerta didn't really fit that profile either. Whatever the case, Freda was most concerned for Guy when the masculine personality was dominant because he thought of himself as having the *wrong parts* which was, of course, inescapable.

Most parents faced with the birth of a child with ambiguous genitalia opt for surgery to reassign the child female, since that choice requires fewer surgeries and results in a lower cost. Unfortunately, the way the brain develops and the way the body appears are not always aligned, so some young people find that they have been reassigned female when they are clearly male-thinking. In these cases, the suicide rate is alarmingly high and this was partly Freda's concern with Gerta.

For almost a year now, the two of them had been working on a way for the two personas to hear each other, but so far, no real conversation across their perceptual barriers has been possible. Dr. Freda's hope was that, through the use of hypnosis and guided meditation, she could find some way for the masculine and the feminine to begin to blend, or at least perceive each other consciously. If any progress were made it would go a long way toward relieving Guy's depression and could even be a stabilizing influence that might benefit Gerta. For now, the complexity of this case was beyond anything Dr. Freda had read about. She consulted with colleagues at the asylum about the case, but they had cautioned her against expecting any progress, or at least predictable progress, from such a complex personality disorder.

Emil Müller couldn't sit. He paced the waiting room in the St. Elisabethen Hospital for hours, making the other people nervous. An elderly woman seated, presumably with her husband, in the far corner of the room had been giving him disapproving looks for the last hour, but he didn't care. He and Sofie had been trying to have a baby ever since they were married but she had miscarried at least three times, that they knew of. The doctors said it was probably more, but some of the embryos might have been too small to notice. The day their physician sat them down in his office and delivered the news that they would probably never have children was one of the saddest of his life.

But not today. Sofie had carried a baby to full term, and the doctors were beginning to worry about her being past her due date. They felt that her past difficulties might be a reason for concern, but on the day she was to be induced, she had her first contraction and the doctors decided to let nature take its course. They told Emil that it would be several hours before the delivery and that he should go home and rest until they called him, but he could not bring himself to leave the hospital. He was born in this very hospital in 1896 and his mother died here of tuberculosis just three years later, only days before the turn of the century. Now, his first child was being born somewhere behind the double doors before him. He reached into his pocket and pulled out a crushed pack of cigarettes, hoping they weren't broken. He placed the unfiltered paper between his lips and struck a match from a pack he had taken from the club the night before.

It was nearly time for the employees to begin setting up for that night's business, but he trusted his people. He had left word with Elke who would make sure that everything went as planned until he got there sometime after the birth. He turned when he reached the doors leading out of the hospital and when he did, he saw one of Sofie's doctors coming toward him through the glass panes in the opposite doors. The man was stone-faced which could not be a good sign. If everything were going well, wouldn't he be smiling?

"Herr Müller, bitte kommen Sie mit mir," ("Mr. Müller, please come with me,") was all the doctor said when he opened the door, looking directly at Emil.

He stepped through the door the doctor was holding open and waited for the doctor to lead him. The doctor stepped in front and they walked single-file down the long, white, brightly-lit hallway, then left to the delivery rooms. He was excited to see his new baby but held his distance behind the doctor, fearing what he was about to learn. The doctor stopped outside one of the heavy wooden doors and turned to face Emil.

"The baby and mother are healthy, but there is a complication." The doctor's face was still virtually expressionless and Emil actually found this something of a comfort.

If the doctor wasn't emotionally affected then either the complication wasn't a bad one or the doctor had experienced many of them and had grown a thick skin. The doctor opened the door and as it swung inward, he caught the first glimpse of Sofie. She was smiling down at a bundle in her arms and when she heard him enter, she looked up. Her face held a controlled smile and then he knew something was wrong. He went to her, not looking down at the baby, but holding eye contact with her. He stroked her hair and smiled down at her.

"What is the baby's name?" he asked, hoping she would use her uncle's name and that he would have a son.

Sofie hesitated. "I have not given one yet."

Emil's heart sank. He felt weightless as if he had jumped off a tall building but had not landed yet. Not giving the child a name from the ones they had already chosen might mean that the child was either stillborn or not expected to live very long. He began to open the baby's swaddling to check its fingers and toes. Not seeing anything but a normal, healthy baby, he asked *"Was ist los?"* ("What is going on?")

"We will have to choose a name when we know the sex of the baby." She spoke in a measured voice but with a conviction that made it clear that there was no imminent danger. "It is healthy and it is our first born. That is enough for now."

Emil gathered his courage and looked down at the baby in her arms. It was so beautiful, plump, and pink. It had a fuzz of brunette hair on its head and the face looked perfect. He was certain he could see his mother's features in the newborn's face. He looked at Sofie and smiled. His curiosity gnawed at him and he looked toward the doctor who smiled and left the room. They spent the next hour cooing and touching the baby's face. Emil had an almost irresistible compulsion to unwrap the baby to see what the sex was, but he thought this would make him appear like a brute so he resisted the urge.

After an hour or so, Sofie handed the baby to the nurse who was standing by with an incubator which had been plugged into the wall socket at the side of the bed. The nurse squeezed behind the bed and squatted down to unplug the device and draped the cord over the handle of the cart the incubator rested on. She began to wheel the baby out of the room just as Sofie's doctor opened the door. He noticed that she was headed out and held the door for her. Then he came in and shut the door behind him.

"Mr. and Mrs. Müller, I need to discuss the child's deformity with you," he began.

"Deformity?" Emil asked, looking to his wife, then back toward the doctor.

"Yes, Mrs. Müller has seen it but only for a moment. I would like to explain it to you and discuss how we suggest correcting the problem."

Emil looked back at Sofie and then at the doctor, trying to decide who he would rather hear the news from. He indicated to the doctor that he was ready to hear the news and the two of them listened intently. It seemed that about one in every 2,000 children were born with poorly formed sexual organs. The problem was usually under- or over-development of the tissues, but about one in 4,500 children were born with the sexual organs of both sexes or some stage of development in-between the two sexes such that a determination of gender could not be made reliably. The condition resulted in what laymen called a *hermaphrodite* because it often appeared on the outside that they were both male and female, but on the inside this was never true. In the future, thanks to the discovery of DNA in the 1950's, there would be ways to test for the genetic gender regardless of how the fetus developed, but now, in 1943, the technology did not yet exist.

The procedure to correct the deformity would remove the small penis-like appendage and allow the urethra to close properly after urination, but would likely prevent the child, once grown, from ever achieving orgasm. Emil and Sofie knew that they had to do what they thought was best for the child, so they named the child Gerta Leonie Müller. The first name came from Sofie's sister who passed away when they were children. Leonie was Emil's mother's name. Once the surgery was done, healing took no longer than the umbilical cord. The doctor described it as being *simple as a circumcision.*

When Gerta was a toddler, Sofie noticed certain things. Gerta seemed not to pay attention like other children her age. She would sit staring into the distance after being called several times. Sofie tested her hearing by snapping close to each ear and she flinched as expected, so she could hear and she knew her name, but for some reason she sometimes would not respond unless Sofie was directly in front of her.

When Gerta was three, Emil got the last of the permits needed to open their nightclub on the edge of the Red Light District. It had taken nearly two years of negotiating and bribing and talent searching to even get the building ready to work on. They would move into the old triangular building at *Escher Straße 37* and begin cleaning, painting, and building out the bars and stage in just a couple weeks. They would go on to create one of the most diverse and well-known night clubs in all of Germany. They wanted to create a place where anyone from the lowliest worker to the wealthiest socialite could go and both call it *culture*.

While Sofie was home raising Gerta, tracking down performers, and calling them in for auditions, Emil spent most of his time with the construction and painting crews, delivery workers and vendors, to get the club ready for its grand opening. Today, there was someone on a ladder right next to the table he was working at. They were tinkering with the lighting and Emil found it a little annoying, but like any production, one just worked around the problems. Spread before him in the filtered red light were ledgers. He rested his head in his hands after tabulating the last column. The number in the totals space was negative, but he slid one of the other papers over it so no one would be able to see. They knew they had underestimated the expenses, everyone does. Unfortunately, they had not given themselves enough margin for expenses to balloon out of control the way they had.

Sofie and Emil had committed nearly everything they had to this club, yet it was taking even more than that. The little extra money they had in savings was supposed to be money to live on until the club became profitable. If that ran out, not only would the club fail, they would starve on the street. He kept this silent burden hidden from everyone, including Sofie. He knew that a loss of morale at this point would be fatal to the club.

"*Herr Müller?*"

A raspy woman's voice made him look up.

"Yes. May I help you?" he asked. He thought she might have been curious about the construction and wandered in through an open door.

"I am Elke Rossen. I am here for my audition."

Suddenly Emil remembered the name on the appointment Sofie had given him was Elke. But it couldn't be this woman. She was easily over fifty years old. It couldn't be her. "You are here to audition to be a singer?" he asked.

"*Nein, Herr Müller.* I am here to audition for *kleider ausziehen*...stripping performance." Her accent was heavy, but her ability to communicate in American English was excellent; definitely a good skill to have when dealing with international clientele.

"I am sorry, *Frau Rossen....*"

"Elke Rossen, please sir," she insisted politely.

The woman standing before him was the epitome of a proper woman of the world. She stood erect, shoulders back, perfect posture. Her gray wool jacket was cut short at the waist revealing a lighter gray skirt that hung past the knee. Her cream silk blouse underneath was tied at the neck with a powder pink bow and she had a white fur stole draped around her shoulders, probably white fox, very rare. Her hair was tightly curled in the style most popular in the 1920s with curls flat against her forehead and her hat appeared to be from the same period, a dome with a downward-sloping brim and short veil, added as a fashion afterthought. She was not unusually tall or thin as many of the prospective performers were. She was an average height and average weight. What could she be doing here?

"Elke Rossen. I think you might be more comfortable if we rescheduled your audition for this evening...after the construction work is done." He was trying to give the older woman a less embarrassing way to bow out. Clearly she wasn't aware of the type of performance they were looking for.

"Sofie Müller, I presume your wife, set my audition at this time, did she not?" Elke held Emil's gaze without backing down.

"Yes, she did," he conceded.

"Then now is when I will perform for you." Elke turned to survey the room.

Surrounding the dance floor were raised seating areas with benches only. Spaces for tables remained empty but a man with an accordion was sitting on one of the benches. On one side of the dance floor was a bar about one metre from the wooden floor. She walked directly toward the accordion player who perked up when he saw her coming. She handed him a packet of sheet music and turned toward the bar. Marching there, she took one of the brand new bar stools, lifting it easily, and set it in the middle of the dance floor. Then she walked toward Emil and set a single sheet of paper facing him. As she turned away, he began to read. The paper was a long list of venues, some of which he knew well.

Elke reached the stool in the middle of the dance floor which she had purposely set in the center of a cone of light coming from above. The walls of the club were painted black so there was no scattered light. As she sat on the stool, she tilted her head so that her face disappeared into shadow. She obviously knew how to work with lighting. She began to tap down low on the side of the stool, giving the accordion player the tempo and after a few beats, he started playing. It was a song Emil knew well called *Das Lila Lied* also known as *The Lavender Song*. It was a song about hope, about being freed from oppression. Written in 1920 by Kurt Schwabach with music by the Russian composer Mischa Spoliansky, the song was an anthem written at a time when homosexuals were enjoying a short-lived emergence from persecution in the old German Republic of Weimar, before more war-like times crushed the people's freedoms.

It was 1946 and certain communities were experiencing that cycle once again. After the war people became more comfortable with their personal lives and letting others be who they were. It was like coming out of a long, dark night, but the system of reparations imposed on Germany was crushing the economy. Emil had seen signs that inflation was about to explode, but hardship had already begun to affect people's attitudes. More homosexuals were being killed in the streets and fewer people cared. The same was true of certain other groups like the Hasidic Jews who were nearly wiped out by the Nazis.

Elke began to sing, drawing on the loss of her partner, Rosa, to put deep emotion into the lyrics.

Was will man nur?	What do they want?
Ist das Kultur,	Is this Culture
daß jeder Mensch verpönt ist,	that every man is outlawed
der klug und gut,	who is – wise and well –
jedoch mit Blut	however with blood
von eig'ner Art durchströmt ist,	of his own kind perfused
daß g'rade die	that nevertheless this
Kategorie	category
vor dem Gesetz verbannt ist,	is banned by the law,
die im Gefühl	who is in feeling
bei Lust und Spiel	in pleasure and playing
und in der Art verwandt ist?	and in its kind related?

As she sang, Emil could feel the sadness in her voice. He felt her pain as if she were living the lyrics of the song. She slipped her stole off one shoulder, pausing to deliver the next line, then the stole came off the other shoulder, sliding around her arm to the floor. She began to turn and slide off the stool as if she were going to stand, but instead, she slid one arm gracefully out of her jacket, letting the jacket fall from her back, which was now facing Emil. She had not touched the floor, but somehow, she was shifting to come back up to the stool on her other side as the jacket also slid to the floor.

As she continued singing, pausing for emphasis in all the right places, she untied her bow and slid a hand under the blouse's placket, gracefully dislodging each button effortlessly and her hand traveled down. The extraneous noise in the room had died away and, glancing around, Emil noticed that each worker was completely captivated by her movements. She was absolutely confident, and her movements were more enticing than any of the flashy, raunchy auditions he had seen before.

When she unfastened her blouse, she gingerly spread the fabric to reveal her bra-covered breasts and skin.

| *Und dennoch sind die Meisten stolz,* | And still most of us are proud, |
| *daß sie von ander'm Holz!* | to be cut from different cloth! |

She turned to face the accordion player, away from Emil, as the silk blouse slid down her arms to billow to the floor, revealing her back. The music's tempo quickened with the vibrancy of the music, but the deep emotional conviction and delivery of the lyrics continued.

Wir sind nun einmal anders als die Andern,	We are just different from the others
die nur im Gleichschritt der Moral geliebt,	who are being loved only in lockstep of morality
neugierig erst durch tausend Wunder wandern,	who wander curiously through a thousand wonders
und für die's doch nur das Banale gibt.	and who are only up to the trivial.

Wir aber wissen nicht, wie das Gefühl ist,
denn wir sind alle and'rer Welten Kind,

But we do not know what the feeling is
since we are all children of a different
kind of world

wir lieben nur die lila Nacht, die schwül
ist,

we only love lavender night, who is
sultry

weil wir ja anders als die Andern sind.

because we are just different from the
others!

When she removed her bra, Emil wasn't really looking forward to her turning back around. She crossed her arms to cradle her breasts and with a sultry grace, twisted around on the stool with her legs crossed in a move that seemed impossible to accomplish without the use of her hands. As she turned, she began to reveal her breasts and caress her skin softly. Hugging herself and clearly enjoying her body, even in its aged state, she exuded sexuality and sparked desire in every man now watching, including Emil. She continued in this manner, removing her skirt at a luxuriously slow pace, sliding effortlessly from one striking pose to the next without ever touching the floor. At one point, she drew her knees up onto the stool and leaned backward, letting the red light bathe her features in curving shadows as her hat floated to the floor, landing gently as a parachute would after meeting the ground, sliding to the side on a cushion of air before coming to rest.

As the song neared its end, she began to slide from the stool to the floor, slowly, gracefully, and under such control so as to make the difficult move appear effortless and fluid. Just as the music ended, she came to rest on the floor, legs extended with one knee up, breasts out, and one hand gliding up her body delicately tracing the somewhat drooping curves. She came to rest as the music died away and the room fell silent.

She did not move. No one moved. There was no sound other than the muffled noise of the world outside, but in here...silence. Then every member of the construction crew erupted into applause and whistles of praise which continued for long moments before Emil came to his senses. Looking around, he was amazed to see all the young men he employed were cheering and clapping...the one on the ladder, the one behind the bar, the ones painting, even the accordion player had set his accordion aside to stand and applaud in appreciation. Emil also began to clap and stood as he marveled at what he had just seen.

Elke began to rise gracefully from the floor to nod and bow toward each of the men in turn, thanking them for their praise as the applause continued. She treated each man to her undivided attention as she turned to face them, finally coming back around to Emil. Walking toward him, the applause died down, but the men kept staring. She was completely unclothed but showed no sign of embarrassment at all. She stood just a hand's distance from Emil's table facing him in silent expectation. Emil noticed that the men were also still, so he urged them to return to their work. He had just seen the most enthralling performance of his life and it was only an audition. Many of the performers he had auditioned felt uncomfortable with only a few men in the room, saying that they preferred a crowd. Elke clearly did not have that limitation, nor did she favor the flashy, jiggling, bawdiness of the younger performers.

"Elke Rossen," Emil began. "That was amazing. Would you please dress so we may negotiate?"

Elke bowed her head respectfully and returned to the mounds of clothing on the dancefloor, dressing herself as if she were in private, having no care who was watching. Even this act of dressing in view of others left Emil in awe at the woman's power and confidence. While she was dressing, the painter, one of Emil's friends who owed him a favor and wanted to help with the club, came close to him and put his head over Emil's shoulder so he could whisper. He rattled out his appreciation for this woman, her fame, where he first saw her, and on and on until Emil saw that she was dressed. It wouldn't work in Emil's favor to appear to be in awe of her, so he kept his poker face and waved off his friend, urging him to return to his work.

Chapter 24

Kabarett Seks became the most talked about nightclub in Germany. Many other clubs operated as an amenity attached to a brothel. Emil and Sofie had decided before they opened that the *Kabarett* would not be a brothel. Instead, it would be a place where anyone could go, have a drink, and enjoy some rare and unusual performances. It was an eclectic blend of cultures and drew clientele from all across Europe. There were, of course, the local patrons who frequented the club, some on weeknights, others on weekends, but at least half of each night's visitors were well-connected tourists who had heard of the club and wanted to see it for themselves. The club had also become popular with young American soldiers bringing initiates to have fun and then be humiliated by their peers. Too much alcohol and too much yelling was the norm for these groups, but they behaved well enough and never allowed fighting among their ranks, lest they be told they were no longer welcome.

Elke Rossen opened the club with Emil and Sofie and had been the star attraction ever since. She was like a grandmother to Gerta and showered her with love whenever she saw the little girl. Many people came exclusively to see Elke perform and word spread everywhere about the oldest stripper in the business. She drew men who wanted to see a woman of confidence who made them feel sophisticated, not cheap like other strippers. She attracted women who were drawn to her confidence and the comfort she showed with her body. No woman could be young forever, and she showed them that no matter what age they were, they could take pleasure in their bodies and if they were comfortable with themselves, men would be comfortable with them too.

"Mama Rossen! Mama Rossen!" Gerta skipped through the back door of the club followed closely by her mother.

"Be careful, Gerta! You might slip and fall!" Sofie's words didn't even seem to register with the child.

Gerta skipped down the short hallway and grabbed the trim framing the entry to the left dressing room swinging around the corner, lifting her feet off the floor in that instant when she was weightless. Releasing her grip on the door frame, she bounded through the dressing room weaving between the performers toward Elke's vanity. Hearing the girl calling to her, Elke turned to face the entryway. Though she couldn't see her yet, she saw performers parting and suddenly out popped the girl like an antelope bounding directly for her. Gerta leaped into her arms, reminding Elke just how old she was when her back and legs protested the girl's impact.

"My goodness, *Fräulein!* You really are getting too big to jump on me like that." Elke smiled down at the eight year old, holding her like a much younger child and stroking her hair from her face. "And what did you learn in school today?"

"We learned about eggs, then tadpoles, then frogs, then eggs, then tadpoles, then frogs!" shouted Gerta as loud as she was able. Her shrill voice was only partially muffled by the bustle in the dressing room.

"And what happens when all the eggs get eaten by fish?" Elke asked.

"Then the mommy frog is sad and she lays more eggs!" Gerta blurted, knowing exactly what to say and being very proud of herself.

"That's right. That's exactly right. You're getting smarter every day, young lady. Now you run along. Mama's trying to make herself beautiful." She helped the girl to the floor.

Gerta knew the performers needed to be left alone, but not until she had greeted every one, so she slid down and Elke swatted her behind as she sped off. Gerta hugged each performer's legs if they were standing, arms if they were seated, reaching around them unannounced and hugging tightly for a second before releasing them and moving on to the next. Everyone knew what was coming, so those who were applying makeup stopped what they were doing until the disturbance had passed. They all loved Gerta. Even the new performers who were still in their first few weeks and were trying to maintain a defensive wall around themselves, melted when Gerta forcibly hugged them without asking.

The *Kabarett Seks* looked very different in the daylight. The building was on a triangular corner at *Escher Straße* and *Kleine Hartwichstraße* and took advantage of every square metre of space leaving barely enough room for two people to pass each other on the sidewalk. During the day, the rolling doors were raised, especially when it was cool outside. This let in more light as the cleaning crew and bartenders went about their work preparing the building for the evening's business. Critics writing about the club extolled its blend of clientele, the varied music selections, the historical cocktails, and the cleanliness. Even the entryway was talked about in one article. The insides of the doors were fitted with draped velvet to give the appearance of a grand entrance. When fully opened, they fell into depressions carved in the ivy that covered the walls between the windows so they seemed to be surrounded by a living forest. Sofie had always insisted that the club should be as clean and beautiful as her home before they opened each evening so that customers would feel that they were in an upscale bar. In fact, she rarely had to scold the cleaning crew. Everyone at the club took such great pride in their work, from the bartenders, to the performers, to the cleaning crew. Even the lighting positions had long waiting lists for employment because the Müllers paid well and everyone in the industry knew they treated their people like family. Only rarely did the call go out for a new performer and only because someone had to move to another city or go away to school. Everyone who came in was certain the rumors were too good to be true, but once they saw the family atmosphere and the love these people had for each other, their defenses usually dropped away.

As punishment for the war and the investment other countries had to make in equipment, troops, pensions, and repairs, German citizens left behind after the war were subjected to rising prices, falling resources, and falling wages. Many could not understand how *Kabarett Seks* was resisting these hardships. It was actually quite simple. Sophie and Emil maintained a respectable, high-quality environment instead of reducing the quality of the venue as other bars were doing. It was a huge risk, but the result was a packed house every night of the week. If people couldn't get in on a weekend, they would make special plans to stand in line on a weeknight. The lines were always long and the cash flow was always at maximum. The husband and wife team discussed expanding many times, but the expense of moving to another location and the time it would take convinced them that the extra income was not worth the risk.

Now and then they had someone who wanted to reshuffle the pecking order, but when the entire crew turned on them, they usually backed down and stopped trying to dominate. Elke Rossen had been there for six years and was about to turn sixty when one of the unseasoned performers remarked loudly in the company of half of the performance crew.

After one particular incident during which Elke was bruised by a fall, one of the temporary performers made the mistake of saying, "Oh my, Mama Rossen! This means you *must* retire and give someone else a chance to headline."

To which Elke answered plainly, "When the people who come to see me stop coming, I will retire." She never even looked up from applying mascara, but the power of the statement crushed the young upstart's comment and the entire room heaved a collective sigh.

"Girl, she let you off easy that time."

"Please don't make me watch her feed you to the wolves, honey."

"Well that smarts, doesn't it?"

No one questioned Mama Rossen. For that matter, no one dared question the Müllers around Mama Rossen. Those who made the mistake, did so only once before they discovered that a single word from her could cost any of them their jobs. Elke rarely had to use this authority, but when she did it was always to protect the club or one of its people. More than once, she had advised Emil and Sofie not to hire someone because she knew that they had been sent by another club to learn how the Müllers were successful and then take that information back to their real employer.

Once, someone had evaded Mama Rossen's observation and had been reporting back to another club in the Red Light District. It was only a few days later when Mama Rossen had presented this new girl with a matchbook taken from her real employer's club in front of Emil and Sofie, saying nothing. Nothing needed to be said and by looking in their eyes, she knew the charade was over. She marched to the dressing room, packed her things, and left with every performer in the room quietly watching.

Mama Rossen was fiercely protective of her chosen family and everyone loved her for that. Whenever someone was having trouble, whether it was with confidence, or money, or relationships, Mama Rossen was there taking them under her wing, helping to make things better. When she looked into your eyes, you could feel her reaching into your soul. A critic who wrote about one of her performances described it the same way writing, "When she looked into my eyes, it seemed she cared for me as if I were her own husband."

The Jones brothers were a pair of twins from the South of Kenya, brought to Europe by their parents. Wyatt, whose name meant "little warrior," and Asher, "fortunate and blessed," were nearly identical in every visible way, but Wyatt enjoyed the company of younger women while Asher favored older German men. Too often, they had been asked, "If you are identical and one of you is homosexual, then one of you must be hiding." It was sometimes annoying, but both brothers were secure enough in their own sexuality to not care what other people thought, especially the ignorant ones. Their skin was dark...so dark that when the lights were low, no one could see their features. Many of the women who came to *Kabarett Seks* came to see the Jones brothers, to touch their dark skin, to smell their unique odor so different from Caucasian men. On nights when they performed nude, they would conduct a kind of artful dance to exotic tribal music, holding each other in erotic poses requiring both subtlety and super-human strength. In one of their most impressive poses, Wyatt would be upside-down with one shoulder resting on Asher's shoulder as they struck exactly the same pose, precariously balancing in an impossible position. The effect was that of a vertical reflection such as over still water, and when they posed with their cheeks and lips touching, eyes closed, but one brother supporting the full weight of the other, the ladies and homosexuals in the audience gasped with desire. Even the manly men in the crowd stood dumbfounded by the incredible athleticism required to do what they were doing. Erotic or not, their performance was seen as strong and athletic and in no way feminine.

Some nights, the brothers would dress up in identical pinstripe suits or some other classy outfit and tap dance to cheerful music and a rousing beat kept up by the clapping of the crowd. They would perform incredible feats of skill and stamina, often sliding all the way from one side of the dance floor to the other, passing each other in the middle. They were quite a sensation with the early evening crowd out having cocktails before heading off to the symphony or the theatre.

Later in the evening, once the high-society patrons had moved on to their classical performances, Cara and Ciara, the O'Sullivan sisters might perform. Known as "the Siamese Reds," the sisters were from Ireland, and had been joined at the pelvis before birth. Their parents were assured that any attempt to separate them would be fatal, so they had grown up and lived their lives as best they could. Being a part of the Müller's performance family made them happier than they had ever been in their young lives. Both women were now twenty-two and were a vision of youthful beauty in their own right, but side by side, they seemed to be supernatural. Their brilliant red hair and smooth alabaster skin made the women who watched them perform envious of their beauty. When they began to sing, the two sisters were able to tune their voices so precisely that they created haunting, reverberating chords. On hearing this talent, men were struck speechless with desire. When they disrobed revealing their physical connection to those who had not seen them before, there was often a momentary revulsion, but the women moved with a grace and confidence they had learned from Mama Rossen, inviting viewers to examine their bodies, their red pubic hair, their flawless skin.

Ida Gropter was unique. Her loud, bawdy act never went on before midnight. She was a master of burlesque performance, writhing on the floor or swinging from a velvet-covered chain suspended in the middle of the dance floor. She invited stares. She relished the shock and confusion on patron's faces as they tried to figure out what she was. Her huge breasts were usually adorned with pasties to which she would attach tassels, or beads on strings, or feathers. She always kept her groin area shaved close so that those who cared to look could see her womanhood. By the looks on the faces in the crowd when she performed, the women did not really have a problem with what they were seeing, but many of the men were not used to seeing women completely shaven and were curious as schoolboys.

Ida was actually not performing tonight. They took turns being maître d', as was the case this evening. In the dressing room, Ida warmed up her voice, singing scales from low to high, from soft to painfully loud. She would be using her voice all night and all the performers knew how important warming up and stretching was.

"Miss Ida, you sound pretty!" Gerta said as she skipped once around Ida, tugging on her black chiffon practice skirt as she bobbed up and down.

"Thank you, child. Now you run and find your mother." Ida leaned down and gently pushed the child toward the hallway between the two dressing rooms. Her mother would no doubt be scrutinizing the public spaces by now.

Gerta skipped out of the dressing room, hooking her hand around the door frame and swung around to the left, heading toward the main room. Coming up behind her mother, she wrapped her arms around her mother's waist, interrupting a conversation she was having with one of the bartenders. Sofie looked down at her daughter, placed her hand on the girl's head, and went back to her impromptu meeting.

When Gerta was ten, Emil and Sofie decided that the school was not teaching her enough about basic economics so they put her to work. After school each day, it was her duty to sweep and clean the club to earn two *Marks*. She was then expected to save that money so she could buy something she really wanted. Months went by and she collected her earnings in a velvet coin purse hidden in her room. When her parents would ask what she planned to buy when she had saved up enough, she would only answer that she would know when she knew. This was an odd answer for a child, but they decided to let it play out and see what happened. Years went by and Gerta gradually took over the cleaning operation, doing the best job she could do and encouraging the other members of the cleaning crew to do their best too. She never tried to order anyone around. Instead, if someone missed cleaning an area, she would get on her hands and knees and do it herself. This had the unanticipated effect of making whoever had been lax with their duties so guilty that they vowed to never miss anything again.

It was around this time that something strange began happening at home. One morning, Sofie went to wake Gerta up for school, but she wasn't in her bed. The covers had been thrown aside but there was no sound anywhere in the house. Sofie explored the bathroom where she might be brushing her teeth, but she wasn't there. She checked the kitchen thinking the girl might have gotten hungry, but she wasn't there. She wasn't in the living room or the sitting room. Sofie began to panic and rushed back to the bedroom to wake Emil. She knew Emil had just gone to sleep a few hours before once the club had been shut down for the night, but her heart was pounding in her chest.

"Emil," she whispered as she shook his shoulder. "Emil!" she raised her voice.

Emil began to stir, turning over to look at her bleary eyed, wondering what was going on.

"I can't find Gerta!" she stage-whispered. She was visibly panicked now and Emil sensed the urgency in her voice.

Rising immediately and throwing off the covers, he instructed, "You take the upstairs and I will take the downstairs. Open every door, every cabinet."

He rushed downstairs and began his search, taking only minutes to find Gerta curled up in the coat closet in the front hallway. He called to Sofie and his raised voice awakened Gerta. She had no memory of going to sleep in the closet and Sofie noticed that Gerta was listless as she prepared for school. Her movements appeared slow and mindless as if she hadn't gotten any sleep. Sleepwalking wasn't uncommon and they knew that sometimes children went through periods of disturbed sleep which they usually grew out of.

They began to find Gerta in various parts of the house, at first occasionally, then more and more frequently until she was never in bed when they awoke. A few times when either of them would find her and wake her up, it seemed that she did not recognize them for a little while. This was made apparent by a much delayed, "Good morning, mami!" that might come seconds or minutes after she was awake. They took her to her pediatrician who referred them to a sleep specialist who gave his explanation saying, "Sleep patterns are not well understood so unless the condition were dangerous, you shouldn't worry. Use dead bolts in the house and wait for her to grow out of it."

One morning, Sofie found Gerta awake sitting at the dining table in the dark when she opened the pantry door. "Good morning, my dear Gerta," she said with a smile.

"Why do you keep calling me that?" the eleven year old asked with an impetuous look.

Sofie was stunned. She stood immobile looking over her shoulder at the child's face.

"Good morning, mami!" Gerta blurted out after another minute passed and the expression on her face changed entirely.

"Are you playing one of your tricks on mami?" Sofie asked.

"What do you mean?" Gerta asked with genuine-seeming curiosity but Sofie was still suspicious.

At first, Sophie had assumed Gerta was playing games with an imaginary friend the way all children did in their youth, but after this happened several times, Sofie became concerned and finally went to Emil with the problem. What concerned her was how Gerta never seemed to be aware of her imaginary friend.

Emil always slept in late after working into the morning, so they had been sleeping in separate beds ever since the club opened. This meant that he never saw any of these episodes. He listened to her recount various instances with disbelief on his face.

"Stop that," she said.

"Stop what?" he asked.

"Stop trying to think of some way I could be mistaken and just listen to what I am telling you. There is someone else there when she first wakes up." Sofie sat staring intently at Emil trying to judge his reaction.

"Let's take her back to the sleep specialist and see what is going on, but don't alarm Gerta. You haven't told her any of this, have you?" he wondered.

"She's too young to deal with something like this. I thought it best not to worry her. She doesn't seem to be aware of any of it." Sofie agreed with Emil's suggestion, so she scheduled an appointment.

Based on her description, the sleep specialist called in a psychotherapist who recommended that Gerta be put through a sleep study where these instances could be documented by trained professionals so they could attempt a diagnosis, so Sofie made the arrangements. On the day of the sleep study, Gerta went with Sofie to the sleep laboratory while Emil went to work, late in the afternoon. They brought a blanket and her own pillow so there would be items to make her feel comfortable. The technicians connected wires to her head, chest, and arms. How was she supposed to sleep with all these wires hanging from her? They asked Sofie to go home for the night and pick her daughter up at ten o'clock the next morning.

When Sofie went to pick Gerta up the next morning, she asked the technicians if they had found the problem. The technicians refused to answer saying that they would report their observations to the psychotherapist for diagnosis and to talk with him about it. She felt very dissatisfied that no one had told her that was how the process worked, but she already had an appointment that afternoon. This time, she went without Gerta and the psychotherapist tried to explain what they had observed.

It seemed that there was indeed another personality at work, but only when Gerta was not conscious. Parasomnia was not the condition commonly called sleepwalking when the subject wandered around, seemingly acting out simple actions such as urinating in a closet. Parasomnia was different. Patients may hold a conversation or act out very complex behaviours that require consciousness, but the memory centers of the brain do not appear to be storing anything so the patient has no recollection of any of it. Even this did not explain Gerta's condition because the alternate personality that was present when Gerta was not maintained a contiguous memory. When told something in one session, she could recall the information in the next, but at some point during apparent awareness, she would lose access to those memories and be unable to recall the information remembered moments before.

The technician woke Gerta up at the prescribed time after waiting for just the right time in the brainwave cycle, but when Gerta woke up, Gerta was not present. Another personality would coherently answer questions, knew where it was, and would be responsive for several minutes until Gerta awoke, ending the exchange. The child no longer responded in the manner she did moments before and had no recollection of the exchange with the technician.

Multiple personality disorders had been reported, but were very rare and almost always the result of some childhood trauma, sometimes an ongoing trauma. Often these traumas would be caused in females by a male member of the family subjecting them to molestation. Sometimes a tragic event like the death of a loved one would trigger the compartmentalization of the memory along with the defense mechanisms needed to keep the memory from the conscious mind.

Sofie was offended by the suggestion that Emil might have molested his own daughter. He almost never had time to be alone with his daughter and worked as hard as he was able to help the family live a better life than their parents did. He was a good man!

With a level head and a sympathetic tone, the psychotherapist calmed Sofie saying that he was only reciting clinical information that might give some insight into what might be going on with Gerta. He was not trying to imply any wrongdoing, only investigating the known possibilities as a necessary step to understanding the girl's condition. He recommended a series of questions that Sofie should ask Gerta when she awoke. She was to continue the questioning only as long as the alternate personality was apparent and stop when Gerta became aware. Eventually, she would get through all of the questions and then report the answers to him for analysis.

Over the next several months, Sofie would find Gerta asleep in this place or that and wake her. Beginning the conversation where they had left off, the waking personality seemed to have a clear memory of the previous morning's talk. It was aware that Gerta was a girl, but he was a boy. He knew nothing about Gerta that Sofie hadn't told him, but knew what he looked like in a mirror. Sofie tried to make sure that these conversations happened sitting or lying down because when Gerta suddenly became aware, sometimes she would fall down or be frightened by her situation. Sofie noticed something else. These talks with the boy were growing longer. After a couple months, he would be present for several minutes. One morning, he was present for almost an hour before Gerta awoke sitting at the breakfast table wondering how she had gotten there. Emil was curious enough to get up after only a couple hours of sleep to witness this other personality and what he saw made his blood run cold. Sofie had never asked who he was, but Emil couldn't resist the question.

"I don't know my name," the personality answered.

"But you know you are a boy?" Emil questioned.

"Yes," he answered.

"Then how do you not have a name?" Emil asked.

"Because you never gave me one. You just call me *you*, so I guess I don't have a name." He was clearly irritated at this line of questioning.

"Would you like a name?" Emil asked. The male personality looked at him with stupefaction as if he were talking to an idiot.

"Fine. A name then," said Emil as he looked to Sofie for help.

Sofie had been chided and ignored by Emil the whole time this had been happening, so she refused to help, shrugging in a *you're on your own* manner.

Emil thought for a moment and asked, "How about Guy?"

"Good enough." The personality did not even try to contribute or give his approval or disapproval of the name. It seemed he just didn't care.

"Guy it is then. So, Guy, how long have you been in there?" Emil knew it was a silly question the moment it left his lips.

"I'm not *in here*. I *am* here. I already talked to the doctors. If they can't tell you, how am I supposed to?" Guy was growing more irritated with the line of questioning until Emil asked something insightful.

"You said you don't remember anything when Gerta is awake," Emil asked in a preparatorial tone.

"I don't think so," Guy answered. "Why?"

"If you don't share memories with Gerta, then how do you know how to speak?"

Guy sat with his mouth hanging open. He had opened it thinking that an answer was forthcoming, but he had no answer. *That was a good question,* he thought when the dense white cloud consumed his consciousness.

"Papa?" Gerta appeared confused.

"Yes my dear?" Emil asked in as comforting a tone as he could muster. Sofie leaned in closer.

Gerta began to tear up and her chin scrunched as her lower lip began to tremble.

"It's alright dear. You are here with us and you are safe." Emil leaned forward in his chair and scooped the girl into his lap. She was getting too big to do this for much longer, but as the years passed and Gerta grew, Emil had vowed to keep doing it. As the pain in his hips and legs mounted, he had no choice but to gently ease her onto her feet. "It is time to get ready for school, Gerta. Go brush your teeth."

As Gerta moped off to do as she was told, though still confused, Emil turned to Sofie with his own mouth hanging open. "You were serious."

Sofie nodded, but had decided that she wouldn't play the *I told you so* game with him. She leaned forward and asked, "So what do we do?"

"I have no idea." Emil and Sofie sat in silence trying to think of something they might do for their daughter, but the silence remained unbroken.

Emil and Sofie worked faithfully for over twenty years trying to make the *Kabarett Seks* the most talked-about venue in Germany. They balanced Gerta's schooling, a modest lifestyle, and an amazing amount of work tracking down and booking traveling talent and headliners for the club. Nearly every day of the week, the club was at or near capacity by ten o'clock and only on weeknights did it begin to thin out around midnight. On weekends, there was standing room only from well before sundown until closing time.

Kabarett Seks had become Gerta's second home where the staff were family and the patrons were their guests. To her, it didn't seem like work. It was exactly what she would choose to do if it were up to her. Granted, she didn't like having to scrub the floors or pick up the broken glass. She remembered a party early in her college career at the University of Cologne. She had no interest in alcohol since she was around it every day and the students who drank and spilled in the host's home didn't seem to care about the mess they left behind. The same was true of the club, but at least at the club, they were paying for the privilege of being sloppy guests. At the house party, the host ran around stressed all night trying to prevent the inevitable destruction as Gerta tried to help. It was not a fun evening for either of them, but to Gerta, it was an eye-opening experience. She now understood why the club had been set up the way it had. The furniture was upholstered in a way that could not be stained. If it was cut or burned, it could be quickly replaced. The floors, walls, and ceilings were mostly black because black hid dirt well until the bright lights came up. Every detail of the club had been designed to be durable and easy to reset for the next night.

Gerta maintained a very good work ethic in college, outperforming everyone's expectations of her with one exception. As grew up, the Guy personality had begun to emerge more often and for longer periods. At last estimate, he was present about twenty percent of the time and, while he could learn new things just as she could, it appeared that he was not consciously aware of events that had happened to Gerta. For example, when Gerta studied economics, Guy got better at economics but he couldn't recall ever going to classes. Once when Guy was present, he had memorized the names of all the bones in the body, but when Gerta awoke, she could recite the names on demand, but could not remember ever having studied them.

She went to therapy often but the doctors had no idea how to help her, so her parents helped her compensate as best she could. After Guy had awakened a few times at work, causing some confusion and hurt feelings, Emil, Sofie, and Gerta sat everyone down and explained what had been happening. The long-time staff understood and said there were no hard feelings, but secretly, Elke Rossen who was like a grandmother to Gerta, felt left out though she never let it show. The crew began to recognize when Guy awakened by the confused look on Gerta's face and inability to remember what Gerta had been doing moments before. When this happened, whoever was nearby would answer Guy's questions and help him get back to work until Gerta awoke. He seemed to understand that his quality of life depended on how well the club did and he took his responsibilities seriously, but he clearly did not appreciate being there. He also did not have the same feelings for the crew that Gerta did. Gerta adored Mama Rossen, but once, when Elke had tried to take Guy under her wing as she had done for Gerta, Guy snapped at her telling her to "mind her own business." Elke had merely smiled at him and let him continue screwing up what he was doing until Emil had come along and sternly corrected him.

It took Guy a long time to begin trusting the club's staff, but each time he did something incorrectly or made a mistake that Gerta would not have made, they were kind and patient with him. Gradually, he began to curtail the vitriol he would spew at others and he began to improve both as a de-facto inheritor of the club and as a person. It always seemed he was upset at something and he was easy to irritate, so whenever he was awake, the crew would be delicate in their dealings with him. Once someone commented that Guy could never be the leader that Gerta was turning out to be. Guy had overheard, but instead of becoming incensed by the remark, he withdrew and sulked for the next couple hours until Gerta awoke.

The doctors tried to give every hypothetical explanation they could, always thinking that they knew best, but each explanation they gave seemed to be disproven by some quirk of behaviour or realization about Guy's character. Since there was no choice other than to live their lives, Emil and Sofie put great effort and patience into training Gerta, and Guy when he was awake, to one day take over the club. It became clear early on that the one skill in which Guy was lacking was the skill in which Gerta was the strongest: leadership. Gerta engendered loyalty in everyone around her by taking the time to listen, then participate in solutions rather than dictate what must be done. Everyone who came to Gerta with a problem left thinking that they had come up with the solution and gotten Gerta's approval when actually, they had been guided to the solution, and became invested in it with Gerta's help. Guy ordered people around. He was not a leader by any means other than authority.

Emil came in late this afternoon. The crew never needed prompting to begin their work. When there were no Müller family members around, the next most senior person, usually Elke, would open up and get right to work. Everyone pulled their own weight and when someone was late, everyone took up the slack and did more work knowing that one day when they needed help, it would be given gladly. When Emil walked in and sat at one of the tables in the corner, he didn't look well. He walked to the club every afternoon saying that it kept him healthy, but today was unseasonably hot. After several minutes, Elke noticed that staff members were walking up to him and leaving after asking their questions, but he was not joining in as he usually did. He was passionate about the work and was always involved, but he just sat there, and Elke thought he looked a little gray. It could have been a trick of the lighting, but when she approached him, she knew something was seriously wrong. It had been over fifteen minutes since he sat down, but he was still panting and sweating as if he had just come in from a brisk walk in the heat.

Elke sat across from him and asked, "Is it bad again?"

"Yes," Emil answered between breaths.

"It has been months and it's only getting worse. I think it is time for you to go to your doctor." Elke's kind, motherly voice rang true in Emil's ears.

"I know, but it will have to wait for another day," he assured her.

"I want you to go tomorrow. No more putting it off." Elke's attitude had shifted from nurturing to instructing.

"I will go one day when I have time."

"You will go tomorrow or I and the rest of the crew will carry you there." Elke looked directly at Emil's eyes so that when he looked up, he saw how serious she was.

Emil hesitated, trying to think of some way to defer the decision, but saw that he was not going to win this argument. "Yes, Mama. I will go tomorrow before work."

She continued looking into his eyes, letting the emotions of concern, love, and sternness play across her face until she was satisfied he understood that she was immovable on this issue. She placed a hand on his which was still resting on the table between them, and rose to return to work. When he saw her continue to take charge, he knew he could rest a while longer. The team would have all the leadership they needed. Emil rested for nearly two hours before he began to feel better, all the while being watched surreptitiously by each crew member. They were all concerned about him but did not wish to make him uncomfortable by doting over him. It seemed, though, that whenever he looked up at someone, they would quickly look away and go about their business as if they had not been watching him.

The next day, Gerta came directly from school so that her father could go to the doctor. She unlocked the doors before anyone else arrived and was hard at work when people started meandering in. Conversations rose and fell, the bartender made coffee, and Ida Gropter made her customarily gaudy appearance upon her illustrious arrival, which always made everyone laugh. Everyone cleaned until it was time for the performers to begin getting ready. The bartenders brought their bars up to standard and one by one came to Gerta for their inspection. Gerta spent most of the day sweeping up glass and mopping the floors, taking breaks whenever someone else needed help or an inspection. When she was done with the floors and inspections, she called the performance crew to the dance floor, making sure each person knew when they would be going on and which music they would be performing to. The music and lighting crew talked with each performer to make sure their performances would be coordinated, and when everyone was sure about the evening's schedule, she retired to the office to prepare the cash drawers. No one knew how long Emil would be at the doctor's office so they tried not to think about their missing patron.

It was nearly time to open when Sofie came through the back door of the club. She wasn't expected there that night and so everyone knew it could not be good news. She kept her head down, not making eye contact with anyone and went straight to the office, closing the door behind her. A few minutes later, she and Gerta came out. Sofie headed to the dance floor while Gerta encouraged everyone to follow her. The silence was deafening and at-odds with the normally jovial atmosphere of the club. The bartenders came out from behind their bars. Even the lighting crew came down from their ladders and dropped their electrical cords to come to the meeting.

Sofie kept her head down as the team gathered around her, keeping their distance so everyone could see her. Gerta held Sofie's hand and tried to lend her strength to her mother. When everyone was assembled, Sofie took a few deep breaths, steeling herself for the announcement. When she looked up, what she saw did not surprise her at all. Smiles of love and encouragement were evident on every face. Some were tearing up, unable to stand the anticipation. Some of the men were clearing their throats, trying to appear as if they were not about to cry. Sofie delivered the news and there wasn't a dry eye in the room.

"Emil will not be coming back to work," Sofie said. "His doctors say that he has had at least one heart attack and probably more. They say that he must rest and avoid stress and exertion."

There were gasps and whimpers from the circle of friends and coworkers. Sofie turned as she spoke to make sure she included everyone. As she went on about the doctor's requirements for Emil, it became clear to the entire room that if he were to come to the club again, it would only be for the occasional visit. Tears streamed down Sofie's cheeks as she delivered the news with strength and conviction. The club would not only remain open, she would continue to book the best talent she could find and none of them should be concerned about their job. Everyone knew the next logical step, including Gerta.

"As of now, Gerta is the manager of the club. You will all follow her instructions as if Emil or I had given them. Are there any questions?" Sofie gave a respectable pause before continuing. She turned to Gerta, taking both of the young woman's hands in her own and before everyone said, "Gerta, my dear, I know I speak for everyone here when I say how proud I am of you. You have worked so hard to get where you are and never took advantage of your situation, but now we must ask even more of you."

Sofie was no longer able to keep herself collected and began to weep openly as the circle closed in upon her, sharing her pain and showing their support. Those who could reach, placed a hand on her shoulders or back and said a small prayer for her and Emil. Pats on the back as they broke up and prepared to open the club told Gerta that she had their support and as the lights came down and the music began to play, the performers returned to their dressing rooms, the singers attempting to warm up their voices as they cracked with grief.

As everyone walked away, Sofie remained holding Gerta's hands, crying and trembling. Gerta pulled her hands away and embraced her mother, but the hug felt strange, masculine and forced. She raised her head to look into Guy's face.

"Don't worry, Mama. We will handle it." Guy's normally irritable nature seemed to be tempered with sympathy as he drew her close again and she began to sob into his shoulder.

Chapter 25

In 1949, *Kabarett Seks* had its first really good year, coming out of a slump in an overall recession. Attendance was even higher than before, profits were up, and Sofie had a waiting list of performers who kept in daily contact with her, waiting for their chance. Those who lived in Cologne or nearby Bohn would come to the club to see the amazing performances of the headliners, wishing that they could be the next name in lights.

Gerta blossomed in her role as club manager. She started dressing the part each day, wearing all-white dress suits with a jacket cinched at the waist and wide-leg slacks that billowed around her feet so that when she stood still, it appeared she was wearing a long, slim skirt. The baggy legs were helpful for keeping cool in the summer. She spent nearly half the night on her feet greeting guests by name as they entered. In the winter, she could wear insulated undergarments, but in the summer, she could wear far less underneath and be reasonably cool. She had cut her hair into a bob, not in the newer style so popular in America, but in the style of the 1920's with waves flattened against her head like Elke. Her style gave her an air of sophistication and power that the gentlemen found enticing and the ladies found respectable and forward-thinking.

When she arrived at the club each afternoon, she greeted any newcomers, conducted training sessions, checked in with the facility's crews to see if there were any cables, lights, or other hardware that needed replacing, then got on her hands and knees to scrub the floor. If she was needed by the light crew, she climbed ladders without hesitation. When they were a bartender short, she brought out a black and white outfit and stepped in to fill the void and every time she did something like this, the loyalty of her employees deepened. Even when Guy emerged and became confused or frustrated, the crew stepped in to help. Guy was never grateful, but when Gerta returned, she was. It took a long time for her to let go of her embarrassment when she would re-emerge, especially since Guy seemed to delight in spreading his frustration as widely as he could.

Years before, she had developed a system with a psychiatrist she was referred to by her doctors. When they couldn't help her, Dr. Freda Dudek came up with a simple, elegant solution to a very basic problem. When Guy or Gerta emerged, they had no memory of what the other was doing or had committed to when they were unconscious. The solution was to carry a journal at all times and write in it frequently. This way, when Guy emerged he could refer to her notes and pick up where she left off. When she was behind the bar, she wrote the drinks she was supposed to make on a pad before she made them, so that if Guy emerged just then, he would dump the drink in his hand, since he had no idea if it were finished, and start over from the last line not crossed out on the pad. Only the crew knew when Guy emerged behind the bar because Gerta was such a good bartender, she never made a mistake mixing a cocktail.

Using Dr. Freda's method, the two personalities did more than communicate about the last moments of work, they also began to write notes to each other in their daybook; about what they were thinking or what the other should watch for when they emerged. "Burgstrom coming at ten, gets walked to door, needs help walking to table six reservation." If Guy emerged sometime before ten tonight, he would know that Mr. Burgstrom was coming and as soon as he saw someone being led to the door, he should call for an assistant to go meet Mr. Bergstrom before he got to the door, where he, or she, would welcome and entertain him on their way to his table.

Gerta was at the front door at eight o'clock, turning the lock and pushing the heavy metal doors open. The cold air sitting between the doors and the curtain that separated the entryway from the larger performance area flowed out around Gerta's legs causing a light fog to drift toward her waiting guests. The cold air bathed them in relief. It was still nearly midday temperatures after sundown. This was one of Mama Rossen's favourite times of day. She was always ready long before the other performers and enjoyed greeting the eager guests. Rather than do an act of disrobing, for the early crowd, she would tell stories of growing up as a young girl in a performing family, traveling from place to place. When one of her tales included the loss of her dear pet hound, the crowd began to sniffle. Every lady and most of the gentlemen pulled out handkerchiefs and as Elke went on, she lifted their spirits and delighted them at the end. The performers who had been eavesdropping returned to their vanities to retouch their makeup.

Gerta met Dr. Freda in 1961 when she was just eighteen, on the recommendation of her doctors. They had been unsuccessful in treating, or even understanding, Gerta's condition. One of her doctors worked with a colleague who worked with a young and very talented psychotherapist named Dr. Freda Dudek. Gerta avoided psychotherapists for a long time, but Sofie urged her to pursue this young doctor to see if she might be different. After their first meeting, Gerta knew she had met someone exceptional.

Today had been a difficult session, but they worked through some problems with the confusion each of them, Gerta and Guy, experienced when they woke up. Gerta had also gained some insights from Dr. Freda from her last session with Guy that should help her to be more sensitive to his feelings while she was writing to him in her journal. Dr. Freda commented that since this was the first instance of her type that Dr. Freda had seen, she wanted to be allowed to review her journals periodically, so whenever one journal was full, she would leave it with Dr. Freda and retrieve it later.

This afternoon, she was on her way to *Kabarett Seks* to prepare for tonight's contest. Though they never needed to pull talent from the local dregs, they did want to foster a sense of community involvement and participation. It was as if they were allowing the winner of a lottery to bypass the waiting list of headliner talent and take their place among the stars of the burlesque theatre. If she were honest with herself, she had to admit that most nights, she struggled to keep a smile on her face and interest in her eyes while one act after the other flopped horribly. Ending each audition with words of encouragement helped to spread the word through the community that the club had a welcoming family atmosphere and good people working there. This reputation ensured that whenever they had an opening, whether technical, bartending, or performing, there was a surplus of good people in line to take the job.

Tonight would be a series of auditions, granted by drawing. Contestants could submit their forms anytime the club was setting up or open to the public. The callback sheet would be posted each week on the front door along with stand-bys in case one of the callbacks did not show up.

The walk from Dr. Freda's office in the basement of the University of Cologne's *Medizinische Fakultät* to the club took nearly an hour, so instead of walking along the streets, she took the opportunity each week to walk through the *Innerer Grüngürtel*, a park that ran most of the length along the *Innerer Kanalstraße*. The park was beautiful and green at this time of year and the cool breeze today helped to keep the heat at bay. The sun was high and there were many people in the park. Children laughed and played, some throwing balls, others flying kites. Birds sang as flocks flowed from tree to tree. The verdant surroundings made her feel as if she were in the country, which was a special pleasure for someone who was tethered to city life around the club.

As she came to the end of the park, she turned left to meet up with *Innerer Kanalstraße*, then right to take the overpass. She turned left again onto *Eckerstraße* where she was only a few blocks from the club. She waved to the local residents who bustled about taking care of their afternoon business. Children were out of school on their summer break and were playing stickball and tag in the street. Though this neighborhood was one block from a major thoroughfare, it was peaceful with very little traffic. She made it a point to say hello to every person she met and to ask if everything was alright so they would know she was the person to come to with complaints about the club. She also paid some of the local police to work after their shifts to guard the cars parked up and down every street in the neighborhood when the club was operating. She asked these officers to get to know the people in the houses they passed and to ask if they were bothered by the noise. If they were, the police should report that directly to Gerta so she could make adjustments and then visit the next day to let the complainant know their concerns were being taken seriously. This would also help the police improve their relationship with the community without any extra cost to the municipality because she was paying for their time.

In turn, her clientele saw a strong but kind police presence when they parked their cars and often tipped officers who offered to walk them to the club after dark. In this way, the officers made even more money than they were being paid by Gerta and patrons felt safe in the neighborhood. Gerta's parents had never considered that paying out money to a community outreach effort would actually yield more money in the tills, but Gerta had insisted that it would work, and she was right. Even when times were hard, the program always brought in more than it paid out. She even had a waiting list of officers who wanted to work for her, but the program was limited by the distance people were willing to walk on their way to and from the club.

As she came to the club and turned down the adjacent alley, she saw that the door was already open. Asher and Wyatt were holding the door open for Emma and Hans, two of the bartenders, and waved at her as she approached. They were some distance away and she didn't want to hold them up, so she waved the signal to go inside and they did so, letting the door close with a creak and clank behind them. One of the things that Gerta and Guy had learned from working with Dr. Freda was that immediate, clear, concise communication helped teams work more efficiently and respond to challenges faster and more consistently. She and her father, who was now almost bedridden, had worked out a system of hand signals that was nearly indistinguishable from normal movements one might expect from performers. As they developed the system and worked out the issues, they began to hold entire conversations in hand signals, something like sign language, but they weren't working on everyday conversations. Their system was *specifically* for the club and was made of signals that no one but their crew would understand. In this way, they could communicate simple, clear ideas across great distances in poor lighting and over the roaring crowds and music.

As she walked in, she went to her office to make sure her dry cleaning had been delivered. Her favourite gray pinstripe pant suit was in its proper place along with the flowered ribbon she would give to the winner of the contest. She sat down to write some notes for Guy. Thursday nights were very important because the contest helped them maintain a good relationship with the locals. When Guy emerged he needed to put on a big smile and be as gracious as he could.

- Local audition by lottery tonight.
- List of names in music booth *and* receptionist stand.
- BE NICE TO EVERYONE!
- Choose the one that captivates the crowd the most,
  not the one with the biggest tits!
- Emil and Sofie will come to see the auditions. Reserved booth #5.
- Put the ribbon on just before contest and award to winner with
  lots of praise.
- DON'T BE A SCHMUCK!

Love You, Brother!

Everyone thought it was strange that she had started calling Guy *brother* but something that Dr. Freda had said made it seem appropriate. One of the reasons she had teased out of him to explain his general lack of joviality was that he thought of himself as an afterthought...as not worthy of being a person. Dr. Freda felt it would go a long way toward helping the young man feel better about himself if he were not only addressed as a person, but held accountable like anyone else would be. Since they could not come and go at will, this might be a good way to improve their working relationship, and his relationship with the staff.

Gerta awoke standing at the receptionist's stand at the front of the club. The music was loud, the lights were low, and *Frau Bürste* was patting her on the arm as she passed, shaking her head. She didn't stop the elderly woman because sometimes when she did this, Guy had already had a complete conversation with someone and she looked as if she had not been paying attention, so she let the woman go and gave the hand signal for GERTA so her staff would know she was back. Her assistant manager, Gina, saw the signal and repeated it. Then two of the bartenders saw Gina's signal and repeated it. The backstage manager saw the signal and stepped behind the dressing room curtain, snapped loudly so everyone knew to look, and repeated the signal. In less than five seconds, the entire staff knew that Gerta had reemerged and was back in charge.

Gerta's journal was open on the receptionist stand, but she could not take time to read it until she was relieved. She saw Gina heading her way and kept greeting the tide of guests as they entered. It was warm outside so no one needed to check coats, but hats, jackets, and canes were being passed through the little window to a frantic pair of attendants handing out claim tickets. Something brushed her neck and she noticed that she was wearing the ribbon she had left in the office. Her heart began to race. This must mean that the contest was about to start.

"I have this," said Gina as she came up on Gerta's left, stepping between her and the column of guests, immediately shaking hands and calling out names as people smiled back at her or waved if they were too far away to shake hands.

Gerta looked at her watch. It was 7:50 pm. She took her journal and stepped out of the way, so it would be clear that she was not to be disturbed for a few minutes. She turned away from the guests and placed the journal under a light so she could see what Guy had written.

6:00: Opened doors.

6:16: BT Jeremy cut his hand, not serious. Still working.

6:30: Contestants arriving early, gave some free drink tickets.

7:35: Table 4 – Dr. Schäfer plus 3 arrived

7:45: Table 5 – Emil & Sofie arrived

She continued the journal.

7:55: Started contest.

Her momentary panic subsided when she realized where they were on the timeline. She made her way to the space between the dance floor and the bar to order herself a cocktail. The mumbling of the crowd was beginning to build as the contestants lined up against the dividing wall between the large front room and the burlesque room, trying not to block the heavy black velvet drapes that covered the entryway. People began to stream out of the burlesque room to fill every empty space around the dance floor and Tim, the youngest bartender in the club, placed her favourite drink, a French 75, on the bar behind her, knocking loudly once on the bar to let her know it was there without needing her to turn around.

Gerta raised her hands for quiet...an unattainable goal in this setting. As the crowd began to settle down, she turned and took the cocktail, raising it to toast the room. "LIBATIONS!" she called at the top of her voice, holding the champagne flute high.

The entire room raised glasses, hats, purses, and anything else they had handy to join in the toast. "LIBATIONS!" roared the crowd as Tim threw a stack of paper napkins over her head so they filled the air, fluttering to the floor like confetti. Laughing and cheering followed and the thunder of the room's joy gave Gerta a rush of adrenaline making her heart pound. Her smile made the muscles in her face ache, but this was her favourite part of the evening.

With voice and glass still raised, she said, "Before we get started, I want to thank all of you for coming tonight!" to which the crowd replied with hoots and cheers which died almost immediately as she held her glass high. "It makes me so happy to see so many familiar faces!" she said as she singled out one after the other regular guests with a tip of her glass in their direction. "Those of you who are new to *Kabarett Seks* are in for a treat! Tonight, we may find a new headliner!" The crowd exploded in raucous cheers and applause. Giving them time to enjoy their revelry, she raised her other hand, to gesture to bring the noise level down. She kept bringing her hand down and the crowd obliged, lower and lower. Then Gerta raised her hand in the reverse gesture and the crowd began to generate more and more noise, louder and louder until Gerta's short frame could not raise her hand anymore. She dropped her hand and raised her glass, laughing and cheering along with the room.

She took a sip of her drink and repeated, "LIBATIONS!" which the crowd imitated with their own "LIBATIONS!" "Now let's get this show on the road!" Gerta swung her arm down and the music started up as she stepped out of the way.

The first act was a bawdy, classless, writhing on the ground charade that got the crowd clapping, but Gerta had to get everyone's attention from the side of the dance floor to lift the audience participation. It was the diplomatic thing to do when an act was less than stellar.

The second act was a downer. The music was beautiful and the singer could carry a tune, but she left the audience behind after verse one and went into her own little world, not caring about getting any kind of reaction out of the room. Obviously, this woman thought she should be in a studio or piano bar somewhere, not at the *Kabarett Seks*. With compliments and encouragement, Gerta brought the crowd to a respectable volume after the number, but this contestant was not going to win either.

After four more performances, some rousingly fun and one that was so bad the audience started helping her try to remember the words, came Lolita Lipschitz, a drag queen that sang and did stand-up comedy. Nothing could have prepared the audience for the spectacle that took the stage. Lolita was very thin and moderately tall, but carried herself like a man in a dress. There was just no way to put it delicately. He was not padded, so the sequined red dress looked like a vertical column of glitter with a crown of yellow ostrich feather fluff at the top. Her cheeks were sunken and the dark shaving shadow would have shown through the heaviest makeup. Her nose was long and hooked like the wicked witch in the 1939 American movie *The Wizard of Oz*. The expression on her face was a serious attempt at sensuality, but what a tragic farce! Still, she kept a straight face and stood up tall, stepping out onto the stage. Taking a microphone from Gerta, Lolita pulled on the cord too hard and the excess cord that sped her way from off-stage wrapped around her feet and she stumbled, dropping onto the stool at her side and recovering into a surprisingly dainty, pose.

The crowd lost control. When they saw the extra cord headed Lolita's direction, they had gone instantly silent. Seeing her stumble, lose her balance, and somehow end up in a graceful position acting as if nothing were wrong left them cheering and howling with laughter and Gerta crossed her arms with a smile. The music started playing and everyone immediately recognized it as the theme from Doris Day's 1955 movie *Love Me or Leave Me*.

Lolita spent the first few measures clumsily shifting from one supposedly sensual pose to another. The poses, the transitions, they were awful! The audience gasped when during the transition, but before Lolita started singing, she seemed to almost slip off the stool before catching herself and recovering again. Gerta watched closely and thought, *This is no accident.* Lolita had managed to get a cheer before she even started and had the audience absolutely silent and holding their collective breath before the first note came out!

Then the first note came out.

Doris Day performed the theme song of this movie standing on a thrust stage in beautiful green taffeta and diamonds with a blonde bob. She had all the grace and poise of a great movie star from the 40's and 50's, but...

Lolita's graceful pose dissolved from delicately feminine to brutishly masculine and she began in a raspy voice, "You used to tell me that you loved me once." The audience was silent. "What happened, Oy!, what happened?" she pleaded with arms spread awkwardly, palms open, and the microphone falling toward the floor as the cord slipped through her fingers. She caught the cord the instant before the microphone hit the ground and the audience descended into fits of laughter and hysterical hooting. The bartenders, who had been frozen in place by the spectacle, laughed so hard they couldn't breathe. Tim nearly smacked his forehead on the bar, his stomach was so tight with laughter. Even Gerta could not hide the smile that cracked her face.

Drawing herself back up into a regal pose, Lolita pulled the cord sharply causing the microphone to leap back up into her hand, catching it deftly. She brought the microphone to her lips and paused...for a long, long time. The gap she had requested at this point in the music gave her time to give seductive glances and suggestive winks to the audience before the music began again. "Where is all of this coming from? What happened, what *the hell* happened?" she crooned with a smattering of obscenity.

Three lines in and the audience lost control for the second time. As she continued, she played the room like an expert. Gerta watched Lolita closely. Every move, every nuance, was carefully timed and played off the audience's reactions. It was like watching a master at work. Gerta stepped to the side of the bar where she had laid her journal and quickly wrote *Lolita Wins!* before closing the journal so no one could see she had already made up her mind. She looked up just as some other antic drew roaring laughter from the crowd. People were now pressing in from the front entrance and beginning to crowd the dance floor, which was off-limits while performers were performing. Gerta began to move around the perimeter to urge people to step back, when Lolita beat her to the encroaching group. Gerta stopped moving that direction and waited to see what would happen.

Lolita continued to sing, "And you're turning away like you hate me," when without warning, she grabbed the crotch of the man who had intruded the farthest. By the look on his face, she must be squeezing him fairly hard while with the microphone hand, she waved in a motion that let everyone know that they needed to back up. They did so, but the man whose jewels were in her clutches could do nothing but stand there. "Do you hate me, do you hate me, oh," and the man began to grimace and bend at the hip, trying to withdraw his parts from her grip as she scolded him to the audience's delight. When she released him singing "You can take this heart," he was still protecting his sore testicles while she pushed him gently back behind where the carpet met the wood floor with a hand in his chest. She raised her hand to put a finger under his chin and lifting his head to face her, planted a kiss on his lips that raised his eyebrows and made him pull back even farther. As he pulled away, a thick residue of bright red lipstick covered his lips from his nose to his chin. She had obviously open-mouth kissed him while he held his lips shut.

Gerta stood back marveling at how well the situation had been handled. Obviously, Lolita was gifted at dealing with audiences, but she had never heard the name nor seen this person in her club before. The rest of the performance was a work of art to Gerta's experienced eyes. The ups, the downs, the mistakes...it was all carefully played like a violinist plays his favourite concerto. At the end of the number, Lolita had successfully harassed several members of the audience, left one man holding his testicles, and cost the bar over thirty spilled drinks, refilled on-the-house. As Gerta stepped forward to take the microphone from Lolita, the drag queen appeared to slip and stumble toward her letting the microphone slip out of her hand and as Gerta reflexively stooped quickly to catch the expensive device, Lolita caught the cord again, suspending the microphone halfway to the floor. As Gerta's lunge bottomed-out, she stood again, laughing and put a hand on Lolita's shoulder to draw her close enough to hear over the roaring applause.

"I'm going to end up killing you!" She released Lolita who stood erect, eyes wide and surprise paralyzing her face. Gerta only smiled and put a finger to her lips as she mimed *Shhhh.*

The next contestant in line grumbled under her breath, *"Der scheißkerl!"* ("That piece of shit!") before affecting a forced smile and stepping up to take the microphone from Gerta. She knew that following an act like that would not go well.

Chapter 26

"I am very nervous," Gabby said and she fidgeted with her purse.

"That is understandable and entirely normal, Mrs. Gorski. I would like to thank you so much for coming. Your momentary discomfort could be of great benefit to another human being." Dr. Freda's words were practiced and had the desired stabilizing effect.

"Well, I do have to say that I was very disturbed when this man from Auschwitz came to see me at my home." Gabby was irritated, but not deterred. She was naturally defiant in that way and it had gotten her into trouble more than once, but this time she would be prepared. She left instructions for the coachman to be cautious and to prevent this man from coming on the property using any means. In the affluent areas where large estates were, access to law enforcement often took hours. Anton's family had, going back generations, taken responsibility for their own security, but Gabby did not like to be around guns and so most of the estate's weapons were locked away. At Anton's insistence, they would reinstate the previous firearm rules. Each of the coachmen would resume carrying a sidearm and radio just like the guardsmen.

Dr. Freda was not going to play the blame game. There was far too much at stake for that. "Please take whatever precautions you think will keep you safe. If there is anything I can do to help, please do not hesitate to ask."

"Just do me a favor and tell the truth," Gabby insisted.

"Always." Dr. Freda's answer was not a retort but a confirmation and Gabby accepted it with a nod.

"So tell me about Albert. Why did you reach out? Is he in trouble?" Gabby's string of questions did not deter the doctor.

"Yes, Albert is in trouble. He is in a mental institution and someone has tried to kill him." She sat back rather seriously. "I must apologize but I had no idea anything could be connected to you. You may be able to provide the evidence needed to convict his assailant."

Gabby sat thinking for a long moment. Dr. Freda waited patiently. "I can't say that I am happy about this, but if Albert and I are connected through this man, then one day he might have come for me. To tell you the truth, I would rather find out now."

"We can talk about this matter once you have a chance to meet Albert. For now, I would appreciate it if you did *not* disclose this information to him. We do not need to complicate his recovery," Dr. Freda cautioned.

"I completely agree, doctor. How can I help?" Gabby leaned forward and crossed her hands over her crossed legs, listening intently.

"Albert, and you, were brutalized by the Nazis. It was only by the intervention of the Russian Army and The Red Cross, and the charity of others, that you survived. Since then, Albert has been through some very difficult times."

"He's not the only one." The instant Gabby said it, she felt ashamed. "I'm sorry, Dr. Freda. Please go on."

To set the balances straight, Dr. Freda decided to spell out their differences. "Albert faced ridicule, religious judgment, and kept secrets from his mother for many years before attempting suicide, not once, but twice. You, on the other hand, seem to have done well. You have fully transitioned to female. You have a wealthy, prominent husband, and you have good taste in clothes, from what I can see."

Gabby was infuriated. "You have no idea what I have been through," she said in tightly controlled anger. "Tell me how many times Albert has been raped so we can compare notes." She ended the statement with a huff and realized she was hyperventilating. The sudden rush of anger had caught her off-guard.

"My apologies, Mrs. Gorski. I do not mean to belittle your situation, or draw comparisons. I am only trying to help Albert find a reason to live." Dr. Freda's tone was calm and unaffected by Gabby's surge of emotion.

When Gabby returned her gaze to Dr. Freda, she realized that she had flushed. She took a deep breath and let it out slowly. "I'm sorry."

"Please, let us not get caught up in our own emotions when we are both here to help Albert." Dr. Freda's advice was sound and Gabby nodded in agreement. "I do not want your first meeting to be contrived. He is an intelligent man and he would perceive that as an insult. What I would like to see happen is that he meets his old friend again. I would like him to see that you are alive and that he should be too."

"I would like that as well." Gabby appeared resolute.

After discussing Albert's case for a half hour, Freda decided that there was little if any risk to Albert or Gabby in exposing them to each other, so she invited Gabby to go to Albert's room for a first visit.

As they walked down the hall, Gabby's heels made a distinctly loud clacking on the tile floors that stood out sharply amid the soft shuffle and squeak of the staff's shoes. When they arrived, Dr. Freda asked Gabby to wait outside while she confirmed with Albert that he was in the right mood to meet with her. She went through the heavy wooden door leaving Gabby outside feeling awkward.

"Drives you crazy, doesn't it?"

Gabby started at the voice behind her. How had this red haired young girl snuck up behind her so quietly?

"I'm Helga, Dr. Freda's nurse. Well, I'm not actually her nurse, I'm Albert's nurse. Well, you know what I mean." Helga stood waiting for a response with an unapologetic smile.

"I am Gabriella Gorski," Gabby started to answer, but was cut off.

"Oh, you're the one that was with Albert in the camp! This must be such a coincidence! To find someone else from the same camp!" The two were interrupted by the door opening halfway and Dr. Freda beckoning Gabby to come in.

"Let's catch up later," Gabby said in a tone she didn't intend to come out as patronizing. She faced Dr. Freda and took a deep breath. She had no idea what she would find when she walked through that door.

There was a man, about her age, but emaciated and scruffy, sitting up in the hospital style bed. His hair was trimmed but untamed. His bony hands lay in his lap looking like they belonged to an elderly man. There were two scars clearly visible on both sides of his neck and a vacant expression on his face. Deep lines furrowed his sunken cheeks and his eyes appeared dull gray. She stood to face him saying, "Albert, I was Gabriel."

Albert looked up and stared at Gabby, unmoving, studying her. Gabby stepped toward the chair against the wall between his bed and the door, and pulled it toward the bedside. Her purse strap fell off her shoulder, so she set the purse on the foot of the bed at the near corner. When she got situated, she looked back up at Albert. As they studied each other's faces, each began to find features they recognized. Albert's eyes and nose, Gabby's ears and cheeks, they examined each other doubtfully, but with growing acceptance. Then Albert smiled and Gabby couldn't help but smile also. She leaned forward to put a hand on the back of his hand, but he reached for her with open arms, so she got awkwardly up from her seat and leaned into his hug, unable to give one back because his back was against the pillows. She rested her arms on his shoulders and patted them as they shared the tentative embrace.

Sitting back down in the chair, she said, "You and I have a friend." She indicated Dr. Freda with a tilt of the head. "Dr. Freda and I have been talking a lot about you."

Albert finally spoke. "I didn't think I'd ever see you again." His chin scrunched and his lip began to tremble.

"Well now you have and I'm so glad to see you again, Albie."

Calling him by the name she did in the camp was too much. Albert descended into gasping sobs and Gabby rose again to hold him, however awkwardly. She sensed a flood of emotions and pain rushing out of him, out of the child in him, and she did her best to absorb it all.

"*Hallo, Medizinische Fakultät,* Dr. Dudek speaking."

"Dr. Freda. This is Gabby."

"*Hallo* Gabriella. How are you?" Freda noticed that Gabby's voice was quite cheerful.

"I am well. I called to tell you that we have a mutual friend," Gabby teased.

"Really? Who would that be?" Freda mentally reviewed the proper protocols for sharing information.

"Gerta and Guy Müller from *Kabarett Seks.* Isn't that a coincidence? I know she's your patient, so keep anything from me if you have to, but I think that is interesting."

"Thank you for understanding my obligations. How do you know Gerta?" Freda asked, quite curious about the connection.

"I will, very occasionally, go to her club...just to see the performances. She and I are the best of friends. She's such a dear."

Those were the words of someone covering something up, Freda thought. "I see. Gabriella, I think there is something we should talk about in person. Would you mind coming to my office on Wednesday afternoon? Would two o'clock be a good time for you?"

"Anytime is a good time for me. I've been wanting to ask you something too," Gabby added.

"And what would that be?" Freda wondered aloud.

"I think that would be best discussed in person as well," said Gabby.

"Very good. Wednesday at two."

"I will see you then." Gabby set the receiver down, concern weighing on her mind.

"*Doktor*, if this really is the same man that hurt Albert, then he will be coming for me as well, right?" Gabby was already certain of the answer, but wanted to see if Dr. Freda might see some way out of it.

Freda hung her head and brought her hands together, knitting her fingers. "I think you are probably right."

"So what do we do?" Gabby asked.

"We make him pay for what he did to you." Freda's words shocked Gabby who sat open-mouthed across the desk from her.

Gabby sat back in her chair with a thud.

"I want you to know that I am very sorry for involving you in this," Freda said.

Looking away, Gabby waved the comment off as if it were a silly thing to say. "As long as there are people like this out there, we are all in danger," Gabby replied. Dr. Freda sat for a long time examining Gabby's face, looking for something but Gabby wasn't sure what. Gabby began to feel uncomfortable with the doctor's stare and finally asked. "What are you thinking?"

Freda steepled her fingers under her chin saying, "I'm thinking that I might want you to get more involved in what I am doing."

"You mean treating Albert?" Gabby asked.

"In tracking down this Nazi and others like him to bring them to justice." Dr. Freda's face was flat and expressionless.

Gabby grinned, then giggled, but when Dr. Freda's expression did not change, she began to understand that Freda was not joking. Her disbelief melted at Dr. Freda's serious expression. She studied Dr. Freda and, though no words were spoken, Gabby read volumes in the silence. She thought about her parents' faces when they were separated from her. She thought about the pain of the surgeries. She thought of Albert being nearly smothered in his room and said in a low, measured tone, "These bastards need to hang."

Freda smiled, leaning forward, dropping her hands to the desk to gently tap the papers there in a definitive gesture. "That's what I was hoping you would say. What about your husband?"

"Anton knows everything about me. He knows what I went through in the camps. He knows I would like nothing better than to put these men on the gallows myself. I won't do anything to jeopardize his practice, but he will be supportive otherwise."

"I want you to be sure you understand what you are saying," Freda continued, very serious again. "If you expose your identity to these people, they could kill you."

Committed now, Gabby retorted, "Then we'll just have to be certain that does not happen."

The two women sized each other up, each gauging the seriousness of the other.

Freda continued, "You must never give secret information out over the phone or in letters. You never know who might be listening or reading your posts."

"Likewise, you must keep my identity secret. You must never let Dr. Nowitz write about me and I suggest that he stop keeping your conversations about this in his journal. He should also be more careful. He was lucky once. It might not go so well if it happens another time."

"Then I think you will be pleased to know that there is a way you can help." Freda sat back in her chair waiting to see Gabby's reaction.

Gabby's face lit up with enthusiasm and a rebellious grin spread across her face. "What do you have in mind, doctor?"

"You told me that Jürgen Żądło gave you his phone number when he came to visit with you."

"That he did," Gabby confirmed.

"Do you think he has any idea who you are?" Freda asked.

"Not a chance."

"Do you think you could get him to tell you what he knows?" Dr. Freda asked cautiously.

In a sultry voice, Gabby said, "I think I could tease something out of him. Are you looking for something in particular?"

It was a terrible risk. Freda was putting her life in jeopardy at the very least, and if Gabby became involved, she would be putting Gabby's life in danger as well. After assessing the situation, Freda decided to explain everything. She told Gabby about Horace tracking the financial transactions of the Nazi doctor Horst Schumann which might have led to Jürgen coming to Cologne to find her and subsequently attacking Albert. She explained that they needed to know why Jürgen seemed to be investigating and if he really was a medical assistant to Dr. Schumann, then he could be turned in to the authorities as a war criminal after they found out any details he might know about Dr. Schumann's current situation.

After Freda's detailed explanation, they both sat in silence for a while when Gabby appeared to hatch an idea. Her face went through several iterations of realization, disappointment, then resolution, round and round until her eyes brightened and she looked back up at Dr. Freda saying "I know what to do."

"Tell me."

"If we agree to bring Gerta in on this, I think we can safely interrogate Jürgen and he won't even know what happened."

Gabby began to explain, but Freda cut her off. "Rather than go over the details now, let's test Gerta's receptiveness first, then we can work out the details with her." Gabby did not realize that there were ethical considerations behind disclosure of that sort of information to Gerta's doctor, regardless of whether the two of them were friends.

Resolute, Gabby nodded in agreement.

"Gerta is coming here for a treatment session tomorrow. If you just happened to be here and we asked her together, then if she agrees, we can work out the details then. Sound good?" Freda asked.

"What time should I be here?" Gabby asked, taking up her purse and pushing her chair back.

"Good morning, Gerta...Gerta?" Dr. Freda asked.

"Yep! It's me." Gerta was unusually cheerful this morning. The previous night at the club had been a blockbuster. Lines down the street were a testament to how well the club was doing and how much talk was going on around town. "I have to tell you, Dr. Freda, the changes you suggested, letting the staff know when each of us emerges, worked out better than I could have expected. It has really helped a lot."

"I'm so glad to hear that, but today I'd like to see if we could talk about something else." Dr. Freda leaned toward the closed door. "Please come in!" Dr. Freda called to someone waiting outside. Gerta turned toward the door and Gabriella Gorski came in.

"Gabby! What are you doing here?" Gerta exclaimed as she rose, pushing her chair back.

The two friends embraced. "It's so good to see you, Gerta. How is the club doing?"

"It's doing great! We're actually starting to have to turn people away. It's wonderful! So what's going on? Why are *you* here?" Gerta's face held a quizzical look.

"Please have a seat, Miss Müller. Gabby and I have something we want to discuss with you."

Jürgen sat at his desk composing a letter for Dr. Schumann. Writing was one of his least favourite things to do. Their letters must include a few coded sequences that meant certain sets of characters had to appear in the right place. He could never keep them all in his mind when he was writing, so he kept having to go back and re-write his letters over and over until he got it right. It was maddening sometimes.

The phone startled him when it rang, partly because it was very close and very loud, but also because he rarely received calls. He picked up the receiver. "*Ja, was möchten Sie?*" ("Yes, what do you want?")

To his surprise, Mrs. Gorski was on the line. "Mr. Jackson, this is Gabriella Gorski. How are you this morning?"

Affecting a professional and gracious attitude, he replied, "Mrs. Gorski, it is good of you to call. I am well. I appreciate your asking. What can I do for you?"

"I was thinking about what you said when you came to visit me. You said if I had any more information that I should call you. Well, I met with Dr. Dudek and I suppose I don't mind telling you about it." Gabby tried her best to sound unconcerned and pampered.

"That would be much appreciated, Mrs. Gorski. What can you tell me?"

"Actually, I would like to meet with you in person if you don't mind. I have a VIP table reserved at *Kabarett Seks* for this evening. Would you like to join me?" Gabby curled her hair around her fingers and cocked her head to one side, knowing that these movements would be conveyed in her voice.

Jürgen was intrigued. He felt some attraction when they first met so maybe he could get under her skirt before things got too serious with the doctor. "I would enjoy that very much, Mrs. Gorski. What time should I meet you there?"

Gabby let girlish glee brighten her response. "I'll let them know to expect you at ten o'clock if that's alright with you."

"Very good, Mrs. Gorski. I look forward to it."

"As do I. You have a nice day, Mr. Jackson."

"Thank you everyone! You're doing a great job. I'm so grateful to each of you for making this club the most talked about place in Cologne! It just wouldn't be possible without this family!" Gerta turned to make sure the entire circle of employees knew she was talking directly to them. She took the time to look each one in the eyes and smile. This took quite some time as the crew had grown from only a dozen to nearly thirty in the past couple months. When she had acknowledged each and every person she said, "Now let's make this another night to remember for the people who give us their hard-earned money!" With a synchronized clap, they dispersed like a soccer team heading for the field.

"Junior, Tim, Adelle and Frank, please stay a while longer." She gave plenty of time for the rest of the crowd to disperse as Gabby and Horace walked over from the table where they were sitting to join them on the dancefloor. When they arrived, Gerta continued "You all know what we are about to do tonight."

They all nodded in agreement.

Horace had been very nervous about the plan when Gabby had proposed it. While she would be putting herself in danger, playing with a man who could kill her if he wanted to, she would need some way to get him to leave of his own free will. That means that a second player had to be Gabby's foil.

"We need someone who can make him feel embarrassed, disgusted, and vulnerable," Gabby said.

When the entire group turned in unison to look at Horace, he threw up his hands, palms out, saying "Oh no! Not me, no thank you!" It was already too late. The group had made up its mind and Horace was actually in agreement. There was no one at the club better suited than him to the task. He grudgingly agreed after much cajoling to work it into his Lolita comedy routine.

"Anyone who wants to back out should do so now." Gerta looked from face to face seeing no dissent. "Alright then. Junior, you will be our protection." She looked at the oversized youngster. "You must stay ready to intervene at any second. Keep freeloaders away from that table, but let them take the chairs if they want them. Tim, you are Gabby's bartender. Keep an eye on them and don't let their drinks run out. Make sure they don't have any reason to get up. Frank, you are our eyes. Keep an eye on them from the bar and if you see any danger, alert Junior immediately. That's your only job. Watch but don't let them know you're watching. Adelle, I hope you won't have anything to do, but yours is probably the most important. If anyone gives you the GO signal, you are to bring the two police officers in to take the man Gabby is with into custody immediately. The only time you will be called on is *if* there is an emergency. Keep an eye on Frank, Tim, and Junior for their signals. Everyone got that so far?"

They all nodded, some saying "Yes, ma'am."

"Alright then. I know we can count on you. Now get to work and stay safe tonight." Gerta felt a heavy weight on her shoulders. Three days ago, when Gabby and Dr. Freda had brought her into this plan, she had spelled out all the details in her journal for Guy in case she wasn't awake at the time it all happened. They would both need to be prepared even if a personality change happened during the operation. She thought this might be a bit like how it felt to the resistance when the Nazis took over Germany, France, and Poland. Three days was plenty of time for Guy to emerge and learn what they were planning to do and though he was often abrasive to her, he trusted Gabby just as she did him.

The previous day, Gerta had awakened in the afternoon sitting behind her desk in her office in the back of the club to find a note from Guy scrawled beside her notes about this Saturday's operation: *Are you fucking serious? Didn't think you had it in you! I'm all in! Hope I get to see some action!*

She smiled at his response. Once again she had underestimated him. There was a checkmark next to each of the hand signals she had drawn for the occasion. These were different from any of the signals already in use by the regular staff and only the people participating in the operation would know what these signals meant. The rest of the staff had been told to ignore any signals they didn't understand and not to get involved.

Ten o'clock came and Gabby was drinking a watered-down martini at her VIP table striking a pose that showed her leg all the way up to the hip. Her dress was a deep velvety green with pearl ropes draping her neck and wrist. Her plunging neckline revealed that she wasn't wearing a bra and sunk almost down to her navel. Her hair had been done by none other than Elke Rossen, their veteran headliner. She had given Gabby's long, golden hair a treatment that made her look like a vision from the 1920's with curls cascading around her shoulders. Mama Rossen had objected to being left out of the operation, but everyone agreed that she was too old to get involved and they didn't want her to get hurt. They did, however, inform her of every aspect so she could keep an eye on them and maybe help out in a crisis.

Every bartender knew that if Gabby were to order cocktails, Tim must be the one to make them. Tim would help to keep Gabby reasonably sober by watering down her martinis, but to her guest, it would appear she was becoming very intoxicated. This would help him feel as if he had the upper hand, but what he wouldn't know was that his cocktails would be spiked with very small doses of Scopolamine. He had been given a dilution in a dropper bottle that would allow him to deliver a very small dose over a long period of time. The small amount of barbiturate would help weaken his judgment without him realizing that he had been drugged and would have the added effect of making the memories of the evening difficult to recall. The effect would be amplified by the alcohol and the effects of the combination could be predicted by someone with the proper knowledge. Tim kept Dr. Freda's handwritten dosing chart behind the bar with the dropper bottle sitting on top so he would know how to manage the doses.

Tim was the smallest man in the club. He was a blonde haired waif of a boy whose knowledge of cocktails from every era was unmatched. His boyfriend, Junior was his opposite in almost every way. Junior had been Gerta's bouncer for nearly two years, hired on a reference from Tim. He was a sight to behold. A caramel-skinned man with a perfectly symmetrical face. His body was so large that no clothes available would fit him. When Gerta hired him, she had asked him to go out and buy clothes that fit the largest part of his body, which were his shoulders for shirts and his thighs for pants. Five pairs of each, paid for by the club and altered to fit by her own personal tailor, and he looked quite respectable. Gerta made sure her tailor got the clothes to fit skin-tight to maximize his appearance of strength. Though his voice was soft and his manner gentle, no one dared refuse him when he asked someone to leave or to stop harassing another guest. Only once in the entire two years had he been forced to use his strength to subdue a knife-wielding jerk with too little sense and too much to drink, and he had cried for hours at the end of the evening, after his duties had come to an end. Mama Rossen had taken him in her arms, or rather, she had tried in vain to reach around his massive shoulders, and consoled him as he cried. He had nearly crushed the man's throat as he carried him bodily to the police waiting outside, who gaped at the huge man carrying the unconscious perpetrator by the neck dangling nearly a half metre off the ground.

The club was nearly full and the performers were taking a break to allow the guests to use the dance floor. While Martin played an eclectic mix of archaic and contemporary music, people young and old danced the night away in a fantasy land of happiness and frivolity.

In the dressing room, Horace was getting into his costume to perform as Lolita Lipschitz, but he was having trouble putting on his eye liner. His hand would approach his eye with the three-haired brush, but before he could apply, he would pull away, his hand shaking so badly he would certainly smear. Seeing his fourth failed attempt, Mama Rossen stood and pulled her chair to his side and took the brush from his hand before sitting down to face him. Thankful for the assistance, Horace turned his chair to face her and leaned toward her, looking up.

As she applied his liner, she saw how much he was trembling and sweating. "Honey, you're going to be great out there. There is nothing to worry about. You've done this many times."

"I know. I know. It's just..." he stuttered.

Sitting back, she asked, "What has you so worried?"

Horace sat back into an upright position. "If I do something wrong, Gabby could get hurt."

"Honey, Gabby's a big girl. She's probably more dangerous than that man out there, so stop your worrying and do what you rehearsed. You are Lolita Lipschitz, damn it!" She threw her head back and shook her hair in the pretentious move they all did when they needed to let go of their nerves.

She had finished his liner and handed the brush back to him, smiling and placing a reassuring hand on his shoulder as she rose to get back to her vanity. He smiled up at her, feeling much calmer thanks to her wise words. He took a deep breath and looked at himself in the mirror thinking "It's time to ditch this man's face and put on the Lipschitz!" He drew a curly brunette bob cut wig over his head and worked it into place, tugging at the edges and tucking his own hair underneath.

It was almost a physical effort not to stare toward the front entry, but Gabby maintained her aloof attitude watching Tim for the *look now* signal as she sipped her cocktail. She thought *I hope I never have to drink watered down gin again!* Suddenly, but smoothly, Tim raised his hand just above the bar surface, from her perspective, and touched his thumb to his pinky with the other three fingers hovering just above. The signal lasted only an instant, but he saw that she had registered it and dropped his hand immediately. The whole thing happened so quickly that anyone not looking directly at Tim from the correct angle would have missed it.

Gabby gathered her strength and casually looked toward the stream of people moving from the front door to the dance floor. Seeing Mr. Jackson, she affected a subtle smile. He saw her too and came toward her, and as he did, she waited for him to see her bare leg under the table. As soon as he looked down toward her leg, she moved to stand to greet him, making sure that the leg remained bare and did not fall under her gown. As she stood, her bare hip became visible above the table top indicating that she wore no undergarments. The bare hip and the plunging neckline conspired to make the man speechless as he arrived at the table, hat in hand.

Jürgen opened his mouth to greet Mrs. Gorski, but no words would come out, so he closed it. Looking her up and down, the woman was obviously delighted that she was having this effect on him. He tried again and this time his mouth cooperated. "Good evening, Mrs. Gorski."

"Gabby, if you please, Inspector Jackson." Her gown flowed around her leg as she spoke, hiding her bare hip, the disappearing skin drawing his eye against his will.

Looking back up at her eyes, he responded "Then I must insist you call me Mason, Gabby."

"As you wish, Mason." She extended her bejeweled hand and he drew it up for a kiss, all the while admiring the exquisite pearl where a wedding ring should have been.

"May I?" he asked, gesturing beside her.

"Please," she invited, gesturing for him to sit. "And what will you be drinking this evening?"

"Oh, nothing, thank you," he dismissed the offer.

"I insist. Let me select something for you if you aren't sure," she urged as they sat down.

"I would enjoy that. Thank you."

Gabby turned toward Tim whose face was pointed down, but his eyes were directed at her. He set the cocktail he was mixing on the bar, explained that it was on the house, and left the line of customers waiting as he stepped out from behind the bar heading toward Gabby.

As he arrived, she asked, "What is your name, young man?"

"Tim, ma'am. What can I get for you?"

"Tim, my guest would like to try a Moscow Mule and I would like another of your delicious martinis."

Jürgen nodded at the youngster and he acknowledged, "Yes, ma'am. Right away." He rushed back to the bar to mix their drinks, adding the first dose out of sight before pouring the drink back and forth between glass and tumbler to mix it.

"I must admit, I was not anticipating your call." He sounded critical and business-like, so Gabby poured on a bit more allure.

Leaning in conspiratorially, she said, "I actually just wanted to see your handsome face again."

He leaned forward, placing his elbows on the table, hands together and smiled. "Well, *Gabby*, to tell you the truth, I was hoping to spend some time with you. That last meeting, you understand, that was just work."

"I do understand and I promise I won't hold it against you." She giggled a little and Tim returned with their cocktails, putting them in front of each of them. She placed a hand on Jürgen's thigh, out of sight.

Jürgen didn't flinch. Instead, his smile broadened and as he took up the drink with his right hand, he put his left hand under the table and rested it on hers. After a sip, he said, "Well, now Gabby, I'm impressed." Setting the cocktail down with an appreciative look, he continued, "That is delicious. You really do know how to read a man."

Gabby only nodded in appreciation as she leaned toward him, placing her free elbow on the table and resting her chin on her curled fingers, making sure her favourite pearl stuck out beyond her cheek. She gave a wink and a smile to Junior who was shifting his weight from side to side catacorner across the dancefloor. He realized he was appearing nervous and tried to force himself to relax, thankful that her encounter was going as planned.

Gabby and Jürgen laughed and took turns wooing each other with seductive glances and suggestive innuendos as they drank. She toasted the evening and as she raised her glass for him to clink with his, Junior gave the *GO* signal to Adelle who was standing outside the dressing room. She ducked through the black velvet curtain and found Lolita. Looking in Lolita's reflection in the vanity, she signaled with five fingers up. Lolita would take the dance floor in five minutes. She took a deep breath and, satisfied with her makeup, exhaled forcefully, gathered her wits, and stood, heading for the curtain.

"Well, I was curious about that. When Dr. Dudek told me that she was looking for someone, I didn't realize she was looking for you. That's so interesting." Gabby was having fun watching Jürgen's faculties become like soft clay in her hands.

With a bit of a slur and his eyes beginning to blink a little slower, he said, "Oh, no. She's not looking for me. She's looking for Dr. Schumann. He's this guy I used to work with a long time ago. You don't want to hear about all that stuff. It was wartime."

"No, I do want to hear!" she objected as she moved her hand further up his thigh. When he removed his hand from hers, he was indicating that he hoped she would continue moving upward. "I am so fascinated by medicine. Tell me, did you and Dr. Schumann work together for a long time?"

"Yes. The whole time we were at Auschwitz, I was his medical assistant." She reached his crotch with her slowly sliding hand and felt that he was growing firm under her touch. He was so distracted by the contact that it took him several seconds to recover. "He taught me all the things they don't teach you in school...about how things really work...and not just with medicine."

"You must miss him very much. Were you friends?" she asked as she scooted her chair closer to his for easier reach without too much being visible to other guests.

"Oh, yes. Good friends."

His sentences were getting shorter so she knew the drug must be working. As he downed the last of his Mule, Gabby signaled to Tim to bring another for each of them. She didn't need to turn her head to know that he had seen the signal. Gabby's team were professionals.

"Have you been to visit him recently? I'm sure he misses you too." Gabby was taking her time steering him where she wanted him to go and making him harder with delicate strokes of her fingers.

"Nah. He's too far away for that." Jürgen looked like a little boy missing his mother.

"Well maybe we could go see him. I love to travel and I am so lonely when I do. I have no one to go with me." She baited the hook delicately now. No one could be sure how far she could go without him realizing that he was being interrogated.

"Aw, I don't know if that would be a good idea," he discouraged.

"And why would that be?" she asked, giving him a squeeze and feeling a spot of slick wetness beginning to form on the outside of his pants. She rubbed her finger across the spot and Jürgen's concentration was broken by the sensation.

"Sudan...that's near Africa I think...is not a place for a lady to go. Plus I hear the savages down there stink and don't bathe."

"Oh, my. Sudan is a big place. I would love to go there!" She snuggled up to his shoulder, placing a hand on his chest while she worked his arousal even higher.

"It's this little place called Khar...something. Anyway, it's not the best place to go. Maybe we can find a place closer to the coast. You know, they've got nice hotels there and we could get to some place private." He snuggled her back and placed a tentative kiss on her cheek.

Khar...something wasn't good enough, but it would have to do. She took his cheek in her hand and kissed him deeply as the lights went down and Marin began to announce, "The Incomparable Miss Lolita Lipschitz!"

Jürgen took another sip of his cocktail and placed it back down on the table a little too hard, causing it to splash over the side. He leaned back into Gabby's inviting gaze and brought both of his hands up to hold her face while he kissed her. She could tell that he was intoxicated after only three drinks by the way his kisses became wetter and sloppier. As she groped him, he slid one hand under her gown and cupped her breast, oblivious to the performer or the rest of the room.

"Mason, my dear, we mustn't do that quite yet." Gabby slid his hand out of her gown and placed it on her thigh. As she looked over his shoulder to the dance floor, she locked eyes with Lolita and gave the signal. She brushed Mason's shoulder as if she were brushing off dandruff and Lolita knew it was time for him to go.

"So who out there is meeting for the first time?" The question elicited cheers from a smattering of tables and standing guests, some of whom raised their hands. She looked toward Gabby who raised her hand and encouraged Mason to raise his as well. As he looked up and realized he was surrounded by people and a performer was walking toward them, he mounted a great effort to collect himself. To prevent him from regaining his wits, Gabby gave his crotch a gentle squeeze that made him groan under his breath.

He turned to her saying "You're so bad," as Lolita came up to their table.

"My, my, my! Honey, you look fabulous! What is your name dearheart?" Lolita praised Gabby who responded sheepishly for the audience.

"Gabby" she said in a quiet, demure voice.

"I'm sorry, hon. These ears are a little old. What was that name again?"

"Gabby!" Gabby said with her voice raised as she withdrew her hand from Jürgen's leg.

"And who is this rugged stud with you?" As Lolita approached their table, the two of them were bathed in the spotlight, causing Jürgen to squint and raise his hand to shade his eyes.

In slurred speech, he said "Jürgen. I'm Jürgen." Then he got a look at Lolita's face as her head blocked the spotlight and his face gave his revulsion away.

It had happened! Not only had the impostor inspector given away Schumann's location, if they could figure out the city name from his garbled words, but he had forgotten the fake name he gave to Gabby and used his own. Gabby knew that the liberating forces had captured many of the Nazi's records and, from them, they would probably be able to positively identify this man. Now they were in real danger.

"Ooh, Mr. Jürgen. Do you mind if I join you?" Before he could object, Tim had a chair ready which she took with one hand and slid beside the surprised man, hopping up into the tall cushion and placing a large, masculine hand on Jürgen's thigh. Jürgen froze. He did not want to pull away from a performer. That would make him look bad in front of the other guests. He definitely didn't want this man in a dress touching him, but if he didn't keep calm, he might not get between Gabby's legs tonight. It seemed he had no choice but to play along.

Turning to the audience, Lolita launched into a soliloquy about a man who she loved and who loved her until he found out that she had a little extra block and tackle. With a suggestive nod to the crowd, Lolita moved her hand up to Jürgen's crotch and gave him an uncomfortably hard squeeze causing him to wince. Looking down at the erect man's lap as though looking through the table, she said "Ooh I'm having dessert tonight!"

Gabby threw her head back and laughed along with the audience while Jürgen grumbled and tried to laugh, but halfheartedly.

Addressing Gabby, Lolita said, "You keep him warm honey. We'll share him after the show." The audience roared with laughter and Gabby found herself genuinely laughing, despite the pressure of the mission. Lolita had played her part perfectly so far.

Jürgen turned to Gabby asking, "He's joking, right?"

Gabby put on her best look of provocative desire and shook her head. She leaned forward to whisper in his ear, "I think we should take him with us."

Jürgen's eyes went wide and he pulled back to look Gabby square in the face. She was serious!

"Think how much fun that will be," she suggested. "I think I would enjoy seeing the two of you together."

Jürgen's revulsion deepened as Gabby continued with the game. If she and Lolita could get Jürgen to choose to leave, there would be no need to remove him and he would have no idea he had been interrogated. In the best-case scenario, none of the security they had prepared to use would be needed.

Lolita's performance ended but before she left the stage, she twisted her upper body toward Jürgen and Gabby, pointed at them and promised, "Don't you two go anywhere. I'll be right back."

Jürgen began to get up, but Gabby sensed he wasn't ready to storm out just yet, so she caught his hand and urged him to stay. "Haven't you ever done that before? Wouldn't you like to be with me?"

He couldn't say that he didn't want to be with Gabby, so he let her draw him back to his chair. He wasn't going to be able to leave with the erection he was sporting anyway, so he sat back down. Gabby nuzzled his neck, kissing him and teasing his ear with whispers of what she wanted to do to him. She placed her hand back on his crotch and he closed his eyes with the strained pleasure of the moment.

A few minutes after the lights went back down and the dance floor was again crowded with revelers, Jürgen was lost in Gabby's touch.

"Well hey there, handsome man!" Lolita's raspy voice broke Jürgen's oblivion. She sat down in the chair still empty next to him and roughly put her hand on his leg.

Jürgen opened his eyes, seemingly unaware that Lolita was there. He looked into Lolita's manly face, her hand and Gabby's hand squeezing his hardened manhood, and made his decision. "No, no, no! I am not doing this."

Gabby affected a hurt look as Lolita moved in closer to deliver the final line. "You know, it takes a man to know what a man really wants," she rasped heavily in Jürgen's ear as Gabby released her grip giving Lolita room to squeeze harder.

Jürgen bolted up from the chair trying to get around behind Lolita but had trouble freeing himself from her grip. Lolita released him saying "Aww, honey. Don't be like that!"

Jürgen took his hat from the table and covered his erection with it as he made for the door, pushing through the crowd on the dance floor, toppling one woman and eliciting angry shouts from a few men. Junior had drawn closer as he saw the scene playing out and, when Jürgen leapt from his chair, Gabby gave the *out* signal. Junior escorted Jürgen, but all he really had to do was follow the man as he stumbled toward the door. As the two of them emerged from the entrance, Jürgen pushing his way through the inbound crowd, Junior was close behind. The two officers policing the front door came to attention and moved to intercept them, but Junior gave them the *OK* signal as he helped Jürgen collect himself and walk off down the sidewalk.

"Honey, I don't know about you, but having a bulge like that and letting it go? I must be slipping!" Lolita teased Gabby.

Gabby looked at Lolita seeing that she was trying to cover her nervousness with humor and said, "Thank you. I owe you one."

"You owe me way more than just one, but we can square up another time. Right now, I need some *honey in my cocktail.*" With a suggestive saunter, Lolita was off toward the burlesque room leaving Gabby sitting at the table alone. She motioned to Tim who came over. "May I have a *real* drink now, please?"

Tim laughed and said, "Right away, Mrs. Gorski."

"And don't call me that!" she called to him as he walked off toward the bar. "It makes me feel old."

"What do you mean you can't find him?!?" Ida yelled over the music as she dropped to her knees, leaning back on her ankles using her hands for support. Flinging her hair to one side, she shot Gabby a disbelieving look but instantly saw that she was serious. "Ten minutes *Du alte Prostituierte!*" ("...you old prostitute!")

As Ida went back to gyrating her enormous breasts, the men surrounding her swayed to follow her movements in the swirling lights and pounding music. The tiny raised dance floor in the burlesque room was littered with *Deutsche Marks*, enough for a month's rent. Ida was out of breath and sweating like a pack animal, but the men around her were eager to put their *Marks* anywhere she would allow them to touch. She struck poses worthy of an Olympic gymnast in twelve centimetre heels and teased just out of reach of the grasps of the too-enthusiastic younger men. The older men admired her while standing with money in outstretched hands which she would take from them, placing it where their propriety would not allow them to place it. The burlesque room reeked of body odor, cheap cologne, rancid perfume, and alcohol and as the lights and hair twirled to a crescendo, the music finally broke in a blast that echoed through the ringing in Ida's ears. Just before it ended, Ida grabbed the man nearest her, the one with the most bills on display, and buried his face in her breasts. The sweat made his face slip between rather easily, so he could not breathe and she teased him, holding him there rubbing his face back and forth before releasing him with a satisfied squeal. The affronted man reeled back in delight, catching his breath, laughing and cheering so loud his voice echoed off the walls after the music faded. He reached into his pocket and grabbed his entire fold of cash, flinging it to disperse over Ida's head as she bowed demurely placing a pinky between her teeth and giggling like a schoolgirl.

A young, shirtless man came out from behind the music booth with a black bag to help her collect her take as the Maître d'Noir came out to work the crowd back up into a frenzy for the next performer. As Ida passed behind the character, she tucked a roll of cash into her hand and the Maître d'Noir deftly concealed it under her corset for later retrieval.

Ida headed through a back doorway draped with a black curtain gesturing to Gabby to follow her. They didn't have a single *decent* liquor in the burlesque room, but she was handed a vodka martini by a sweet young thing that saw her when she entered and rushed to get her a drink. Now that she was passing by the bar, he worshipfully handed her the cocktail raising his voice above the new performance music to say how much he loved her dress and her hair. *"Ich wünschte, ich könnte genauso sein wie Du!"* ("I wish I could be just like you!") he bleated like a wheedling child. She stopped to face him, took a sip of the poorly made cocktail, smiled, placed a hand on his undeveloped, hairless chest, and pressed him backward until he fell onto the stained and burned red velvet loveseat behind him. He fell into it dramatically, wailing in admiration and ecstasy as she flowed through the black curtain drawing every eye in the room with her as she went. Even the current performer could not help looking where everyone else was looking as Gabby disappeared behind the drapes following Ida.

In a voice just loud enough to be heard over the music, but not so loud as to be heard by anyone else, Ida said "You two were supposed to be working together! What do you mean you *lost* him!"

"Lost *her*, my dear. Lolita is nowhere to be found," Gabby corrected. "We finished the operation, and did a damn good job of it too, when I saw her come in here."

"Did you look for her?" Ida felt stupid the moment she asked the question and Gabby dropped her chin. "Right, of course you did." She thought for a minute about where Lolita might have run off to. Since Lolita was a performer, not a licensed sex trader, she was not restricted to the Red Light District. "Who drove?"

"I did, but she might have gotten in someone else's car," Gabby said.

"Don't worry. I'm sure she's not *that* stupid," Ida reassured. "Did she buy all her drinks herself?"

"Even *I* know she's not that stupid," answered Gabby.

"Alright, alright. I was just checking. You were there. I wasn't. What else can you tell me?" Ida asked.

"We're in deep shit, I can tell you that!" Gabby alarmed Ida with that response, but followed "...that has nothing to do with this situation. We just need to find Lolita and make sure she's alright!" Her voice was becoming hoarse quickly having to yell over the loud music.

Ida set her jaw with conviction and reached for a black silk robe hanging on a nearby wall hook. Taking Gabby by the hand, they pushed their way through the crowd heading for the front of the club to find Gerta. They smiled artificially as they wove their way between groups of guests cheering, dancing, and toasting the evening. Finding Gerta near the front receptionist stand, Ida placed a hand on Gerta's shoulder. The look on her face when she turned to see who had touched her informed Ida instantly that Guy was awake. They explained how the operation had been successful, but now they could not find Lolita and were worried about her safety.

Guy immediately took action waving over a couple of the club's security men as well as the two policemen just outside the front door. Guy described what he wanted from each of them in a commanding voice, encouraging each of them to stay in contact with each other during the search so as not to place themselves at unnecessary risk. He showed genuine concern for their safety as well as Lolita's. When everyone understood the plan, he sent them out into the night, remaining behind to coordinate their efforts. He suggested that Ida and Gabby remain in the club for their own safety, but when Gabby refused, he instructed to Junior to join them.

"Stay with Junior!" he shouted over the music. He leaned on tip-toe and pulled Junior close, speaking into his ear so only he could hear. "Don't let Gabby out of your sight, understand?" His look was stern and serious as he lowered himself to his heels. Junior nodded his understanding and motioned to Gabby to head for the door. As they left, Gabby turned back to Guy and mouthed the words *Thank You*. She felt a new appreciation for Gerta's alter-ego as he smiled and shooed them out of the club.

Over the next few hours, Gabby, Junior, and the staff who could put their duties aside for a while scoured the neighborhood around the club as they coordinated through Guy, but they found only a broken heel and some red feathers smashed into a muddy puddle nearby.

Chapter 27

The sun had gone down hours ago leaving Freda's flat in a quiet, peaceful darkness. The only sound was the occasional clink of the gin bottle against the rim of her favourite teacup. Pouring in the dark had proven to be a messy affair, but Freda didn't care. It could be easily cleaned up later. The dark and stillness were preferable now. Though a faint glow penetrated the lace curtains, it was not enough to illuminate anything in the room. As she raised the cup to her lips, the intense fragrance of juniper filled her nostrils along with the sting of alcohol. This time, she missed her lower lip and sloshed a small amount of gin against her chin before she corrected herself and moved the brim to her lips. Earlier, she had been sipping, but now she drew a mouthful, held it for a second, then swallowed it down. She set the teacup down a little too hard this time, judging by the momentary ring it emitted. She would have to be more careful to avoid breaking it during what she knew would prove to be a long night.

As the evening had come and the light faded, Freda reviewed the plan over and over in her mind trying to think of all the ways things could go wrong. As each disaster scenario formed in her mind, she would mold it, plotting and testing various decisions until the next disaster occurred to her. She knew it was too late. The plan had been thoroughly discussed by everyone involved and every possible contingency had been discussed. Her colleagues were competent people, each possessing a useful set of skills. They would be fine, but she could not avoid thinking that if anyone were hurt tonight, it would be her fault for involving them in the plot.

She tried to find some way she could be part of the evening's activities. Gabby had tried many times to dress her in fine clothes, bringing scarves, bags, and other items of clothing to her office. A few times, she had even tried them on, but it was no use. Her frumpiness was even more obvious when she was draped in taffeta and her manner was so obvious as to be a risk to the operation, so they had all agreed that she should not be present. In any case, it would be too difficult to hide her from their target and seeing she and Gabby together would certainly reveal their collaboration.

The group discounted her protestations of responsibility for the risk of approaching him because he had already come to Gabby's house in the guise of an investigator. He was certainly the one who broke into Dr. Nowitz' office, and the attack on Albert left no doubt in anyone's mind that they could all be targets. Nevertheless, as she drank in the silent darkness, she was unable to numb the nervousness and guilt and her mind raced with creative ways by which the plan could go wrong. It seemed a supreme effort of will just to sit unmoving tonight and wait.

✸　✸　✸

Through the open door to the back of the office Helga could see that she had left Dr. Freda's old brass goose-neck lamp on overnight giving the room a lonely yellow-green glow. Darkness always carried with it memories of loneliness and shame from her childhood, and even though she was an adult, happy with herself and her hopes for the future, she could not suppress the memories. She understood from her studies and from working with Dr. Freda that the loneliness suffered by patients, and by herself, contributed just as much to her personality and emotional defense systems as instances of persecution and fear.

Helga disliked the darkness so she poked her head through the doorway and flipped the light switch on the wall even though she would not be spending any time in Dr. Freda's office. Helga startled with a bark as she slapped her hand over her mouth, trying to control herself lest she give an embarrassing display.

"Well is that any way to greet a lady?" asked the woman in red, suddenly revealed by the light. Lolita was reclining in Dr. Freda's chair with her legs crossed on top of the desk, one heel aimed at the door, the other heel missing. Helga couldn't help bursting with laughter at her own fright and the gaudy red feathered dress Lolita wore.

"My apologies, ma'am. I didn't think a lady would have broken in during the night," Helga snarked. Over the past year, once she had come to trust her and Dr. Freda, Lolita had essentially come and gone as she pleased, locked door or not. Early in Horace's treatment, Helga had been uncertain and distrustful of Lolita's antics seeing them as an affectation and perhaps dishonest. One day, months before, Lolita had called the office and discovered that Helga was home with the flu. Somehow, she had found Helga's address and shown up with a basket of hot chicken soup, fresh bread, and milk. She was dressed in a nurse's uniform complete with white bonnet and red cape. Helga was too ill to object strongly when Lolita insisted on working Helga's shift at the hospital.

"You can't work at a hospital in those!" Helga complained pointing at the ruby red high heels Lolita wore with her stark white uniform.

"Honey," replied Lolita with a perfect poker face, "I don't have anything nearly as dull as you!" pointing to Helga's white Mary Jane shoes on the floor but looking her in the eye allowing the double entendre to linger before twirling around, flinging her cape over her shoulder, and prancing off for a day's work at the hospital. When Helga returned to work a few days later, she discovered a spotlessly clean, well-organized office with supplies restocked, records in order and properly annotated, and Dr. Freda thanking her for making sure her shifts were covered. After that, Helga felt that she had to rethink her prejudices about people who dressed up as someone else. Maybe they weren't lying. Maybe they were protecting themselves by inhabiting a character that had the traits and strengths they wish they had.

As Helga mused and her laughter abated, she saw that Lolita wasn't smiling. The realization squelched her laughter and Helga straightened her posture, observing Lolita more carefully. In the light, Helga now noticed a large bruise partially covered with makeup. She came to Lolita's side and knelt down for a closer look. Lolita did not move, keeping her face toward the door but her eyes on Helga. As she realized the depth of the bruise, Helga took a long breath and sighed placing her hand on Lolita's.

"Are you OK?" she asked.

"Never better," Lolita remarked, turning her face toward Helga's, punctuating her words with a forced, jerky smile.

On closer inspection, Helga realized that the feathered dress bore signs of a struggle. Smudges of dirty wetness had flattened the feathers and dried near her shoulder where a nasty scrape was bleeding red droplets through a layer of oil-based foundation. She stood and walked without a word into the front room as Lolita waited stoically. Lolita took her feet down from the desk and remained seated, waiting for Helga to return. When Helga reappeared in the doorway, she had the tray she had brought to the office but this time it contained cotton gauze, a small glass bottle of alcohol, and several white hand towels. She began cleaning Lolita's wounds without asking what had happened.

As Helga worked, Lolita became uncomfortable with the silence. As Horace, he could sit for hours listening to some boring accountant speak of business without the need to move or speak at all, but as Lolita, she was rarely ever quiet. She was always attracting attention and sometimes that attention was unwanted. She had come to understand that her looks made her ridiculous as a woman but unremarkable as a man. When he had first dressed up in women's clothing it had taken him weeks to procure the materials, the makeup, dresses, accessories, and then the practice took even longer. He was terrified that he might be discovered and have his career ruined, so he worked on a convincing result for over a month before trying it out. He was so careful he even chose a moonless night on which to go out the first time. Avoiding lit or crowded areas, he was certain not to make eye contact with anyone in the clubs in the Red Light District. It wasn't long before Lolita began to emerge, always quick to twist a phrase and never stingy with flamboyance.

Helga could see Lolita wrestling with what to say first and gave her the time she needed to start talking on her own. Lolita described a lavish evening of drinks and smoke-filled clubs, after leaving *Kabarett Seks* earlier in the evening. She tilted her head away from Helga, presumably so she could work on the bruises and scrapes more easily, but the motion was fraught with wistful longing.

"I just wanted so much for him to like me...to want me," sighed Lolita.

A young man had taken a fancy to her at the last club she went to and as they spent time together laughing and toasting the evening away, he became enamored with her. As his eros turned more lustful with each drink, Lolita eventually found herself guiding the handsome younger man out of the club and around a dark corner. She knew it was a foolish thing to do, but she had longed so much for someone to accept her as normal, if only for the night. At first, the young man was confused by what he found. When her gentleman had already gone too far, he looked at her in disbelief at first, then with revulsion. He looked down at himself, still mostly dressed, as if he had been contaminated. She could see it in his eyes. Instant, angry sobriety. He straightened up, drawing something from behind. Despite the surrounding darkness, Lolita saw a glint of light near his hand.

"Well let's just say he won't be calling on me anytime soon," Lolita added flippantly.

"I'm so sorry," was all Helga could say. She knew the anguish Lolita was going through but didn't want to seem presumptuous.

"So you met Dr. Freda when you were in college?" Lolita asked, changing the subject.

"Yes. It was my first year in my associates studies before I went to nursing school," confirmed Helga.

"Then when did you...*do the deed?*" Lolita asked with a completely inappropriate suggestiveness in her voice giving the universal scissor snipping motion with her fingers.

"I wasn't even thinking about it back then," Helga said. "I was suffering so much from trying to be someone other than who I was that I was a long way from that point when Dr. Freda came into my life." She paused, contemplating those early days with Dr. Freda. "She helped me understand that I was making myself suffer by trying to make other people happy."

"Well at least she showed you how *not* to dress!" quipped Lolita.

"Very funny," deadpanned Helga. "I'm sure you knew how to dress on your very first day, did you?"

"Honey, of course I did! I didn't spend all those years in the closet for nothing!" Lolita tossed.

Helga's serious demeanor broke and the two of them shared a giggle. It was refreshing.

"See? *There* she is. Freda loves you, honey," Lolita said, her voice falling to a soft, matronly tone. "You don't smile enough, little girl! How else are you supposed to get these wrinkles if you don't smile?" Lolita waved her hand under her own chin as if to display her gorgeous countenance before resting her eyes back on Helga's. "So tell me. Why would you do something so drastic...and painful? I like my precious little soldier too much to cut him loose!"

"Well that's because you have a man's life to go back to," Helga replied. Suddenly realizing that what she said might have been insulting, she followed, "I'm sorry. I didn't mean that."

"Yes you did. And you are right to say so," Lolita assured. "So...the snip, snip?"

Helga's eyes went wide and Lolita knew she had found the stab wound. She turned to look into Lolita's eyes with urgency. "We have to get you upstairs to the emergency room." As Helga shifted her weight to stand, Lolita placed a hand on her shoulder. Helga reversed her motion and went back down on one knee, looking at Lolita imploringly.

"I don't want to answer questions about this." Lolita did not have to explain. She knew Helga was a smart girl. She would figure it out.

Helga searched her thoughts and realized that this incident becoming public could finish Horace's career. She leaned in close to examine the cut. It had filled with blood and clotted, but the clot was still shiny so it would be easy to remove. She would have to probe the wound to determine how deep it was so Dr. Freda could decide if any of the underlying shoulder structures had been compromised. From the apparent angle, the bursa may have been punctured and that would require more advanced treatment.

Helga went to the front room again and returned wearing gloves and carrying a pair of thin forceps, several long swabs, and a brown bottle of iodine solution. She stood before Lolita, wishing she did not have to hurt her. She applied the iodine liberally and some dripped down Lolita's arm. "Well," Helga began with an exasperated stare. "I'm sorry but I need to clean this cut out. This is going to hurt."

She raised a swab to the wound.

"A sweet young thing like you couldn't begin to hurt me...sssss!" Lolita sucked in through a grimace as Helga pulled the cut open to clean inside with a swab.

"This is going to require stitches after Dr. Freda has a look," Helga informed her.

"Do everything you can to preserve this beauty, honey. Its expiration date is coming up fast!" Lolita joked, but Helga could see the concern in her eyes.

Helga turned her attention to her work with a smile, but she sympathized with Lolita's flippant statement. Even at this age, she was beginning to realize the fleeting nature of life. She would sometimes ache a little after a long day of hard work and hangovers seemed to be lasting longer lately too.

Helga paused working, realizing something. "You know, you've never asked me about my transition before. Why now?"

Lolita had her face turned away, Helga thought to bear the pain of cleaning the wound, but when she turned to face Helga, Lolita's eyes were glistening. She blinked and a tear fell onto her cheek, making its way downward through the thick makeup. "Because you know who you are and I'm still lost."

The coffee smelled strong and the aroma of fresh pastry baking helped Freda tamp down the nausea from last night's drinking. The sun was too bright and the echo of the scattered conversations off the walls of the small cafe were especially piercing this morning. Her headscarf helped to shield her from some of the light, but nothing could be done about the noise.

The waitress, Zofia, knew a hangover when she saw one and did not try to strike up a conversation. Freda had been coming to her mother's cafe for many months and had become a welcome sight most mornings. Her brother ran the cafe in the evenings, she in the mornings, but the secret to its popularity was their mother and father. Gretta grew up in Poland around the turn of the century and, as she told the story, was a master baker before she was ten. Piotr had been making sausage since he was a boy and when they met in war-torn Austria in the twenties, their passion for food was a dominant theme in their relationship. Married for nearly sixty years, they rarely spoke, but worked together like the most seasoned athletic team, weaving around each other in the kitchen and even passing pots and pans to each other without being asked. They simply knew what had to be done and did it.

"May I bring you anything else?" she asked Freda as she set down a plate with a croissant, honey, and butter.

"No. Thank you, dear." Freda looked up to see the sympathy in the girl's eyes, but could not tolerate the light, so she quickly looked down again.

The old wooden door creaked loudly as someone entered, then a shadow fell over Freda's table as a masculine figure with heavy footsteps approached. He pulled the chair out and sat down roughly. Freda very nearly became ill when his body odor wafted across the table, so she brought the coffee to her lips hoping the strong aroma would drown out the offensive odor. It helped a little so she held the cup longer after taking a sip.

In a heavily accented blend of French and German, he observed with a sigh, "Well, it seems someone had a rough night."

"I don't know what you mean." Freda was only half joking, knowing that her present condition was obvious to anyone who had experienced it for themselves.

"Of course you don't." His gruff reply was typical for him, but she understood that his response was a caring one.

He took a flask from his vest pocket and held it out to Freda, but the thought of putting her lips where his had been, stinking the way he did, nearly made her vomit. Viktor was a kind and gentle man, but Freda was certain no one would ever know that by looking at him. His face was greasy and dirty as usual and his clothes were easily three days old and caked under the arms with white salty patches and yellow stains dried into the brown fabric. He was probably younger than thirty but his sun-aged skin bore the wrinkles of time and grief.

He got comfortable as the waitress approached with a subdued scowl on her face. No doubt she thought he might be some sort of vagrant and didn't appreciate having him here, but he and Freda had business to discuss.

"Coffee and bacon please." He did not look up, but clearly expected her to have heard him. He drew out a crushed pack of cigarettes and slid one out of the pack. It appeared to be as mangled and dirty as he was. He flicked his lighter and sucked the flame deep into the end as the cigarette glowed brightly. He held the smoke in for a moment and blew to the side; a gesture that Freda greatly appreciated. He sat looking at Freda, waiting for her to collect herself.

As Freda drank her coffee and Viktor smoked over his cup, she became aware of him staring at her. When she finally looked straight into his eyes, she knew something was wrong. His kind eyes were hard, as if he were containing something, deliberately being stoic. Freda's own discomfort subsided somewhat as her instincts told her to prepare herself.

"So I have something to tell you." Viktor took his coffee with his cigarette hand which had a centimetre of ash already cracked and ready to fall. He swigged his coffee as if it were rough liquor and when he set the cup down the ash dropped onto the table. "You know the young man Liam, do you?"

As Freda leaned forward, Zofia was suddenly there and reached between them to refill their cups. The silence of the suspended question hung heavy in the air while they waited and once the waitress walked away, Freda leaned further forward. He did not. He maintained a relaxed, or perhaps tired, posture leaning back against the uncomfortable chair. He put his cigarette out as she responded.

"I do." Freda waited.

"Liam is dead." Viktor had no patience for prevarication or drama. That was for city boys and women. His vocation was more substantial, or at least that's what he thought. He looked Freda directly in the eyes and held them for a long moment.

Freda felt that this was an appropriate expression of respect coming from him. She met Liam just after he joined their group. He was an angry young man, filled with frustration and hatred, but as they worked together she saw his rage soften and his wisdom grow. She knew that, given time, he would come to accept all the bad things that had tainted his life and would one day be happy again.

"Liam is dead?" She wasn't stunned. She only wanted confirmation.

"Yes," Viktor replied with a curt nod. "We found him this morning." He drew his cigarette pack out and lit another.

"May I ask how it happened?"

Viktor drew on his cigarette in such a way that he would get as much out of it as possible without burning his fingers. The wince on his face and the smoke that seeped from between his teeth told her he had misjudged this one. He crushed the cigarette out and leaned back again.

"He was on a watch last night and someone caught him. We found him with a knife in his back. His target has disappeared."

Freda sat back in her chair and looked down at her coffee, which she hadn't sweetened yet. It didn't seem right for the two of them to be sitting there enjoying coffee, croissant, and bacon when poor Liam had just been killed.

"I'm so sorry," Freda offered.

"I'm sure he would thank you." Viktor pulled out the next cigarette when his bacon arrived. Instead of putting the cigarette away, he lit it and picked up a rasher. "I'm telling you this because I don't want you to find out from someone else and get upset." He crunched as he chewed. Freda's stomach flipped when he took a drag of his cigarette through a mouthful of bacon.

As Freda and Viktor both recovered from their evening's trials, they got caught up on current events in the group. Spread across most of the European countries and down through Africa, Nazi hunting teams worked on the nearly impossible task of bringing escaped war criminals to justice. His particular cell did mostly information gathering since they operated in the major cities in Germany. They observed, often for weeks, sending their information through the network where it somehow got to the appropriate people who would sometimes ask them for more direct intervention.

Liam had been on a team that was observing a character they thought to be funneling money to a group of Nazis in Argentina. He was hiding in a tiny apartment overlooking the street on which his team's target lived. He showed promise and demonstrated discipline so his team leader decided that he didn't need supervision for this target, but he was wrong. Liam or someone else from his team must have been seen getting into position sometime over the last week and Liam paid for that mistake with his life. The flat was a single room, so there was no way he would have missed someone entering. From the position of the body, it appeared he had been held down from behind. The knife had been expertly placed into his heart, but anyone who has seen men bleed to death know that it doesn't happen that quickly. Since no one in the adjacent flats had been disturbed, Liam must have been kept quiet somehow as he died, but there was no sign of a struggle, no sign of forced entry, and nothing left on the body or in the room.

Freda took a thick envelope from her jacket pocket and passed it to Viktor across the table. She did her best not to appear nervous as she did so and Viktor watched her in amusement as she exposed herself trying to be clandestine with an envelope under her hand on the table top in plain view of the entire establishment. He even made her wait a moment before leaning forward to take the envelope, just for the entertainment. As he took the envelope, he spirited it to his own pocket in a fluid movement that made Freda's puerile attempt at secrecy seem even more obvious.

"I put a little something extra in there for you and the group," Freda smiled graciously.

"I told you to stop doing that." Viktor gave her a stern look, but an appreciative one. "It is very kind of you," he tempered his reprimand with reluctant thanks. His gratitude may have been grudging, but not because he was ungrateful. Freda well knew that this was a calling, a vocation. Each of them had their own reasons and they did not need rewards to do what they did. He could see in her eyes that his thanks had been received. She was one of the few women he knew that he could be himself with and not think that she would take offense. There was something else. He could tell she was hesitating. "Out with it," he demanded.

"I want some information on a man who may be a danger to me, and some others." She took out a small picture twice the size of a postage stamp. It was Günther Schumacher's employee portrait taken when he was hired at the Wiesenhof.

She slid it across the table to him and he leaned forward to take it with a sigh. He was becoming a little impatient with how obvious this doctor was being. He picked the small square up and examined the image.

"What can you tell me about him?"

"I think he was a medical officer at Auschwitz. I will know more about him later today, but it is not him I want information about. Horace has uncovered some transactions that may lead to the man he worked for. Horst Schumann escaped Germany, but we may have gotten close to finding him. He transferred over one hundred thousand *Deutsche Marks* to the man in the photograph and then this man attacked one patient, visited another at home, and may be responsible for breaking into an associate's office. This seems like too much to be coincidence."

His eyes wide with interest now, Viktor said, "I agree. You might want to think about going away for some time."

"I can't do that. Last night, some people who are helping me drugged him in a club. I am going to find out what they know later this morning."

"You *drugged* him?" Viktor was incredulous. He examined her face more closely and seeing that she was being entirely truthful, sat back. "Didn't know you had it in you."

Freda appreciated the back-handed compliment. As she laid out what Horace had explained to her, she found herself becoming confused. Understanding the intricate details of international financial transactions was not one of her strengths, so when she could see that he was also becoming confused, she decided on another course of action.

"Would you come with me to meet them?" Freda's invitation came out like a child hoping a parent would grant them a wish.

"Ya, sure." Viktor hadn't even looked up when he answered. He was drawing out another cigarette.

Helga and Lolita heard the front door open with a crack of sticking paint as Dr. Freda arrived. Neither of them moved for a long moment and Dr. Freda came in sorting through the post she had retrieved from the mailroom on her way down. As she walked through the inner door, she stopped short. Lolita was sitting in her chair with Helga kneeling next to her dabbing at an abrasion on her shoulder. Freda's heart dropped when she realized that the previous evening must not have gone as planned. Her mind raced, but she did her best to suppress any visible sign of what she was thinking.

Recognizing Dr. Freda, Helga went back to work sanitizing and dressing the shoulder wound.

"Good morning, *Frau Lipschitz*. It appears you had an eventful night? Have you been here a long time?"

"Yes, *Doktor*." Lolita didn't indicate which question she was answering leaving Freda in silent panic, but Lolita's eyes darted to Helga and back to Freda indicating that she would explain later when they could speak in private.

"How are you feeling?" she asked.

Helga did not give Lolita the chance to answer. "Several bruises and abrasions and I am working on a stab wound. She won't let me take her to Emergency."

Dr. Freda's eyes belied her concern as she came closer to see the wound. Helga gave her room and manipulated the opening of the cut so she could see down into it. "Have you given her something for the pain?"

"Not yet. Once this is clean, I was going to apply some lidocaine."

"It seems Nurse Helga is taking good care of you. Would you agree?" Freda asked. Her voice trembled with something like anguish and Helga glanced up at her. She realized that she had not maintained her professional detachment and Helga had noticed the momentary lapse.

Freda realized that Helga was becoming suspicious. In this short exchange, she had already stolen a few glances at Freda's and Lolita's faces. She was a smart girl and she was beginning to figure out that something was passing unspoken between them, so Freda decided she had to give Helga a plausible reason to leave the room. "Helga, would you please reschedule any appointments I have this morning? I am expecting a rather eccentric guest and Mrs. Gorski will be joining us as well. Also, please call the orderly station and ask them to send young Master Frank to Mr. Krämer's house to bring suitable clothing and shoes," Dr. Freda requested with authority.

Helga could tell that she was being dismissed, but she stood obediently saying, "Yes, doctor." She used some alcohol and a fresh gauze pad to clean her hands, then collected the bloodied cotton and swabs with a clean cloth and went to the front room to dispose of them. As she pulled the door closed, her eyes met Dr. Freda's and in that instant the doctor knew that it wouldn't be long before Helga began prying. Sooner or later, she would require an explanation for the meager funds even though the practice was thriving, for the unscheduled visits with strangers who were not patients or faculty, and for why she seemed to spend an inordinately long time in meetings with a few select patients.

Setting the post down on the corner of her desk, Freda moved to the spot Helga had occupied and, kneeling quite a bit more slowly than the younger woman, she resumed treating Lolita's wound. She didn't know where to begin. Her heart was pounding and the feelings of guilt and of not knowing what had unfolded the night before threatened to overwhelm her. She took some fresh gauze from the tray, doused it with alcohol, and set about cleaning the shoulder laceration so she could determine if stitches might be needed.

"What happened?" Freda asked without looking up at Lolita's face.

Lolita could feel Freda's fear through her touch and placed a hand on the back of the hand Freda was cleaning her shoulder with causing Freda to hold still.

"It's alright. Everyone is safe and no one got hurt, at least during the mission. It went pretty much as planned."

Freda looked up into Lolita's eyes and the smile Lolita wore told of her sincerity. She cast her eyes downward and took a deep breath which helped to calm her nerves. Then something occurred to her and she looked back up at Lolita.

"Then how did this happen?" Dr. Freda asked.

"Let's just say that I don't like leaving a man unsatisfied, so after we got rid of her date I went out on a little mission of my own. Unfortunately, *that* mission had casualties."

There was a commotion as someone came through the front door, then cast a shadow on the frosted glass. Gabby flung the door open frantically looking for Freda, but when she saw Lolita, her panic abated.

Lolita flashed a catty grin at Gabby who rolled her eyes and gave an exasperated sigh as she closed the door behind her. Gabby draped her fur coat over the back of a chair as she pulled it away from the visitor's side of the desk. From Freda's perspective, she could see that the bottom of the coat was wet and soiled.

Gabby collapsed into the chair locking eyes with Lolita as she did so. "I have had a team out searching for you all night!"

"Keep your voice down," Dr. Freda cautioned.

Gabby gave Freda a knowing glance, lowered her head, and took a deep breath to calm herself. After several seconds, she looked up at Lolita who was expecting a verbal lashing, but instead of berating her, she simply said, "Well, I'm glad you aren't dead."

Freda saw the looks they shared and she knew all would be well between them once they calmed down. She determined that stitches would not be necessary and she began to close the wound with butterfly bandages, taking great care so Lolita would have minimal scarring. When she finished working, she set the used gauze and swabs on the tray, placed a hand on the side of the desk, and heaved herself to her feet. It wasn't that she was getting old. She was just in mid-life, but Freda did not exercise, did not eat as healthy as she should, and drank too much. She knew these behaviours were beginning to catch up to her.

She stood there for a moment, waiting for Lolita to get the hint that she wanted her chair back. Once she realized this, Lolita rose and the two squeezed past each other in the small space. Freda sat in her swivel chair and Lolita moved to the chair at Gabby's side, where she sat patiently waiting. Once all were settled, Gabby began speaking, but Freda held up her hand.

"We have a lot to cover this morning, but that will have to wait for a little while. This morning I met with Viktor. He has some unfortunate news, so I have asked him to join us this morning. He should be here any minute."

They looked at the door where they heard the front door open followed by someone talking. Then they saw someone approach, casting a shadow on the frosted window before the knob turned. Master Frank stepped through with a garment bag of black canvas draped over one arm and a pair of fine black patent-leather shoes in the other hand. Lolita gave him a seductive wave of her fingertips and a silent pucker that made Gabby roll her eyes.

"Thank you, Master Frank. Please leave them on the chaise." Freda gestured to the far side of the room. It took a moment for Frank to come to his senses, staring at Lolita's smeared makeup, bandages, and dirty gown, before he did as Dr. Freda asked. As he did so, Lolita rose, composed herself, and sauntered around the desk, catching Frank before his exit so he had to pass close by her to escape. She clearly enjoyed the young man's discomfort. She collected her *Horace* clothes from the chaise and headed for the door. As she approached Helga in the front room, the young woman gave her an intensely curious stare.

"Just stop, honey. That is none of your business so don't be asking," chided Lolita with one finger raised instructively. With that, she headed for the front door tossing the garment bag over her shoulder. Without looking back said, "I'm off to the little boy's room."

As Freda's eyes focused from Lolita's receding form to Helga's face peeking through the door, she realized that Helga was staring at her with an impatient, demanding tilt to her head. Freda gave a kindly frown shaking her head back and forth slightly sending the signal to Helga that now was not the right time to inquire. Helga got the message and the demanding look melted from her face as her trusting professionalism once again took hold. Helga moved out of view to the left as the wheels on her stool squeaked in protest and Freda felt her respect for the girl increasing. She had underestimated Helga, expecting the wheedling of a child, but instead had been given a rather adult level of deference. She would soon have to show her the same respect by including her in the group, but not today.

Gabby rose from her chair to move to the open door. Closing it slowly and quietly so as not to alert Helga, she put her ear close to, but not on the window, since doing so would be obvious if viewed from the other side. She allowed a few moments of silence to pass before she returned to her seat.

"She's so young!" Gabby remarked in a hushed voice so Helga could not hear her if she happened to be listening.

"Yes, she is. Far too young to get involved," replied Freda as she met Gabby's eyes.

"Can you tell me what happened to Horace last night?" Freda asked.

"He got sloppy," Gabby snapped with a tinge of anger. Then, softening, she added, "He could have been seriously hurt." She looked away so Freda could not see the concern and anguish in her eyes. Maintaining a stern voice, she added, "I had no idea what happened to him last night."

"Well, he is here now and he is safe. I didn't see any serious injuries...at least he hasn't complained of anything serious." Freda realized that the last statement wasn't helping. She could see the concern rising in Gabby's face. "We can go into the mission later, but how did you two get separated?"

Gabby told Freda what she knew of what happened after Jürgen left *Kabarett Seks*, but she carefully avoided any details of the mission itself, since it would be disrespectful to Horace if she should start without him. Last night may not have ended well, but Gabby was actually impressed with Lolita's ability to handle the situation. Her timing was impeccable.

With an awful ruckus in the front room, the door opened and Horace entered looking like a million-frank boxer in a fine new suit. Gabby thought the bruises on his face and split lip made him quite manly.

With carefully controlled anger, Gabby gritted her teeth and stage-whispered, "What happened to you last night?"

"I just stepped out to have a little fun. Don't be so upset. I can take care of myself," Horace assured, flippantly.

Horace sat with one knee over the other leg, leaning back in his chair...still acting like Lolita. Seeing the anguish on Gabby's face, he placed a hand gently on the back of her arm and held the touch for a moment. Gabby's anger seemed to evaporate and she relented, placing her free hand on Horace's with a smile and a slow blink. Horace looked at Freda with patient interest.

Just then, they heard the front door open and Viktor's gravelly voice asked for the doctor. Gabby rose again and opened the door, recognizing his baritone. It seemed to Freda, just for an instant, that she might reach out to hug the man, but she stepped out of his way as he crossed the threshold. He looked left, up, right, and appearing satisfied, came into the room. Four people in this office made the space feel cramped and his instincts were warning him that this was not the best situation to be in, but he trusted Freda and she trusted him. He looked at Gabby, standing beside him, still holding the door knob, touched the brim of his grimy beret with a little nod. She directed him to her chair, but seeing the fur coat, he decided he would rather stand and let her have the chair back. He stepped behind the chair and pulled it toward him, offering it to Gabby. She closed the door and took the chair with a grand flourish, overdoing the high-class lady act, making him smile.

"So is the girl going to sit out there?" Viktor asked bluntly and a bit too loudly.

Demonstrating the controlled volume she expected of him, Freda answered, "Yes. She doesn't know much and I would appreciate keeping it that way for the time being."

"Good." Viktor's manner was not approving or disapproving. He was merely acknowledging her decision. "So, Liam is dead."

Freda closed her eyes and bowed her head. The man had no tact whatsoever.

Horace and Gabby were stunned. Gabby, still in the afterglow of his chivalry, went pale and all emotion and energy drained from her. Horace, who had been about to say something comedic at their exchange, closed his mouth and the Lolita character fell away. The room remained silent and they were all content with that for a while.

"How..." Gabby began.

"How did it happen." Viktor's interruption wasn't a question. It was a statement that belied his impatience. He would have to recount the murder of his young friend once again.

As Viktor described how Liam had been found and speculated about how he might have died, he gave details and answered questions as they arose. It had been less than half a day and he had already begun to feel distant from the events of the previous night. He wasn't upset with himself for letting this happen again. He was just observing how much more quickly it was happening with each friend lost.

"Mrs. Gorski, you and Liam were close, weren't you?" Viktor asked.

Gabby had a strong sexual attraction to Liam, but every time they met, she sensed the handsome young man harbored such strong anger that she did not dare try to get close. Still, she reasoned that if he were that angry, it was unlikely that he would choose to be close to anyone, so she flirted with him, teased him playfully, but never went too far with him.

Once, she had come down a hallway at one of the cell's safehouses and saw Liam through an open door at the end of the hall. These were the sleeping quarters for the men and the doors on the occupied rooms should be closed, but this was one of the only places the men could be careless without risk, so they often were. She had slowed her pace, being careful not to click her heels on the floor as she approached. He was facing away from her, pulling his boxers up and flinging the sheets over where he slept. He obviously slept nude. His body was beautiful. Gabby had to consciously hold her mouth closed as he stretched, reaching over his head and back, loosening the sleep from his muscles. His rump was firm and the two dimples just above each buttock made Gabby's hormones rush. The juvenile beauty of his body held her captivated as he bent over to pick up a shirt from a trunk beside the bed and, pulling it over his head, the contours of his side and chest were highlighted by the overhead lamp. As he brought the shirt down around his torso, he turned his head and saw Gabby standing there.

He wasn't embarrassed, just shy. He smiled with his head tilted down and his eyebrows raised in the most adorable puppy dog look and she found herself in total and complete lust for him. She didn't let that show. She only smiled modestly as she turned away and retreated back down the hall. The image of his beautiful body would be burned into her memory forever, but now that beautiful body was a form of cold, dead flesh, violated by another man who meant him harm. He would never grow out of the anger he bore. She would never get the chance to kiss his lips. At such a young age, he would never again know intimacy with a woman. She regretted not trying to get to know him better and felt guilty that her thoughts of him were so carnal.

Horace was heartsick. He felt guilty that his careless sexual escapades were probably going on as Liam's life was ending. That beautiful boy. Gone. It was just horrible that someone could do something so despicable while he was out gallivanting around being led by his dick. He felt ashamed. The value he placed in clothes and feathers and drinking and men...were unworthy pursuits. He suddenly had the thought that Liam couldn't possibly be the first man killed in the cell. He wouldn't dare ask Viktor how many he had lost, but he began to wonder, just how many lives does it take to turn a man into Viktor, distant and cold?

Viktor had no wish to let the group suffer in silence, so he broke in. "Our friend, the doctor here, has been very generous to my team and it seems now is the time to repay her. She tells me that someone may be after you and it seems that you've carried out a little *operation* of your own. Let's begin by you telling me what you learned from your *unsuspecting* spy." His inflection of the word *unsuspecting* let everyone in the room know that he was having trouble believing either that he was unsuspecting or that they had found a spy, but he was willing to listen.

As Gabby and Horace took turns describing what they had done to Jürgen, drugging him and playing with his hormones to extract information, Viktor and Freda sat listening, nodding, and thinking. When Horace began describing how he and Gabby had toyed with the man's arousal under the table, Viktor raised an eyebrow, but said nothing. The slightest twist at the corners of his mouth was the only indication that he found the episode humorous. Gabby confirmed how each drugged drink had affected the man's control and Freda's nodding indicated that they had dosed him properly. They continued to the point when Gabby lost track of Lolita. Of course, she could have gone on longer, but though she was angry at having lost track of her, she felt no need to embarrass him in front of Viktor simply for the righteous thrill.

"You are some of the luckiest people I know," Viktor responded after a pause long enough for him to be sure they were finished. He didn't say it with admiration or humor. The room was silent as Gabby, Freda, then Horace gradually figured out that his tone was reprimanding. Each in turn lowered their eyes as he stared them down.

"I like you people. I would not want the last thing I know of you to be some..." he gestured with his hand in loops punctuating "...*cowboy operation*..." with a subdued flourish. Looking directly at Freda, he stated, "You should have called me." Now it was his turn to look down in disappointment.

Gabby felt she was being scolded which inflamed her conviction. "We are not children," she blurted before she could stop herself.

"No, you are not. That is why you should have known better." His rebuke stung just enough to remind the group that they were, in fact, amateurs at the very thing he risked his life doing every day. "I could have had men in the crowd to protect you if something went wrong, but instead you decided to act on your own. I could have made sure you didn't get hurt." Looking directly into Gabby's eyes, then into Freda's, his chivalry was apparent and his concern was not about the operation, but about his friends.

The group sat quietly, considering the parts of their plan that could have benefited from having experienced men there. They knew they were in the wrong here and no one felt like arguing.

"So you think you have identified Schumann in Sudan. You have records that say it is him, but you do not have a visual confirmation. Schumann has apparently hired someone to track you down and this person has all the information he needs to get to all three of you because your inquiries were discovered." Looking at Horace now, his eyes showed his accusation.

Freda broke in. "That is all correct. What we need to know is where to go from here."

"Whatever you do, I suggest not being so sloppy about it," Viktor scolded Freda, but his face held concern, not blame. "You have helped me and my people many times when we needed it, but you did not even think of letting *me* help *you* set your operation up properly." He paused to look among the group. "I want you to promise to include me in the future."

"Why do you think I asked you here this morning?" asked Freda, letting the question hang in the air.

"Fair enough," he replied. "Do you have any plans that you haven't told me about?"

In unison, the group responded "No" and shook their heads. None of them knew what to do now that they knew that someone experienced in torture and murder was coming after them.

"First, we tie up the loose end you let walk out of the club last night." Viktor's voice now rang with the timbre of a school teacher. "I would have had men outside to take him and hold him. It sounds to me that you left him in no condition to put up a fight." He smiled unexpectedly. "Now that is something I would like to have seen." He chuckled to himself, grudgingly admiring the little troupe of spies before him. He took out the small picture Freda had given him earlier and showed it to Gabby and Horace in turn. "What can you tell me about his appearance now that is different from this picture?"

"In that picture, he had a bit of a beard. He shaved that before I met with him." Gabby squinted in the dim light to see the picture more clearly. "The picture is recent, so his skin is the same."

"He might be walking with a limp after last night," Horace added jokingly, sharing a smile with Gabby.

"Now what can you tell me about the man you think is Schumann?" Viktor asked, putting the picture back into his breast pocket.

Horace took his cue and began explaining the various financial transactions he had traced back to Schumann including the recent payment to Jürgen. He explained how each bank kept its records and how those records connected together to form a trail, but as he got into the intricacies that *he* found fascinating, he saw Viktor's attention begin to falter, so he began to dumb it down. As he took them through the various connections that led to Schumann translating each into layman's terms, Viktor began to understand that there might be a way he could help.

"Could you send money to Schumann yourself? Maybe an unannounced gift from a sympathetic Nazi collaborator?" Viktor appeared to be hatching a scheme in his mind.

"I don't see why not," Horace confirmed.

To Freda, Viktor asked, "Could you provide some money for such a payment?"

Freda considered it for a moment and then replied, "I think I can put enough together in a few days' time."

To Horace again, he asked, "Would you be able to tell me exactly when the transaction would show up at the bank in Sudan? What city did he say?"

"We think he meant to say Khartoum. If I sent the money with special instructions, yes. I think I could make it available with about a day's notice."

"How would we bring Schumann to the bank if he isn't expecting the money?" Viktor was out of his element on this.

Horace thought out loud. "We would have to notify him. It would have to be something that would not alarm him. Maybe from someone he already knows...but how would we find someone he already knows?"

Viktor's eyes gleamed and his eyebrows popped up suddenly. "You have already met someone he knows."

Realizing that Viktor meant Jürgen, Freda was intrigued. "But how would we get him to send money to Dr. Schumann if Schumann was sending him money?"

"My men should be able to find out where he receives letters." Looking at Horace, he continued, "Do you think you could intercept his banking channels?"

Horace considered carefully and confirmed, "I think so."

"Now this part is important. Can you redirect a message coming through the bank so Jürgen never sees it?"

"I am certain I could," Horace responded.

"Could you send a message back in his place?" Viktor asked.

"Yes." By now, Horace had thought through the entire process of bank communications and was certain he could take over as Jürgen's intermediary.

"Then here is what we will do." Viktor spent nearly half an hour laying out his idea to use Jürgen's banking connection to Schumann to manipulate Schumann's movements in Sudan. "There is just one problem left," he admitted after the lengthy explanation. "Someone who knows him will have to visually identify him when we capture him."

Gabby looked around the group. "Well, other than Albert, I am the only other one who could identify him."

"It would mean that when the time comes, you would have to go to Khartoum to work with our men down there." Viktor gave Gabby a look indicating that this was not a decision to be taken lightly.

Freda broke in saying "When the time comes, we will all go see him brought to justice."

Gabby looked quizzically at Freda. "You know that the trip will take weeks?"

Freda nodded.

"What about your practice?" Gabby wondered why she would want to go through the trouble and expense of being there herself, but Freda did not answer.

Chapter 28

"Thank you so much for meeting me so early," Dr. Freda said. She rose from her seat as Hugo and Maria approached the table in the cafe. Zofia was pouring a fresh cup of coffee for the doctor, so she stepped back and waited for the older couple to take their seats. The three shook hands in turn and sat, asking for coffee and bagels which Zofia went to retrieve.

"You said you had some information for us about one of the boys you were searching for?" Maria asked, trying not to think the worst.

Dr. Freda heard the worry in her voice. "It is not anything bad, just...different. I thought it might be better to discuss this in a more relaxed setting before we head over to the Wiesenhof." She saw Maria's worry transform to curiosity, so she continued, "I told you on the telephone that in addition to meeting Albert, you would also meet Gabriel."

Maria smiled and sat up straighter. She was not hiding her anticipation for the meeting. "It has been so long. I wonder if we will recognize him."

Dr. Freda's forehead wrinkled and her eyebrows raised. "I don't think you will." Hugo and Maria looked at each other questioningly and then at Dr. Freda in confusion. "Gabriel is not Gabriel anymore. He was blessed with some opportunities to, let's say, improve on what was done to him."

Now they were even more confused. Hugo asked, "So was he able to reverse the surgery?" Maria looked at him askance, knowing that no such technology existed. Hugo, seeing her reaction, adjusted his statement. "I mean to say." He paused, searching. "Well, I don't know what I mean to say." He surrendered hoping either Maria or the doctor would take control.

"To phrase it succinctly, Gabriel Köhler is now Mrs. Gabriella Gorski." Dr. Freda hoped she would not have to explain. While there had been much progress in the field of sexual psychology and surgical intervention, the uncomfortable nature of the topic meant that the public was generally ignorant of the possibilities. The Social Health Programs instituted after the war included education of the public, but that education was skewed toward things that concerned the general public, not specialties. Dr. Freda watched realization dawn on Maria's face but when she turned to Hugo, she saw only a blank stare as if he had not heard her.

She sought confirmation from Hugo. "Do you understand?"

Hugo felt that the whole room was staring at him. He saw that Maria did understand so he tried to quickly guess what Dr. Freda was trying to say. "But why would he get married if he could never..." He trailed off as the look on Dr. Freda's face told him he had guessed incorrectly.

"No, *he* did not get married. Gabriel is now Gabriella," Dr. Freda clarified slowly.

"Then who is Gabriella?" Perhaps Gabriel had found a missing relative? That must be it. Hugo felt that was probably it, but again, he could see that he was wrong.

Maria leaned toward him and placed a hand on his arm. "Gabriel is not a boy anymore." She watched Hugo's face as he stared at her. He wasn't grasping this simple idea. *Trying to talk to men sometimes requires a bit more patience,* she thought.

"Well, of course not. We both saw what was done to him." Hugo wondered why Maria felt it necessary to remind him of what they already knew.

Maria took a calming breath, resolving to try again. "Gabriel, the boy, became Gabriella, the woman."

Hugo replayed what she had said in his mind. *But boys grow up to be men, not women,* he thought. Then he began to think that maybe they were talking about the same person. *If Gabriel became Gabriella, that would mean he would have had more surgeries to give him...*

Finally, Dr. Freda and Maria began to see realization begin to take root. They exchanged glances with each other, mutually deciding that they should not do anything that would shame the poor man. His mind was just now going to a place it had not been before.

"How are you feeling this morning, Albert?" Dr. Freda was glad to see him sitting upright and writing in his journal. By the number of pages turned, she could tell that he had been hard at work. Still, she couldn't help but feel a little anxiety at seeing him with a sharp writing instrument in his hand.

Albert looked up after a moment of intense concentration, obviously finishing an important thought. He smiled at seeing Dr. Freda standing in the doorway. "I feel good today."

"May I come in?" Dr. Freda had begun treating Albert as if he were a guest instead of a patient. It might take many more months of treatment, but sooner or later he would have to be discharged and she wanted to keep that thought in his mind. Her attitude would have a motivating effect on his behaviour.

Albert invited her in saying, "Please," and gesturing to the chair at his bedside.

She stepped into the room toward the chair, slid it away from the wall, and sat facing Albert. "So, you know what is to happen today?"

"I have some visitors, don't I?" Albert's reply was one she might expect from someone looking forward to the event, but she could hear trepidation in his voice and in the subtle wave of tension that gripped his shoulders.

"You do. How do you feel about that?" she asked.

"Better than last week." He paused, averting his eyes.

Albert's reply carried with it a tinge of shame at the panic attack he had during their last session. Apparently he was not doing as well as he had previously thought. In that session they had discussed the memories that Hugo and Maria's impending visit brought up. At first, he was glad to hear of their plans to come to see him in Cologne, but as they talked through the memories, his heart began to race and he began to hyperventilate. He had recognized the physiological responses and begun to control his breathing without prompting which Dr. Freda had praised him for. They did not stop simply because he was having a strong emotional response. She taught him ways to control the severity of the attack, so they continued talking as she monitored his condition. They discussed that a similar response might happen during the actual visit and he promised to do his best to control his responses then too. They therefore considered the session a rehearsal for the upcoming visit.

"Give yourself some credit, Mr. Novak. You handled yourself quite well and you continued to function despite the discomfort. The important thing is that you did not let it overwhelm you."

He nodded in grudging agreement. "When will they be here?" he asked.

"They are checking in now. I will meet with them for a few minutes and then we will come to see you."

Albert nodded again and Dr. Freda rose just as there was a knock on the open door. An orderly had arrived with two extra chairs wanting permission to bring them in. Freda motioned to the other side of the bed and the young man hoisted the chairs over Albert's feet with some effort. Dr. Freda rolled her eyes at the orderly's carelessness as she headed out the door. Walking toward the front of the asylum, she heard the orderly close Albert's door with a loud thud that echoed around the large corridor.

As she approached Nurse Mila's station in the lobby, she could see an older couple talking with her. When she came close, they looked up at her expectantly. She came to stand with the desk between them.

"Good morning Mr. Jaeger and Mrs. Stromberger. I hope your trip wasn't too taxing." Dr. Freda held a rather stiff posture but extended her hand over the desk to each in turn.

The two decided not to change either of their names. He had built fame for himself, both before the war and during, and his name seemed to have escaped the rage now directed toward Nazi collaborators. He was seen more as a journalist who was allowed into the Nazi party but wasn't really a part of it. Maria had become known as *The Angel of Auschwitz* and though she had given up nursing by the time they married, she still preferred that the stories of what she had done not fade so quickly into history. Her keeping the name was a way to honour all those she could not save.

Maria was unable to contain her smile as she took Dr. Freda's hand. A single, slight shake of the hand and Maria's smile softened as she looked into the doctor's eyes. Freda found the woman's attention to be somewhat intense so she looked downward breaking eye contact as she stepped around the front desk. She raised her eyes to Hugo who looked at her stoically, but warmly. It seemed he wanted to take in her impression before he shook hands and the slight smile on his face showed that he approved. He squeezed her hand quite firmly, not shaking it. The expression of gratitude was apparent.

Hugo was a small man, about the same height as Freda. His glasses were tinted slightly, making his eyes a bit difficult to see. The frames were gold and black tortoiseshell with wingtip accents at the upper corners. He removed his hat and his hair was cut close with the hairline having receded long ago. Freda imagined that, at 63, he seemed the classic city dweller, worldly and sophisticated. His suit was a brown tweed with darker reddish cords woven through in a pattern of large squares and his vest and hat were made of the same. She knew little of his life before his personal fame was subsumed by the work he did as Hitler's personal photographer, but clearly he was a man of taste with good fashion sense. Still, Freda had the sense that he was a man burdened by memory. When approached by Hitler's staff and while following the brutal dictator around, he hadn't refused the work, or the pay. He didn't try to escape or avoid being around people who were suffering under the Nazi regime.

Maria radiated a love charged with energy and strength, but it was clear to Freda that, at 65 and suffering from heart disease, her body was no longer keeping pace with her mind. She was stooped and was still breathing heavily from the walk to the lobby. She was perspiring and her skin was pale. In their correspondence, Freda learned that she had suffered a major heart attack in 1957 which had nearly killed her. Her recovery took several years and her doctors were constantly telling her to rest and not to exert herself or she might have another heart attack. Just from these few moments in the woman's presence, Freda knew that she was not the resting type. It was clear that Maria lived and loved with gusto and would do so until her final breath.

"Our trip was just fine, thank you, Dr. Dudek. We both appreciate what you are doing here," said Hugo.

"Would you please follow me?" Dr. Freda turned to head back toward Albert's room, but knowing that Maria would become winded easily, she walked at a leisurely pace. She expected the two to follow behind her as Albert's parents had done, but they came to walk beside her, Maria on her left and Hugo on her right. Rather than feel affronted, she felt two kindred spirits were beside her. Maria's decades in nursing showed clearly given her comfort in this place. Unlike the average visitor who was often a parent, family member, or friend, Maria carried herself down these halls as a colleague would. Hugo had worked for one of the most frightening men in the world, so of course he would also be unphased by the stark surroundings.

As they came to Albert's room, Freda slowed about five metres short of the doorway. Hugo and Maria came around her and turned to take a position facing her with their backs toward the doorway. They stood listening as if ready to accept instructions from a commander, formally at ease.

Dr. Freda folded her hands in front of her, one over the other, as if she were about to give a speech. She looked each of them in the eyes allowing the seriousness of what they were about to do sink in. Hugo and Maria understood completely. They were not nervous, so Freda relaxed a bit. It did not appear to be necessary to prepare these two the way she had prepared Albert's parents and she did not want to insult their intelligence with a review of basic treatment concepts.

"Do you have any questions before we proceed?" Freda's words echoed in the hallway and faded away as Hugo and Maria considered. They looked at each other and a conversation appeared to pass between them in an instant of stillness. Then they looked at Freda, both resolved.

Hugo spoke for them both saying, "I do not believe so."

In truth, Maria was experiencing something strange. It had been a very long time since she had served in a nursing capacity. Certainly being in this place was no reason to feel what she was feeling. There had been many times when she would be threatened or even beaten for letting a patient die, or helping them live. There was no threat here, but she was almost certain she could hear the sounds of war. Doctors barking commands like soldiers, patients wailing as procedures and amputations were performed without anesthesia, the smell of death and decay.

Freda laid her hand on Maria's arm asking, "Are you alright?"

Maria realized that she must have been overcome by memories long enough for Freda to notice. Hugo was now looking at her with concern in his eyes. Maria placed her hand on Freda's. "I am." She collected herself and looked into Freda's eyes with confidence and conviction. "I am ready."

He could hear their voices outside his door. Freda's was easy to recognize, but the other two were almost too quiet to hear. He felt his heart rate beginning to rise when he heard the squeaking of Dr. Freda's shoes come to a stop in the hallway. It seemed that they were taking far too long to come in, but they also were not having a conversation, just some words exchanged, but the voices stirred memories. He couldn't understand the words through the door, but it seemed he could hear more than just the three of them. He couldn't help hearing of the sounds of the medical barracks where he had been altered. The smell of the sweat mixed with gunpowder on the soldiers when they came close. A shadow came over him as he sat on a blood-caked bench waiting for Dr. Schumann to examine his work, to see if he was healing. The stink of hot urine wafted up to his nose and he felt something wet cooling on his chest. His breathing came in short gasps and the room was spinning.

Albert had worked so hard to gain some modicum of control over himself and now he was devolving into a sniveling child again. This would not happen. As he became more aware of the room around him, he clamped down on the memories. He felt his stomach muscles tighten and he physically forced the memories down. He began timing his breathing and quickly realized that a breath every few seconds was not enough. His lungs were screaming at him to breathe faster, but he refused. This is all you can have. I will tell you what you can take from me...no more. A deep inhale...slowly now...holding the breath but not closing the throat...and gradually reversing the flow of air, slowly exhaling and pausing with lungs empty. His lungs were screaming at him to speed up. "No. *You* slow down." Talking to his body as if it were a child helped him to realize that what it thought it needed was not necessarily true. As his slower breathing reduced his heart rate, he realized that he had regained control.

The door cracked as the paint around the frame released it. It opened slowly revealing Dr. Freda and a shorter man standing behind her. As she came in, he came in behind her, but because he was the same height, Albert's perspective obscured the man's face. As Dr. Freda came in farther, he could see a woman's form behind her. As Dr. Freda stood to the side and the elderly man came in with his hat in his hands, Albert's heart leapt in his chest. The man smiled in a very controlled, almost apologetic way as the woman worked her way around him. She was impatient and when she came into view, she stopped suddenly. She looked at Albert for a moment, not sure of who she was seeing. Albert recognized her immediately. The man too.

"So it is you." Hugo tipped the hat in his hands toward Albert in a confirming gesture.

"Mein Lange vermisst." ("My long-lost one.") said the woman.

Albert let a breath escape as a gasp. He felt a tear slowing moving down his cheek, but he did not wipe it away. The couple stood in the doorway looking at Albert for a long time. Then, he realized they were waiting on him.

"Please come in," he said as he gestured to the extra chairs and Dr. Freda stepped back to allow them room to pass.

They made their way, she rather clumsily, and he dignified but halting, around the foot of the bed and to the chairs, but neither of them sat. The woman had a look of desperate restraint but she couldn't contain herself anymore. She rushed forward, wrapping her arms around Albert and lifting him upright so she could get her arms behind him. She poured all the love she had into the embrace and Albert felt the defensive control he was so committed to, melting away.

As he became aware of her scent, the room faded. He was cold, shivering, and he was wet. A man in a white coat stood over him gesticulating and shouting, but Albert could not see his face and his voice was muffled as if he were yelling through a pillow. He dared not look up or the man might kill him for being disrespectful. Suddenly a searing hot shock of pain spread out from his right ear, rapidly encompassing his jaw and neck. A loud ring further obscured the angry man's voice.

A woman's voice began to reprimand the man, shrill and equally as angry. The man did not seem to be accepting her authority. The muffled voices were arguing, that he could tell from their tone, but he still couldn't understand the words. The argument ran its course and the shouting subsided. Then a dark form came before him and stooped down to his level. Albert saw Maria's face. She had a sympathetic smile as she stroked his shoulders comforting him.

He could see that Maria was talking to him, but he couldn't quite hear through the ringing in his ears. He noticed that his surroundings had changed. He was now looking down at his adult form covered by a sheet. Maria was holding him by the shoulders and as she repeated herself, he began to understand her words. Dr. Freda stepped into view at his side placing a hand on his arm. He looked up at her.

"Yes, thank you, doctor. I am fine." Albert's voice trembled with restrained emotion. "I am sorry. This is all a bit overwhelming." Albert took a deep, controlled breath.

Constantly aware of the pounding in his chest, Albert realized that he was in a better condition than he thought he would be. He wasn't having to exert himself as much to regain control. It was only a memory. He slowly raised his eyes to meet Maria's and felt a weight rise from him that he hadn't realized was there. He expected this to be a tearful moment, but Maria's eyes were dry. So were his own.

Maria smiled and reached toward the chair immediately behind her. She drew it to the right so it aligned with Albert's head but she didn't bring it closer to the bed. This was an obvious cue to Hugo that it was his turn to assail Albert. A little slow to recognize the proper timing, Hugo stood in the corner holding his hat. A few heartbeats later, Maria turned to look at Hugo with an anticipatory expression and he edged forward.

"It is good to see you, son." Hugo addressed Albert with a reserved compassion as that of a father reuniting with a son long estranged. As he approached, he laid his hat at the foot of the bed and came to stand between Maria and Albert. Their shared discomfort with the ritual was obvious to all, so Hugo merely patted Albert's arm a few times, smiling. He retreated to the chair Maria pulled up beside her own and sat.

Maria was a champion no matter what situation she was in. Albert could see that the passion for making others' lives better burned just as bright in this woman as it had in the nurse who held his hand when he was recovering from surgery all those years ago.

"Will you please excuse me? I will be back in about an hour." Dr. Freda made a semi-formal bow, hands folded in front, and turned toward the door. Just as she was about to pull the doorknob, she heard Maria behind her, so she turned to look over her shoulder.

"Thank you," Maria said. "Thank you very much."

Dr. Freda nodded in acknowledgment and without a word, left the three alone in the bright, cold room. The latch clicked so loudly that it echoed around the room for several seconds as the three sat.

Maria began to speak, leaning forward, almost raising a hand and then interrupted herself, sitting back again.

"*You* have nothing to say?" He shook his head. "I knew I would see it *someday*, but I thought it would be on my deathbed."

Maria turned to look scoldingly at Hugo, but the love she felt for him radiated through the sourness and the two smiled at each other. Maria rested her hand on his as she turned to Albert, this time resolved to acquaint herself with the man he had become.

"I am so sorry you have had difficulties." She paused. That probably wasn't the best way to begin, so she tried again. "I have not seen you since you went to live with the Rabinowitz family. Please tell me about them."

The time passed quickly. Albert told Hugo and Maria about his two adopted sisters, about how he and Ernst had hid the periodic maintenance of his condition from Lena. He told them about Selma and Etta and how much he missed Selma when she went away to school; about leaving Etta when it was his time to go. He asked about what happened after they were separated. Hugo told Albert about being racked with fear as he carried photographs of the most hated man in the world with him through American occupied territory. Maria told him how she had continued to serve at The Red Cross hospitals after the Soviets liberated Auschwitz.

Just before she met Gabriel, Albert, and Lukas, she had fallen ill from a type of vasculitis that happens when people stand too long and lift too much weight over and over. It commonly happens to nurses, but can also happen to people addicted to certain narcotics which she was administering at the camp. She was ordered to leave by the commandant but when she made an impassioned plea, she convinced him to let her stay. It was only later that a patient told her that the French resistance had tried to get her out with a false claim of addiction. It seemed she had missed a chance to escape, but she was no stranger to risk.

In 1944, the Auschwitz complex was huge, encompassing ten blocks. Each block had its own commander, staff, and barracks. It spanned over a kilometre from end to end and was almost always a mud pit. Everyone there had accepted that from the moment they arrived, they would be muddy up to the knees. It was important not to stoop down or the mud would find a way to climb higher. Even though the commanders were not strict about mud on uniforms below the knees due to practicality, they still expected perfectly maintained and clean uniforms above.

As she made her way from block one to block ten, she struggled against the suction of the mud, expending the precious energy she needed to treat patients. She arrived a bit early to her station where three of the other nurses were just finishing their night shift. Usually, not much happened during the night shift, but Dr. Schumann had come in very early today to begin a new experiment and the nurses were all talking about it. One of them was in the surgical ward, which was just a room full of metal tables, and assisted Dr. Schumann. She was now pale with disbelief and recounted her observations to the other nurses under her breath when no one else was around.

Three boys had been sedated and taken to the surgical ward when no other surgeries were going on. Dr. Schumann did not simply castrate the boys. That was common, but he had completely removed their external sex organs. The procedures were so invasive that infection was a certainty. It would be the nurses' job to clean the wounds after the procedures and to try to prevent, or treat, any infection that might occur. Generally, those who became diseased or infected after sterilization were gassed and incinerated, but not these three. Dr. Schumann left specific instructions that these three should be retained and treated to the best of the nurses' abilities.

Maria read her assignments for the day, collected supplies in a bin, and prepared to begin her rounds. She packed some extra alcohol and gauze hoping that the man she had been treating for a gash on his leg was still alive. The wound itself was not bad, but the infection could become a problem and if it did, it would be a death sentence the minute any of the guards or doctors noticed.

She made her way through the bustling rooms in which were offices, examination rooms, nurses' stations, and inventory areas. Though it was well-organized, it was all packed in so tightly that it appeared chaotic. She wound her way from this area to that, turning corners carefully so as not to be run down by someone heading the other way. She emerged from the barrack doorway to find that several of the beds were empty. These would be filled again today by new patients with the old ones being incinerated by afternoon. The daily routine had been established ever since Rudolph Höss had solved the problem of burial space by installing incinerators adjacent to the gas chambers making the operation much more efficient.

Three beds stood out to her. About two-thirds of the way down the east wall were three young boys, struggling and moaning in pain. She checked her area quickly and finding no critical cases, she walked toward the three beds. Standing over them, her heart ached with sympathy for their suffering. She set her bin down at the foot of one bed and came to stand beside one of the boys. He did not seem to be fully aware yet when she took him by the arm. Turning his arm over, she matched the number tattooed there to one of the papers she had collected from her station. She read the details, checked his pulse, high; checked his temperature, slightly elevated; put her stethoscope to his chest, good clear breathing sounds. She poured a mixture of alcohol and water on a small cloth and wiped his forehead.

The boy's restless movements calmed and he opened his eyes slowly. He turned his head to look at her and she returned his gaze with a comforting smile.

"Wirst du mich sterben lassen?" ("Will you let me die?") the boy asked in a pitiable, squeaky voice.

Maria was not certain if he meant to ask her help to die or if she would prevent him dying, so she answered generically, *"Ich werde tun, was ich kann."* ("I will do what I am able.") She rested a hand on his arm in a soothing gesture and he seemed to relax, closing his eyes and whimpering softly. She prepared some gauze in a dish with alcohol added so she could dip the gauze and her fingertips into the solution without contaminating the whole bottle. She lifted the blankets from the foot of the bed rather than uncover the child. This would help him to feel both warm, still covered by the blanket, and distant from what she was about to do. She knew it would be painful.

As Maria was treating Gabriel, the boy tried his best to remain still, but there was so much seepage and the sutures were very sloppy. The skin was certainly not going to close properly. She talked with him as she cleaned his wounds. She thought a kind voice might distract him from what had been done to him.

She saw Hugo Jaeger come toward her from the staff area and she glanced up at him, giving him the briefest smile, hoping no one would ever see the way they felt about each other. He had two cameras strung around his neck. He was already perspiring from exertion and he seemed to be in a rush. As he came up behind her, he placed a hand on her shoulder.

"Meine Liebste. Ich bin froh, Sie zu sehen." ("My Dear, I am happy to see you.")

She knew that he wanted to express his affection openly but could not. She did as well, but it would not be safe to do so within the camp. It could be used as leverage against them by the Nazi party or any commander wanting to extort them. Catching Hitler's favourite photographer in a compromising position might be a great feather for someone's cap, so they were very careful to keep their feelings secret.

He dropped a small black metal canister into her skirt and she closed her knees to conceal it. Reaching between her thighs, she retrieved the canister, tucking it into a concealed pocket sewn into the folds of her skirt. The negatives would not change anything now, but in the future, they could be used as evidence against the Nazis. In either case, they would have to be hidden for now so as not to expose one of their most valuable insiders who could easily be located behind the lens if the images were disseminated too soon.

"Do you still have the picture I gave to you?" Hugo's question was blunt, but kind.

"I keep it here," Albert said as he reached across his chest to pat the journal lying on the side table. Then he realized that Hugo might like to see it, so he grasped the heavy volume and slid it into his lap letting the pen fall onto the sheets. He opened the back cover and drew the photograph out of its pocket. "I used to keep it in an old book my parents gave to me...the Rabinowitz'...*The Brothers Karamazov.*" He turned the photograph so Hugo could see it.

Hugo rose from his seat, peering through the bottom half of his bifocals, inspecting the well-worn photo. Stooping was uncomfortable, so he sat down after only a moment. Albert tucked the photo into the back pocket of his journal and placed the book back on the side table, setting the pen on top.

"I would like to tell you why I gave you that photograph." Hugo's tone was serious and Albert felt the room grow cold.

"Why did you?" Albert asked hesitantly.

"I thought that if you had some evidence of what had happened to you, that one day you might find your own justice."

Hugo's voice was tinged with guilt at not helping the boy more, but Albert the man had a very different opinion of Hugo as he thought back to his final months in the camp.

It was so cold that morning. The doctors told him to stay warm, but under a blanket caked with dirt and speckled with moth holes, it was impossible, so he shivered throughout the night. He awoke early that morning when a clap of thunder and a bright flash illuminated the room. The sparse gray light penetrating the clouds and diffusing through the small windows left the room barely bright enough to see. The rain splattering in the mud outside and pelting the corrugated metal shell of the barracks filled the room with constant, deafening noise. Albert was shaded from the glow of the window in the far wall by a shadow of a man standing over him. He gathered his covers to him and cowered against the head bars as a beaten dog cowers at the anticipation of pain.

"Keine Angst. Ich bin es." ("Do not be afraid. It is me.")

The man stooped beside the bed and put his hand on both of Albert's hands clasping the blanket to his chin. Albert relaxed when he realized it was the photographer. He wanted to reach up and hug him, but he had been warned how dangerous that was. Albert realized that the hand that clasped the two of his had something in it and Hugo was tucking the object out of view. It felt like a playing card but was sticky on one side in the wetness.

"Sie müssen dies versteckt halten. Lassen Sie sich von niemandem sehen, der es betrachtet." ("You must keep this hidden. Do not be seen by anyone looking at it.")

Albert brought the picture under the blanket and slipped it into the pocket of his prison uniform. Hugo patted his chest where he had seen Albert hide the picture and smiled just as a blinding flash of lightning lit the barracks so brightly it hurt their eyes. The clap of thunder that startled them both told them the strike was close and the shell of the building heaved.

Later that day, Albert huddled with Gabriel and Lukas against the wall between two beds. They collected their blankets over them to try to trap the heat of their breath. The many holes in the blankets let a lot of heat escape and the occasional breeze of cold penetrated their covering quite easily. Albert kept watch through the holes as he drew out the picture. He had no idea what could be so important that

Hugo would risk his life to give it to Albert, but he wanted his two friends to be with him when he saw it for the first time.

In the dim light of the moth holes it took them a while to understand what they were seeing. It was the picture Hugo had taken of the three of them standing against a wall shortly after Dr. Schumann had cut them. As they saw what had been done to them from the new perspective, they each began to weep quietly. Gabriel reached toward the picture and laid his fingertips on the surface where his privates should be. Albert put the picture back into his pocket knowing that they could be surprised at any moment by a curious guard. They held each other as the reality of their cold, dark future closed in on them.

Maria was emotionally crushed by the things she witnessed in this place, especially the three boys. She spent many evenings staying up late, explaining her feelings in her journal, exploring the horrors she had not wanted to believe until she had seen them for herself. When the Nazis gained control over the press throughout Germany, they suppressed any mention of the atrocities they were committing. A few personal accounts that seemed somewhat plausible had caught her attention, though she didn't really believe them. She did however, feel a compulsion to head toward, instead of away from, the source of the accusations.

"Is that your journal?" Maria asked.

"Yes," Albert replied. "I guess you could call it that."

"What do you mean?" Maria asked.

"Dr. Freda has been helping me deal with so many things lately. She says that I am improving and I think I am also, so when she suggested keeping a journal, I thought I might also write about what has happened to me in the past." He hesitated, then set about explaining. "A journal is supposed to be something you write in every day, but I could not have brought one to the camp when I was young."

"I think that is a wonderful idea. So you are writing in your journal daily now?" Maria began to lean forward, very interested to know more.

"Yes, but anytime I remember something from my past, I write about that too. That doesn't really count because Dr. Freda says that our minds edit our memories each time we recall something. If a detail is lost or remembered differently, the memory is forever changed, so you couldn't really call that a *journal entry*."

Albert's explanation seemed perfectly logical, but Maria began to shake her head in disagreement. "I must beg to differ, Albert. Those are *your* memories. Whether they are accurate is not the point of journaling. The point is to capture memories in whatever state they are right now. Right or wrong, they are who you are today and that is something to be cherished."

"Yes, yes," Hugo affirmed, raising his hand as he spoke, then resting it back on his knee.

The outburst was out of character for Hugo, so it made Maria pause and turn to him. She then turned back to Albert to continue.

"Are you a writer?" Maria asked expectantly.

"Oh, no. I'm no writer. Dr. Freda thought it would help my treatment. Writing about the bad memories makes me feel that they have moved out of me onto the pages." He paused, hearing the ridiculousness of his own words. "I am sorry. That doesn't make any sense."

"Young man, I think you have a bit of trouble believing in yourself." Maria's statement was not meant to be an insult. The tone she used was one of certainty, but not cruelty.

Albert began to speak, to refute her assertion, but realizing that she was perfectly accurate, he stopped himself, mostly out of deference to her.

When she saw that he had accepted her assessment, she continued. "Albert, I keep a journal," she stated in a soft voice. The admission left her feeling vulnerable so she paused to gather her strength before continuing.

"When I began hearing stories of what the Nazi party was doing, I did not believe them. I thought there was so much hatred and loathing on all sides of politics before the war that some people were just making up horrible stories about the side they hated. That is, until I was treating some patients who were being moved. They were being taken a long distance, so they were transferred through the hospital where I was working. When I came to check on them, they told me about some things they had seen. I was incredulous, so they challenged me to go see for myself. Since nursing is a service that everyone needs sooner or later, it was easy for me to move from hospital to hospital. I found the doctors who could get me into the military medical facilities and worked for them, a month here, a week or two there. One day, I was treating a man with a severe acid burn. The burn was so bad that the transversalis fascia was exposed in some areas, that's the layer between the inside and the outside of the abdominal cavity," she said, putting her hand to her own abdomen and to the right to indicate where the man was burned.

"The pain he suffered was so intense that even the strongest sedatives could not keep him from struggling. I was wiping him down since he was constantly perspiring from the pain when he awoke and looked at me. I asked him how it had happened and he told me that one of the Nazi doctors had done this to him while he was strapped down in a hospital. I was so shocked I couldn't speak, so I just finished my work. When I came to the other man, he said that I obviously didn't believe the first man, but that it was true. This man had his entire leg amputated up to the hip including the entire femur and ball joint. He said the same, that it was done by a doctor but he had been perfectly healthy before."

Maria sat for a long moment trying to remain calm and not let the memories overwhelm her. It was beginning to seem to Albert that she was making a confession.

"I didn't believe anyone could be so cruel, so I started writing what I learned in my journal. I thought that I could piece together how such horrible things could be rationally justified, so I decided to get assigned to one of the camps that had opened under military control. I was transferred to Auschwitz to care for the *Leichenkommandos* during the *Sonderaktion 1005*. This was before the Nazis began incinerating bodies and they had apparently realized that they were running out of space. These *corpse commandos* were tasked with digging up the bodies of prisoners to burn them, but with all of the decay and rot, infections were common. As I worked,

I learned that everything I had thought was false was true. The reports were not propaganda. The Nazis really were as horrible as people thought they were.

"I felt so guilty at the way I behaved toward my family and friends who insisted that the Nazi party was good for Germany. I yelled at them and called them names trying to get them to see the truth, but nothing worked. They were so committed to the propaganda they had been fed that they were unwilling even to listen, so I knew that I had to do whatever I could on my own. I wrote in my journal every day. It almost got me in trouble once. I didn't know that someone had read one of my notebooks and some resistance sympathizers tried to get me out of the camp, but I didn't know what they were doing so I fought to stay where I was. Then one day, I met you, Gabriel, and Lukas."

She leaned forward in her chair, stretching awkwardly to place a hand on Albert's wrist.

"I had sunk to a very dark place. I knew it was too late. The Germany I knew and loved was dead, strangled by the Nazi beast. I was about to leave nursing behind and go back home when you three showed me that even though you were in pain, having terrible things done to you, you could still be kind to others. I thought that if these three boys can withstand the horrors of war, then so could I. You three kept my heart beating. My journal kept me sane. When I wrote in my journal, I knew that those memories would never die, even if I did. I still have my journals."

Albert smiled at Maria. "Why don't you write a book? You must have so much in your journals to work from."

"Oh, no. No, no, no. It is much too painful even to go back and read them, but I do keep all my old notebooks. Maybe someday if you become a writer, you could put them to use."

Albert lowered his head, not wanting to accept her suggestion, so they sat for a few minutes in silence. They heard someone approach the door with their shoes squeaking on the floor outside, then the doorknob turned and Dr. Freda entered.

Coming to stand at his bedside she asked, "Albert, how are you feeling?"

"I feel good, thanks." Albert's cheerful reply was a possible sign that he was not finding it necessary to control himself, which would be very welcome news indeed.

She looked at Hugo and Maria. "Have you had a good visit?"

Maria beamed, "Yes, very good. Thank you so much for helping Albert."

Dr. Freda smiled, nodding at the group, and formally brought the meeting to a close. "Albert needs his rest now. Please come with me."

Hugo looked at Maria in acknowledgment and began to rise. As Maria placed her hand on the side of the bed to lift herself to go with Hugo, Albert sensed something. She was winded even though she had been sitting still for over an hour.

As they came to stand between Dr. Freda, who was standing in the doorway heading out, and Albert lying in bed, they both came to a stop. She took Hugo's hand in her own, looked into his eyes and smiled. She turned to Albert still holding Hugo's hand. "Thank you, Albert. Thank you for letting us spend some time with you."

She turned, tucking her arm under Hugo's, and they followed Dr. Freda out into the hallway.

Dr. Freda took up a slow walking pace, headed toward the atrium. She thought that since the couple had just spent an hour in the confined space of Albert's room, they might enjoy some time outdoors. It was a beautiful day, with the sun shining and a cool breeze. As they came from the hallway into the open common area, the glass wall on their right revealed the expanse of green grass and pristine landscaping in the central courtyard. When Dr. Freda came to the external door on her right, she pulled out her overly large key ring and searched for the proper key. Hugo and Maria stood waiting, her hand still tucked under his arm.

Dr. Freda opened the door and held it for them as they walked out onto the brickwork patio. They paused, waiting for Dr. Freda to lock the door behind them. She turned from the door to face them. The three talked for a long while about how the meeting went, about Dr. Freda's prognosis and planned treatments, and about making these visits more frequent since it seemed to go so well.

"So you offered your journals to Albert?" Dr. Freda asked Maria.

"Yes, but now that I think about it, that might not have been such a good idea. They contain some entries that anyone would find extremely disturbing, so I don't think I will do that just yet."

"My sentiment exactly. Thank you Mrs. Stromberger."

"Maria, if you please."

"Maria, then. After what I just saw, I think I will give my permission for the two of you to visit Albert anytime you want. I will leave word with the front desk." Dr. Freda was actually ecstatic at the wonderful outcome, but she maintained tight control over her emotions, trying to project an air of professionalism.

Hugo was content to observe the ladies' conversation, but he seemed to be itching to say something. "Doctor, would you walk with us, please?"

Dr. Freda nodded and gestured to her left down the brick walkway that ran the perimeter of the courtyard and came from the middle of each of the four walls of the courtyard to a central rotunda made of stone or concrete. Hugo released Maria's hand so he could walk beside Dr. Freda since the walkway was too narrow for the three of them to walk side-by-side.

"Doctor, you know that I was a photographer before I was hired by the Third Reich?" Hugo asked.

Dr. Freda nodded with an affirmative "Mmmmm."

"You also know that I escaped being captured by the occupying armies."

She nodded again.

"What you may not know is that photographers are very particular about protecting our work. It does not take much to ruin a photograph or a negative."

Hugo glanced from the path to Dr. Freda and she saw his eyebrows raised before he looked forward again. It seemed as if he were giving her the chance to figure something out.

"You must have a stash of pictures in your possession, then," Dr. Freda concluded.

The statement brought Hugo to a lurching halt on the brick path. He stopped so quickly that Maria nearly ran into him. After one step, Dr. Freda also halted, turning back to look at Hugo. "I am correct, I see."

Hugo began walking again, a little unsure of himself. "You see, I couldn't possibly take all of my negatives and prints with me or someone would have noticed, so I took as many as I could fit in a satchel. I knew I would be unable to stop for a long time, so I also packed my best bottle of brandy. That was a lucky thing because it drew attention away from what I was carrying. I have been thinking about doing something for several years and perhaps there could be some benefit to you."

Dr. Freda was intrigued. "How do you mean?"

"When I was finally away from the Third Reich, the Russians, and the Americans, I buried the prints and negatives. I left them there for nearly ten years, but there was some argument about the land, so before anything could happen, I moved them to a bank vault. I have been talking with some people at Time magazine and showing them a few pictures. I might think about letting them print some, but you could use them for another purpose. The man who attacked Albert? The doctor you think he was working for? I may have some of the evidence you need to bring them to justice."

"Dr. Freda came to a slow stop over several footsteps. Her imagination raced as she considered what impact access to this type of evidence would have on their attempts to capture Schumann."

Hugo came to stand by her side, waiting for her to emerge from her thoughts. Maria stepped up behind her and also waited. Dr. Freda looked slowly up at Hugo, then back and down at Maria. "I think I would like to introduce you to someone," she said conspiratorially.

Dr. Freda, Hugo, and Maria walked to the rotunda in the center of the courtyard and sat. The doctor explained about Viktor's team, the men and women trying to bring Nazis to justice, and their plans to entrap Dr. Schumann. She explained that Schumann had already been recognized once in Spain and immediately went into hiding. It was crucial that when he was confronted again, that there was no way out; no way to physically escape and no way for him to cast doubt on his identity or the crimes he committed.

"I am going to tell you something, doctor. I do not want you to repeat it to anyone without first checking with me." Hugo looked into Dr. Freda's eyes with deadly seriousness.

"I agree, *Herr* Jaeger." Dr. Freda's answer left no question she would honour his request.

"In 1956, I dug up my collection and moved them to a vault here in Cologne." Hugo let the information hang in the air as Dr. Freda contemplated it. When she realized that she was being offered access to such a wealth of evidence, she smiled, looked Hugo in the eyes to demonstrate her sincerity, and leaned toward him, placing a hand on his arm.

"Thank you, *Herr* Jaeger. Your offer is very generous."

Chapter 29

The stately, black Bentley pulled slowly around the corner and up to a small sidewalk parking area in front of the old bank. The building was only a few decades old, but the bank within was nearly 200 years old. The Oppenheim family had founded the original institution, but lost their shareholder stake a couple generations later. Immediately after the war ended in 1945, the Oppenheim reopened, free of Nazi control and the family regained their controlling ownership.

Ben came around to the building side of the car and opened the back door standing at attention as he did so. Gabby took his offered hand allowing him to use his bulk and strength to lift her to her feet on the sidewalk. She looked up into his squinting face and realized he was looking directly into the sun.

"Poor boy. Don't squint like that or you'll age before your time." Gabby's voice was sultry and soft.

As she approached the building, she heard Ben close his door just as someone opened the front door for her. He was such a conscientious bodyguard. He was always making sure she was safe before he went to park the car. The man holding the outside door was finely dressed and tipped his top hat to her as she entered. Her heels echoed throughout the atrium only slightly dampened by the indoor greenery being fawned over by a groundskeeper.

"Welcome to the *Salomon Oppenheim*, Mrs. Gorski." The man waiting just inside the double entry atrium was dressed in the finest suit, even better than those she bought for her husband. His shirt was starched and crisp white without a wrinkle. His moustache was curled and waxed so perfectly that it seemed artificial. His gray and black pinstripe slacks had knife-sharp creases as did the backs of his white gloves.

"Aww. Aren't you sweet?" Gabby teased as she walked past him, brushing her finger under his rigid chin as she passed.

As she strode gracefully into the atrium, he took in her luscious figure. Gabby's heavy black dress clung as if it had been sewn onto her. The velvet dripped with black satin ribbons studded every centimetre with a white pearl. He saw rich people all day, every day, and he knew real pearls when he saw them. Her fur stole didn't quite cover the plunging back of the dress and he could see a triangle of bare porcelain skin beneath. As her hips shifted left and right, he was hypnotized by their perfect teardrop shape. The dress seemed too tight at the knees for her to walk, but she did not seem to be having any trouble. He didn't immediately notice when she slowed, but when she stopped suddenly, he looked up.

"I'm up here, handsome." Gabby fluttered her eyclashes and gave the most seductive smile she could muster. The young man liked what he saw. His cheeks flushed and his ears turned a bright shade of pink when he realized he had been caught staring at her bottom. He quickly glanced at the lobby boss who was glowering at him. He would certainly be reprimanded for his behaviour.

Gabby didn't wait for him to apologize. She turned again, heading for the heavy wooden door to the back of the lobby, in the right corner. Between the left and right corner doors was a large stage-like service counter with the floor raised so the clerks were nearly half a metre taller than the customers, leaning over the counter uncomfortably for each interaction. The man who should have been leading her, finally decided to go around her just in time to pull the door open for her. As he turned to face her, pulling on the ornate vertical door fixture, he saw that every man in the room was looking at Gabby, yet she seemed not to notice.

As Gabby walked down the narrow, but unusually tall hallway, she noticed how old it seemed. The lobby was, of course, where the bank did the majority of its transactions, but the majority of its money was actually exchanged in these back rooms. The young man holding the door once again scampered ahead of her, all pretense of dignity abandoned. She enjoyed doing that to men and each time it was as sweet as nectar. He reached the end of the corridor where the passage turned right and disappeared around the corner. Gabby did not quicken her pace for servants, so she maintained her comfortable walking pace and when she rounded the corner, he was standing at attention facing her about ten paces down the hall. As she approached, he reached for the door handle, but since he was still intent on drinking in her image, he forgot to look and missed, smacking his fingertips into the door just behind the handle. He winced and corrected his aim, looking at the door this time. He stood straight and brought the door handle to his side, so that he blocked the hall giving Gabby only one direction to go.

Rather than proceed through the door, she came to a stop before him as if she weren't ready to enter just yet. She smiled and he felt his heart pounding in his chest. She raised a black-gloved arm, placed her fingertips on his chest, and turned to walk through the door letting her fingers trail across his chest until they fell away. He let the door close behind her and when it finally latched, he let out the breath he had been holding to make his waistline look smaller. He was out of breath, not from the effort of walking, but from doing so with his shoulders drawn up and his chest puffed out. He leaned forward placing his hands on his knees and exhaled, panting. Just then, the lobby boss came around the corner to find him in another undignified position. As he stood erect and the disapproving man passed him with his persistently sour look, he thought, *This day is not going so well.*

"Mrs. Gorski! It's so good to see you again!" The deep baritone voice boomed as it echoed around the room.

An older, well-dressed gentleman pushed his chair back from the table that filled the majority of the room. His heavy-set form barely fit between the wall and the table with enough room for the chair under him, but he managed to extricate himself and come toward Gabby with his hand outstretched.

"Hello again, uncle." Gabby took his hand and tried to maintain her dignified posture while he shook her hand so vigorously he might have knocked her completely off balance if she did not keep her grip on him. "Has Hugo arrived yet?"

"Not yet, my dear, but soon."

His white hair was cut short as was his moustache. His suit, though made to fit the large man, was still stretched in folds around his middle. His clothes fit so tightly that the vest buttons were all turned sideways and looked ready to pop at any instant from the strain. His plump face was deeply lined, as an overstuffed pillow might be, and his rosy cheeks were speckled with blood red spots and splotches looking rather raw. He finally released her hand after standing there smiling at her for a long time.

"Please have a seat, Mrs. Gorski." He offered one of the chairs to her with an open hand.

"What makes you think I could sit in a dress like this?" she asked.

He turned even more red than he was already and bubbled with laughter as his bulk jiggled. "Right you are, my dear! You are quite a vision today!"

As he continued to giggle, he made his way back to the chair. The exertion was making him breathe heavily and Gabby could see that he had started to perspire. The poor man was going to eat himself to death. Still, he was sweet and kind and deserving of all the respect and love Gabby could give him.

The pressure in the room dropped suddenly as the door opened. Hugo came in holding a rustic looking beige tweed Fedora in his hands. His suit was a burgundy so deep it was almost black. As he stepped into the room, the clerk let the door close behind him. He seemed preoccupied with something.

"Guten Morgen, Herr Jaeger." Gabby tried her best to curtsy but the dress restricted her movement.

Hugo looked up at Gabby and seeing her smiling at him helped to focus his attention. "Good morning, Gabriella. How have you been?" He stepped forward to place his hat brim-down on the table next to Gabby. He took a deep breath and exhaled.

She stepped toward him and, taking his hands in her own and asked, "What has you so troubled today?"

"It is nothing."

Gabby could tell that it wasn't *nothing*. He was definitely being affected by something. As Gabby held his hands, she could sense tension, fear, and...also guilt? She wasn't certain. "Thank you so much for doing this, Hugo." Gabby's voice was free of pretense and he looked into her eyes to see the abject sincerity in her gaze.

He had not meant to let so many people know where he had moved his photographs to and he was feeling guilty for not trying to use the photographs to bring people to justice until now. He should have done it long ago, but he was afraid that if he exposed himself in that way, either people would accuse him of being a Nazi and prosecute him, or the Nazi sympathizer network would find him and kill him for betrayal. Neither was true, but when people come looking for you, they have already made up their mind about your guilt, no matter what crime they accuse you of.

In 1956, he had taken his map and a shovel out to the area where his negatives and prints were buried. He had put several prints into each jar, about thirty of them, and buried them in a random pattern under the canopy of trees. His hope was that, without the map, someone might find a *few* of the canisters, but not all of them. With his map, and compensation for ten years of brush growth in the area, he found each of the canisters with one or two strokes of the shovel. He collected all of them into burlap bags and took them home. He opened each canister and cleaned the dirt from the pictures and asked Maria not to enter the dining room of their small house. He knew exposing her to these pictures would bring back bad memories.

"Did you see Dr. Freda on the way in?" Gabby asked Hugo.

"Yes, she will be here in a minute," Hugo confirmed.

"Let us just wait for a few minutes before we get started then, shall we?" boomed Gabby's uncle.

"Levin, this is Hugo Jaeger, the photographer." Gabby gestured from Levin to Hugo, intending them to shake hands.

Hugo could see that rising from his chair would be an effort for the big man, so he approached to shake Levin's hand. "Thank you for not calling me the *Nazi photographer*," he said to Gabby over he shoulder. "I'm convinced that that's the only thing anyone will ever remember me for."

"I am certain that is not true, Hugo. You did wonderful work, both before and after the war." Gabby's assurance might have been heartfelt, but it rang hollow. Even she knew that he was probably correct. His legacy would certainly drown in the ocean of Nazi history.

The door opened again and Freda ambled through. Gabby and Hugo had both dressed for the occasion, but the doctor was, as always, wearing her rubber-soled white shoes, heavy woolen skirt, and scarf covering her hair. The only color on her was the dingy pink hand-knitted sweater she wore.

"Good morning, Dr. Dudek!" Levin's voice was still booming, but with people in the room, the echo was much reduced. He worked his way to standing and came around the table, passing behind Hugo who turned to observe the meeting. He barely fit between the wall and the table, so Hugo had to move back to give the two appropriate space.

Freda extended her hand looking up at the dapper man. "Thank you for helping us with this, Levin."

With an enthusiastic shake of her hand, he said, "Not at all, *Doktor*. If there is anything I can do to help, I insist you ask." His face beamed with kindness and sincerity and his vigorous handshake transmitted trustworthiness...which was making her shoulder hurt, so she resisted so much movement. He immediately detected this and reigned in his enthusiasm, apparently just now realizing that his exuberance made her uncomfortable. "I am glad I can contribute."

As Levin turned and made his way back to his chair, he slapped the steel door on that side of the room. It was an unremarkable metal panel with rivets around the perimeter and a recessed handle reminiscent of a bulkhead door on a ship or submarine. A heartbeat later, the door opened outward and the four of them leaned to see around each other through the vault door. Another man like the one who greeted them at the door came through the opening, bathed in amber light from behind. He was much younger than the others, with a clean-shaven face and a boyish smile, but he was tall and stocky like a rugby player. He carried a large metal box and set it on the table after taking a step to the left, toward Gabby, Hugo, and Freda's side of the room. As a second young man came through the door, the first slipped behind him and disappeared back into the vault room. Their carefully choreographed movements cast beams of warm light on the far wall across the table. In all, they brought three shallow, long boxes, lining them up on the table so the edges and corners met to form a raft. Their presentation completed, the two young men disappeared into the vault room and the door closed, shutting out the amber light.

"I do not like doing this," remarked Hugo as he stepped forward. He slid his hand to the left corner of the table and leaned to draw the closest box toward him. He flipped the latch on the right side and lifted the lid. The long lid reached nearly up to his own height and he carefully lowered it back toward the table being careful not to let the metal hit the table too forcefully.

There was silence in the room. Hugo stood looking into the box filled with pictures. Some were in pristine condition. Others were cracked or brown. Still others were peeling as the emulsion separated from the paper backing. Each of them cautiously leaned forward to see. Gabby put her hand to her mouth with a controlled exhale through the nose. Her heart was racing but she needed to see what was in the pictures. Hugo stepped to his left to allow Freda to view the contents of the box.

As Freda came around Hugo, looking into the box, she felt lightheaded and cold. She knew that her blood pressure had just dropped, but the emotional response couldn't be avoided. She knew that these pictures could bring dozens of escaped war criminals to the justice they deserved. Feeling her heart pounding and speeding up instead of slowing down, she contracted her abdominal muscles to push blood back up toward her brain.

Gabby was not holding up as well as Freda. She felt dizzy. Her heart was pounding. She knew she couldn't sit or the dress might be damaged, but she had to do something so she pulled the chair from around the corner of the table and perched on its edge, trying to keep her legs straight and supporting some of her weight with one hand under her.

In a soft, sympathetic voice, Levin asked, "Are you alright, Gabriella?" He leaned forward and appeared to be ready to get to his feet. His concern helped her to regain control.

"Thank you, Levin. I will be fine."

Hugo thought this moment would alleviate some of his guilt, but it didn't. These two ladies would certainly be upset at what they were about to see. Now he had a new reason to feel guilty, but he continued on the path they had chosen together. As he lifted images out of the box, he organized them in piles of like subject matter. Prisoners he put in one pile; nurses and doctors in another; soldiers, commanders, and structures in another. When the first box was empty, he closed it and slid it to the side to make room for the next box.

Gabby saw that Freda was having trouble with what she was seeing. Her skin was pale and she looked unsteady, so she put her own discomfort aside. Lifting herself to her feet, she adjusted her stole and assumed an erect posture. She took two steps, coming up beside her, and tucked her arm under Freda's.

"This must never happen again," Gabby whispered.

Chapter 30

Dear Nephew,

The family has come to a final decision and wishes to dispose of the family properties. Please tell your mother in no uncertain terms. We would appreciate hearing back from you when she has been informed. Be sure to learn everything she has to tell you before you leave.

On a personal note, I was quite upset to read of your encounter with Mrs. Gorski. I had hoped you would take better care of the family's affairs while you are visiting Cologne. If you require assistance with the formalities, we can send someone to put you on the right track. We wish you better luck in your endeavours.

Sincerely,

H

Jürgen's blood ran cold as he slowly lowered to a seat on the edge of the bed. He took no notice of the envelopes at his side which slid to the floor one by one. He read the rough script of Dr. Schumann's hand and the meaning behind the words. He no longer had the luxury of waiting to take care of the doctor. Whether or not he would ever be able to get to Albert again was a problem to solve later. He knew that if he did not take care of the doctor and report back soon, he would probably not live more than a month or two.

The Nazi network was still very strong in Germany and enjoyed the unstated support of many government officials and many more citizens than world leaders were aware of. Jürgen understood how the various cells were all connected but as a minor functionary, he was not important enough to have contact with anyone other than his little group. It was Dr. Schumann himself who had arranged accommodations and scheduled informant meetings before he was ever ordered to Cologne from his hometown. He worried about his own dealings in Frankfurt. Were his associates keeping up with collections or was his neighborhood going soft, possibly letting another protector move in? There was a lot of planning to do, so he couldn't worry about his own problems right now.

The next step was to find out where she was frequently alone at predictable times. Then establish when would be the best time. He would carry a gun, of course, but even a silencer could be heard. If he could immobilize her, then slitting her throat would be the quietest way to dispose of her. He reached for a map he kept folded on his nightstand and finding the University of Cologne's medical facilities, he began to trace the streets in the surrounding area in thick black lines. This helped the roads stay fresh in his mind. He would focus on the web and imagine the map disappearing so he could only see the black lines and shapes. If he needed to get away quickly, he would know where he was going even after several switchbacks.

Gabby's face beamed with happiness. The way the light from the huge atrium windows fell on her as she approached Hugo and Maria made her glow with a timeless beauty. Her flowing sundress was bound around the waist by a white Chanel belt with a circular buckle. Her white high-heeled shoes gleamed where the light struck them sending patches of mottled light dancing across the walls. As she extended her hands, palms down, Maria stepped toward her with hers extended palms up. The two wrapped fingers and Maria's smile grew, as though Gabby was passing happiness to her through their touch. They held each other's eyes for a long moment before Gabby addressed Hugo over Maria's shoulder.

Hugo took a step to close the space between them, extending his hand to shake hers, but Gabby did not grant him the formality. She took his hand in both of hers, one on top and the other underneath, and squeezed. He smiled, accepting the gesture as a sign that Gabby wanted them to feel comfortable. The last time he had been in such a grand home had been while he was traveling with Rudolph Höss to an audience with Hitler. A Jewish family's manor had been confiscated by the Nazi party after the Jews were all ordered to retire and the owner had been ousted. In 1933, the Nazi party passed a law that de-naturalized all Jews to non-citizen status, allowing the party and all German citizens to take whatever violent actions they wished against Jewish families without any consequence or fear of reprisal. It also allowed him to win his second election by an overwhelming majority. Hitler wanted his most influential men behind him. Hugo was to capture the grand ceremony on film so it could then be used by the Nazi propaganda machine, further convincing Germans that the world was good, Germany was good, and they would be looked after by the Reich. He wondered if something similar might have happened to this place during the war.

Gabby bid them to follow her to the place she had prepared for them in the garden. As they followed, Maria couldn't help looking up and around. Her curiosity made it obvious that she rarely, or maybe never, visited homes like this one. Hugo glanced back toward the car, but seeing the chauffeur Ben deftly handling their luggage and the door, seemingly without effort, he realized that they were in good hands and there was no need to worry. As they passed through the central ballroom toward the rear lobby, Gabby diverted their path toward this object and that. A painting of Anton's grandfather in a commander's uniform painted between the two world wars. A statuette of a Greek goddess which was a sculpture carved by his late wife, Amelie Koch Weber, who discovered her talent quite by accident when she spent time recovering from an illness. She created wonderful works of art and gave them all away to friends and family, but this one was Anton's favourite and would never leave the manor.

As they strolled about the room, Ben took their luggage upstairs, turning around the corner pillar to follow the banistered gallery to a room at the front corner of the house. The angle was just right so that when Ben threw the upstairs door open, Hugo could see the far corner against the ceiling. He imagined that the room must be luxuriously huge if he were estimating the distance between the door and the corner of the house accurately. Maria was oblivious to Ben's activities upstairs. She marveled at each object d'art, inspecting each closely, all the while fascinated by Gabby's narration.

What Hugo admired about Gabby was not the objects she now possessed, but that she had carefully learned volumes about each and could answer questions about the family's history and ancestors without hesitation. When she was Gabriel, his entire family and its history had been taken from him. Now, Gabriella cherished a new history and that made Hugo very happy. It showed the character of the woman she had become.

They continued in this way, taking their time ambling down the short hallway until it opened into the rear lobby. To the right of the door was a sparkling chrome cart stocked with linens, glasses, a pitcher of deep rose colored liquid and a heavy looking silver box with rounded corners and a knob on top. As they approached, two girls came from the hallways at the far corners of the room. One held the door and the other took the cart by the handle. They waited for Gabby and her guests to pass through the door and the girl with the cart came through behind them. They crossed a landing outside with steps descending to the garden path below, but Hugo didn't see how the maid would follow them. Perfectly on-cue, Ben came down the hallway from the front of the house, out the door at a brisk walking pace, and picked the entire cart up just after the maid stepped aside. By this time, Gabby and Maria were already nearing the bottom of the steps, but Hugo was lagging behind and Ben passed him on his way to the cobblestone path below. Hugo's eyebrows raised as the strapping youth passed, noticing that he wasn't even breathing hard. Ah, youth did not understand its own impermanence.

The girl who had manned the cart before, made it to the bottom of the steps and took possession of the cart from Ben while he bounded back up toward the house taking two steps at a time. Gabby continued her slow pace through the carefully landscaped and manicured garden. She continued to explain which family ancestor had planted various ornamental bushes and rows of flowering lilies. As they came over a rise in the path, Hugo and Maria were relieved to see a clean white tablecloth draped over a circular table with big, bold flowers embroidered around the hem and heavy iron chairs padded with embroidered seat cushions. Maria was especially grateful to see a comfortable chaise resting on one side of the paved clearing. Just the walk from the car to the garden had left her winded and her legs were beginning to swell uncomfortably.

As they arrived at the clearing, Gabby, who had been clandestinely glancing back at her guests, realized that Maria was indeed very tired and pale, so she stepped to the side of the chaise and extended her hand toward it, inviting Maria to recline there. Once Maria was situated, Hugo, who was standing patiently, followed Gabby's gesture to the chair between the table and the chaise. He pulled it backward a bit so as not to block Maria's line of sight to the table and sat, thankful for the thickness of the embroidered linen cushion. His hips had begun to ache during the train trip to Cologne and he knew that Maria must be feeling the strain as well. Gabby sat in one of the two remaining chairs as the maids parked their cart and began to transfer its contents to the table.

There were linen napkins, silver chargers and beautiful yellow and gold Mottahedeh china plates, tea, cakes, and finger sandwiches. A partitioned tray with olives, celery sticks, caviar, and other morsels remained on the top level of the tray and the lid was transferred to the bottom shelf of the cart. It all happened in a choreographed blur of motion. When the maids came to rest, one beside the cart and one behind the table, Gabby clapped her hands together silently and asked what Maria would like. Maria hoisted herself up again, but Gabby motioned for her to lie back and tell the maidens what she would like.

"Is there cream cheese and salmon?" Maria looked hopeful.

"Ma'am, the cream cheese has a touch of lemon and dill and the salmon is smoked in applewood," said the girl beside the tray.

"Oohh! May I have some of that, please?"

Gabby leaned forward saying, "I've had the most delicious pomegranate juice brought in. Would you like to try some?"

"That sounds lovely." Maria began to relax. Gabby knew that the two of them were unaccustomed to luxury and it would take some time for them to begin to treat the estate as their own, but she was glad to see them beginning to relax. She noticed that Maria was enjoying being pampered with childlike abandon. If they were at a high-society event, Maria would have been the topic of every conversation for the snobbish elite until they tired of her child-like antics. Gabby didn't see her that way. Instead, she saw her behaving unabashedly.

Hugo requested the same as Maria. Gabby did not give any instructions and yet her plate was prepared and set before her. Hugo admired that she had left nothing to chance.

"Thank you for putting up with us while we are in town," Hugo addressed Gabby as he opened his napkin, laying it across his lap. His posture was still rather stiff and formal.

"I want you two to think of this as your home. If Anton and I are away, that should not deter you. Just call the house and tell them you are coming. Ben will take you wherever you want to go and will bring you to and from the train station. He's very reliable and, as you saw, has little trouble handling heavy bags." Gabby smiled, looked into Hugo's, then Maria's eyes with a nod to indicate that she was serious and would take offense if they did not do as she asked. "I think Albert is doing so much better since seeing you again. I want to do everything I can to help him...and you."

"Yes, it was so nice to see little Albert, all grown up." Maria realized her oversight, amending, "...and you. You have done quite well for yourself." The added statement left a look of embarrassment on Maria's face, so Gabby acted quickly to soothe her.

"I have been blessed with so many good things and I feel so fortunate that I got to meet you again after so many years," Gabby sighed, momentarily lost in memory.

There was one question left unspoken and they all knew that there was no point in bringing it up. They even imagined the young boy Gabriel's soft voice asking, *Why didn't you do anything to stop them from doing this to us?* Gabby had done everything she could to make Hugo and Maria as comfortable as possible on their first visit to Cologne in over twenty years, but there was no ignoring that question, and no way to answer it either.

As the sun sank lower and the temperature began to fall, they had their fill of refreshments and rose to return to the house. Gabby motioned to the maids indicating that they were finished and the maids gracefully relieved the three of their plates and glasses, returning to attention around the clearing.

"Do you feel well enough to walk back?" Gabby asked Maria.

"Oh, yes. Thank you. I am quite alright now." Maria was indeed feeling better. Her color had returned and she seemed much stronger.

Gabby rose and came to Maria. Holding out her hand in a request, Maria placed her hand in Gabby's and slid to the edge of the chaise, standing with difficulty. She was grateful for the support. Hugo rose also, but stood back, letting Gabby and Maria precede him on the path back to the house. During the slow walk, Gabby explained when dinner would be served, breakfast in the morning, and they were to call for lunch anytime they wished. She encouraged them to visit the extensive gardens around the property and offered to give them a tour after they had rested.

The music coming from the open door of *Kabarett Seks* echoed off the buildings around him. The little cafe on Jürgen's right looked busy as he came up the street. There was an orange glow projecting from its open door, casting the shadows of its patrons across the street. On the left, *Kabarett Seks* was awash in blue light which made the heavy red doors look almost black this late at night. He was feeling a little tipsy already, his altered vision making it a little difficult to make out details. It was as if his eyes were blurry with a sleep he could not wipe away.

As he came to the street corner, he saw someone far ahead in the line waving at him to come forward. He ignored the look of disdain from the patrons who were made to wait in a line down the sidewalk and around the corner of the building. The huge bouncer wanted him to come forward, so he straightened his jacket and tried to maintain an upright posture as he walked toward the door. The bouncer leaned down to say something into his ear over the loud music, but all he could understand was "...is waiting for you!" All the rest was drowned out. The bouncer gently pushed on his back, guiding him toward the door where clouds of smoke lingered just beneath the awning before escaping around the edges, upward into the night sky. As he passed the threshold, he felt bathed in music. It vibrated against his skin and his bones resonated with the low, thumping bass.

The short girl at the front, what was her name? He couldn't remember, but she obviously recognized him, immediately stepping toward him. Her oversized pants suit flowed around her ankles like white silk as she stepped past him, tugging on his sleeve as she went ahead. She turned left at the dance floor, walking close to the raised booths built in an arc tracing the dance floor. At the last booth, closest to the bar against the far wall, sat Gabriella Gorski, waiting for him. She was positively radiant. In fact, she seemed to emit a soft glow of her own, accentuated by the dimly lit corner booth. Following the Maître d'Noir, he brushed past people dancing with arms waving and smoke trailing up to the ceiling from cigarettes held high here and there. As he came to the booth, the woman leading him was nowhere to be found. She must have slipped away through the crowd. Gabriella finally noticed him and when she looked up at him, his heart leapt and she seemed to glow even brighter. *Verdammt!* She was beautiful! Her hair was perfect, wavy and blonde. Her dress was open in the front, the neckline so low it disappeared into the shadow cast by the table. Her white fur stole was wide enough to cover her, but she had let it slide behind, revealing her bare shoulders.

He was too distracted by the smooth shape of her beautiful neck to realize that she was talking to him. When he looked up, he could see that she was asking him something. She was inviting him to sit beside her. The white glove on her right hand was slowly patting the red vinyl cushion beside her, but he couldn't hear her words over the music. He stepped up to the raised platform the booth rested on, and then moved to sit where she indicated, all the while fixated on her beautiful face.

As he sat, she leaned toward him to say something in his ear. She placed a hand seductively on his arm.

"I want you," she breathed into his ear, voice raised just loud enough to be heard over the din. She withdrew her hand and sat back to observe his reaction. Her breath seemed to linger around him now; strawberries, vanilla, and vodka.

Drinks came and glasses collected on the table as the night went on. They were engrossed in some silly conversation about the arts or something like that, but all he could think about was squeezing that pretty neck as she begged for him inside her. When she had worked herself into a receptive way, she pointed to the wall opposite them on the far side of the club. Heavy black velvet drapes covered the wall, but he could see a second set of bouncers allowing people through. When the drapes parted, he could see that the space behind was dark, with intense splashes of pink and blue lights just visible before the curtains closed. Smoke billowed out with each person exiting. He felt her pushing him out of the booth, so he made way, standing beside the booth, helping her down from the platform.

They bumped and jostled their way through the crowd, as she led him by the hand. They finally reached the heavy black drapes and shuffled through. It seemed there were many layers of soft black fabric he was passing through. He didn't understand how one curtain could be so thick, but in a moment they emerged into a darkened space. Flashes of colored light randomly pierced his vision preventing his eyes from adjusting to the darkness. There were bodies all around him, but Gabriella still led him by the hand and she still seemed to glow with a light from within. While he was bumping and stumbling through the crowd, she seemed to flow through it. The press of bodies seemed to part under the pressure of the light emanating from her.

They reached the back wall, along which there was a hard concrete bench that encircled the room. It was painted black, but still showed the ashes and spilled drinks of the previous few hours. Gabriella glided into a seat and he fumbled his way to the bench beside her. She was dressed almost entirely in white, yet she did not seem to mind that the seats were filthy. As he came to rest, he looked at her. She gazed into his eyes and smiled with her lips slightly pursed. She placed a hand under his chin and drew him close. She closed her eyes and he did the same. As their lips met, the softness of her kiss enveloped him. With his eyes closed, she stroked his face with the tips of her fingers. She held his face so their lips remained touching as she whispered unintelligible things. As her lips brushed his, he found the contact intensely arousing and his manhood swelled until he ached. They continued kissing and whispering lip-to-lip as her hand traveled slowly from his cheek to his neck, then down to his chest.

He ached for her the way he had for no woman before. The way she knew his body but restrained her attention was maddening. As her hand slid down his stomach to his lap, there was no missing the mound there. She slowly closed her hand around him and squeezed. His vision went white. An explosion of ecstasy overtook him so quickly that he thought he might have spent himself already, but as his vision returned she was still smiling at him. His eyes continued to adjust to the darkness and he could see her faint glow. Her hair had changed. He could have sworn that Gabriella was a blonde, but the hair before him reflected only darkened glints of the pink and blue lights in the room. The color of her lips had changed too...and the shape. Her lips were crooked now as he examined them. They didn't seem right. He looked up into her eyes and recognized Lolita, the performer. Lolita was just then the ugliest sight to see and then he squeezed. The drag queen had a grip on him where Gabriella's hand was before and there was nothing he could do to stop himself. He began pumping with relief and horror at the same time, unable to get away as Lolita put all her weight on him, nearly rolling on top of him. He wanted to get away, but his body did not move when he ordered it to. As he continued throbbing, his vision went white with each surge until finally it stayed white and he woke breathing heavily, blinded by the beam of early morning sunshine that streamed through the open curtain beside the bed.

He lay there for a minute, trying to process the dream when he noticed a cold, wet sensation in his lap. Without thinking, he reached down and was surprised to find a sticky, cooling area of wetness. He sat upright in exasperated revulsion. What kind of man would let a filthy whore of a drag queen get hold of him like that, but in the back of his mind he tried to make sure to preserve the memory of being taken like that. He was disgusted with himself but could not resist the urge to remember that moment. He began to curse and rant as he climbed out of bed and went into the bathroom to clean the mess.

It had taken nearly two weeks to stake out the hospital. Dr. Dudek's office location was particularly problematic. Since hers was the only office in the basement and there was very little traffic, he had wandered around down there acting as if he were lost. It wasn't as bad as he thought it would be, though. He was only stopped once by a guard and the young man didn't even check his identification before escorting him out and wishing him a nice day. While he was exploring, he picked several of the locks on the doors lining the basement hallways. The main hallway to Dr. Dudek's office actually ran down the north wall of the basement, not down the center. The hallway that led to her door, turned left, went to the far corner, then another left, then another and you were back at the stairs that led up to the lobby. The area was nearly always dark indicating that only the hallway to Dr. Dudek's office was ever in use. Some evenings, she worked late and when she did, the staff left the hallway light on so she could find her way to the lobby since turning out her own light plunged the hallway into utter darkness, especially if the lobby lights had been turned off.

If all went well, tonight would be the night she took her last breath. If not, he would take care of her some other night, but he knew it had better be soon, before Dr. Schumann ran out of patience and sent someone to finish off the doctor and him too. He knew Dr. Schumann wasn't stupid enough to leave his loose ends untied. He kept his breathing slow and steady as he stood in the darkened basement room with the door cracked just enough to see if anyone passed by. The room was heavy with the odor of dust, papers, and old glue.

Helga was running late for a study session with her classmates, but she promised Dr. Freda that she would have this stack of charts sorted and filed before she left. As she slid the last one on the top-left of the roll-out shelves, she tapped on Dr. Freda's window. She could see the yellow and green glow of the goose-neck lamp through the frosted glass and when the doctor gave permission, she opened the door.

"Are you leaving, Helga?" Dr. Freda knew that Helga had stayed late, but the girl would not shirk her duties no matter how late she had to stay.

"Just finished. Is there anything else I could do for you?" Helga was hoping the offer would be ignored because she needed to head out immediately if she were still to have some hope of being on time.

Dr. Freda finished writing the line she was working on and looked up. "Thank you for staying so late, young lady. Now off with you!" She shooed Helga away as if she were annoyed, but the capricious smirk on her face told Helga otherwise.

Helga pulled the door shut with a gentle click and reached for her purse and wrap-around smock. Hurrying out the front door, she fumbled with her tinkling keychain, feeling for the right key. They had all been taking extra precautions since Albert was attacked. Keeping the doors locked was one of the habits they had adopted.

Jürgen looked up when he heard the clack of a door closing down the hall. The tinkling of keys was clearly audible even through the cracked door and he could hear the rhythmic chirps of rubber-soled shoes becoming louder. He stood upright from leaning on a nearby desk and slowly approached the cracked door. Standing behind the door, he heard the footsteps stop just outside. *Iss Scheiße und stirb!* (Eat shit and die!) he thought as the shadowed figure stood just on the other side of the door.

Helga was fumbling with her notebooks, smock, and keys when she nearly lost control of the collection. She paused leaning far to one side in order to balance the mess in her arms. After a while, she regained control over the sliding stack and began to shift the notebooks to bring their center of gravity back in line with her own so she could walk. She nearly dropped her keys in the process and she pinched the ring against the bottom notebook with her middle finger trying not to drop it. As she righted herself, she continued walking but something didn't seem right. Had she heard a door creek behind her? As she turned, she thought she heard it again.

Setting her books down on the steps leading up to the lobby, she pocketed her keys and began walking slowly back toward Dr. Freda's office.

Jürgen didn't hear footsteps anymore *but* he hadn't heard them go up the stairs. That meant whoever it was might be waiting for him to move. He controlled his breathing and stepped behind the door just as it began to creep open causing his eyes to open wide.

"Hello?" Helga didn't want to lock anyone in the dark if someone had been looking for old files, but the light didn't seem to be on in the office. As she pushed the door open a bit more, she could see old desks stacked with boxes and a few lab coats draped in the dim light spilling into the room from the hallway. Maybe someone had been there earlier, but no one was there now, so she pulled the door shut with a firm clack and checked her keyring to see if she had the proper key. She didn't so she resolved to inform the information desk that someone had left the office unlocked. She didn't have time to do anything about it now.

Jürgen felt his body prepare for the coming encounter. The door started opening and as soon as he saw any part of whoever it was come into the room, he would grab them and pull them in. He was fully capable of subduing most people with his bare hands, but he also had a garrote wire wound in his hand, ready to use. Adrenaline surged through him as he leaned forward, ready to heave the door open, pulling the intruder in with it, but the door reversed direction and closed with a clack. Then he heard a female voice grunting as she lifted a heavy load followed by footsteps heading up toward the lobby.

He sighed deeply several times to replenish his oxygen. He realized he had been holding his breath for the last minute or two, not something you want to do if you are about to do battle. Whoever it was had not locked the door, so they must not have had the right key. On his side of the door, the lock was a T-shaped knob that could be unbolted from the inside. He carefully surveyed both sides of several locks down here and compared those to the one on Dr. Dudek's door. He had practiced on the others that looked like hers and he was confident he could open the lock silently. He planned to open the door swiftly but quietly and if no one was in the outer room, he would rush to open the inner door before the doctor had time to react. He had no idea when she planned to leave for the night but he resolved to do this quickly instead of slowly to narrow the chances of getting caught.

Since the office light was on at the end of the hallway and its reflection off the floor would light the way, Jürgen turned the hall lights out once he had closed the dark office door. The eerie greenish-white light scattered off the shiny floor and he could see imperfections in its flatness causing the light on the walls to be distorted into irregular shapes. He had his lock picking tools ready as he walked down the length of the hall. Not only did he need to keep his footsteps quiet so as not to alert the doctor. He also needed silence to hear any footsteps approaching from behind. If the lights suddenly came on, he would pocket the tools and ask whoever it was to help him find his dropped glasses. Then, when their back was turned, he would escape.

He halted once when he heard a thud from ahead but realized it must have been a drawer shutting or a heavy book being closed. He resumed his progress toward the door at a quickened pace and stopped half his arm's length from the door. That way, he would not cast a visible image through the frosted glass. He inserted the straight pick, then the angled one. He wished he could spray some oil into the lock to make the movement even quieter, but he didn't have the luxury of time right now. As the mechanism aligned and tripped, he slowly turned the lock counterclockwise while also turning the straight pick to support the tumblers. There wasn't any sound that he could detect. He grasped the handle and pulled gently but the door did not move.

This usually meant that a door was stuck to the paint around it or the door jam was out of square. In either case, there would be a noise when he opened the door. He prepared himself.

Dr. Freda's eyes were getting heavy but she knew this would be a long night. She did not want to be drunk when Viktor and the others arrived, so she had restricted her gin intake to a painfully low level. The tea cup beside her silently called to her. She refused to look at it and yet, being to the side of her vision, the cup was receiving more of her mind's attention than the forms centered in her field of view. She found this both interesting and annoying. In the time between Helga leaving and the Nazi hunting group meeting, she would have plenty of time to finish her paperwork for the past week. She knew she would feel terrible if she wasted that time, so she strained to focus on the task at hand.

Helga must have forgotten something. Dr. Freda heard the outer door's sticky paint release the door with a crack. Whatever it was, Helga knew her way around. She would ask for help if she needed it. There had only been a second since the outer door opened but Helga was already opening her office door. Maybe she had a question to ask instead of forgetting something.

"Yes, Helga. What is it?" Dr. Freda kept her focus where it belonged, giving the girl time to formulate her response, but nothing came. As the silence dragged on, Dr. Freda was feeling imposed upon. She set her pen to the side of the form and looked up, but it wasn't Helga. It wasn't anyone she knew. A man in his fifties stood in her doorway. He was clean-shaven and wore a tan overcoat despite it not being cold or wet outside. He looked her directly in the eyes and it seemed he was trying to assess her somehow. Then the eyes gave him away. She had given a picture to Viktor with those eyes; different face, maybe lost a beard? She was certain now. This man tried to kill Albert and he was standing over her right now.

By the time she pushed her chair back and began to shift her weight to stand, he was already standing on her foot, reaching for her. He must have been waiting for Helga to leave so there would be no one to hear her. She channeled her strength into a sideways swing at his head with her right hand, using her left hand to hold the chair for leverage. The blow landed, but the force of it was absorbed by his arm. He now had a hand on her left arm holding that side of her body in place. He was rapidly gaining control of her and she knew that if she did not change that, the outcome would not be good. She tried to wrench her body under his, trying to slide off the chair and hopefully pull her arm free in the process, but the pain that stabbed her elbow told her his grip would not be broken so easily.

He was so close she could smell his smoky breath. The odor mixed with the gin she had been drinking and her stomach began to object. He used his weight and pushed her down into the chair. She was unable to resist but continued to struggle to free herself.

"Be still, *Fräulein*." His instruction carried a deadly seriousness and she immediately ceased moving. "If you force me to hurt you I will, *understand*?"

Freda nodded cautiously. She looked up into his eyes, but he was too close for her to focus on his face.

"You will tell me what I ask you to tell me and I will let you go unharmed. Now, doesn't that seem fair?" His grip tightened and her elbow throbbed. Her hands began to tingle from the pressure. She did not acknowledge him, but felt his grip relax. Maybe he thought he had gained control and would let his guard down. She would have to be vigilant for her chance.

"You know who I am, do you?"

"Yes," Freda confirmed.

He chuckled and leaned in close. "I didn't mean to hurt little Albie, but he said that he would tell others that I was there. He wasn't thinking very clearly, so I had to help him understand." Stooping even closer, he whispered in her ear, "Now you will not tell that I was here, will you?"

She shook her head indicating the negative, but not speaking. She was trying to give off as many fear signals as she could while still seeming plausible. That would help him lower his guard.

He slapped her hard across the face, releasing her left arm just long enough to complete the motion, then holding her down again. The blow stung and she tasted blood on her tongue. Her reading glasses careened across the desk then off the other side and her ear began to ring almost immediately.

He instructed her to remain seated and with his left hand, he reached for the overcoat pocket. The fabric was draping oddly since he was stooped over and he fumbled for a moment. This was her chance. She channeled all her strength into an upward thrust with her palm turned up. She was aiming for his nose in a move that Viktor had shown her. If it landed, it would kill the person instantly. Even if it didn't land, she would crush his nose. It seemed to take a long time for the swing upward to connect but when it did, the bones in her hand flashed with agony. He had tipped his chin up at just the right instant to catch the blow with his teeth clenched tight and his neck muscles ready to receive the force. He only lurched backwards a little, releasing her left arm. She would have moved just then but the pain from her hand had stunned her momentarily. He twisted his body, winding up to strike the insolent doctor. With a grunt, he slapped her as hard as he could, but open-handed so he did not damage her too much to be able to speak.

Freda felt the impact on her cheek and jaw and found that she could not take a breath. The intensity of the pain was too great. The room faded through a red glow into a blackness she could not escape.

It was almost time for the meeting with Viktor. The Bentley glided over the wet, black pavement that seemed to disappear unless the light glared just right off the road's surface. Ben was taking extra care around turns, driving at a relaxed pace. He learned to do this when he noticed on his own that passengers were being flung from side to side in the powerful car. No one had ever criticized him, but he thought this was the best job anyone could ever have, so he tried very hard to make everyone comfortable. Gabby told him that his *sixth sense* was coming along nicely. That made him feel good and whenever she was comfortable, she paid bonuses generously.

In the rear view mirror, Ben could see Lolita sitting on the car's right. A view of Gabby was blocked by his own head, but she would lean where he could see her if she needed anything. Lolita was not a vision of beauty, but she was something to look at. She had grown far more *herself* over the last year and much of that was to Gabby's credit. She included Lolita when others didn't. Tonight, she was dressed in a glamorous one-piece that had pinkish-gold reflective squares with rounded edges hanging from clips or stitches or something stuck into the fabric. They dangled in unison as she moved and Ben knew it must be terribly uncomfortable to wear something like that. The ethereal shafts of glowing pink light the dress cast around the car's interior made it seem warm and exciting.

There was no way of passing Lolita off as a woman. When shaven, he still had the shadow of a beard. His eyebrows were thick with gray hairs that stuck out at random angles. His nose, his makeup, the way he walked was humorous to watch, but none of that mattered. Ben had seen some of Lolita's comedy performances at *Kabarett Seks* when chaperoning Gabby and his confidence and sympathy with others succeeded in bringing the audience to tears of laughter. There were so few people in the world who stood out like Lolita.

"Thank you so much for letting me tag along," Lolita said, bowing her head in a gesture of grace. Tonight was going to be their first night out in almost two months. They had been so busy working with Viktor's men and helping Freda plan the excursion to Sudan that they hadn't really had time to just be together without some pressing obligation. In that time, Lolita and the whole group spent weekends at the Gorski Estate where they enjoyed lavish meals, large private rooms, and an expert staff.

"I just hope this meeting goes smoothly so we can go out and have some fun afterward." Gabby was as pent-up as Lolita and despite having a staff to take care of the mundane tasks, was still glad for the respite this evening would provide.

As they pulled through the circular driveway to the path leading to the *Medizinische Fakultät* at Cologne University, the headlights swept across some parked cars. Many belonged to various faculty members and doctors who were catching up on their work and wanted their cars close when they were ready to leave. This left no spaces large enough for the Bentley except at the opposite side of the half-circle. Ben would wait for them and once their business with Viktor and Freda was completed, he would take them to *Kabarett Seks* first, then to any other bars they wished to visit. As the headlights swept across the parked cars, Gabby saw a BMW 2000 Touring M40. She remembered the make and model from Jürgen being at her estate, but in the darkness and glare of the lights, she couldn't quite tell if it was blue or green.

"What is it?" Lolita asked, noticing the expression of concern on Gabby's face.

"I'm not sure. I thought I recognized a car." Gabby tried to brush off the odd feeling she was having, but it wasn't working.

Ben pulled all the way around the semicircular drive and parked against the sidewalk that traced the perimeter, joining at the center with a perpendicular path leading to the steps up to the hospital. This was not the entrance used by patients, but by doctors, teaching faculty, and staff. The parking lot to the side of the facility was almost completely empty as it always was after dark. Ben came around the car to open the door closest to the walkway. He held his hand out, first for Lolita, then for Gabriella. He would stand there observing them until they entered the building, since he was responsible for their security as well as being their chauffeur.

Faint shafts of pink light continued to reflect off Lolita's dress, which caught the dim light from the street lamp, some seventy-five metres away. As they walked, arm in arm, their forms faded to silhouettes against the dimly lit glass windows covering the front of the structure. Ben thought it poorly planned, that there were no lights on this side of the building for better visibility at night.

At the top of the steps, Gabby turned back toward the driveway and the car she had seen. There was so little light that from this angle, the car looked nearly black. She just couldn't ignore the sense that something was amiss.

Lolita reached for the door handle and pulled, taking the stance of a bellman saying, "Let me get the door for you, Miss." She gestured down an imaginary red carpet and Gabby played along, crossing the threshold with overdone glamour and pompous, bounding steps. The two laughed at their own childish behaviour and took each other's arms again as they walked through the lobby lit only by an overhead globe. The cocktails they had while getting dressed and doing makeup at the estate had mostly worn off by now and both of them were craving a fresh round, but business like this was too important to take lightly. They reached the opposite end of the expansive lobby where it narrowed to the large open end of the hallway that penetrated the building all the way through to the other side, where the hospital's main lobby was. It was still lit and they could see the occasional person crossing the hallway off in the distance. This end of the facility always shut down earlier than the other, but when they came to the stairs leading down to the basement, they were both a little put out. They knew that Dr. Freda would be working between the end of her workday and the start of the meeting and the basement was seldom used for any other purpose, but it seemed disrespectful of the staff to turn the lights off while the basement was still occupied.

Gabby flipped the switch on the wall illuminating the stairs after a flicker and buzz from the light tubes. Both of them squinted at the sudden increased light, then began to descend the stairs. Gabby noticed that Lolita was watching her closely as she turned to her left, stepped down with her right foot, then crossed her left foot over her right to land on the next step down. She slowed the movement and gathered her dress up to about knee height so Lolita could see more clearly. After a couple more steps, Lolita turned to her left, stepped down, then crossed over, very slowly and awkwardly descending the stairs. Gabby smiled at Lolita's application of a bouncing, grandiose style to the movement and she was certain this would somehow appear in her next comedy performance. She released the satin fabric of her gown which flowed around her and swung a bit back and forth as it fell to the floor. Raising her wrists, she pretended to wave at spectators, blowing kisses at the bare hospital walls and catching an imaginary bouquet of roses.

Lolita chuckled as she imitated her girlfriend and confidante. There were few people in Lolita's life who appreciated her for who she was. Gabby was kind, generous, but most of all, honest from their first meeting and they were becoming very good friends. Gabby had even invited Lolita to a couple social functions, but Horace felt that it would not be respectful to cause a scene at a social function, so he went in a very expensive suit he purchased that day. He knew how he looked in a dress. No amount of makeup would change the reality of his appearance. Tonight was a different story. Tonight, they were sisters, equals, and friends.

They reached the bottom of the steps and their irritation at the staff doubled. The hallway light was out too, even though Freda's office at the end of the hall was clearly occupied. Lolita stepped to the middle of the hallway as Gabby adjusted a shoe that wasn't fitting quite right. A moment of tugging on the strap and she was ready to proceed. She looked up at the light switch and raised a gloved hand to flip it up when Lolita's hand suddenly smacked her hand down. Appalled and not understanding why Lolita would be so rude, she looked up at Lolita's face and felt the blood drain from her own.

Lolita had one index finger pointing up and placed on her lips and the other slowly swaying from side to side. Gabby looked over Lolita's shoulder at the distant door and noticed something strange. In addition to the glow that would be expected from the frosted glass window and the slit under the door, there was a bright shaft of light projected vertically against the wall catacorner to the office door. Lolita reached down and slipped her shoes off, discarding them quietly to the side of the hallway. Gabby took the cue and removed hers as well, dropping them on top of Lolita's. Lolita began to walk toward the office down the dark hallway, being very careful not to make a sound and Gabby stayed directly behind, keeping her distance.

As they approached, it became clear that the shaft of light was indeed coming from the office. The door had been left ajar, but they still couldn't see how wide, nor did they see any movement or shadows beyond the door. Lolita crossed the hallway, hugging the right wall. Gabby realized that this would be the best angle of approach to avoid being seen through the gap should someone be behind the door. She followed and when they reached the corner where the hallway turned left, Lolita moved to a position just to the right of the shaft of light cast across the floor. She leaned left, into the shaft of light and back upright, then turned to look at Gabby who was coming around her right side. Gabby feared that someone had broken into the office. If they were still there, or if Freda had been kidnapped, or worse, they did not know.

Jürgen was disappointed in himself. He had not meant to hit her as hard as he did. Even if he could wake her up, she would be groggy for a long while. He should learn to control his strength better. At least he would have plenty of time to search the office before slitting her throat. Then he would head to the Wiesenhof Asylum to do the same to Albert. In the meantime, he would do what he must here. He reached into his pocket and withdrew a skein of cord wrapped several times around the middle. He stepped behind the chair, lifted her into an upright position and passed two loops of cord around her shoulders. This allowed him to hold her upright with just one hand while he threaded her hands through open spaces beneath the chair's arms. He tied her hands behind and under her and pulled the shoulder loop taught with a knot at the top and another looped around the knot that bound her hands. With just three knots he had anchored her so that even if she came to, her center of gravity would be too far back for her to get any leverage against her bonds.

He started with the stack of manila folders beside the ledger in the front office. This was the assistant's station so whatever she was working on would be the most recent activity. Some recent contacts might be helpful, especially if they contained something about Albert. To his surprise, Albert Novak was the name on the first folder. He set the entire folder aside to take with him. He began going through the other folders. The first one was for some girl named Gerta. Lots of long medical terms he didn't understand actually made it easier to scan the documents quickly. He picked out words that made sense to him, *personality disorder, second personality, childhood corrective surgery,* boring stuff. He slid that folder to the left, but since there was no counter top to catch it, the folder tumbled to the floor scattering a fan of papers that each went their separate ways when they hit the floor. The next folder and the next were cast to the floor as well.

The next folder had a name on it that intrigued him: Viktor Greko. His smile was crooked and filled with loathing. He knew this name. Viktor was the name he got out of that stupid boy, Liam. The youngster who thought he could become a spy was no match for him. He had known he was being observed for over a week when he decided to pay them a visit. He was able to see the way they changed shifts by moving to a position a couple blocks away. In the early morning hours, he noticed that one man entered a nondescript door on the side of the building and about 5 minutes later, one man came out the same door. They weren't even smart enough to come and go in a way that would not be noticed. Viktor had not trained his men well and this had made them easy to dispose of.

He had gone in the same door and since he knew where the room was, he only had to wait until someone left without being relieved and he could set up his own spy operation. A few nights later, it happened. Maybe the boy had been late. He waited a few minutes and entered, trying to move quietly on the creaking stairs and narrow hallways. Rats scurried along the baseboards and he could see three pathways. One on the left and the right for the rats and a large one down the middle where people had kicked the dust aside while walking. He found the room and, confirming it was unoccupied, entered and found a place that was completely hidden in shadow between the open door and a cabinet that was too large for the room, preventing the door from opening completely.

When Liam had arrived and Jürgen had him immobilized on his knees with his weight pressing down and his knife piercing about a centimetre into Liam's back, he had convinced the youngster that he would let him live if he provided names. The boy was weak and gave the name Viktor Greko before Jürgen had slowly pushed the knife into the boy's heart. With the blade turned sideways, it slipped easily between his ribs and he knew when the tip entered the boy's heart because he could feel the heartbeat through the handle. It was something he had never experienced before, so rather than leave the boy to bleed to death on his own, he stayed, holding him in place, asking his name, how it felt to die, what did he regret. As Liam's life drained away, Jürgen felt an exhilaration he had never felt before. Killing for him had always been a lethal blow and a swift exit, but this was something new and he found that he craved that feeling.

When he was done sorting papers and it was time to cut the doctor, how would she react to the knowledge of her impending death? Would he relish it as much as Liam's? He would have to speed things up. He set Viktor's file on top of Albert's and continued sending pages splashing to the floor as he scanned pages for words he could read. When he was done with the nurse's stack, he moved to the doctor's office through the middle door. Dr. Dudek was still where he had left her, head lolled off to one side in a position that was certainly going to hurt when she woke up.

He pushed her and the chair to the side. The old wheels resisted the direction he wanted, turning the chair around to the left as he pushed. He leaned over the desk. There was a bill on top of a stack of papers. When he spread the papers across the desk, some falling off the side to the floor, he saw that they were all bills. The last name on the ledger before him was the same name he had seen on the top bill. He continued to move papers around. What he had already found would be of great interest to Dr. Schumann and would help him gain the old man's appreciation, so he continued to dig for information, scattering papers and pushing books off the desk as he went.

Freda had no idea how much time had passed when her vision began to return. She knew that she had been unconscious for a while and her jaw was throbbing with each beat of her heart. It must be very swollen by now. She did not move, even though her head was cocked uncomfortably to the side. She saw a sideways view of her desk with Jürgen leaning over it, making a mess. Obviously he was searching for information and she knew that this was not just about her anymore. The information he got from her office could well put other people in danger, people she cared about. She would have to try to delay him until the others arrived, but how long would that be? What if Viktor was not the first one here? If Gabby or Lolita arrived, they would be no match for Jürgen and they might be hurt or even killed along with her.

Lolita motioned to Gabby to back up and after a few seconds, Lolita began to back down the hallway while keeping an eye on the doctor's front door. When they were about 20 paces away, Lolita stopped and Gabby came close so she could hear.

"There are papers on the floor and I think I saw someone moving," Lolita whispered in Gabby's ear, still keeping her eyes locked on the office door.

"What should we do?" Gabby's question was not frantic. It was purposeful.

"Freda is either alive or dead. If we wait too long, she will probably be dead, so we have to take care of this. You go tell Ben to bring the police while I try to surprise whoever has broken in." Lolita took Gabby by the shoulders and pushed her to the side, expecting her to turn and run, but she resisted.

"I am not letting you do this alone!" Gabby's whisper was dangerously loud and

Lolita shot her a scowling glance so she would lower her voice.

Seeing that Gabby was not going to back down, Lolita said in a gravelly whisper, "Just stay behind me." She began to advance toward the office door, stepping softly on the balls of her feet. The stockings made her feet slippery against the polished floor. This would be a problem if she was about to confront an assailant but it was better than fighting in heels.

Lolita schemed and planned, working through different scenarios and what she would do in each case. Since she was dressed the part, she would take advantage of the Lolita costume and persona if at all possible. Maybe she could lull whoever had broken in into a false sense of security, but she and Gabby both realized who it probably was.

"The car!" Gabby whispered over Lolita's shoulder, realizing that she *had indeed* recognized one of the cars. It was too coincidental that the same exact car Jürgen was driving when visiting her was now parked outside and Freda's office had been broken into.

Lolita only nodded, so Gabby assumed that she understood. Lolita spread her knees wide as she prepared to barge through the door. An upward lunge would give her the momentum she would need to make it all the way into the back office in a single stride, even if the door between them were closed. He squatted down, positioned his hand under the doorknob, and prepared himself, but now he could hear someone talking. It was a man's voice, but it was so low and muffled that he couldn't make out what he was saying. Then a woman's voice, soft and quiet, was audible. Freda was still alive. He remained crouched, straining to hear anything that might help their situation.

"Ah. You are awake."

Freda lifted her head and stretched her neck, bending her head to the opposite side. The muscles were sore and protested her movements. She felt the tension of the cord holding her to the chair and pulled her hands to test its strength. Jürgen was no fool. He had not used thick ropes which were easy to untie. He knew that a small cord would hold a knot better and was easily strong enough so that she had no hope of breaking it. She glared at Jürgen.

"I didn't mean to hit you that hard. I hope you will accept my apologies." Jürgen's tone might have seemed sincere if the situation were different, but in her current predicament, she knew better than to take anything he said as fact. Nevertheless, she would need to take advantage in any way she could. She didn't respond right away so he drew a new package of cigarettes from his pocket, unfolded the foil at the top, and flipped his wrist so several of the cigarettes leapt upward, sticking out of the pack. With his lips, he selected one and pulled it free while with the other hand he retrieved a lighter from his pocket. Striking the lighter, he put the yellow flame to the cigarette and drew just enough to light it. He put the lighter away and took the cigarette between the fingers of his left hand as he inhaled deeply.

"You don't know your own strength," Freda said as she worked her jaw open and closed.

"I am glad I did not hurt you too badly. I have some questions to ask you." There was a touch of menace in his carefully balanced tone and he breathed out puffs of smoke as he spoke.

"I might be able to help you if you tell me who you are," Freda bluffed.

He froze for an instant. "Don't do that. Don't act stupid. You know who I am." He let the intensity of his hatred for her flow out in those few words and Freda knew that if she was not found soon, she would die. "There. You see? You gained nothing by lying to me," he remarked as he watched the effects of his intimidation crush her hopes for escape. He needed to bait her now; to give her some hope so she might trust him. "I promise I won't hurt you if you just answer my questions."

"I will answer if I can," she said reluctantly.

"How do you know a Mr. Horace Krämer, the banker?"

Freda's blood ran cold. He knew exactly how Horace had helped her which meant he would be Jürgen's next target. "He helps me with my banking." As soon as she said it, she was ashamed at how obvious the lie was.

Jürgen stooped and leaned forward to put his face very close to hers. The stench of cigarette smoke wafted from his lungs, invading her nose. He brought the glowing orange cherry of the cigarette up to her face, keeping his own face close. He slowly moved the lit cigarette closer and closer to her right eye, just to the right of her field of view. This was a technique he had practiced over the years. The movements of a person's eyes when a danger was approaching would help gauge how susceptible to fear and intimidation they were. Dr. Dudek did not look at the cigarette, but held his gaze unblinking. This frumpy old Jew would not be as easy to interrogate as he had hoped.

"Do not lie to me again or I will put this out in your eye. Understand?" He paused moving the cigarette closer, holding it just a centimetre from the white of her eye. At this distance, she could feel the heat radiating from the tip and see the orange glow. This usually helped people to make up their minds to be honest very quickly.

Freda began to sort her thoughts into two categories. If she simply confirmed what Jürgen already knew, that would create no higher risk to anyone else. If she gave him new information, she could be putting others' lives in danger. She vowed to herself that she would not let that happen. He was waiting for an honest answer about Horace, so she decided to begin doling out bits of harmless information.

"Mr. Krämer helped me trace some suspicious transactions. I am certain you are aware of at least one of those." She hoped the statement would get him talking. Anything that might waste time would help her, so playing to his ego would be beneficial just now.

"I don't know what you mean," was the answer that he gave, but he poured menace and threat into the answer so she would know that she was treading dangerously.

"Dr. Horst Schumann paid you over one-hundred thousand *Deutsche Marks* to bring you here. I think that means he is worried someone might be looking for him." Jürgen's obvious look of surprise confirmed for Freda that she was indeed piquing his interest so she added, "I imagine that he sent you here to find out who that might be."

"You could be on to something there," Jürgen said. Taking his time, he smoked his cigarette and considered his next question before asking, "How would a pampered socialite be involved? You know the one...Gorski."

On hearing Gabby's name through the two doors, Lolita knew she must act to protect both Gabby and Freda from whatever this bully had planned. She lunged upward which gave her leverage against the door on her slippery feet. The door swung open, but she did not let go of the knob. She brought the rapidly moving door to a stop at right angles to the door frame as she headed for the inner office door.

"Yoo hoo! Dr. Freda? Are you there?" Lolita braced her shoulder to strike the inner door as she called out in a carefree, innocent voice. If she could cause just a moment's hesitation, she might be able to surprise the intruder, but just as she reached for the doorknob, the door swung wide giving her nothing to transfer her weight to. As her motion continued forward, she lost her balance and fell face-first onto the floor.

Jürgen thought he heard someone so he left the doctor sitting quietly and moved to the door so he could see through the gap into the front room, but the angle was too extreme. Just then, he felt the pressure in the room change so he pulled the door toward him. He had intended to use the door as a club against whoever came through, but it happened so quickly he had no time to react. A woman in a sparkly dress came careening through and smacked the floor so hard he heard the woman's skull impact the floor. She rolled over on her back and he recognized her as the crossdresser in his dream. This was the one who had toyed with him the night he went to *Kabarett Seks* to see Gabriella Gorski. This might have even been the one who had drugged him that night, maybe as a prank or to take advantage of him after he left the club.

He turned to face her as she tried to lift herself against the back wall. He had not wanted to use a gun, but this situation required a speedy resolution and escape. His hatred for this man in a dress boiled and he flung the right side of his coat open, clasping the handle of his Luger pistol and drawing it out of its holster. One shot each should finish them both. Then he would have to leave quickly since the sound would surely be heard by someone. As he took aim, Lolita's eyes went wide. She knew this was the end but her last thoughts were not of embarrassment at being killed in a dress. They were of how she might still tackle Jürgen with her dying breath so that Freda and Gabby could escape. Jürgen aimed the pistol carefully but did not fire. Instead, he crouched down, getting closer and closer until the barrel of the gun was touching Lolita's forehead.

He snarled in her ear, "People like you make all the rest of us unclean. You don't deserve to breathe the air that I do. Now, I am going to fix that."

Just then, he heard something behind and he turned his head for an instant. All he could see was a shadow blocking the door so he quickly rotated his body to take aim at the intruder and shot as quickly as he could.

An unexpected impact to his shoulder shoved him toward Lolita, knocking the pistol from his now stinging hand. His whole arm went numb the instant before he noticed that his ears were ringing from the deafening sound of two shots, not one. As wave after wave of pain mounted in his back, penetrating through to his chest, he realized that he had been shot. The crossdresser was still holding his wrist so it couldn't have been him. Maybe Dr. Dudek had freed herself, but when he looked, she was still tied to the chair. He continued turning toward the open door where the beautiful Gabriella Gorski was standing, surrounded by the glow of the lights from the front room.

A thin trail of smoke rose from the right barrel of the *Röhm* RG-17 double-barrel .38 Special Derringer she held at arm's length, still pointing at him. A moment before, her left side appeared to be shoved backward, but she did not lose her balance. Her left arm hung oddly at her side and she let out a sound like a grunt and a scream forced between gritted teeth. She retrained the weapon on Jürgen's head. She had one more shot ready and he knew that she could kill him at any second. He shifted his weight, preparing to spring toward her when he felt someone tap his injured shoulder hard causing him to see stars and wince in pain. He turned around just in time to see Lolita's fist coming at him fast. The blow connected and Jürgen's jaw broke cleanly with a sharp snap. As his vision faced, he could feel where his jaw had split between his two lower front teeth, spreading them apart and the left half of his jaw turned at an odd angle to the rest of his face. He could no longer support his weight, so he began to fall over toward Gabby. He was no longer conscious when his face whacked against the floor.

Lolita sat on the chaise where she had been through many sessions of hypnosis under Dr. Freda's care. Gabby lowered the gun and looked at her arm, then at Freda who was sitting silently, mouth agape. Freda would later describe how lucky she was that the bullet had only bounced off the side of the bone, cleanly breaking it in half. If it had struck more directly, the bone would have splintered and been much more difficult to fix. Lolita saw another dark shadow occlude the doorway behind Gabby and a deep, rumbling voice called out. All three ladies yelped in unison as they were startled by the new intruder and Gabby aimed her gun but did not fire.

Viktor carefully raised his hands. "I will be sure never to underestimate you ladies again, but I would appreciate it if you didn't kill me just yet." Viktor came through the door, hands still raised, and stooped to survey Jürgen's form on the floor. He rolled the unconscious man on his back and put a hand over his mouth. "He's still breathing." Looking up at Freda, he asked quite sincerely, "I could kill him for you. It would be very quick." His eyebrows raised and the pleading look on his face almost had Freda convinced he was serious, until a smirk crept into his expression.

"Thank you for the offer, Viktor, but I think we will let the authorities take care of this one."

They heard the sound of feet running down the hall toward them. No doubt someone in the main lobby had heard the shots and was coming to investigate. As the person running arrived at the office, he came to a sliding stop on the papers strewn on the front office floor. Ben caught himself with both hands on the door frame and poked his head through. Gabby smiled, happy that Ben had come running to her rescue, but as she prepared to protect her arm from him, he searched the room frantically. He looked over Viktor and, seeing Lolita sitting there cradling her arm and bleeding from a cut on her forehead, he rudely shoved Viktor back so he could pass. He went down on one knee and began to inspect Lolita for gunshot wounds. He roughly turned her head to one side, then the other, inspecting her neck. He reached up under her wig, feeling for any other areas that might be bleeding. He gently slid a hand under her cradled arm, and looked up into Lolita's eyes, tears welling in his own. Lolita didn't say anything. She raised her hand and, placing it on his cheek, gave a look that silently said, "Thank you for caring."

Gabby watched the heartfelt exchange. *"Verdammit!"*

Viktor looked at Gabby with a smile on his face. "Let the boys have this moment. We need to get that looked at," he said, indicating her bleeding arm. He turned and walked toward the front office door where more people were arriving. Someone turned the hallway lights back on and three orderlies were looking over an older nurse's head to see what was going on. "I think you should call the police," Viktor remarked as he headed back up the hallway. Everyone there thought the situation had been resolved, but as Viktor climbed the steps to the lobby, he planned out the observation points his men would move to, just to make sure there wasn't a cleaner following behind to either kill Jürgen or finish a job he failed to complete. He crossed the lobby and sat at a padded bench on the opposite side of the room. He took out a cigarette and lit it. It was going to be another long night, but at least this time he wouldn't have to watch another friend be carried away in a bag. He motioned *all's well* to the spotter hiding somewhere outside. He trusted his men not to make any rash moves. He did not want any of them to have to deal directly with the police if he could avoid it. They would have many questions.

Viktor watched as the police arrived, one officer, then another, eventually almost a dozen. They were already in a hospital so after a while Ben appeared, helping Lolita up the stairs and carrying her shoes. All the while, Lolita protested his doting but Viktor could see that she secretly appreciated the young man's attention. They went off toward the main lobby and emergency entrance to have her head looked at. They never looked up at Viktor. Likewise, Gabriella came up the stairs assisted by a nurse who had a firm grip on her other arm just in case she experienced a psychogenic blackout as often happens after a physical or mental trauma. She was also too preoccupied to see him.

Jürgen was brought up on a gurney being carried by two huge orderlies and surrounded by four officers. Viktor could see that his left wrist was handcuffed to the frame of the gurney and when they dropped the wheels after reaching the top step, the jolt brought a cry of pain from Jürgen's prone form. Viktor was certain he had earned that small retribution for trying to kill his friends. He felt more invested in the hunt for Dr. Schumann than he had before this incident and he promised himself he would do whatever he could to see that he was captured and made to answer for his crimes.

He talked to one officer who came into the lobby, but since he walked in after everything had happened, he didn't have any first-hand information to offer. The officer walked away as another appeared coming up the steps, steadying Freda. As Freda's head came above floor-level, she saw Viktor sitting across the lobby and smiled. He was standing guard. Even though he had not stopped Jürgen, he was not going to simply walk away when attention wasn't on him. As she reached the top of the steps, she patted the officer's hand supporting her elbow, assuring him that he could go about his business without worrying about her. She walked toward Viktor and he stood to walk toward her. They met in the middle of the lobby and he took both her hands up in his own.

"You are a lucky lady."

Freda blushed for the first time in many years. He smelled just as bad up close as he always had, but just now, it didn't seem so offensive. He lifted her right hand and tucked it under his left elbow as he turned toward the main lobby and they walked slowly, saying nothing.

Chapter 31

He went through one operation to fix his shattered shoulder blade and a second to control some bleeding that was most likely the result of a bone chip piercing an artery just enough to weaken it but not enough for it to bleed so they missed it the first time. They kept his pain medication low so he had not slept more than a couple hours at night. He would awaken when the injection wore off and they would leave him suffering until his next scheduled dose. He despised being under the control of these doctors and the two officers who stood guard took turns with meals and breaks so that he was never left alone. At least they stayed outside the blue curtain that was suspended knee-high from the floor by beaded flexible metal cords in an overhead track. They had not taken his handcuff off even once, but that didn't mean he was all alone.

He had left word with his contact in the network that he would report back at a specific time. When that didn't happen, they came looking for him and found him under guard in the hospital, upstairs from where he was to have assassinated the doctor. Because of that mistake, they were both under guard, as were Albert Novak and Gabriella Gorski. The operation had devolved into an amateur mess, but the network was patient and resourceful. There was no need to dispose of Jürgen until his doctors approved his interrogation. A cleaner would make sure the body was lost in storage, and would then begin the long task of eliminating the local players to protect Dr. Schumann.

Jürgen was very drowsy after several days of little sleep so he didn't see the young officer come through the curtain. The dark form looming over him disturbed his fitful sleep, so Jürgen opened his eyes and looked up. The officer stood at attention right next to his bed, which was odd because the police didn't act that way to prisoners. The officer said nothing, but slid a pad of blue stationary under his cuffed left hand and worked a pencil between his thumb and forefinger. Jürgen realized that this was a member of the Nazi network giving him a chance to get a message out undetected. He scribbled quickly, only stopping to think for a few seconds now and then. The instant he was done, the officer pocketed the stationary and pencil, and stood back at attention with an empty clipboard. "Who should I send this to?" he whispered.

"Schumann, in Khartoum," was Jürgen's answer.

The officer stood at attention as a nurse entered. Jürgen was impressed that the young man was not phased by the unexpected intrusion. They never asked permission to enter, which was irritating, especially when he was trying to relieve himself with one arm in a cast and the other hand chained to a rail. He would finally get some relief from the pain and get a couple hours of sleep once the pain medication started working, but he began to feel strangely stupefied and drunk, not like the normal morphine haze he enjoyed. As his chest began to feel tight and hot, he opened his eyes to see the nurse looking at the officer, both standing at attention, observing. His breath began to come in short gasps, each breath shorter than the last. He tried to take a deep lung full of air, but found that he could only pant shallowly. As he began to struggle, the nurse put a hand on his chest and held him still. He couldn't make a sound because he couldn't take a breath and even though he was a strong man, he didn't have enough strength to sit up or even kick his legs. As his panting grew faster, his vision narrowed to a long tunnel surrounded by blackish-red walls. The curtains before him began to draw off into the distance as the tunnel became longer. The sounds of the hospital became distant echoes and his body began to relax as his breathing stopped. Jürgen saw the face of the nurse and then the officer looking down the ever-lengthening tunnel and he wanted to call out to them, but he was unable to move or make a sound. The end of the tunnel began to fade; darker and darker until there was nothing.

Chapter 32

Saturday, 17 February, 1962

I find myself sitting alone in the grass on a cool, breezy day in the courtyard of the [Wiesenhof] asylum, overcome with a feeling of profundity. My thoughts attempt to expand enough to allow for the possibility that what has happened to me has not been by chance. To have suffered so greatly as a child, losing parents and siblings, then being institutionalized is not something unexpected, but to then find the most gracious and forgiving Dr. Freda Dudek who not only does her best to make me whole, she gives of herself to the limit of her stamina. She leaves me in awe. I see it as even more incredible that after so many long years, my dearest friend Gabriel should find me bringing with him stories of life, love, and liberation that warm my heart. Then two who were swept along by a river of hate, yet who showed me the deepest kindness at their own great peril, come to my rescue once again and give of themselves so that I might be lifted from my own personal pit of despair.

My mind considers that the universe might revolve around me, given the extreme rarity of coincidences. It is an odd state to be as an outside observer, seeing my own awakening and analyzing it as I am. I harbour a fear that the mind, in its complexity, could fool itself into a sort of temporary healing by faith alone; that such healing might vanish like a wisp of smoke at the next trauma. Would I succumb despite the sacrifices of those who love me? I must believe that I would not, yet I doubt my conviction even before the ink on this page is dry.

In times when doubt prevails, Dr. Freda reminds me to write an account of something uplifting. Thinking on the frequent visits of my friend Gabriel, now Gabriella, a smile possesses my lips. The warmth of his love radiates even more strongly through who he has become. It is as if his trials somehow cleared a lens through which his love for the world now shines even more brightly. His trials did not break him. They created her. The cruelty of life pushed him to transform, not away from himself, but toward a better version of himself, which happens to be female. Her challenges have been little different from my own in their principal, so I am forced to conclude that in my past, perhaps hidden from my own memory, are the seeds of experience that can make me whole again.

"Albert?" The raised voice startled him and his pen faltered mid-sentence. He realized that a shadow had approached and covered the page, but he hadn't seen it. He looked up, maneuvering to place the sun behind Hugo's head so he could see his face. Albert smiled, closing his journal and setting it aside on the grass, resting the pen on the cover.

Albert rose and wrapped his arms around Hugo, who tolerated the overt display and reluctantly reciprocated. Albert then turned to Maria who had kicked off her shoes and stepped into the grass to Hugo's side. She beamed with happiness and spread her arms wide. Albert moved to embrace her and gently hugged her as she stood on her toes to reach his level. He guided her back down and she held him at arm's length to examine him from head to foot, showing her pride in him.

"My boy, you seem ready for today." On Hugo and Maria's most recent visits, Albert had been progressively more coherent as Dr. Freda reduced his narcotic medications, replacing them with a new class of antidepressants and mood stabilizers. Though the success rate with these medications had only been a little more than sixty percent over the first few years of trials, Dr. Freda and Albert agreed that the risks were worth the potential benefit and Albert turned out to be one of the lucky ones.

"I am ready. It will be so good to get out into the world again." Ever since the news of Jürgen's death, he had been noticing a new urge to get away from the confines of the asylum. He hoped the authorities could question him and impose justice on him, but complications stemming from the gunshot wound had led to a blood clot that killed him a couple days after surgery.

For today's excursion, Albert had chosen a tan American-style blazer with patches sewn onto the elbows. The informal fashion had been adopted recently by academics and Hugo told Albert it made him appear worldly. Navy slacks and turtle shell frames on his reading glasses did make it seem that he might be a student from the nearby university campus taking advantage of the peace and tranquility of the isolated courtyard for study rather than a patient writing in his journal.

"Ben is waiting for us in the car," said Hugo to the group and he turned to lead them back into the wing once Albert had collected his journal. They turned left through the glass doors which were locked behind them by the orderly who escorted them to find Albert. They walked down the long hall until they came to Albert's door on the left where he stopped to deposit his journal. Then they continued toward the lobby.

As they approached the front desk, Nurse Mila heard them coming and peeked her head around the corner to see who was there. She knew that today would be Albert's first time out of the Wiesenhof since his arrival over three years ago. In that time she, like many of the staff, became quite attached to Albert. Seeing him heading for the door brought an immediate upwelling of happy tears. She put her hands together in front of her mouth in a praying motion and nodded her approval as they neared. Albert came to the end of the hallway where it opened into the spacious lobby and saw that Nurse Mila was not alone. Standing off to the side and now moving toward his path were Nurses Jean and Curtis, the orderlies Timothy and Kent, and a few others who had begun to consider Albert family. Hugo was leading, but now stepped to the right to yield the floor to Albert who stopped even with the front desk. Albert took a deep breath and began to walk toward the door.

In unison, the staff stepped up in a line to pat him on the shoulder as he passed, saying that they were proud of him and they were so happy for him. Albert could not help the smile on his face, though he didn't think that walking to the door should be worthy of so much praise. He felt more embarrassed than anything, but he understood how they felt. Each of them lived to see this moment for each of their patients. One by one they completed their congratulations and stepped back to allow Albert to continue on his way, symbolically leaving them behind. As he approached the huge glass doors being held open by the two newest and youngest orderlies, Hugo came up behind him on his right and Maria on his left.

"Let us go have some fun today," Hugo said, giving Albert a proud pat on the shoulder as a father would his son.

Ben drove them along busy streets to the center of the city where most of the museums were clustered. They spent the day roaming vaulted halls and large darkened rooms with paintings and sculptures illuminated in the darkness. Albert had not been to the museums since he was a child and marveled at the grandeur of these huge structures.

He walked the halls with a new clarity of mind he had not experienced in a long time. He found that on the new medications, he could think about things that were prone to overwhelm him with emotion. Now, he could examine what happened to him and analyze it. It felt as though he had an adult's control but there were times he wished he could just sit and cry. He had tried crying a few times but found he was unable to. Dr. Freda had explained that the antidepressants would reduce his ability to experience strong emotions and give him a way to deal with his emotions in a more constructive way.

A few days before, Dr. Freda had formally requested a meeting with Albert after today's outing. It was time to talk about the upcoming changes in his life. He couldn't live at the asylum once he recovered and he didn't want to be a burden to his parents. He was considering two options. He could either go out and get a job to support himself like any grown man, or he could accept his father's offer to send him back to the Budapest Seminary. He was a bit old for seminary school, but there were men older than he who attended. His theological background would probably not have much value in the job market and without a degree he was unlikely to find a job that paid well. Possibly, he could find factory or clerical work through family or friends.

Hugo and Maria had also been invited to the conference, as were Gabby and Anton. They each expressed their happiness at Albert's recovery and he was glad that they would be there. For months, Hugo and Maria had been coming to Cologne for week-long stays during which they visited with him for hours. Albert felt that their interactions filled a void he had thought to be bottomless. Often, their visits were part of treatment sessions with Dr. Freda during which he would tell the group about his youth and his time in the camps. After each tale, they would converse, exploring the nuances of his fears. Sometimes these sessions would last all day and into the evening until the windows grew dark and the asylum began to shut down for the night.

Gabby was growing weary of the constant attention from the staff and from Anton, but she understood, their concern came from how much they cared for her. Dealing with the cast was tedious, but she was managing. She would be so happy when she could get back into some of her favourite gowns, but for now, it was a focus of conversation. When the socialites would see her in public with her cast, the talk was not of scandal, but of the heroic Mrs. Gorski and her deadly aim.

Hugo had recently accessed a vault where he kept pictures he had smuggled out of Germany at the end of the war. It had been almost twenty years since he had taken them and he was considering releasing them to the world. He decided that Time magazine in America was the most effective means to disseminate the historical pictures, his goal being to not allow them to pass out of memory. Already, the ranks of Holocaust deniers were spreading around the world and he felt it was his duty to present evidence to refute them. Occasionally, Hugo would bring envelopes filled with photos, spreading them out on the small table Dr. Freda had moved into Albert's room. At first, Dr. Freda insisted on being present while they discussed the pictures, especially the ones of Dr. Horst Schumann, which caused in Albert a welling up of hatred and a desired vengeance that she knew was only under control because of the medications.

Hugo, Albert, and Maria had a wonderful time exploring the museum district and had a light lunch at a nearby cafe. It was a weekday but because the museum district was in the center of Cologne, it was bustling with people. Men rushed around with briefcases heading from this building to that, crossing the museum properties but not taking time to appreciate them. Albert thought it was sad to see people ignoring the beauty before them. They talked about the politics of the pre-war era which Albert did not really care about when he was young, but which now provided some insight into how some people could be so horrible, while otherwise good people did nothing to stop them.

The sun shone and a light breeze caused the tablecloth to swirl around their knees. The hostess gave them a table some distance from the cafe where they could enjoy some privacy and spend time talking, giving Maria a chance to recover from all the walking around. A small vase with two miniature mums on long, naked stems threatened to tip when the wind sporadically changed direction. They had coffee and croissants with honey butter made by the cafe's owner who came out to visit them personally once they had settled. He invited them to stay as long as they liked, but they were due back at the Wiesenhof in a couple hours and they still wanted to visit some of the smaller museums.

As noon drew closer, they approached the Gorskis' Bentley. Ben, leaning against the driver's door basking in the sunlight, saw them coming from far away. He opened the passenger door, standing at attention for nearly ten minutes as they walked at Maria's pace. Maria and Albert both thanked Ben as they climbed into the back seat but Hugo did not wait. He rounded the back of the car and let himself into the passenger front-side door. Ben gave him a pleading look, but Hugo was accustomed to serving himself and being waited on made him uncomfortable. Most often, Hugo would find that Ben had expertly anticipated their needs before they knew they had them.

Albert was feeling a touch of nervousness as they traveled the city streets. Seeing the look of concern on his face, Maria placed a hand on his. He looked at her and, seeing her compassionate smile, placed his other hand on hers saying nothing. They both looked forward and enjoyed the calm silence for a time.

The three slowly made their way toward the doors of the asylum while Ben took the Bentley around toward the side parking lot. Gabby had given instructions to wait for them until the meeting was over. She and Anton drove themselves into town and when Ben drove around the side of the building, he could see the small Mercedes parked among the other cars. In the back of his mind, he hated how cramped that car was, but it was one of Gabby's favourites and to her it seemed spacious. He selected a location away from the other cars where he had a clear line of sight to the roadster and settled in for a long wait.

"Why don't you get the picture Dr. Freda asked you to bring?" Hugo suggested as the three came to Albert's door in the asylum hallway. He patted Albert on the shoulder saying, "catch up to us on the way there."

Albert opened the door to his room and stepped in as the others continued down the hall toward the conference room. He closed the door and stood for a moment viewing the room not as a resident, but as one who is renting quarters. They had begun to seem overly sterile to him since he spent more time in the courtyard. Today, after viewing great works of art in grand buildings that were works of art themselves, he felt like a stranger here in this tiny room. He went to the closet, reaching up to the shelf above his clothes. It seemed almost comical to him that only three sets of clothing hung on the wooden bar, as if he were a traveller only staying for a few days. He brought down his copy of *The Brothers Karamazov* and held it for a long while. The edges of the cover and the corners of the pages had been worn so smooth as to feel like soft cloth against his fingertips. The binding had begun releasing pages after decades of use, but he had kept every single page in its proper place. Where the loose pages stuck out, they had been worn smooth as well, becoming softer and their exposed edges had picked up stains from two decades of frequent handling.

He held the book to his chin and closed his eyes, inhaling deeply. The smell of the paperback roused memories of home and family, of love and guilt, and of life-long hatred for the Nazis that had taken his birth parents. Some day, he vowed to find and punish the men who violated him, if they were still alive. With his eyes closed, he allowed the emotions to swirl within him. He felt the ebb and flow as his mind grappled with unspeakable images that appeared above the flotsam of his thoughts and faded away as new images bubbled to the surface. One vision was always there, clearer than the others, something he had never told Dr. Freda. Perhaps today would be the day. He had been feeling lately that this memory of something he had done might be one of the last to conquer before getting on with his life. The thought of confessing this particular sin sent a shiver of fear through him. Would she be appalled? Would the others abandon him for this thing he had done as a child? He might find out shortly.

He retrieved his journal from the nightstand before heading for the conference room. Turning right, he saw Hugo and Maria ambling in the distance and began walking the same direction. He passed through the common room which opened to the left as part of the hallway. A mother who was cradling a boy of nine or ten years old looked up and smiled a silent greeting as he passed. The boy's mouth was slack and his skin was gray. A lone patient was standing in the middle of the room mumbling as if conspiring with someone nearby.

On the right, the glass wall that separated the common room from the courtyard radiated the warmth it had stored up while it was in sunlight. It was past noon now and the shadow of the rooftop was moving away from the glass wall, slowly consuming the courtyard. In another month, the cool breezy days would give way to the cold, gray days of winter. A boy, Timmy was his name, was trying to fly a kite but the courtyard was surrounded on all four sides, never allowing enough breeze close to the ground to fly a kite. Nevertheless, the child ran and laughed all the while dragging the kite upside-down and skittering along on its tip, blades of grass flying up behind it as they were plowed up. He couldn't remember her name, but Timmy's mother stood nearby smiling and shaking her head at the child's hopeless battle against gravity. Albert tried many times to help the boy launch his kite, throwing it up as hard as he could just as the string went taught, but the kite never caught enough air to fly. Albert remembered the frightening day he saw Timmy shudder and fall face-down while running with the spool of kite string, not even trying to catch himself. The boy's seizures were so severe and sudden that he might never be able to live a normal life, but Albert made the wish like a daily prayer, that Timmy might one day be able to live a young man's life with a wife and a family of his own.

Albert proceeded to the other side of the common room where the hallway narrowed again and seeing the closed conference room door, stood outside. This was what he had been working toward, what they all had been working toward for so long. Opening this door meant closing so many others. He reached for the doorknob, but found he did not want to turn it. Just a few more seconds of...whatever he had in this place. No. It was time to move forward. He turned the knob and the people he had come to regard as his extended family came into view as the heavy door swung silently open.

Gabby stood on the left holding Anton's arm. She was positively radiant in a white cocktail party dress with vibrant yellow lemon and green leaf print. It flared out from the waist ending at the knees, showing off her flawless legs and impossibly high white heels. Ten years ago, this type of dress had been new to American fashion, but now the fashion was being discovered here in Germany. Anton's charcoal grey coat draped the black leather chair nearest him and he looked up from Gabby whispering something in his ear. Gabby looked toward the door and smiled coyly at Albert.

Hugo and Maria were just inside the door and turned toward each other so they could see Albert coming in. They both smiled and headed off to the right side of the table. Dr. Freda was at the far side of the table standing. She had uncovered her hair for the occasion, but her clothes were no different than any other day. Albert wondered if she had anything other than wool skirts and shawls. His breath caught in his throat. Ernst stood with his hat in his hands. He looked from Lena at his side, up to his son and a broad grin slowly spread across his face. Lena was covering her mouth and nose with a white handkerchief and tears were streaming down her careworn face. Albert recognized Ernst's only charcoal suit. It was the same one he wore to the synagogue for somber ceremonies like weddings and funerals. Lena wore a heavy black wool skirt that hung to the floor with a cream top with baggy sleeves and a floppy black bow tied around her neck.

Ernst and Lena came to Albert and wrapped their son in a heartfelt embrace, nearly knocking the books from his hand. Ernst slapped his hand down on Albert's shoulder several times to punctuate his pride and Lena squeezed the three of them together. Ernst reached to take Lena's arm which was still grasping Albert's. As she released him, Albert turned toward the table. He felt underdressed, but he didn't yet have very many choices in his closet. As he pulled out his chair, those around the room pulled theirs out too.

Everyone situated themselves comfortably around the table except Dr. Freda who remained standing, one hand over the other. She looked at the faces around the room one by one and when she was satisfied that she had everyone's attention, she took a deep breath, held it a moment, and let it out. Albert thought surely she had been in this situation many times. Why would she appear nervous this time? As she began to speak, he heard trepidation in her voice. Perhaps his condition had not improved as much as he had thought. He resigned himself to hear her out with an open mind.

"*Herr* Albert Novak." She stopped and collected her thoughts further before continuing. She knew this must have been a moment Albert had been anticipating for many months and she did not want to spoil it for him. Vindication was a necessary reward that encouraged further growth and social engagement and she would see that he had his. She started again. "I am so very grateful to have met you, *Herr* Novak. Being your doctor has helped me grow more than you will ever know. Seeing you begin to accept responsibility for your life and to deal with past events is something I will cherish for the rest of my days. I speak to you now as your former doctor and your forever friend."

Gabby began clapping heartily. After a slight delay, everyone joined her in making a cacophony in the small space. Dr. Freda held up her hands in a calming gesture. Albert was embarrassed but committed to see this through so he tolerated the attention with a sheepish grin. Dr. Freda came around the table to the empty chair at the corner between Gabby and Albert. She stood for a moment, appearing to weigh her next move. Albert wasn't sure what was happening. He thought maybe this was just her style of letting patients go, so he watched her without speaking. A look of resolution came over her face and she pulled the chair out to sit down. She did not move up to the table but instead slouched forward informally.

"I am going to tell you something that may be a bit upsetting, but it needs to be said." Dr. Freda paused waiting for Albert's approval to proceed. He nodded so she continued. "Do you have the picture Hugo gave you in the camp?"

He had turned toward her in his chair as she rounded the corner and was still holding the novel and his journal in his lap. He retrieved the picture from the back pocket of the large volume. It was the picture of him, Gabriel and their friend Lukas from Auschwitz, emaciated and emasculated. Holding the picture out to Dr. Freda, she took it gingerly and turned it so she could see. She placed her hand over the picture as if sensing something from it. Albert was still a bit confused, but he listened intently. Gabby let Anton's arm go and moved her chair to be closer to theirs, putting a reassuring hand on Dr. Freda's arm. Freda closed her eyes as she gathered her conviction but opened them at Gabby's touch, removing the hand covering the photo. She placed her hand on Gabby's, hesitating.

"Go on. It will be alright." Gabby's sincere reassurance made Albert think the worst. Was he unsalvageable? Had she found something else wrong with him? His heart began to race and he began to feel fear creeping into his thoughts.

One morning very early, Gabriel and Lukas were awakened by the mouse-like sounds of Albert crying. They were both afraid that the soldiers would come and put a bullet in his head if they heard him suffering, so they climbed out from under their crusty blankets and came to him asking what was wrong but he would not tell them. The night was bitterly cold. They were all chilled to the bone as was every other prisoner. Albert would not tell them why he was crying. If he was in pain, they could tell the doctors and maybe Albert could get treated for whatever was wrong. They were Dr. Schumann's pet project, so as long as they helped the butcher catch problems early, they still had value to his sterilization experiments and would probably be allowed to live.

They climbed under Albert's blanket, one in front, and one behind. The three of them barely fit on the thin, lumpy pad, but Gabriel and Lukas would gladly suffer some minor discomfort if they could keep Albert warm until the medics arrived in a couple hours. Between them, Albert was racked with silent sobs which seemed to worsen for a while, but as Albert tired, he began to drift off to sleep. Not knowing what was wrong with him, neither Gabriel nor Lukas could sleep so they just kept still, pressing against Albert to keep him warm. They were both very concerned.

Sometime just before sunrise they must have fallen asleep because they were both awakened by Albert's trembling sobs. They pleaded with him to tell them what was wrong so they could get him help but he insisted he did not want to involve the doctors. They sat up and huddled together under the blanket for warmth as the gray light of morning filtering through the clouds began to illuminate the dirty barracks window. The camp was so cold that even the soldiers were reluctant to move around. The boys' breath rose from the holes in their blanket like wisps of smoke. Albert was becoming tired again and he stopped crying. They asked if the soldiers had done something to him. Was he in pain? He refused to answer, falling into a dreamy stupor, both from exhaustion and from some trauma unknown to them.

Gabriel and Lukas were glad when they saw Maria making her rounds. They had been carrying the burden of anxiety for hours now and it was beginning to turn to real fear. They knew better than to give any outward sign of distress, so they waited for Maria to make her way around to them. When she did finally come to them she was immediately alarmed by the looks on Gabriel's and Lukas's faces and moved quickly to sit with them. As she went through the motions of checking their overall health, Gabriel and Lukas described their concerns about Albert in panicked whispers, aiming their faces away from a soldier in the corner of the room to conceal their conversation. When Maria came to Albert, she saw that he was lethargic and bleary-eyed. Her heart sank when she saw how pale he was. The moment he was no longer useful to the doctors, his body, living or dead, would be dumped outside to freeze until they could collect him for the incinerator.

Maria felt Albert's forehead and neck. He didn't seem to be running a fever. His eyes were coordinated and pupils responsive. She listened to his breathing. There was a risk that Albert could be coming down with Typhoid and if that were the case, he would be immediately executed and burned since that was how the Nazi party controlled outbreaks in the camps. No medical treatment was ever given to prisoners if they were thought to be contagious, but to protect the soldiers and medical personnel from contracting Typhoid, they would simply cull the prisoners who had it, but Albert didn't seem to be showing the classic symptoms of the disease.

Maria sat back, baffled. "Albie?" she addressed him. The boy did not move, so she repeated, "Albie? *Was ist los?*" ("What is wrong?") He still did not move. She took him by the elbow and squeezed firmly to try to get his attention without letting anyone else know that something was awry. Albert turned his head slowly toward her and gradually raised his eyes to hers. At first, they were dry but as she watched, a heart wrenching look of abject horror consumed his face and his eyes welled up with tears. It frightened her but she gave no outward sign. She had learned not to react visibly or others might suspect her of being a sympathizer.

What she saw on Albert's face was clearly a terrible trauma he had experienced recently. This often happened to the residents here because they had seen such unspeakable atrocities. Sometimes it broke them. She took Albert's face in her hands, which was a very risky thing to do, saying, "Albie, you must tell me what is wrong so that I can help you stay *alive*." This seemed to shock Albert out of the abyss he appeared to be in and he began to collect himself.

He stuttered terribly as he began to explain, but she understood enough to follow him. As she and his two friends listened, he told her about the boy he had tricked into being taken instead of him when the doctors came for the three of them. He described how, less than an hour later, they had come back for him and taken him to the room where Gabriel and Lukas were lying on two tables and the body of the boy who had been taken by mistake was lying broken and bleeding on the floor under the table where the doctor was leading him.

He said that the boy appeared to be looking at him, watching him, judging him. The dead boy's eyes seemed to stay fixed on Albert as he came toward the steel table. The doctor told him to stay where he was. He stood rigid, still looking at the dead boy's eyes under the table knowing that he had died because of Albert; that Albert had killed someone just to buy himself another hour. The boy had come to Albert in his dreams, in every dream since the surgery. He described the haunting of his waking hours, of seeing the boy just outside his view but when he looked, there was no one there. Maria wanted so much to take him into her arms and hold him, rocking his fears away as a mother would. Instead, she rested a hand on his small hands as he wrung his fingers. Feeling her touch, he began to rock back and forth, but she implored him to get control of himself.

"Albie, there was nothing you could have done. The only reason you three are still alive is that you are subjects of Dr. Schumann. Look around. Do you see anyone from your group still here?"

Albert looked around and realized that there were none left from his group. Everyone here had arrived after the surgeries.

"Do you know what happened while you were in surgery?" She looked at him questioningly.

"*Nein,*" he answered softly.

Maria continued, "Everyone who was here that day was taken to the mass grave to help dig up bodies. Those who could not dig were killed in a line outside the barracks and a new batch of prisoners was brought in. Someone was showing symptoms of disease and they didn't want their officers to get sick, so they disposed of everyone." She paused, waiting to see if the young boy would make the connection, but after a few moments, she saw that she would have to make the connection for him. "You may feel very bad for what you have done, but he would have either been killed an hour later or worse, would dig up bodies until he died or was killed." She placed a finger under his chin and lifted his head to face her directly. "My dear boy, you are in a terrible place with very bad people. There is nothing you could do here more wrong than what is being done to you. That makes it difficult to tell the difference between right and wrong sometimes."

Albert pulled his chin down so he would not have to meet her eyes. Gabriel and Lukas each reached forward to place their hands on Albert and his tears began to dry.

"You just remember what we told you about the photograph. If any of you escape, you must keep this picture as evidence of what was done to you. Someday we may be able to use it to bring some of these men to justice." Maria lifted Albert's hands in her own in a prayerful way before setting his hands back down as Gabriel and Lukas withdrew.

Albert's anguished look dropped away suddenly and confusion took its place. "How could you know all this? How could you possibly? Did someone tell you that story?"

"No, Albie," Freda answered. "No one told me anything."

Albert was even more perplexed and his eyebrows scrunched together as if he could force the pieces together by sheer effort, but something just wouldn't fit.

"I was there, Albie." Freda leaned toward him and placed her hand on his, but he pulled away looking down at where she had touched him.

"Lukas?" he asked. It could only be Lukas. If she were his friend, then why had she not told him before now? He felt a wave of hot anger wash over him dulled by the medications so he still felt in control of his temper. His lips pulled tight and looked up at her asking sternly, "Why have you said nothing before now?"

Freda was ready with her answer. "You were a suicide patient when I found you. What was I supposed to do?" Freda shrugged her shoulders unable to answer but she knew how deeply this could impact Albert's mind.

Albert looked at Gabby. It wasn't anger, but suspicion on his face this time. "How long have you known?"

Gabby answered calmly and with as much compassion as she could. "When I first met Freda, I knew immediately." She gave Albert a respectful nod letting him know that keeping this from him had not been easy. "We talked about you, how your treatment was progressing, and why she had not told you yet." Gabby sat back in her chair. With firm resolve she said, "I agreed with her. It was obvious that you needed time to heal before learning who she was."

Freda continued, "In order to be able to help you, I needed to be a stranger to you." Freda allowed the assertion to hang in the air for a moment before asking, "What do you think, Albie? Was this the right thing to do?"

Albert sat back in his chair studying Freda and Gabby with a judgmental stare. They could see conflicts and resolutions flashing across his face as fast as they occurred to him. They patiently waited for his thoughts to play out and grow quiet again. "Yes, I think it was the right thing to do." His face softened and he leaned forward again, taking one of Freda's hands in his own. "Thank you for not giving up on me." He held her hand tightly and, sensing the course of his emotions, Gabby added her hand and for the first time in almost twenty years, he felt the touch of his two best friends, and they were both alive. They sat in silence like this for a long time. Anton, Ernst, Lena, Hugo, and Maria all sat still, eyes downcast in reverence. They all knew what would come next. It was time to let Albert in on the rest of the secret and hear his decision.

Minutes passed and eventually the three looked up. Examining Freda's face more closely, Albert saw traits that she still possessed from childhood. The shape of the nose and the lips, though her nose was more mature and creases now radiated from her mouth. How could he not have seen? "What happened to you after the war?" Albert asked sheepishly.

Freda knew this question was coming. One of the reasons Albert had difficulty recognizing her was that she appeared significantly older that himself.

"After I was adopted, my new parents brought me to Hungary and for a few weeks it seemed that the nightmare was over. They knew I would have special medical needs, but I doubt they were prepared for what happened. About two weeks after the adoption, my legs began to hurt. I ran a low-grade fever for the next month while doctors tried to discover what was wrong with me. After more tests than I can remember, I was diagnosed with Osteonecrosis which is a type of bone infection. By the time it was discovered, the damage was done. They treated me for the infection and I got better, but my bones were brittle in the places where the infection had damaged them.

"The pain was sometimes so bad I wanted to drop out of school and stay in bed, but I knew that was not any kind of solution, so I lived with the occasional fracture. I suffered through it and refused to let it take the rest of my life away the way the Nazi doctors tried to."

Albert felt ashamed that he had allowed his own trivial concerns bring him down. He felt guilty for all the time and effort he had demanded of others and a scowl came over his face.

"How are you feeling, Albert?" Freda asked.

He rose from his self-pity with a new conviction saying, "Better than I have felt in a long time." Albert let out a sigh and she could see that he was absorbing today's revelations well.

"I am glad to hear that." She paused for a heartbeat and then added, "We have more to tell you."

Albert sat back aghast. "More than this?" he asked, incredulous.

"I am afraid so," Freda answered. "The reason I asked you to bring the picture is because it is time to put it to use." Albert gave her an inquisitive look so she continued, "Maria has something to say to you." Freda stood and made her way back to her chair. "Maria?"

Albert swiveled his chair from Gabby to face Maria, who had stopped weeping but was still drying her eyes. She smiled as she prepared to jog his memory. "Albie, do you remember what I told you when Hugo and I gave you the picture?" Albert nodded but said nothing. "It is finally time for the picture to serve its purpose." He sat waiting so she continued. "Freda has found Dr. Schumann." Again, Albert sat in shock, mouth hanging open in stunned silence. He turned to face Freda who only nodded.

Hugo began to explain. "I know it must have been a difficult thing for you to carry that picture all this time, but I am so very glad you did. I gave you that picture so that one day, we might bring those horrible men to justice. Now we have a chance to make one of the *worst* of them answer for his crimes."

Albert looked down at the picture he was still holding and noticed that his hand was trembling. There in the picture was the evidence. The three boys had been stripped naked so Hugo could document the experimental procedure, but Albert saw much more than that now. He began to see that the three of them were not merely able to recount stories of what was done to them. They could prove the physical damage to a court. The fact that they were still living meant that their testimony would be impossible to refute. If they really had found Dr. Schumann, they would be able to firmly hold him accountable for the atrocities he committed. He asked without looking up from the cracked old photograph, *"Where is he?"* Albert surprised himself with the intensity of the rage in those three words.

Freda was pleased with how the meeting was going so far. Albert had not only recovered and accepted who she was, but seemed remarkably well balanced for someone in his position. When she started to speak, Albert looked up at her and everyone in the room turned to hear what she had to say. "Dr. Schumann fled immediately after the war and the authorities have been unable to locate him, but we have. We have all been working with an underground Nazi hunting cell. Because they do not report to the government, they can keep their information secret until an arrest happens. Too many fugitives have escaped because they were informed by Nazi sympathizers within the ranks of the government." She paused for emphasis. "Dr. Horst Schumann is the director of the Komfo Anokye Hospital in Khartoum, Sudan."

She didn't need to explain that they were planning to apprehend him. That was obvious, but Albert asked, "What can I do to help?"

Freda was very happy to see how strong Albert's mental faculties were, and his reaction aligned with the best-case scenario they had all discussed prior to this meeting. "We would like to invite you to join us. We still have much planning to do, but Gabby and I are hopingN77d19J1o

to be there when they capture him so we can look him in the face and he will know that justice is being served. If you would like to be a part of that, you could come with us."

Albert didn't need any time to think. "How soon can we go get him?"

At his reply, Freda nodded at Gabby who rose and went to the door. She opened it and beckoned to someone apparently waiting outside. "Albert, this is Viktor."

Gabby gave a gesture of presentation, but rather than go through the motions of ceremonial introduction, Viktor walked straight to Albert and offered his hand to him before he could stand saying, *"Kumpel von mir."* ("Glad you are better, buddy.") His grip was almost painful, and his gruff manner was a little off-putting, but Albert's impression was that this man was a doer, not a talker. Viktor's accent was not pure German and his voice was gravelly. It sounded as if he had spent time in Italy, probably smoking since he was five years old.

The group spent two hours informing Albert of recent events and their parts in the cell's operations. Freda told him how she contributed everything she had earned from her practice and when Gabby joined the group, she had donated food, moved them to better quarters, and even offered to fund the trip to Africa.

When it came to Jürgen's fate, dying in the hospital and the body going missing, Viktor said, "Yes, about that..." Viktor reached in his pocket and produced a folded piece of tissue-thin blue stationary. He spun it so it would be upright from her perspective and slid it across the table. Freda picked it up, gave Viktor an inquisitive look, then turned her attention to the paper. Inside, she read the sloppy writing.

DEAR UNCLE,

MY CONVERSATION DID NOT GO WELL. SHE INTENDS TO KEEP THE FAMILY'S PROPERTIES AND IS SEARCHING FOR OTHERS IN THE FAMILY TO HELP SOLIDIFY HER POSITION. I FEAR THAT SHE WILL WANT TO HAVE A TALK WITH YOU, PERSONALLY TO TRY TO RESOLVE YOUR DIFFERENCES. THERE ARE SOME WHO ARE SYMPATHETIC TO HER WISHES ON THIS END. THEY WILL BE CONTACTING YOU SOON.

I AM SORRY THAT I WAS NOT ABLE TO MAKE HER SEE REASON, BUT MAYBE ANOTHER FAMILY MEMBER WILL BE MORE EFFECTIVE. I WILL BE UNAVAILABLE FOR A LONG TIME, BUT I HOPE YOU WILL REACH OUT TO ME ONCE I AM FREE OF MY CURRENT OBLIGATIONS.

SINCERELY,

J

"This is from Jürgen?" she asked.

"It is."

Viktor's short answer left Freda hanging, so she prodded him. "Is Schumann, 'Uncle?'"

"Yes he is," Viktor answered, again without elaborating.

"It seems to be about me. How did you get this?" Freda's eyes were bright with curiosity.

"I told you that a fixer had taken care of him so that his body would not be found. I did not tell you who the fixer worked for." Freda looked at him, stunned. He just shrugged and said, "I asked you to let me get involved. I did not say that I would tell you everything *I was doing.*"

Viktor explained that they had seen to it that the dead man's mail was collected and his bills paid. Once each week they would mess up the room and have a maid clean it so that if anyone was watching the apartment, reports would go back to Schumann that there was normal activity. A man looking a lot like Jürgen frequented the apartment with a hat and turned up collar to hide his face. Now they had to decide what to do with this resource, and quickly. The fixer found Jürgen's stash of letters so they had a good sample of his handwriting but not a primer. He must have memorized how to encode the letters, so that was a problem, but they should be able to keep a convincing correspondence going, at least for a while. Eventually, they might find a way to use this against him, to manipulate him somehow, but Viktor cautioned, "We do not have much time. I am certain that Schumann is expecting a reply to his last letter. We need to decide what to do about that as soon as we can."

Albert was not overwhelmed. He wasn't even anxious. As he watched the group get down to the business, he felt a new sense of purpose and realized that his family might have just expanded by one. They went back over some previous decisions explaining the relevant information. They knew where Schumann was, so why didn't they just have a cell in Khartoum capture him? Freda explained that so many people had been killed or had died since the war, that many criminals were not convicted if there was no direct evidence of what they had done. That was one reason why Hugo was planning to publish his pictures. In Schumann's case though, they had photographs placing him at Auschwitz and showing the results of his crimes, but now they also had three eye witnesses, not just of some random atrocity, but of the one recorded in the photograph.

There was also the concern that the tribal systems at work in Sudan might allow Schumann to talk his way out of extradition. Freda and Gabby were planning to travel there once all the arrangements had been made and the proper people paid off. They offered Albert the chance to join them and he emphatically accepted.

Albert was given the job of maintaining correspondence with Dr. Schumann. When he volunteered, Viktor explained that this was no simple assignment. He would have to study every nuance of the letters for word choice as well as the physical marks on the page. Everything had to be perfect or Schumann might detect that he had been found and flee Sudan. Then they might have no way to find him again. It was vital that their plans involve the local police in Khartoum, backed up by the militia of the ruling party, and that he be visually identified by the three of them so there could be no denying who he really was.

The cell in Khartoum was monitoring Schumann's movements, finding that he kept to a predictable schedule. They knew where he worked, where he ate, and where he lived, but he must not become aware of their activities. They must send that first letter immediately, so Albert would begin working this very evening.

As the meeting wound down and everyone confirmed their understanding of their part to play, Viktor said he had somewhere to go. Eventually, Ernst and Lena rose and bid their farewells with many hugs and promises to call often. Then Hugo and Maria thanked Albert for helping them do some good for the world again. Anton excused himself, slapping Albert on the shoulder as he passed saying, "I'm proud of you, son." He closed the door leaving the three alone in silence for a long moment. Gabby and Freda waited for Albert to speak first since this was really his graduation ceremony. Albert bowed his head.

Freda began to feel awkward waiting for him to speak when she noticed a tear fall from Albert's lashes. "I am sorry if this is all a bit much to take in," she apologized.

Very softly, Albert said, "I missed you."

It was too much for Gabby to stand. She took Freda by the hand, and brought her around the table to hug Albert, still seated and weeping softly. Gabby and Freda squatted down to Albert's level and the three put their foreheads together like they did when they were children, surrounded by suffering and death. This time though, there was only love and purpose.

Gabby began to chuckle, causing Freda and Albert to look up at her, each with a questioning scowl on their faces. Gabby stopped chuckling and explained, "Look at the three of us. A nymphomaniac, an alcoholic, and a basket case!"

"*Former* basket case," corrected Freda.

Gabby acknowledged the correction with a nod to Freda and put a hand behind Albert's head, drawing him closer and touching foreheads again. Albert was so filled with joy at finding both of his friends. He could not speak. He could only smile and weep silently as they held each other.

Chapter 33

Albert had been working furiously for the past few days. Gabby and Anton had welcomed him to their home so he could work without distraction. He couldn't stay at the asylum anymore and his work, though subtle, could be the deciding factor between success or failure. One would think that all he would need would be to copy the handwriting precisely, but Viktor explained that there would be coded information hidden in plain sight. On the first evening, Albert had discovered that every eleventh *letter e* was separated from the next character by slightly more space than the others. Viktor called this a primer and it acted like a key letting the reader know that it came from a trusted source and not an impostor. Albert would have to study every letter they collected from Jürgen's apartment, practice writing like him, and discover every hidden detail or their subterfuge would be exposed.

Meals were brought to him in his room and stacks of blue stationary were brought in and out. Once marked up, they would be burned to ensure that they were never seen by anyone. He practiced the phrasing and writing for nearly three days with only a few hours each night to sleep. Gabby and Anton gave instructions that he was not to be disturbed unless he asked for something which was contrary to the staff's habits of service, but they left him alone until two days later.

The sun turned orange as it sank low in the sky. Albert opened the door to his room, looking disheveled and greasy. He was holding two pieces of blue stationary. One had fold lines on its back and was darkened around the edges. The other was fresh and new. He held them side by side as he came down the hallway toward the main stairs. He wasn't watching where he was going. Instead, he was looking back and forth between the two papers. He was walking slowly, so when he emerged from the hallway headed for the top of the stairs, Gabby noticed him from below. Seeing the look of concentration on his face, she ascended the stairs cautiously, staring at him. He did not see her until she blocked his path at the top of the stairs.

He looked up, and turned to stand beside her. He held the two sheets so they could both see. Gabby's eyes went wide and she leaned forward, squinting, examining. Her eyes went wide again and she stood erect, facing Albert. "It's amazing! You've done it! I can't tell the writing apart. I think it's ready." The two of them went to Anton's office to call Freda and tell her that they would be coming to see her tomorrow with the letter to give to Viktor. They already knew what to communicate. That had been provided by Viktor, but it would now be Albert's job to write it as Jürgen would have with all the secret flourishes and wording that Schumann would be looking for.

Albert's parents invited him to come back home to live with them while he returned to his seminary studies. The offer was appealing, but he wanted to stay close to Cologne until they captured Schumann, so Albert Novak became another temporary resident of the Gorski manor. When they needed to see Viktor or Freda, Ben would take them into the city and back. Somehow, Gabby always found a way to inject some shopping into the schedule and she delighted in outfitting Albert with some stylish new clothes. In his free time, Albert began studying, working toward the day when he would re-enter the seminary. After more than one suicide attempt and years in an asylum, it was unlikely he would ever be elevated to rabbi, but there were other ways a seminary eduction could be a benefit. He loved writing, spending at least an hour every day writing in his journal. He loved history and spent whole days at the libraries around Cologne researching their upcoming trip to Sudan and the cultures of the area. When he first joined the rest of the group, he thought planning a vigilante trip would be fun and action-packed. Instead, what he found was long hours of diligent research. Pouring over maps and correlating observations made by a distant team as they planned out their entrapment. It could take months or even years of slow progress until they were ready, but if they waited too long, something might happen to warn Schumann of their activities, but if they rushed in, they could lose men in a failed operation.

When Hugo and Maria came to visit, Gabby made sure that Freda and Viktor were invited. Horace was frequently present when the group gathered for a dinner or cocktail party, but he was atrociously inattentive when Ben was in sight. The two could not stop making eyes at each other and Horace missed entire conversations to distraction. Still, it was nice to see two people getting to know each other and enjoying each other's time.

Two months passed. Albert kept the correspondence going with Schumann, consulting with Viktor on what information to communicate so they might manipulate him later. He also became fascinated by the history of cryptography. He had, of course, learned about Enigma machines and other devices used in various wars, but what piqued his interest were the techniques of encoding information into handwriting by communicating to an untrusted reader one thing but to the trusted reader, something else.

Elke Rossen, the star of *Kaberret Seks*, passed away in her sleep on the fifth of February, 1962. Her services were attended by admirers and colleagues from across Europe. Lolita had reluctantly become the matriarch of their troupe of performers and entertainers, and her comedic drag stylings left patrons howling with laughter night after night. Thanks to Gabby, Lolita's fashion sense, makeup, and tastes continued to improve, but she never felt like being a woman interested her. He always felt that dressing up as Lolita was an outlet, but he was beginning to discover that there was a whole community in Cologne built around drag performance and he was glad to have helped some fledgling careers with a night performing at the *Kabarett*.

It was in late July when Viktor called for a meeting. Dr. Freda asked the group to meet at the hospital after hours. They assembled and waited for Viktor, exchanging exciting news about the trip planned for the following month. Albert's correspondence with Schumann was going as well as they hoped and Gabby found the ship they would travel on as well as the estate where they would stay when they got there. They were in high spirits when Viktor arrived. As usual, he didn't knock.

He entered, but not in his usually bullish manner. He was holding his beret in his hands and looking down at the floor after closing the door behind him. Freda had a bad feeling. Gabby turned, laughing but her laughter died suddenly when she saw Viktor standing there.

"What is it, Viktor?" Freda asked in a low voice.

"He's gone." Viktor's answer was flat and final.

"Can you be more specific?" Gabby asked gently.

"Someone said they saw Schumann and went to the authorities in Khartoum. It was some old woman, a prisoner at Auschwitz. She insisted they arrest him, but before that could happen, he was gone."

Gabby lowered herself slowly onto the chaise. Freda put both hands flat on her desk in front of her and looked down in disappointment.

"I don't think he found out about what we are doing. It seems like the woman's claim is legitimate. She really is from Auschwitz. It appears we are the victims of bad timing." Viktor looked up at the group saying, "I am sorry."

Chapter 34

Saturday, 5 May, 1962

　　I'm feeling very humble just now. Gabby and Anton insisted on having a celebration at the asylum for me. I can't say I don't understand what is so special, but I just wish it weren't directed at me. I was embarrassed, but I went because all of my friends and family would be there. Selma and Etta came into town with their families. Mother and Father came in from Budapest. Gabby, Anton, Lolita, and Hugo were there, but Maria could not come. I do hope she can recover from her latest heart attack.

　　All the people who helped me when I was unwell were there. Even a few of the doctors and nurses who had moved on to other jobs attended. Despite my abject abhorrence of being the center of attention, it was touching to see so many. They will, no doubt, go on to treat other patients and live their lives and eventually they won't think of me anymore. That is the way of things, but I will never forget. Each person contributed in a profound way to my reclaimed health. Even Jude who did nothing more than hold my hand while waiting for my medications to take effect, gave of her strength and caring to help me recover on my own. Now, I feel the need and the responsibility to pass that strength on to others.

　　I have to write that I am still a bit angry at Freda for not telling me who she was earlier. I am not sure if I am more angry at her for keeping the secret or at myself for being so chauvinistic as to not see it myself. I suppose we all see the world through our own filter of assumptions and I can't come up with any reason why knowing sooner would have been the proper course, but that does not negate the feelings.

　　I feel a deep disappointment in Gabby that my heart insists on forgiving, but my mind wants to remember endlessly. She knew the whole time and even after she told me who she was, she did not tell me who Freda was. I would have done the same, knowing how unhinged I was. She has shown me so much kindness. What she said to the room tonight brought me to tears. She gives selflessly. She opens her heart completely and holds back nothing.

I had a chance to talk in private with Hugo. He explained why he would take such a terrible risk giving a prisoner one of his pictures. We talked about it before, but he hadn't explained his motivation completely. Maybe losing track of Schumann brought this out of him. He said that too many criminals get away with what they do because the evidence against them is not strong enough. By giving us the picture, he hoped one day to have three things seal the fate of the criminals at Auschwitz: photographic proof, Nazi records, and eye witnesses. Having all these at the same time, there would be no chance of escape. That is exactly what we are going to do if we ever find him again. All three of us will stand before this monster and he will know that justice is unavoidable.

July was a hard month. After receiving the news from Viktor that their target had disappeared, they did some investigating. The arrogance of Dr. Horst Schumann had finally caught up with him. He had been nearly caught once before when he applied for a German passport through the consulate in Japan. Incredibly, they had issued the passport without asking any questions and only later did they realize that they had a wanted war criminal in their control and had let him go.

Other than acknowledging that they had indeed issued the passport, the Japanese government refused to confirm anything else. Further attempts at diplomatic investigation indicated that heightened interest would only be met with heightened resistance, so the matter was dropped. While Schumann was hiding in Khartoum, the periodical *Christ und Welt* (Christ and the World) run by Giselher Wirsing, a former SS officer, printed an article about a Sudanese hospital and Albert Schweizer. The hospital in Khartoum served many thousands of people and was heralded as a great achievement, but unfortunately for Schumann, the article pointed out that many of the Nazis who escaped capture after the war were hiding in plain sight throughout Africa and someone had recognized him.

It didn't seem that there was any sign of Schumann in the Nazi-hunting network or in the public media. Albert had been particularly aggressive in his research, pouring over magazines and newspapers sent to him from across the world.

While he could only read German, Viktor had introduced him to Mikel, their cell's journalist and researcher. Albert couldn't understand why this man would be working with Viktor. Mikel was a small, slightly built, and timid man, but what he lacked in physical stature, he made up for in resourcefulness. He lost his entire family in the war. Not all of them had died. Half of them had been either Nazi sympathizers or officers whom he now considered dead. Despite the occasional accusations arising from his family history which he bore with stoic silence, everyone knew that his passion for the network was partly fueled by the guilt of having Nazis in his family.

Mikel became fascinated with Albert's work trying to reconstruct the path

Schumann's life had taken since the war. He began introducing Albert, by correspondence, to acquaintances in Africa, America, and across Europe. Albert's project turned out to have quite a broad appeal and many of his new long-distance friends began sending him annotated newspaper articles and other periodicals they thought might be of interest. They were quite liberal with translations and some of their word choices left Albert gasping in laughter or rolling his eyes. Nevertheless, he refused to criticize them. They were helping in the best way they could.

Weeks went by but there was no sign of Schumann. Albert's efforts to find him began to make up the background repetition of a day's work as other priorities began to intrude. He decided to take Ernst's offer to support him while he completed his seminary degree. To be closer to the Budapest Seminary, he moved back into his parents house. Lena resumed mothering him as if her little boy had just resurfaced, but Albert was over thirty now. He felt self-conscious when he caught her cleaning his room or preparing elaborate meals while refusing his offers of assistance.

Occasionally, Albert would wake up early to prepare breakfast for his parents but invariably, Lena would hear him or the smell would wake her up and she would try to take over. This morning, Albert was frying latkes in the heavy cast iron pan he remembered from his teens. Cholent was bubbling gently in a small copper pot and slices of challah were toasting in the oven. He allowed himself to be carried back to his childhood by the smells and sounds of cooking. When Lena approached the door, she saw that Albert was lost in thought, staring down at the stove. She usually swooped in to take back her kitchen, but today, she stopped just shy of the kitchen door. She stood silently watching for several minutes remembering the frightened little boy she brought home from The Red Cross orphan placement center. She remembered the first time she heard him laugh, the first time he came home with skinned knees, the first time he asked about his family.

Albert felt someone watching him and turned to see Lena just outside the kitchen. He smiled warmly and she dipped her head. He expected her to come in, take the spatula from his hand, and try to usher him out of the kitchen but instead, she came in, went to the cupboard, took down her favourite coffee cup, and came to stand beside him while she poured herself a cup from the heavy percolator Albert was tending on the stove. After replacing the pot, she stood to Albert's side, admiring his cooking technique. He felt as if he were a novice being scrutinized by a master chef. Any moment she would begin making corrections or issuing instructions, but she said nothing. She did not offer to help or try to take over. She just watched quietly, sipping her coffee. Eventually, she reached up to place a hand on his shoulder. Pausing only for an instant, she then turned to go back to her room and finish dressing for the day, leaving Albert to handle the rest of the cooking on his own. When she left without saying anything, Albert felt something. He felt like a grown man.

Ernst always made a racket when he was preparing for the day. This morning, he was attempting to convince Lena that he could wear his favourite black coat one more time before washing it. Albert could hear Lena saying that she would not allow her husband and prestigious community leader to stink like a farmhand. Albert could imagine her clutching the coat as he wheedled like a child not getting his way. It brought a smile to his face as he remembered how often this argument occurred.

Ernst never got his way in this matter, yet he still tried the litany of excuses that had never worked before. Grumbling to himself, he continued to justify his position to no one in particular. Albert could hear him coming down the stairs, then groaning as he stooped to pick the post up from the floor.

As Albert took the baking sheet of challah out of the oven, Ernst came into the kitchen. Albert set the bread on the stove and looked toward his father who was standing there holding a letter. Albert could tell who the letter was from by the look on Ernst's face. Viktor had arranged to redirect any post that was not bills to pay from Jürgen's apartment in Cologne to Budapest, Hungary nearly twelve hours away. When Viktor forwarded newspapers or magazines that might have some information about Schumann, he would send an overstuffed manila envelope. Today, it was just a regular envelope.

"Please set it there," said Albert, looking at an empty spot on the corner of the counter beside the stove. He took up the spatula and began flipping the latkes which were beginning to smell wonderful.

Ernst stepped toward the counter and deposited the envelope. He observed that Albert was alone in the kitchen this morning and raising an eyebrow in mock interrogation, he said, "I see that you have been permitted to cook without supervision."

Albert looked up from the sizzling potato cakes and seeing the satirical look on Ernst, decided to play along. "I think the chef has decided I am beyond hope." They shared a conspiratorial chuckle before Ernst took the rest of the post to the dining room to read.

Albert would get to the letter after breakfast. He took out three plates, set them beside the stove, and began portioning out the meal. After they ate they talked about Albert's studies and Ernst's duties at the synagogue while Lena cleared the plates. Albert went back to the kitchen to retrieve the letter from the counter while Ernst continued reading the newspaper. Albert returned, sat down, and confirming that the letter was addressed from Viktor, tore it open.

He slid a blue envelope from inside the white one and his eyes went wide. The blue envelope was of the same type used by Schumann and Jürgen and then by Albert while he was impersonating Jürgen. He examined the front closely as he set the outer envelope to the side. The return address was from "Uncle H" which had been Schumann's *nom de plume* in all the letters. Albert knew that the mail was not actually being forwarded by Viktor himself, but whoever was forwarding it wrote Viktor's name as the sender. It was likely that Viktor had not known that the letter had arrived since they had lost track of Schumann. If he had seen it, he would have called Albert immediately.

Without taking his eyes off the blue stationary envelope, he reached for the letter opener imagining that this letter could contain something of too much importance to just be ripped open. Ernst noticed Albert reaching blindly for the letter opener and he helpfully slid the wooden handle toward his grasp. Then he saw Albert staring at the blue envelope with his eyes wide and his mouth hanging open. A wave of concern overtook him and he set his newspaper down. Albert's hand found the handle and he slowly brought the blade to the letter. His hand was trembling slightly as he slipped the blade under the flap and gently sliced upward. Setting the letter opener down, he glanced at Ernst who was focused on Albert's letter.

The smell released by the envelope left no doubt of its authenticity even before Albert had read a word. He gingerly eased the folded blue tissue paper from its sheath. Before unfolding the letter, he carefully examined the front and back of the blue envelope, then set it on the table so he could unfold the letter with both hands. He took a deep breath smelling the stale tobacco odor of the paper and willed himself to relax.

Dear Nephew,

Now that I have settled, I should inform you that I was required to move quite suddenly, having lost title to my quarters in Khartoum. Any correspondence you have sent in the last several months should be considered lost and I must ask you not to send anything to my former address. Please resend any important correspondence to my attention at the Krachi West District Hospital in Kete-Krachi, Ghana.

I wish to learn of the outcome of your final meeting with your mother. If further action needs to be taken, please let me know and I will attempt to help you from here. In such a remote area it may take longer to exchange letters, but I will patiently wait to hear from you.

H

Albert went white. "Son? What does it say?" Ernst was very concerned now and leaned forward to place a hand on Albert's arm.

The touch startled Albert. "Oh, it is nothing bad." A triumphant smile began to spread across his face. "Actually, the news is very good!" He clutched the letter in his fist. "I have to call Freda!" Without further explanation, he leapt up, the legs of the chair moaning as they slid against the grain of the wooden floor. Albert went to Ernst's study and closed the door behind him, not even registering the look of intense curiosity on his father's face.

Albert set the letter beside the phone. His fingers trembled as he dialed each number. He was too excited to sit.

"Yah?" came the answer.

"Would you please put Viktor on the line? This is Albert."

"Yah, stay on," the male voice said and Albert could hear muffled voices in the background when the man covered the mouthpiece.

"Viktor."

"Viktor? This is Albert."

"I know. What do you want?"

Albert was not offended by his gruff greeting. That was Viktor's way. He calmed himself before continuing. "I think I have found Schumann," Albert said flatly. There was a long silence. Albert thought they might have been disconnected. "Are you there? Did you hear me?"

"Let us discuss that in person. Can you meet at Freda's tomorrow evening?"

Viktor was just being cautious, Albert knew, but he was right. They should not say too much until they were face-to-face.

"Verdammit! Bist du sicher?" ("Damn! Are you certain?") Horace nearly threw the chair backward as he stood, slapping his hands down on the table in frustration as he bolted up and turned away.

Viktor understood his reaction and held his own demeanor steady rather than respond emotionally. "Yes, I am certain. This is not something we will be playing around with, you understand me?" The tone of his voice made Horace turn back. He examined Viktor's face. The stern set of his jaw and the sincerity in his eyes told him that he was not exaggerating in any way, so he tried to calm himself. "The Head of State is a tribal dictator named Kwame Nkrumah. He has been sympathetic to the Nazi regime and we know he is harboring several war criminals from Germany, Austria, and Japan. He is not a man to be underestimated."

Horace turned away again, crossed his arms, and his heavy breathing made it clear that he was trying to control his temper as he began to pace. Viktor and Albert sat side by side waiting for the group to regain composure. Gabby appeared numb, staring at the table and not reacting at all, hands folded between her knees as she was before hearing the news. Freda sat back in her chair and bowed her head disappointed, trying to collect herself. She turned her head to the side, not looking at anything in particular, but deep in thought. She inhaled slowly and deeply. She exhaled slowly. She sat motionless for over a minute. Albert was starting to feel very uncomfortable while he waited in silence for someone to speak.

Then Freda leveled a resolute stare at Viktor saying, "We will do what we can until the day the situation changes. Do you agree?"

Viktor was taken aback. He had expected her to admit that Schumann was beyond her reach. This Nkrumah had the title of Head of State but in actuality, he was a warlord. Yes, he put on suits and went to diplomatic meetings, but in his territory if he wanted you gone, no one would ever find your body. "Freda, I know how much this is costing you. This could go on for *years*, do you understand?" His forehead scrunched with genuine concern. She could be a great doctor with lots of money if she didn't give it all to him, but looking at her face, he could see her unwavering commitment. He watched her for any facial expression for what seemed a long time and, seeing nothing, shrugged his shoulders. *"In Ordnung."* ("OK.") He sat back and folded his hands in his lap.

"Could we not buy someone or bribe someone to let us go in and take him?" Gabby asked.

Viktor looked at her in amazement. "You think you are the only one trying to get to someone there?" He didn't mean to, but he let anger color his words. "What do you think happens to the other operations there when you go in trying to get what you want by throwing money around?"

Gabby recoiled at his stern reaction. "I'm sorry," Gabby admitted.

"You should be." Viktor's words stung, but Gabby knew he was right to be angry with her. "These men put their lives at risk every day. This is not a game." Viktor crossed his arms. He sat for a few moments, no one willing to intercede.

"I *am* sorry," she repeated, leaning forward and placing a hand on his crossed arms. "I spoke without thinking it through."

He began to relax saying more gently, "Of course. I am just saying that there are other things to consider. A mistake could cost lives. Remember there are other groups like the Israeli Mossad who are hunting these men. Their methods are sloppy and they cause a lot of collateral damage. We *don't* want to get in their way." He remembered the innocent secretaries and assistants the group had bombed, gassed, and poisoned without capturing their targets.

Horace had been standing away from the table facing the wall, trying to regain control during the exchange. Viktor spoke to his back. "Can you trace his financial transactions in Ghana?"

"I doubt it," Horace replied, discouraged.

"Could you tell me why not?" Viktor's question could have been testing Horace's expertise, but when he turned to examine Viktor's face, he saw no judgment or suspicion there.

Horace turned to rejoin the table, thinking carefully. "The banking system in Ghana is under the control of the tribal rulers. They use it to launder money and rather than hide their own transactions specifically, they have obscured all identification and location information from all international transactions." Horace sat down heavily, pulling his chair back up to the table. He continued to think hard, trying to come up with some way this could be done.

Viktor seemed to have an idea. His face brightened and he asked, "What if we could trigger a transaction of a known amount?" As he said this, he tilted his head toward Albert who realized immediately what Viktor was suggesting and he too looked at Horace with renewed hope.

Horace reviewed the structure and protocols of the various international banking systems, concentrating intently, but came to the same conclusion. "Even if we knew the amount, we would only ever know that it came from Ghana. We would not be able to use the information to locate him within the country unless we had access to someone within the Ghanaian government who could re-attach the information after the outbound transaction was completed.

Viktor considered this, but dismissed the notion saying, "If we had someone like that, they could just send the information directly to us, but we don't have anyone in the government that could be trusted not to warn him. We might lose him again."

The room fell silent and everyone tried to think of some way to circumvent Schumann's sanctuary. Many minutes passed but no one had any ideas.

Freda spoke up, breaking the silence. "Then we are left with only one course of action. We watch and wait."

Chapter 35

Helga rushed through her morning duties trying to ensure that she would finish early. Struggling to concentrate on the stack of forms before her, she kept her head down and focused as best she could. Dr. Freda would be expecting this paperwork to be delivered before Dr. Benjamin arrived for his meeting and at this pace, Helga knew she would probably be able to meet that deadline, but she wished she had more time. She kept a schedule that would be grueling for an older person, but she was still in her twenties and seemed to her elders to have boundless energy. In actuality, she had been blessed with a lower sleep requirement than most. With only four hours of sleep per night, Helga was able to out-perform many of her peers and those who required eight or nine hours of sleep were simply not suited to medical practice.

In the last several months, she had been dividing her time among three major projects. Dr. Freda had finally received a promotion at the University of Cologne School of Medicine and had asked Helga to help her to reform the Department of Sexual Deviance into the Department of Sexual Health which would blend the practices of psychology and sociology with the physical sciences of surgery, and endocrinology to form a single department under which one could receive treatment for any condition relating to human sexuality. Their patients would include German citizens and foreigners who could not legally receive treatment in their own countries. For example, the list of requests for treatment Dr. Freda had received but could not satisfy numbered over fifty from Denmark alone. They ranged from cross-gender dressing to complete transsexual evaluation and transformation. Dr. Benjamin's work had been invaluable and progress in the field around much of the developed world had accelerated over the past decade, but there was still much to do.

Helga's second project was helping to administer the Weber Foundation. It was not a year old yet and had not even been dedicated, but the plans laid out by Gabriella and Anton Gorski were well thought out and progress was moving swiftly. Seven of the ten new clinics already had locations purchased and the existing three clinics had received an infusion of capital to upgrade their facilities, equipment, and staff. Her main area of focus was the staff. It was her job to find and vet nearly one-hundred nurses, doctors, and technicians and be prepared to hire them as each facility began to operate. The goal was to have all thirteen facilities fully built-out and staffed by the end of January the following year and it was beginning to look as if it would actually happen on time.

On top of all this, she was continuing her nursing courses. She was half way through her Bachelor's of Science in Nursing program but was probably going to spend another three years on the degree since her time would be even more constrained when the clinics began to open.

She was so focused on her work that she did not even notice the time. When she finally finished and set her pen down with a sigh, she looked at her watch and blinked. Looking again, she saw that it was nearly three o'clock. Even walking quickly would not get her to the meeting on time, but running without a genuine emergency was not tolerated in this hospital. She hoisted the stack of folders and headed for the door. The stack was not so unwieldy that she had trouble managing the door, but she was careful and moved slowly knowing that she did not have time to stop and clean up a pile of spilled papers.

Gabby felt much better now that she and Anton had decided how best to honour Dr. Johan Weber. Gabby thought of him as a grandfather. Anton missed his friend and would often chuckle when they were talking about him. Gabby longed to know everything Anton could tell her about her dear departed mentor and it was clear to her that Johan and Anton had been much more than professional colleagues. Anton would often recount adventures he had experienced with Johan, weaving tales of the mischief the two would get into. It warmed her heart to see the joy Anton relived when talking about Johan.

Anton had been the one to tell Gabby when Johan passed away. The anguish she felt at his passing still brought tears to her eyes, but now she would be doing something in Johan's name that would help countless people, and it was all thanks to his selfless generosity. The executor of the will, a Mr. Phineas Burlingson, invited Gabby and Anton to his law offices for the reading of the will. To Gabby, it seemed somehow disrespectful to talk about a man's property after he passed away, but in practicality, someone had to make certain his wishes were carried out. With no family, the two of them were closest to Johan.

Gabby and Anton sat quietly in the hallway outside Phineas' office. Through the closed doors they heard several heated exchanges, but they couldn't make out what was being said. Phineas had asked them to wait, presumably until some previous meeting was completed. Anton appeared relaxed and she was certain that he was accustomed to this sort of setting. The hallway was carpeted in luxurious burgundy wool with an oriental inlay. The walls and ceiling were all made of hardwood and the paintings lining the walls made this office seem more like a museum. Every piece of furniture was antique, or maybe they were just old and ornate.

Gabby jerked with a start when the heavy wooden double doors to Phineas' office thudded against the doorstops. If the metal latches intended to catch the doors and hold them open had not been bolted through the carpet into the floor beneath, Gabby was certain her hand would have been crushed against the rail of the wooden bench she and Anton were seated on. A group of relatives looking very much like each other emerged from the office yelling and arguing with each other. They ignored Gabby and Anton as they bickered and fought on their way outside. Gabby felt sorry for them. Nothing as unimportant as money should divide a family like that.

"Mrs. Gabriella Gorski, please enter," boomed Phineas' voice from inside the spacious office.

She rose and smoothed her black satin dress. She turned toward the door while Anton came to her side. They walked toward Phineas' desk and Anton closed the space between them with a laughing greeting and hearty handshake. Gabby was overwhelmed. The lawyer's office was palatial. The ceilings were at least 6 metres high capped with intricate molding all around the room. A large set of wooden book shelves spanned the wall behind the man's desk and was even outfitted with a wheeled ladder on a track. Gabby couldn't help but look around the room trying to take it all in. To Phineas, she looked like a young girl lost in a big world.

Phineas said, "Please have a seat, Mrs. Gorski." He gestured to an empty chair left askew by the former occupant. Anton was already making himself comfortable in one. Before sitting, she straightened one of the chairs beside Anton. Then she gracefully lowered herself onto the cushion and folded her hands in her lap. She was trying very hard to hide her nervousness, but Phineas saw through the facade.

"Relax, Mrs. Gorski," he said in a softer, friendlier voice than before. "You are not in any trouble."

Gabby saw a flash of embarrassment cross his face and sensed that he thought the last statement might have sounded condescending. She decided to alleviate his discomfort. "Well, if I am in trouble, I know you are the person I would come to for help. Johan was very particular about whom he trusted."

He had to admit that the image of the gold-digging young temptress certain socialites tried to push on him just did not fit the person who was seated before him now. He was an excellent judge of character and as he studied her he felt his skepticism dropping away. She was not simply the most beautiful vision of a woman he had seen in a long while. She was also kind and thoughtful.

Over the next hour, Phineas explained Johan's wishes. He had to explain to her what a *codicil* was and how it affected the execution of a will. "Think of it like a trump card you hold back until every other card has been played, except in this case, a codicil is like an ace card. Nothing beats it." They spent time talking about a timetable for the conversion of the real estate and larger items like cars and furniture. He explained that, according to the terms of the will and codicil, she could not keep the house or anything else. The situation was heartbreaking but Phineas was a conscientious man, stopping to let her catch her breath when he saw she needed to.

When it came time to talk about his clinic, she discovered that he actually had three. They all served the underprivileged and the elderly as well as the sex workers who could not always afford medical care or who were afraid of the stigma that being seen in a clinic might bring. As he described the assets, the payroll, and other technical features of the medical practices, Gabby felt her eyes welling. She drew out a white handkerchief as she attempted to contain her emotions. What would the employees do now that his clinics would have to be liquidated? What about the people who relied on those places when they were sick or were too poor to afford their medications? It was overwhelming. As she brought the handkerchief up to the tip of her nose, she bowed her head slightly and shut her eyes. The heavy tear that fell into her lap did not go unnoticed.

"Please do not worry about the staff and patients, Mrs. Gorski." His voice was soothing but not patronizing and Gabby imagined that he must be very experienced in the art of handling people when they face these choices for the very first time. "I have some good news here. According to the will and codicil number three paragraph forty-seven, the clinics are owned by a trust and the trust is owned by the estate. The codicil effectively protects the clinics from liquidation and keeps them operating. Now, they can't be left in that condition. Sooner or later you will have to take some kind of action to either preserve or dispose of the trust, but for now, they will report to me and I will report to you."

Johan had thought of everything. He was such a gem of a man. They missed him dearly and talked about him often. They would make certain his legacy would continue far into the future. On receiving the funds from the execution of the will, Anton helped Gabby set up The Weber Foundation. At that time, they decided to leave the funds alone and let them accrue interest. The clinics were operating mostly on donations from well-established benefactors, many of whom Anton also knew personally.

Gabby brought her mind back to the present. It had been a few years since Johan's passing and she thought he would be proud of them both. Anton publicly credited Gabby with their success, but she knew it would not have been possible without his connections. The guests had already begun arriving but she was running a bit behind schedule. She was seated at her vanity, bright lights eliminating all shadow. She finished dressing a while ago, but now she sat on the swayback vanity bench collecting her courage. This would be her debut as a public speaker and her stomach was feeling queasy. She looked down, tightened her grip on the emotions and fear, and looked back up at Mrs. Gabriella Gorski, Philanthropist. As soon as the thought crossed her mind, she rolled her eyes at her reflection. Hopefully today's event wouldn't induct her into the *pompous socialite* club.

"Ma'am. It is time." The maid had been flitting back and forth, splitting her time between helping Gabby dress and checking for the signal from the opposite wing that Mr. Gorski was ready. Gabby placed her hands on the edge of the counter and stood erect as the maid slid the bench from under her. Shoulders back and confidence in her gate, she walked slowly toward the bedroom door. The maid held it open for her and when Gabby stepped into the hall, she turned to see Anton at the opposite side of the ballroom's second floor gallery. They walked slowly toward each other, arriving at the top of the grand staircase at the same time. The room that had been filled with the sounds of conversation and clinking glasses fell silent below them. He offered his arm and she rested a hand on top. She looked into his eyes and he looked into hers.

"I am very proud of you, my dear. This is a wonderful thing you are doing." He knew compliments embarrassed her so he didn't wait for a response. He looked down to the room of black and gray suits and dresses. Many of them were friends, some were acquaintances, but the majority were strangers; people who were as well-connected as he was, but in their own circles. Nearly everyone who had pledged their participation was here today and the level of generosity they discovered over the last year had been a delightful surprise.

Anton moved to descend the stairs and Gabby took her cue, stepping in perfect time with him as they came down. Four steps from the bottom, where they could still see people arriving at the front door, they stopped. Anton took a deep breath so that his voice would carry and said loudly, "Ladies and gentlemen! If you would please begin moving to the West Garden, we will make an announcement shortly!"

The crowd acknowledged and began moving toward the west wing where the French doors spanning that side of the house were all opened, giving access to the elevated landing and the steps down to the path leading to the garden. Even more realized their drinks needed refreshing and instead turned toward the various bars set up around the east wall of the ballroom. Noticing the two-axis flow of the crowd, Anton raised his voice again. "There is plenty of champagne available in the West Garden, but please take your time!" The implication was, of course, that they should not dally, but should attend to their comfort before heading outside.

Gradually, the crowd parted, leaving an opening for Gabby and Anton to descend into. They walked arm-in-arm to the ballroom floor and signaled to their valet who made his way toward them with two lead crystal flutes of champagne as they greeted pockets of guests and thanked them for their attendance. With champagne in hand, they encouraged the stragglers to head for the garden.

It was the time of year when the afternoons were cooling down and as they drew closer to the open doors, Anton signaled to another of the valets with a white arctic fox stole draped over his arm to come forward. He moved toward the valet and met him halfway as the last of the crowd flowed toward the door. Gabby was distracted talking to an older man and his wife when Anton came up behind her and draped the stole over her shoulders. She hadn't even realized that she would need it, but appreciated Anton's forethought.

The brief warmth of the high sun was already beginning to cool, but it seemed that everyone was prepared. Black wool coats, hats, heavy stoles, and light fur coats were abundant in the river of guests and patrons below them. In time with the others, Gabby and Anton slowly made their way along the path leading away to the West Garden where rows of folding chairs were arranged. All along the path, waiters refilled glasses of champagne and wine, never asking permission. They knew each beverage by sight and swooped in so swiftly that a guest might turn their head just for a second and look back to a full glass. The path emptied into the seating area with outdoor carpeting spread in all directions so people could navigate freely without mussing the grass beneath.

As Gabby and Anton reached the seating area, they turned to the right and walked to the front corner of the chairs, then left toward the center aisle where a carpeted riser was. Seated in the front row were Freda, Horace, Helga, and Hugo. Sadly, Maria was too weak to make the journey this time. Front and center sat Dr. Harry Benjamin talking with his protégé, Freda. He looked up and smiled warmly as the two approached. Gabby and Anton smiled and nodded at these and many other friends dispersed throughout the crowd but continued toward the riser. There would be plenty of time afterward to visit and chat.

Three small steps led up to the riser's platform. Anton advanced ahead of Gabby and turned his back to the riser, raising his hand and letting Gabby lean on him as she took the steps. She released his hand when she reached the top and he followed to take his position beside her facing the crowd. In unison, the waiters and valets stepped back to the edge of the carpeting, suspending their service and indicating to the guests that something was about to happen. The crowd hushed so that only the occasional mumble could be heard. Everyone looked up at Gabby and Anton.

Anton waited until he was certain he had everyone's attention and spoke loudly and clearly. "My friends, dear benefactors, and honoured guests, we thank you for coming together today to help us honour the memory of Dr. Johan Weber, Jr.!" There was a muffled, but enthusiastic round of clapping from the audience. Anton began speaking just as the clapping began to wane. "It is because of his generosity and commitment to ensuring the ongoing support of the community that we are able to honour his name today!" Stronger applause. Anton's part was done, so he passed the audience's attention to Gabby with a bow as she stepped front and center.

The champagne that she had on the walk out to the garden helped to calm her nerves and dull the chill of the afternoon. She stood for a long moment without speaking, thinking of Johan and seeing how many of the people he loved were here today. She closed her eyes and bowed her head for just a few seconds and the crowd, reasonably quiet, fell absolutely silent. She imagined that there was no one here but her and when she opened her eyes, she did not see rows of people. She saw the love and laughter that Johan had brought to so many people's lives. She looked up taking a deep breath and her voice rang out clearly, with a conviction and strength that surprised her. "My dear Johan!" The audience was rapt and several of the ladies lifted kerchiefs to their faces. "You found me when I was lost, alone, and afraid! You lifted me out of despair! You gave me hope for a better future!" She felt herself beginning to tear up, but that would not do, so she swallowed her emotions and willed herself to continue. "I am just one, but we will never know how many others you helped, how many people you saved! In your name, Dr. Johan Weber Jr., we establish The Weber Foundation which will begin by opening ten new clinics across Germany to serve the elderly and underprivileged free of any cost."

Those with glasses set them down to join in the rousing applause. She continued even louder, "The Weber Foundation will uphold the principles you stood for and reach out into the community to provide assistance with education, housing, job training, and legal expenses for the unfortunate!" Dr. Benjamin could no longer contain himself. With tears streaming down his face, he leapt to his feet clapping as loudly as he could. The crowd followed his lead and a wave of ovation spread to the farthest corners. The applause lasted for nearly a minute before Gabby began to speak, indicating that guests should restrain their adoration, but it still took many seconds for those who knew Johan well to settle down. She knew why those involved in their plans were so enraptured by the idea. A dedication of a foundation was hardly new, but this particular foundation was unique. "Thanks to your generosity and kindness," she swept a hand across the crowd, palm up to indicate the guests, "your matching contributions will make this the first foundation of its kind in Germany!" The applause this time was deafening and several abandoned their composure giving shouts of praise with the occasional obscenely loud whistle of celebration.

Those in the audience, perhaps ten percent of the guests, had been so enamored with Gabby and Anton's idea that they gave as much as they could to amplify the effects of Johan's estate. The two had carefully orchestrated the collection and arrangement of funds, trusts, and real estate purchases so that a very important threshold had been reached. Not a single *Deutsche Mark* of the foundation's principal would ever be spent. Instead, all of their plans, all of the clinics, all of the medical care, education, administration, and indigent costs would be paid for by the interest alone, and any remainder would be funneled back into the foundation, thereby compounding its influence and power over time.

Gabby was unable to hold the tears back, but she did not let them distract her. As the applause faded again, she raised her hands to calm the crowd. "None of this would have been possible without you and we thank you from the bottom of our hearts!" Gabby reached back, taking Anton's hand, and he stepped forward.

They continued with gestures of thanks as the crowd expressed their gratitude and as the din fell, Anton cleared his throat. Gabby looked sideways at him and saw that he was tearing up and trying very hard to hide it. "It is a great honour to have such wonderful people here today. Let us make Johan proud as we help the people of Germany!" The clapping rose and fell modestly so he continued, "Please stay and enjoy yourselves!" He gestured to the perimeter where the waitstaff were stationed with new glasses of champagne so guests could deposit flat or empty glasses and take a new one.

The crowd began to disperse. Some headed toward the heart of the West Garden, walking the labyrinthine paths and pointing at various sculptures and plants. Others meandered back up the path to the manor house to get out of the cold. Gabby turned to face Anton taking both of his hands in hers. "Thank you, my love." Anton bowed his head, embarrassed by the tears he was still shedding despite his best efforts. She raised a hand to his cheek to wipe a tear away with her thumb and to lift his face so she could look into his eyes.

"None of this would have happened if it weren't for you." Her praise was both sincere and forceful. He released her hands and took each of her arms in his grip. Looking deep into her eyes he said with all the conviction he could muster, "Johan would be so proud of you."

They were interrupted by Dr. Benjamin coming toward them followed by Freda, Horace, Helga, Albert, Hugo, and several others. "You young people make this old man glad to be alive!" exclaimed Dr. Benjamin as Freda laid a reassuring hand on his shoulder. When he felt her touch, he raised his own hand to pat hers and turned to see her smiling.

Chapter 36

"But I think this label denotes a category with still more subsets within. For example, one man may derive sexual arousal or pleasure from the act of dressing in women's clothing. Another may require the risk of discovery for the same degree of pleasure. This would be separate and distinct from the man who dresses in women's clothing as a demonstration of liberty or principle though he might not derive any sexual pleasure, do you not agree?" Dr. Benjamin leaned forward to take up his tea. At seventy-eight his hand shook a little, but it was still manageable. He held it up to his nose as he reclined in the heavy leather chair. He inhaled the orange and spice-laden steam rising from the delicate china cup, giving Dr. Freda time to ponder his statement.

She did not speak. Matters this complex required focus and discipline, so she merely raised her hands to tent her index fingers over her lips and thought as Harry sipped his tea. Her friend and mentor was visiting from America and would be traveling across Europe to attend to various matters. He was consulting on several books as well as writing another of his own. He was also called upon to provide expert testimony in court proceedings in countries where gender dysphoric dress or actions were still illegal. He looked quite handsome in his brown and green twill suit and vest. His espresso colored London Fog trench coat lay across the corner of the table beside him. He declined to let anyone take it from him when he arrived. Freda was actually a bit warm, but she did not want to remove her black wool jacket.

"It seems to me that there could possibly be an infinite number of distinctions made if an infinite number of cases were available. Therefore, the choice should not be among the distinctions themselves, but how easily these distinctions would be accepted academically. Consider that the distinction of a man who dresses in women's clothes may now be accepted as valid by a significant proportion of medical and legal professionals, but the distinction of a man who dresses in women's clothes without an arousal component but with a *libertarian* view and other specific complications might not be accepted by others as distinct, even though you and I might see it as such." Freda leaned forward to set her tea down as she continued the thought. "In order for your work to be accepted by the target audience, it would have to be at some degree of complexity which correlated with their own level of understanding, beyond which those who do not understand would rather discount your interpretations rather than increase their knowledge or experience."

Harry did not acknowledge her statement, but continued enjoying his tea. This was the practice of learned men and women; to allow plenty of time for an idea to be expressed, then digest the information dispassionately, and formulate a response that contributes to the discussion or further develops the main topic. It was nothing like a common people's conversation. It was a slow, methodical process that the both of them enjoyed immensely. He groaned with the effort as he leaned forward to set his cup on the saucer and reclined again. He considered for nearly a minute before he spoke. "So I now understand that my credibility and sales of the book will suffer if the reader is too stupid to comprehend, yah?" He paused so she could fully appreciate the joke and they began to smile at the feigned defensive retort.

"I have missed you, old man." Freda looked up at him with admiration, chuckling. He let a high-pitched, bouncing hum out through his nose as he tried to chuckle inwardly and failed.

The door burst open and Helga entered, apologies already on her lips. Harry stood with some difficulty waving her protestations away with both hands. She stopped when she saw him waving and coming toward her. The door, which was closing steadily behind her, punctuated her awkwardness with a loud *clack* as the latch engaged. Harry ambled toward her.

"My dear, my dear," he wheezed. He wasn't having trouble breathing. He was trying to resist laughing. He became more collected as he approached and, taking hold of the stack of folders, tried to take them from her. She didn't let go. She wasn't resisting him. She just didn't understand that he was taking them from her. When she realized this, she tipped the stack slowly toward him. He turned, set the stack on the table, and waddled back to her, his hand extended. She extended her hand. He took her hand, then placed his other hand on top of hers and stood gazing into her eyes.

This would normally have made Helga extremely uncomfortable, but not with Harry. When she looked into his eyes she saw trustworthiness, brutal honesty, and a touch of twisted humor. The grin gave that part away. "My dear, it is your time to become a mentor. You must learn to relax." She began to object, but he silenced her with a raised hand. Then they stood there. He looked at her expecting something, but she didn't know what.

"Why did you stop talking?" he asked, standing as erect as he could, pulling his shoulders back as he posed the question empirically.

"Because you raised your hand," she answered, wondering what else it could possibly be.

"No." He took a breath and explained. "You stopped talking because you see me as a mentor." Glancing back at Freda, he continued, "We have been discussing the responsibilities you are taking on and how your career is progressing. We are both very proud of you, but you must understand." He paused and his look became serious. "There will be many people looking to you to be their mentor. Show them what peace looks like." He patted the back of her hand and let it go, turning to head back toward his seat.

Helga looked over at Freda and saw her smiling and shaking her head. She poured a third cup. "Please come sit," Freda said. We have a lot to go over while Harry is in town." Giving a nod to Harry, she asked, "Have you decided on a title yet?"

"I think I have. How does *The Transsexual Phenomenon* sound?"

"Like the butt of many jokes, I can be certain." Freda's smile threatened to break out into laughter but she maintained her composure.

Helga came up to the table and took the cup and saucer. The room was empty except for the three of them. In less than two months, this conference room would hold fifteen doctors, but for now, they enjoyed the luxurious furniture all by themselves. They spent hours discussing how The Weber Foundation would function, outlined scenarios that would need preemptive solutions, and talked more about Harry's upcoming book. Over the course of the meeting, Helga began to feel less like an observer and more like a participant of the decision making process. Her change in attitude did not go unnoticed.

Eventually, it came time for Harry to leave so he could prepare for a dinner conference that evening with Reed Erickson, a wealthy man who was preparing to fund the Erickson Educational Foundation the following year. Mr. Erickson was considering transitioning from male to female and, of course, he wanted the most experienced person on the planet to guide his transformation. That was Dr. Harry Benjamin.

As he rose, Helga leapt to her feet and came around behind him. She took up his coat and when he stepped free of the chair, helped him dress for the cold weather. He thanked Freda for the tea and gave Helga some parting words of encouragement. Once he was gone and the door closed behind him, Freda and Helga sat at a corner of the long conference table and spent more time discussing some of the specific tasks Helga was working on. Helga seemed to think that the problems she was facing were cause for Freda to be concerned about choosing her for the position, but halfway through her explanation of one particularly sticky personnel choice, Freda leaned forward and placed a hand on Helga's.

"Relax. You are doing an excellent job. The only real problem I have seen so far is that you doubt your own ability." Freda's criticism peaked Helga's self-doubt and fear until Freda squeezed her hand and repeated, "Relax." Helga looked up from the various folders she had spread on the table to see Freda smiling with a calm, confident expression. "Remember what he said?" Freda asked. "He didn't mean don't let anything bother you. He meant that others will bring their turbulence and stress to you. As their mentor, you must help them calm the chaos and bring clarity to their thoughts."

That evening, Harry arrived at his hotel in the back of a taxi. The driver opened his door and stepped out into the dark, cold drizzle that seemed to thoroughly soak everything. The trees across the street drooped, weighed down by the weather. The driver expanded a large umbrella, opened Harry's door and covered him while he exited. The doorman, seeing a guest arriving, came toward them with another large umbrella.

As he ambled down the long hallway to his room, his thoughts began to wander. He felt lonely on these long trips from America. Gretchen was probably having the same feelings at their home. He wondered if she was as fulfilled as he by their decades of marriage. He turned the key in the lock and opened the door. In the middle of the week, occupancy was low, but he had still requested a room in the center of the building. Maybe it had something to do with being caught on a ship in wartime.

He entered and locked the door, came in to stand before the coat rack and removed his trenchcoat. Hanging it, he considered how many times he had done this same sequence of actions over the years. He never wanted to travel this much, but the world was awakening to the natural complexities of human sexuality. Prejudices were becoming simply a majority opinion instead of the only accepted way of thinking and the world was moving away from tyranny. He hoped young people like Helga would make sure it kept going that way.

Chapter 37

It was a lovely spring day in April, 1966. The sun was high. Birds were singing in the trees outside the School of Medicine, and flowers perfumed the air, but Dr. Freda had just spent the whole morning consulting on one case after the next. She hadn't even gotten to see the sunrise which had become her morning custom on the way to work in the spring and fall. Today, there was simply too much to get done for normal work hours, so she was in before sunrise and would probably not get home until late in the evening. She needed a clear head the past few weeks, so she had forced herself to go without a drop of gin. *It had not been easy!* The sweating and weakness had not abated until just a few days ago, and when it did, she realized that what she experienced was indeed withdrawal symptoms. Once they passed, the chemical dependency would no longer be an issue. It was now merely a psychological tendency to return to drinking. Maybe sometime in the future. For now, there were too many people depending on her decisions.

She was reading a newspaper article a colleague had translated about recent changes in the American laws regarding the treatment of transsexualism when the phone rang. She leaned forward, her favourite old chair from the basement office creaking and twanging in protest. She set the newspaper and the typed translation down as she picked up the receiver.

"Are you sitting down?" Viktor asked without greeting or introduction.

Freda sat up straight. "Yes. Why?"

"Kwame Nkrumah will be deposed when the government is overthrown. The military is planning a coup in less than a month." He stopped and waited for this to sink in. He knew it would take a moment or two.

Freda did sit holding the receiver silently for many seconds. Coming to her senses, she took a calming breath. "Let's go get the bastard," she said in a level, clear tone. "When can you meet?"

They set a meeting for the following day. Freda's schedule was already full but there was no choice. They had to move quickly. If Schumann perceived any danger from the change in power, he might disappear again. Viktor had a team in Ghana that had been watching Schumann for nearly four years. He had fallen into an almost unbroken daily routine and Viktor hoped that routine would remain regular. Schumann was in charge of the Krachi West District Hospital near the coast of Ghana and had been living in the area for over three years. Nearly every day he frequented the same coffee shop and passed through the same market on his way to the hospital.

Freda called Gabby and Albert first. She thought that was only proper. It would be a hardship for Albert to come to Cologne on such short notice, but when she offered to delay he flatly refused saying they shouldn't waste a minute. Gabby and Anton assembled a travel plan and contacted all the proper people to get there quickly and in style. Gabby would later admit that it was all Anton's doing. Albert still communicated with Schumann from time to time, and Freda was still paying the rent, both on Jürgen's apartment here in Cologne and his home in Frankfurt. The costs had been mounting over the years and it was beginning to wear on her, but she repeatedly refused Gabby's financial assistance saving the offer for when times really got bad.

"Maria?" The voice was distant and muffled.

"Maria?" A bit clearer now. She struggled against the exhaustion. She wanted to see who it was, but her mind felt so sluggish. She began to see some light, red through her closed lids. She struggled to open her eyes.

"Maria?" It was Freda's voice. She struggled harder and began to resolve some details from the shadowy figures around her, but she also began to feel the pain again, a throbbing in her chest in time with her heartbeat.

"Let me know if you need anything." That was the nurse's voice...Nurse Margaret. So sweet.

Freda's face came into focus and a moment later; Hugo came into focus over her shoulder.

"My love? I have brought some guests to see you." Normally a stoic man, Hugo had trouble keeping the heartbreak from his voice. She thought he was such a sweet man. He should show that side of himself more often. The room grew dark again and she closed her eyes to rest, just for a moment.

"Maria?" Someone was trying to wake her. Someone was jiggling her arm. She was a little irritated and struggled to waken to see who it was. Freda was still here. How long had she been asleep?

"Hugo?" Her voice was dry and weak. She licked her lips as someone held some ice to them. It was so soothing and made her mouth feel less sticky.

"I am here. So are Gabby and Albert and Freda," Hugo replied.

She opened her eyes wider and saw that Freda was holding the ice. "Oh, thank you my dear. You are so kind."

Gabby was standing closer to Maria, which gave Albert the chance to turn away behind her so he could wipe away his tears without anyone seeing. Gabby wanted to cry but she had her emotions strapped down with iron belts. Freda was smiling warmly. It was infectious and it made Maria smile too.

"We wanted to come see you before we left." Gabby reached awkwardly toward the bed and placed a hand on Maria's arm, being careful to avoid the tube and needle taped to the back of her hand. She could see the skin through the surgical tape, purple mottled with the yellow and green of a days-old wound. She stepped closer and began to relax a bit.

"Where are you going?" Maria asked, her eyebrows knitted in confusion.

"We're going to Ghana to capture Schumann," Gabby said.

Maria's eyes went even wider, but there was a fogginess in them as she looked up at Gabby. She looked to the other side of the bed at Freda who nodded her agreement.

Maria knew she could not sit up, but she put all her strength into raising her arm to grasp at Freda. She managed a handful of shawl, but that would have to do. She tried to take a deep breath but found that she could not. The pain was too great, so she used what little breath she had to push out the words "Go get that bastard!" Freda helped lower her hand to the bed.

They each found a place to sit while Hugo cleaned her face with a damp washcloth and straightened her hair with his fingertips. She was so sorry she could not spend more time with him. It seemed that their lives had been cruelly delayed by the war, keeping them apart during the vital years of their youth when they might have had a family, children, maybe even grandchildren. She began to fade again, so the trio rose to leave. Before they could get to the door, Maria woke calling for Albert who came to her side, tears streaming down his face. When he thought they were leaving, he had released his grip on his emotions and now he couldn't stop weeping. Seeing her trying to reach for him, he took her hand carefully, protectively.

She opened her eyes and pushed herself to consciousness with a valiant effort. Her eyes became clear and she focused them upon his. "Make him pay!" she forced out with all her might, then she faded again.

"We will. I promise you, we will." Albert's tears abated as he made her this sincere, last promise.

Chapter 38

Even though it had been winter for over a month now, the sun was bright and the breeze coming off the Gulf of Guinea was warm. Dr. Horst Schumann sat on a chair woven from reeds and grass stalks. He didn't call it wicker since that would imply some artistry was involved. Everything in the village of Kumasi was impermanent, from the mud dwellings to the furniture and clothing worn by the natives. It was just as dusty as Khartoum but these savages put even less effort into making their surroundings livable. It had been some time since he wrote to Jürgen to let him know where he had escaped to. To be certain he received the message, Schumann sent one letter to Jürgen's apartment in Cologne and another to his home in Frankfurt. A month later, he was greatly relieved when he received the reply that the Jew, Freda Dudek, had been taken care of. In this part of the world there was little information from the developed countries, so Horst had not been able to find any news from Germany and something as inconsequential as one more dead Jew probably wouldn't be printed in any papers.

When he was discovered in Khartoum, he was forced to flee immediately. There was no time to go to his home to pack belongings. He boarded the first train he could and headed south, toward the heart of Africa. The Nazi network knew of a man named Kwame Nkrumah could be counted on to provide a safe-haven for exiled men and women. He had considered going to Argentina, but news of several captures of former officers dissuaded him so he headed for what was formerly called the Gold Coast. Nkrumah was a visionary who, like Adolf Hitler, had united the factions and elevated the former colony to the status of a country in 1957. While Nkrumah was merely a dark-skinned savage himself, he *had* successfully brought the two largest factions, the Gold Coast People's League and the Gold Coast National Party, together under the ideal of Pan-Africanism and they had repaid him by making him the first Prime Minister of the independent country. He later became its first President. In just four short years, he was meeting with heads of state like the American president, John F. Kennedy.

Nine years later, Nkrumah used what he learned during a formal education in America and then in London, to parlay Ghana's only export of consequence, cocoa, into an international commodity. He recognized that the rich countries of the world would not accept slave-grown cocoa for much longer, so he helped to abolish the practice on the mainland, bringing many of the slaves from São Tomé and Príncipe where the majority of the world's cocoa was grown to the Ghanaian cocoa farms as indentured servants. This helped to elevate Ghanaian cocoa to the largest source of foreign capital in the country.

When Horst first arrived in Ghana, he spent several days in Nkrumah's compound in Accra recovering from the trip. On the Sunday following his arrival, he was surprised by a guard who flung his door open and ordered Horst to remain in his quarters. The guard stood watch while three other men ransacked his room. Finding nothing, they straightened up a bit, throwing the blanket over the crumpled sheets and standing chairs upright. Horst could do nothing but remain silent and watch. Things were done the same way in the Nazi empire, so he understood that this was a prelude to the arrival of someone important. He did not query the guard who stood at attention once the others left. Horst stood motionless as almost an hour passed. When the heavy iron door opened again, the guard snapped to an especially forceful attention and five soldiers swept into the room joining the first to form two rows of three against the walls to either side of the door.

In came President Kwame Nkrumah. He was shorter than Horst imagined an African leader to be. What hair he had was thick and kinky but rapidly receding and his skin was one of the darker shades of the common people. He was smiling, but Horst did not feel happiness from the man. He felt deadly confidence. When he spoke, he spoke in British English with touches of an American accent. His speaking had a musical quality which probably came from the influences of his tribal language. Instead of being dressed in tribal garments, Nkrumah wore a gray pinstripe suit and starched white shirt open at the collar. He stepped toward Horst extending his hand in greeting.

"Doctor Schumann. I am glad to finally meet you," Nkrumah said.

Horst stepped forward and took his hand. One stately shake, and they broke their grip. "Thank you for your gracious hospitality, sir. How may I be of service to you?"

Turning to his guards, he ordered, "Wait outside." The soldiers turned in unison and marched out. Horst noticed that their formation had been misaligned and now their marching was crowded and disorderly. These were not the same caliber of soldier as in the Nazi empire. "Please tell me how you came to be in my country."

Horst gave Nkrumah an abbreviated account of the events from his discovery in Khartoum to his sanctuary here as an exile. "I am grateful for the hospitality you have shown me. Please allow me to repay you in some way."

Nkrumah tilted his head slightly and smiled again. "You are an experienced doctor, correct?"

"That is correct, sir." Horst realized that this was not a conversation. He was being questioned by a powerful and dangerous man.

"Of course you are," Nkrumah confirmed flippantly with a wave of his hand. "It is my understanding that you were one of Hitler's doctors, were you not?"

"Yes, sir. I was stationed at Auschwitz, Block 10 and at Birkenau." Horst did not elaborate, but when he saw Nkrumah look up at him with his head still tilted, he realized the man was waiting for more. "I was in charge of radiation and other experiments studying reproduction and medical intervention." This answer seemed to be satisfactory.

"And how much administrative experience do you have?" Nkrumah asked.

Horst felt as if he were being interviewed for a job. He saw how Nkrumah lifted his head and pulled his shoulders slightly back waiting for his answer. This posture was meant to project authority, Horst knew, but coming from the shorter, balding man the body language did not have the intended emotional effect. Still, Horst knew that this man, savage or not, held his life in his hands. "I was in charge of a staff of twenty and was responsible for the X-Ray equipment, the surgical rooms, and the collection of research data. I was also responsible for the nursing staff in my block. In Khartoum, I was responsible for running the Komfo Anokye Hospital in Khartoum, Sudan until I had to leave suddenly."

"I want to be candid with you, Dr. Schumann. I know why you are here. You served a leader that more powerful countries refused to accept. You are here because you think I will protect you." He saw that his words rang true with the exiled doctor so he continued. "We maintain several hospitals throughout Ghana so we can let the people see that I am helping them. I want you to run one of them for me." Nkrumah paused to let Horst appreciate the offer. When he saw the look of realization pass across Horst's face, he continued. "Do not thank me, doctor. You are not going to like where I am sending you."

Horst's enthusiasm deflated and he knew that Nkrumah had seen it on his face. "I will be honoured to go wherever you want me to," he answered.

Nkrumah studied the taller man's face and determined that he did indeed have Schumann's loyalty, at least for now. "I want you to go to Kumasi to the north. It is a small village today, but it is located at an intersection of roads that will be important to my country. The hospital there will serve the population for one-hundred kilometres in every direction. I want you to build a hospital there."

Horst was flabbergasted. He had run medical departments and hospitals and even served as a doctor on a ship for a while, but he had no idea what to expect from a hospital in a village. He certainly did not have any experience in the African bush.

That was in 1962. After four years, a building had been renovated, staffed, and was fully operational as a hospital, yet the indigenous population was still suspicious of modern medicine and only sought medical attention for the most serious illnesses. Consequently, the hospital had a high death rate. Patients often arrived long after anything could be done for them and this fueled the suspicions of those who lived out in the wild bush country. Here in Kumasi, the resident population was beginning to trust his doctors and even to admire him personally. In reality, anyone from the Aryan race received top-notch medical care. Treating the savages was just a necessary function if he wanted to keep the protection of President Nkrumah and, of course, his anonymity.

He watched from the shade of a thatched umbrella as villagers traveled on foot to and from the central market. It reminded him a lot of Khartoum, but it was much smaller and not at all congested. He set his coffee on the ground beside the chair. The hut owner would come to get it once he had left. There was no need to go to the market today, so he walked the dirt streets weaving his way through the mud and wooden structures, trying not to brush against them. He despised how dirty this place was and he never seemed to be able to stay clean as he made his way to the Kumasi Central Hospital.

Chapter 39

Freda was finally getting used to her new quarters. She made significantly more money at the hospital ever since her promotion and she had finally convinced herself to move from the small flat to something more comfortable and closer to work. She still saw patients, so she had to make certain she stayed close to the hospital and being able to rest more comfortably would improve her efficiency at work. That is how she recalled the internal argument. Today, she would not be going in. She had informed the staff of her trip and delegated everything to the other doctors and staff. Every patient was accounted for and Helga was doing a wonderful job with the nursing staff. Freda had complete confidence that all would be well during her trip to the "Wilds of Africa" as everyone called it. They had no idea that she was going, not for vacation, but for a much more somber task.

She was spending extra time in Cologne University's library, but she wasn't doing medical research. She was reading essays and books on Ghana and the tribal traditions of Africa. So much of it seemed strange to her and many of the accounts were clearly preposterous but they also had profound and long-lasting effects on Ghanaian culture. Ghana had only gained independence from British rule in 1957 and the man who made it possible, President Kwame Nkrumah, was complicated. He was a warlord, a statesman, an authoritarian, and a Pan-African, meaning that he wanted to elevate all of Africa to free country status. He would apparently do this by both diplomacy and brute force. He was also formally educated. When she first started reading about Nkrumah she had immediately felt a dislike of the man. As she learned more, her feelings became more conflicted about him. How could a man guilty of such brutal dictatorship-style acts also be the one to bring independence and freedom to a country in the African jungle?

As she tried to decide what to bring, she laid out sweaters, shirts, dresses, and skirts. Carefully examining the clothing spread across the bed, she began to retrieve scarfs from the closet, draping them over the wrought iron foot grill. In the scalloped waves of the metal, she arranged the scarfs in the same order as the outfits on the bed. She blamed Gabby. Freda never thought about clothes. Everything was white, gray, brown, or black so outfits were easy to put together. What she saw spread before her was definitely Gabby's fault. Blue, red, and teal now resisted matching with the random scarf and demanded premeditation.

She started at a hard knock on the front door. She placed a hand on her chest and breathed deeply to slow her heart. She tossed the scarfs over the other clothes and went to the front door. She still found it odd that she had to walk down a hallway to reach the front door. In her old flat, the only door was within five steps of anywhere inside. She approached the front door and could tell that Viktor was outside through the mottled frosted glass that she understood was the fashion in newer households. She opened the door and as he came into view, she saw Viktor removing his beret.

As the door swung inward, Viktor appraised her silently saying, "You look well."

Freda couldn't be sure, but for him, the greeting was gratuitous. Was he hiding something? Viktor never visited her at her home, either at her old flat or here, and she knew the reason he was here now. All the arrangements had been made, all the introductions had been done, and all the papers were in order yet Viktor had repeatedly expressed concern over their plans to witness Schumann's capture for themselves.

"Please come in, Viktor." Freda stood back from the open door giving a sweeping gesture to indicate his path. He hesitated, looked up, then to both sides, then behind. Freda marveled at how deeply ingrained his caution was. He always seemed suspicious and some people took his manner as unfriendly but she knew him well enough to realize that his suspicion came from repeated loss, not lack of trust. As he stepped carefully over the threshold, he looked around like a child at a museum before noticing the table in the middle of the entryway. He stepped toward it and laid his beret on the new wooden surface.

She came up to his side, and noticed that he wasn't looking up from where he had placed his hat. "You are concerned."

"Yah."

She placed a hand on his shoulder and he looked at her askance. She got the impression that he was more than simply concerned. She imagined he thought she was going on a one-way mission but was too proud to discuss his feelings. "Come with me," she said as she headed back to the bedroom. He reluctantly followed, sneaking a peek into the kitchen at the end of the hall before they turned down another short hall. He could see around her that she was in the process of packing. He could see stacks of clothing and an open suitcase on a high bed. As he came into the room, he saw that there was a complex operation in process with clothes hung on door handles and drawer pulls, and folded stacks laid across the bed. She stepped around the wrought iron bed frame, lifted a scarf from the rail, and went into the closet, presumably to return it to storage.

"I see you have let Mrs. Gorski get her hands on you," he deadpanned, looking at the splashes of color around the room. It was not as if the room were painted with clothes of every color, but for Freda's normal style, this was a lot to take in. Freda looked around knowing that she had stepped far outside her comfort zone, but she was beginning to enjoy the small pleasures Gabby had been showing her.

Freda looked up from the arrangement of clothing on the bed to meet Viktor's eyes and smiled. That was all the answer she felt she needed to give. The tilt of his head and playful smile matched her own and they shared a subdued giggle, both nodding to acknowledge the moment. It became quiet.

Freda looked up again and saw that Viktor was lost in thought, seemingly frozen at the end of the dying smile, imagining the worst. His face went grim and his eyebrows came together as his forehead wrinkled. He took a deep breath and let it out. She recognized the technique she had taught him to calm himself and she knew the mantra that he was reciting in his head. Without looking up, he said, "You know, you don't have to go." He knew he was wrong the instant the words came out, but he pressed on. "I trust Esam. I know he can do the job. You don't need to go."

She let him have his fantasy for a moment as she smiled sympathetically. "You know I do. I have to be there so he knows it is me." Freda's answer was gentle but firm. He still did not look up, but she saw his face progress through various stages of grief before settling into acceptance.

He looked up without raising his head, trying to catch her looking at him. "You are not going to analyze me again, are you?"

"I am sorry," she said playfully. "Would you like me to make room for you to lie down so you can tell me what is troubling you?"

"That's not funny," he said, looking down, trying to suppress a smile and failing.

"Yes it is." She knew that now was not the time for serious talk. They had been through the dangers. They had made plans for the disposal of their property and remains if the worst happened. They had said their goodbyes already, but it seemed to her that he needed something more. She had no idea what that could be just now, but he was presumably here for that purpose. She would let him take her where he wanted to go in his own time. As the silence dragged out, she picked up a shawl that was not tidy enough for her taste. As she waited for him to speak, she looked up at him, then down at the shawl, fold, flip, back up at him, repeat with the next sweater.

He finally looked up at her and seeing the heavy orange sweater in her hands said, "You do realize it is never cold in Ghana."

"Oh, this is not for the mainland. It is for the cool ocean breeze." She continued folding and stacking. He nodded and frowned, conceding the point. After another long silence, she picked up one stack, placed it on another and brought the taller stack around the bed toward him, bound for the suitcase. "You should see the bikini I packed."

"No, thank you."

She was already facing the suitcase but turned quickly at the blatant insult and caught his smirk which he feigned trying to hide. This was how their friendship had gone over the last few years: jab, parry, retreat, but always in good fun. She turned back toward the suitcase and dropped the stack inside, heading back around the bed for the next stack. "Tell me how you know Esam."

"What?"

"You told me about what he does in Ghana and how he can help us, but you haven't told me about the man. So, where did you first meet him?"

Esam Lumo had been a skinny child. Growing up as a slave on the cocoa farm on São Tomé left little time for play or studying. His parents, also slaves, had not been born on the island. They had been taken as payment of a debt owed by their parents and placed together by their master. Then just a few decades later as the chocolate buying public began to voice displeasure with the practice of slavery, Kwame Nkrumah, then a tribal and social leader, arranged for Esam and many others to come back to Ghana as indentured servants rather than slaves. The British company, Cadbury, was the company with the most buying power and their intention to exclude cocoa produced by slaves was clear. Nkrumah was instrumental in keeping a good portion of the world's cocoa supply in Africa.

Indentured servants, he argued, were not slaves. Rather, their worth would be calculated and any prior family debts added to arrive at an amount. The indentured servants would be "paid" for their labor and the amount would be deducted from their worth until they essentially purchased themselves, like a modern corporation buying all of its own stock back a little at a time. When their balance was paid, they were free. They could then continue to work and get paid in cash or, more often than not, the indenturer would have no use for them and bring in someone younger or cheaper. For many, this practice left them unemployed and unsupported at a time when their bodies were wearing out.

When Esam was allowed to come to Ghana, he worked as hard as he could. If the master allowed him to start early, he did. If the master allowed him to work late, he did. He started moving the large trays of drying cocoa beans with teams of other young men. While there was more modern equipment available, the men worked hard to be faster and more agile than the tractor lifts. As Esam grew, his master saw value in feeding him and his team more and as they reached adulthood, their bodies became physically formidable. Some masters were afraid that strong men like Esam might try to overthrow them, but Esam's master was good to his servants. Instead of trying to control them out of fear, he celebrated them by starting a grappling contest. Within a year, word of the contest had spread and servants began traveling to the region with their masters' blessings, hoping to gain recognition and prestige.

Esam was always a favourite at these events and though he did not always win a purse for his master, he brought in more than he cost. After one particularly grueling bout with an opponent much larger than he, Esam remained bedridden for three days. He was afraid that his indenturement would never be paid off if he could not get back to work, but his master brought him a doctor and one of the women was tasked with caring for him. His master said that it "was a sound investment" and never said anything about it again. Finally, the day came when Esam was no longer indentured and his master became his employer.

"I was stupid, arrogant, and men died. Esam saved me when he could have left me to die like I deserved." Viktor kept his head down the entire time he told the story and the scar she had seen only a few times before now took on new meaning.

"Is that what happened to your head?" Freda asked.

Viktor's hand jerked up to cover the scar that parted his hair like a cowlick but before his hand reached his head, he staunched the reflex and lowered his hand. His body was covered with scars, yet this one still elicited embarrassment. "Yes. A bullet grazed my skull hard enough to knock me out, but not hard enough to kill me." Freda could see he was becoming angry at himself. He clenched his fists and breathed hard, finally turning away. "I killed those men." Freda let him stew for a while as she watched, respecting his feelings of guilt. There was nothing to say when the truth had already been said. This was something he had lived with for two decades.

"I understand why you trust him so much. Thank you for telling me about him." Freda spoke softly but with conviction. "It makes me feel much better about the situation we are going into to know that there is a good man waiting for us there." She shook out an unruly espresso-brown linen dress with white chenille collar and sleeves, trying to figure out how she should fold it. She laid it on the bed and began to experiment. "To tell you the truth, I am afraid. It is possible we could be hurt or kidnapped, but I have to be there. I have to look into his eyes and see him hang." She realized that she was clenching the dress in her hands, creasing the brown linen, so she released it marveling at how quickly the suppressed anger had overtaken her despite her years of training and experience, just as Viktor's had overtaken him.

"Thank you for opening up." Freda resumed folding.

"So are you going to send me a bill?" Viktor snarked.

"Absolutely."

Chapter 40

Gabby and Anton arrived in Barcelona after over a day traveling east through a stop in Frankfurt and changing trains in Strasbourg to head west toward Paris. They passed through Montpellier stopping only briefly at the border between France and Spain. Once through the checkpoint at Cerbère, with passports in order and all luggage accounted for, they proceeded to Barcelona, Spain. They arrived a week before the others would be joining them to board a ship bound for the South African coast.

The *Zukunft* would be setting out to sea in a few days but tonight they were enjoying themselves. Most people in France and Spain knew English enough to hold a simple conversation. Thanks to Anton's medical practice, he was able to speak passable Spanish with his patients. Their limousine pulled up to Gloria's and squealed to a stop. The brakes were wet from the constant rain. If you did not know there was a club here, you might miss it. The rain pattered on the roof and the windows scattered the outside lamps filling the cabin with a dreamy light like a starlit night sky. These last few days seemed as if they were in a world of their own, like young sweethearts. They knew when their relationship began that it would be an unusual one. The legal act itself required a complex arrangement of trusts and assignment of powers and cost far more than a conventional marriage. Before that, they had honest and frank discussions about sex, their feelings, and how they might involve other parties without destabilizing their relationship. Anton was delightfully surprised to find that Gabby was so enlightened despite her young age. He imagined that she had been through much more than most people her age and had earned for herself the status of *old soul*.

Last night's escapades with a strong Spanish youth left them both hungry for more. The young man's beautifully muscled, panting nakedness had entertained them for hours. Anton had long ago learned, with Gabby's help, to enjoy the beauty of two lovers even though he could no longer participate. He derived the most pleasure from the unbridled passion that Gabby put into her performance, making sure he could clearly see her lover's penetration and looking into his eyes as much as the eyes of the evening's catch. She made him feel included, wanted.

On the street in front of Gloria's the rain left them two choices. They could either wait for the driver to escort them with an umbrella or they could make a dash for the door. Gabby turned to look mischievously at Anton. "Fuck him," she said and Anton barked a loud laugh as she flung the door open to make for the club. The driver had moved too slowly and seeing that his charges were impatient, tried to get to them, but they did not care, laughing and ducking as they were soaked on their way to the entrance.

The doorman saw them coming too late and could not get the door open before they got there. Gabby grabbed the door and heaved it open and they came staggering into the lobby, dripping and laughing. Anton was out of breath, but

Gabby was invigorated and charged with energy. It had been far too long since they had shared an intimate experience together and these few days of ecstasy in each other's company had rekindled their passion. She was determined to make the most of their time in this wonderful old city. Two stewards brought them towels and they continued laughing as they dried themselves.

The club was not on the main strip. Its performers were not well known. The audience was not prominent. What they were was genuine. There were no wall flowers. There were no Dutchess impostors. There were good people here. Locals and knowledgeable visitors. The owner of the club was a former patient of Anton's. The gracious Miss Regina threw a curtain over her shoulder as she flowed toward them in a sparkling, floor-length, blue sequined gown accented with white ostrich feathers.

"Oh, he-e-ell no!" she blurted as she occluded the spotlight streaming in from the room behind her. "You two babies are messed up tonight!" She approached and Anton's laughter abated, but Gabby's did not. Anton looked up at her, water dripping from his black hair, and smiled.

Anton closed one eye to stop the room spinning. "You know, you are very tall," he slurred. Miss Regina leaned down to his ear so he could hear her clearly over the throbbing music echoing around them. "And don't forget that I could kick your ass. Got me?" As she stood, she lifted his chin with a finger. A loving, benevolent smile spread across her face and he knew he was in a safe environment. By now, Gabby had stopped laughing and was watching their exchange with a smile of admiration. Miss Regina turned to look at Gabby and seeing her face, instantly recognized real love. Her smile broadened as she released Anton's chin and moved toward Gabby. Taking both Gabby's hands in her own, she leaned down to her ear. "I think he loves you, sweetie."

Miss Regina waved off her staff when they tried to charge an entrance fee. She beckoned toward a young, curly-haired man who immediately came close and stood on the balls of his feet to hear her. She gave instructions. He asked a question. She answered. Anton could not hear a single word over the cacophony of music filtering through his alcohol haze.

"First, coffee." Miss Regina's voice was so loud that it not only overcame the background noise, it actually hurt his ear.

A man was stepping up to Anton's side. He lifted Anton by the arm. Miss Regina was lifting him up by the elbow. The lights bounced around behind his closed lids and he realized that he was too drunk. He allowed himself to be lifted and guided, trying to follow whoever was pulling him and stepping with as much dignity as he could muster with his eyes closed. He wondered if Gabby was being taken care of. He felt someone very strong take him by the arms and help him into a padded booth. There was a table he could feel before him, but he could not see it. He smelled the rich, acrid aroma of coffee and another aroma he knew but did not recognize.

"Honey, are you OK?" It was Gabby's voice, close, soft, and so beautiful to hear. "Honey, there is some coffee here for you. Open your eyes." Anton opened his eyes with great effort. "You just need some refreshment. I'm not done with you yet." Her voice carried both concern and passion and he knew the night was not over yet. As he took in his surroundings, he saw Miss Regina standing at the edge of the table.

He suddenly felt as if his mother were giving him a scolding look and he poured all his effort into composing himself. As his head cleared, the muffled music became clearer.

He sipped his coffee and followed Gabby's orders whenever she told him to drink water, he began to worry that he had embarrassed her. "I'h sorry," he drawled when she leaned in to see what he was trying to say to her. "Don't be sorry, my love. Come back to me and let's make this a night to remember." He sat back up, looking at the loving grin on her face. Her beautiful eyes reflected the pink and blue spotlights twirling around the room. He nodded and took a deep drink of water without being asked to, putting the glass down empty. Now he recognized the aroma. Miss Regina had the bartender put a couple drops of bitters in his water to settle his stomach.

Early on in their relationship, Anton and Gabby began talking *about* their relationship rather than just living in it. Though his specialty focused on surgical gender reassignment, he wanted to treat the whole person. It wasn't a good idea to try to do both, so he worked with several therapists and psychologists to help his patients achieve the best possible outcomes. This gave him a unique perspective on relationships since most of his patients did not fit the established template for marriage or heterosexual relationships.

Communication was the key to understanding and if two people do not fit some socially agreed upon template, then they had the opportunity to define their own. He knew that couples of all sorts drifted apart when their individual expectations did not match their partners. Good communication allowed couples to learn and understand what they shared and what they didn't.

Anton had been clinically impotent for a long time now and he had accepted that there were certain things he could not do for Gabby. Likewise, he thought that it would be nice to have children, but even though he could still ejaculate when he was flaccid, Gabby would forever be incapable of bearing children no matter what kind of medical intervention they might employ. They discussed what would satisfy each of them, agreed on certain boundaries, and revisited the topic periodically to make sure that reality was living up to expectations.

They were quite mature about the whole thing, yet Gabby felt uncertain about something. While they didn't always share a lover and she was free to have encounters on her own, it was always close to home. They would always sit and talk after an encounter, whether mutual or her by herself, and she would recount the lovemaking in vivid detail for him to enjoy. He often suggested things she might try and various ways he might participate in some later encounter. Gabby was about to go to Africa and they would not be able to share these experiences with a fresh memory.

Over breakfast in their room, he could tell she was preoccupied, but he let her sit in silence as she ate, not looking up at him. When she finally did look up, she caught him watching her and smiling.

"What?" Gabby asked.

"You are wondering if I would be offended if you had a lover away from home," Anton stated.

"Damn you. I can't even have a secret for a minute, can I?" Gabby tried to keep a straight face but failed miserably. Her smirk was plainly visible and Anton chuckled.

Chapter 41

The *Zukunft* had been gently rocking back and forth for a long time, but for the last few minutes, the motion had intensified as the wake from a large ocean liner passed. Even though the speed of ships was limited near the eastern port of Barcelona, the sheer displacement volume of some of the newer ships caused waves that made writing difficult. In truth, Albert's handwriting had noticeably degraded and it was becoming increasingly difficult to concentrate. He wanted to keep writing, but the undulating cabin was playing tricks with his innards. The tiny porthole made the dock seem to swing up and down, so he could not look outside to calm his nausea.

He had the steward bring him some tea and warm towels, but to no avail. As he cleaned his face and stared into the mirror, he could not bring any more ideas to mind. Maybe he was trying too hard. Maybe another stroll around the deck would clear the blockage. He had never written a book before, but since his decision, writing in his journal seemed more critical than usual.

Maria had given him some advice about journaling when he came to her about buying a typewriter. She said, "There is an ineffable quality to experience that can only be captured by handwriting, by your thoughts flowing onto the page through your own hand." He decided to continue with handwritten journaling.

He heard the mooring bell ring for the next round of boarding and looked out his water-level window to see Gabby emerging from a limousine with the door being held by Anton. From this low, he could not see the entire scene, but it appeared that they were followed by at least two other vehicles that parked off to the right. Anton took Gabby by both arms and spoke to her as men loaded carts with luggage.

"I want you to have a good time. It is just unfortunate you can't come back with that man's spine." His voice had a guttural quality and a power she had seen unleashed during the past week in Barcelona. He was vigorous, passionate, and strong. He drew her close with an arm around her waist. He looked deep into her eyes. "Come back with some good memories."

She placed both palms on his chest. She could feel his breathing and his heartbeat. She could see the longing in his eyes. She bowed her head to place her forehead on his chest. As cart after cart of matching luggage wheeled by, Anton began to wonder how much she had packed. He looked over his shoulder at the trucks and saw at least five carts filled with matching Louis Vuitton luggage. He looked back at Gabby with an inquisitive expression. "You did say to be prepared?" she asked rhetorically. He just smiled knowing that if there were an argument to be made, he had already lost.

"I look forward to hearing about your adventure," he said with finality, holding her by both arms at a distance. Feeling his emotional control slipping, he tried to bring the farewell to a close.

"I bet you do!" She gently but firmly removed his hands, putting them around her waist instead. She closed the space between them so they were hip to hip.

She took his face in both of her hands and drew him toward her for a passionate, lengthy kiss that left him seeing spots. Noticing that his control was about to fail, she reached down to pick up her favourite vintage piece, a 1901 LV Steamer bag, and turned to walk toward the gang plank. The ship was not large for a cargo vessel, but its passenger accommodations were adequate. The men with the carts stood to one side as she approached the wide bridgeway leading into the side of the ship. The captain had come to welcome some of his more prominent passengers aboard and he watched Gabby and Anton's exchange dispassionately. Now that she was approaching him, he thought she must be the most beautiful woman he had ever seen. Her cloak fluttered in the sea breeze and twisted around her as she walked giving her an ethereal quality.

"Welcome aboard the *Zukunft*, Mrs. Gorski. I am Captain Timisson." He stepped toward her and took the gloved hand she offered, bowing slightly.

"Captain, thank you for meeting me in person," Gabby replied with a curtsy.

Looking at the row of luggage carts and their attendants waiting off to the side he asked, "Is this all yours?" His face betrayed his disbelief. The uniform bags of varying sizes seemed to be duplicated over and over on each subsequent cart, enough to fill one of the smaller cabins to the ceiling. The first mate, a tall young man with light-mocha skin and kinky blonde hair and eyebrows, came up behind the captain. "Bruno?" He turned to see Bruno was already there. "Ah, Bruno, please see Mrs. Gorski to her quarters."

Gabby saw Bruno steal a glance before returning to forward-looking attention. "Yes, sir!" he barked. Clearly the youngster had been trained in some military capacity. Gabby marveled at the way his blonde lashes curled so tightly. They were so light that they caught the sunlight, gleaming against his haunting hazel eyes.

Captain Timisson stepped aside and Gabby passed him in a swirl of fabric and perfume. Bruno turned and walked toward the elevators but Gabby saw Mr. Asher Robinson come into the reception lobby from the far hallway and immediately, their eyes met. Asher smiled broadly and the melancholy of whatever had been occupying his mind melted away. As they walked toward each other, they each tried to contain their happiness to see each other. She knew this man. They met when he was working for the bank where Hugo was hoarding his photographs. He was a capable young man with his whole life ahead of him so it was no surprise that Gabby and Anton should find his name on the crew manifest. Anton's research into her trip had been meticulous. When she asked about his planning activities, he had told her that he would take care of it. When he was finished, he presented her with names, dates, ports of call, contacts in foreign ports for money, clothing, food, wine, and servants. It was quite a stimulating rush to see his attention to detail as he arranged for her every comfort. His list included talents as well. Asher was known for his knowledge of wines and had been instructed to bring aboard a sufficient supply of his own selections for the group. No expense had been spared, but Freda and Albert refused to travel in luxury, thinking they did not deserve the treatment. This had forced Anton to make some concessions like sending them on a cargo vessel with quarters instead of chartering a ship. Still, the rooms were spacious and the amenities were luxurious.

While Gabby was examining her room and giving Bruno instructions on where to put this and that, Freda arrived at the terminal. She was nervous about going so far from home, but she wasn't worried about where they were going. To her, it did not matter how dangerous the area. She would face the man who had harmed so many like her. Arrangements had been made which she would review with Esam as soon as they were settled in Accra proper, but until then, she was taking her cohorts into danger. She knew that, thanks to Viktor and Esam's interventions, Ankrah's people would keep them as safe as they could, but the larger culture into which they were traveling was not so easily controlled as here in the civilized world.

The agent on the other side of the counter raced through a ledger with one hand and held the passport, picture facing her, in the other. The woman's navy blue uniform was clean, freshly pressed, and from her epaulets hung loops of gold rope with tassels at the ends. Her dark hair was pulled tightly into a bun tied with a white cord. Freda stood silently waiting until the woman scribbled some notes and looked up. *"Disfruta tu viaje,"* she said nodding toward the row of doors that led out to the dock. Freda took that to mean their business was concluded so she took her passport from the woman's outstretched hand, tucked it into her handbag, and hoisted two matching suitcases at her sides.

On the dock, the cool ocean breeze twirled her woolen skirt around her ankles and she felt a slight chill in the air. The captain was gesturing for her to approach. "Welcome aboard the *Zukunft*, Dr. Dudek. I am Captain Timisson." He beckoned to a valet who was already approaching. The young man in maroon waistcoat and slacks took her bags and stood a few metres away, eyes forward standing at attention, waiting. It seemed odd that a cargo ship would have such crisp looking deck hands, but she understood that the crew who dealt with the cargo would probably not be the same as those dealing with passengers.

Anton had described how the trip would unfold at an evening gathering. They drank wine and laughed as he described the ship and hotel accommodations. That is, until they were all sufficiently anesthetized to discuss the grim task ahead. They knew the details, the political climate, the risks of being Caucasian in a mostly dark-skinned part of the world. She remembered feeling a pang of guilt at the comparison of races, but she had to face facts. She was a former male from an oppressed and brutalized race. She was the "other" and yet she still thought of the Ghanaians as "others." It seemed there was no hope of humanity overcoming this persistent failing.

Captain Timisson brought her aboard, describing the layout of the ship in general terms. Pointing toward the bow and up through the ceiling, he referenced the bridge. Pointing toward the stern and down through the floor he described the cargo being held in large voids within the ship, each one closed with a bulkhead door on the top. "Believe it or not, we only need one empty vat in the front and one in the back to stay afloat," he said proudly.

"Won't the vats all be *filled* with cocoa beans on our return?" Freda's question clearly made the captain uncomfortable so he ignored it and continued with his descriptive tour.

"Madam, I have invited your companions to dine with me in the captain's mess this evening. Would you please do me the honour of joining us?"

"Why thank you, Captain. I believe I will."

"Very good then. Dinner is at six, but please come early for some refreshment and conversation." He nodded to the valet who was standing stock-still. The youngster said, "Ma'am, please follow me." He gestured with one of the bags toward the opening elevator doors and Freda stepped past him, taking up a position in a back corner so the valet would be able to turn around after he entered. He set the bags down and pressed the button for the tween deck. They went down past the lower deck, just below the main deck. Gabby's rooms would be on the upper deck, of course, and Albert had wanted to have as much alone-time as possible, so he was in a stern room on the tween deck just below the lower deck. Her room was located toward the bow.

Albert closed his journal and set the pen to the side on the small desk, which was nothing but a shelf set into a cubbyhole in the corner of the small room. A single chair, bed, small bureau, and coat rack were all the amenities the room offered and while he was certain that he could have had a more luxurious room, he wanted a departure from the trappings of wealth that Gabby enjoyed and the recognition that Freda had earned so he made sure his cabin was in the lower decks. His thumb had a persistent bruise from how tightly he clenched his pen, but he never noticed it when he was writing. He rubbed his thumb to get the blood circulating again and pushed the chair back to stand. His body ached from long hours in the same position. He was beginning to notice that his knee clicked each time he stood. His body was starting to feel its age.

Since this was a cargo vessel and would not be stopping at coastal cities until it rounded the west side of the African continent, there were few people other than the crew. He had the promenade deck all to himself and as he strolled around the perimeter, he watched the crew below on the main deck preparing to launch. On the port side he saw four men drawing the loading and passenger planks into the side of the ship with ropes. He could hear the bearings groaning as the weight shifted and sea birds cawed in protest as their perch quaked beneath their feet, eventually taking flight en masse. The morning sun was bright and the sea was calm.

"*¿Puedo traerle algo, señor?*" The young woman's voice startled Albert. He had not heard her coming behind him.

"*Sprichst Du Deutsch?*" ("Do you speak German?") he asked, not holding much expectation that she would.

"*Ja! Darf ich Dir etwas bringen?*" ("Yes, sir! May I bring you something?") Seeing the look of surprise on his face, the young woman smiled feeling quite proud.

"Pardon me," he apologized. "I did not expect you to understand me. May I have some black tea, please?"

"Aye, sir. Will you be on this deck?" she asked.

He promised not to wander off. He thought that must be quite annoying and wondered if passengers led the crew on hide-and-seek missions often. He crossed to starboard and rested his forearms on the railing, letting his mind wander as he tilted his face toward the sun, eyes closed. Birds cried in the distance. He felt the gentle rocking of the ship and through his feet he could feel the bustling below decks. Someone slammed a door or dropped something heavy and he felt the vibration too low to be heard. He heard voices speaking Spanish issuing orders. A bell rang on a buoy somewhere out on the water and with each clang he heard the sound echo off the terminal building behind him. He breathed in the Balearic Sea air.

"Well, here is our lost poet!"

He turned toward Gabby's voice and saw her approaching from the main staircase. Her dress whipped and flapped about her and she drew her cashmere stole tighter. "I just couldn't wait to get out of those clothes!" she said, letting the double entendre hang in the air. Albert only smiled and turned his face back to the sun as she came to the railing alongside him, imitating his stance. "It is so peaceful up here," she remarked softly after a minute or two. He hummed his agreement as they both enjoyed the warmth.

After a while, the woman appeared with a tray, cup, saucer, and pot. He turned the inverted cup over and she filled it with steaming dark liquid. The aroma of the special blend was invigorating. She asked if Gabby would like anything but Gabby declined with thanks. The woman left them in peace.

"Are you afraid?"

He looked down to see that Gabby was facing him with a question in her eyes. "A little. Not much. Are you?"

"Yes." She looked as if she had more to say. "Very much. How are you not?"

Albert had not considered why he was relatively unafraid of standing face-to-face with Schumann, so he took his time answering. "Schumann did what he did because he was surrounded by a system that shielded him from all consequences. He knew that no one would question him whatever he did and so he discarded the veil of respect for human life and showed who he really was. People like that are too cowardly to behave the way they want to without the support of others. His support is gone. The recent coup in Ghana removed any protection he might have had. With President Ankrah taking over, he is once again alone. A coward will not act on his own unless cornered, which we are about to do, but I doubt he will try anything surrounded by guns."

Gabby considered this. Albert could see her come to some kind of decision, but she did not voice it. She put a hand on his arm and turned to go back to the main stairs with a smile and a nod of thanks. He watched her retreat. As Gabby descended, she greeted someone coming up the stairs. The woman with the tray crested the top step and came to offer him more tea. He did not want any, so she offered the tray for him to set his cup down and continued with her duties. He spent another twenty minutes relaxing in solitude until the ship's whistle signaled final checks before departure. He went to join the other passengers on the main deck and when he reached the bottom stair, he saw people waving toward the dock, saying goodbye to loved ones. Gabby was standing beside Freda, waving to Anton. Ben stood next to Anton, giving a subdued wave. The whistle sounded again, the echo off the terminal facade was almost loud enough to hurt their ears. Small ropes were thrown toward deckhands. Two twenty centimetre thick ropes slid from giant cleats into the water to be drawn into the hull through round openings in the side of the ship.

The ship's engines began to push the *Zukunft* out to sea aided by a tugboat that deftly maneuvered around the ship applying thrust where the tugboat captain knew would be just right to make the *Zukunft's* captain's job easier. It was a dance both had performed many times before. As they headed south along the shipping lane toward Valencia, vessels would signal to each other as they passed in the northbound shipping lane. They slowed as they approached the Strait of Gibraltar, where the shipping lanes came close to each other. At one point, the captain's voice came over the speakers. He explained that even though it appeared that the ship ahead was coming straight at them, this was not the case. He named the ship approaching and said that he was in radio contact with her captain and that they would be able to see that the ship would pass to the side as they drew closer. Albert went toward the bow along with other passengers who were curious about the phenomenon.

They explored the ship and periodically, the captain would make an announcement of something interesting or timely. An hour before dinner, they retired to dress. Though this ship never held black tie events, dinner with the captain did call for something dignified. Albert was ready early and went to see how Gabby was coming along. When he approached down the long hallway, the first thing he noticed was that the doors were spaced very far apart, unlike the spacing on his deck. If there were a door into each suite, that would make them huge! When he came to her door, he knocked on the wooden inlay and the soft thud indicated it was wood all the way through, not the metal his door was made of.

"Come!" came from the other side of the door, so he turned the ornate door handle and stepped in.

From where he stood, he could see through a series of openings leading to at least three rooms. This room was indeed huge. The lower deck was almost twice the height of the decks underneath and the rooms were lined with wood panels. It did not feel like a room on the ocean, but felt like a room in a manor house. Gabby's back was turned as she sorted through various stoles and fur coats hanging on a portable rack in the middle of the room. The room was so spacious that she could stand back three metres and still have twice that much space to the nearest piece of furniture. The connected rooms must have spanned a quarter the length of the ship. He couldn't help letting his mouth fall open as he gawked. "Would you mind if we traded rooms?"

"Not a chance! I have seen what you made Anton put you up in. You may as well travel in a suitcase." She selected a white cashmere stole with thick Angora fur edges that wrapped her shoulders, crossed in the front with a giant button holding it in place. Underneath she wore a white Damask dress cut in the American 1950's style of Jacqueline Onassis. He had no idea how she would sit in a dress with no pleats or folds or extra fabric at all, but she would find a way.

At dinner, they told the captain nothing of their real purpose. They listened to the captain's tales of far away ports and exotic places as if they were his everyday outing. Gabby told him of The Weber Foundation and all the good it was doing. Freda described how much the field of sexual psychology had expanded and about her mentors, Anton and Harry Benjamin. They were cautious, but cordial and the conversation lasted into the night over cocktails. When everyone else had retired for the night, Captain Timisson invited Gabby to the observation deck above the bridge. The moon would be rising soon if she cared to see it.

The experience was marvelous. She stood on the exposed deck with countless stars filling her view facing the port side, the bow of the ship on her right. She knew she was facing the upper-most western corner of Africa somewhere outside the islands of Cape Verde off the coast of Senegal. There was nothing but black ocean in the direction he pointed. As she watched, a ring of shimmering purple light, barely visible, raced along the sky toward the spot where the moon would rise. He explained that ice crystals in the air were seeing the moon before they did and to watch the point where the ring would close. She held her breath as the ring of purple diffused into indigo and deepest violet, and a white ring began to appear between them. When they reached the horizon, the rings wrapped downward at the edges and in the center, the first sliver of blue-white light sent a wave of reflections toward the ship , skimming across the water. The light became brighter until it was uncomfortable to her unadjusted eyes, but she refused to look away.

The night air was colder than she had expected and she had begun to rub her arms. The captain, standing a respectful distance behind her, lifted his coat to cover her shoulders. The stole looked warm, but it was more a fashion piece than a practical one. He stepped back. His enjoyment was not in seeing the moon rising. He saw it so frequently. The ecstasy that this beautiful woman was experiencing at this moment...now *that* was pleasure.

The trip around the western coast of Africa was uneventful. The occasional storm passed but none did any more than rock the ship a little. The covered main deck was still enjoyable during a downpour provided the wind was not too strong, but the captain forbade anyone other than the crew to go near the outer railing during inclement weather. Albert passed the time in his cabin writing. Sometimes he would take his journal to the poop deck at the stern where the lights under the canopy were bright enough to write by at night. He was too excited to sleep well, so when he was restless he would spend the early morning writing above deck. As people began to rise, breakfast was served. The food aboard ship was amazing and they all indulged more than was healthy.

During the night, when the moon was not up, they could sometimes see a faint glow over the ocean toward the African coast. The captain explained that some of the major cities were lit with electric lights at night. One of the brightest was Dakar, Senegal which was a major trading destination for many decades but even being the brightest, it was nothing more than a faint orange glow. Once the moon rose, it washed out the coastal lights. One morning while writing on the bow of the main deck, Albert noticed that the sun rose ahead of the ship. They had turned east during the night which meant that they would be arriving at Accra within a day or two.

Albert and Viktor had done quite a bit of research into Accra, Kumasi, and Ghana in general. Viktor had actually visited the region once in his youth but could only guess at the changes from then to today, in 1966. Certainly with the recent coup, there would be some government-driven changes, but the change of power had not been as violent as everyone had feared. They would settle in Accra and after a few days, would travel a few hours north to Kumasi to join the military operation to take Schumann into custody.

The newly-installed President, Joseph Ankrah, was aware of a petition by Schumann to the courts to block his extradition to Germany, but rather than deny his petition, possibly giving him reason to disappear again, Ankrah decided to listen to his advisors who had been in periodic contact with Viktor's group. Schumann had not been made aware of the court's intent to deny his petition, but was instead told to be patient. While the military coordinated with the local police in Kumasi, Esam and his team kept observing Schumann's activities watching for changes or for any sign that Schumann was about to attempt another escape. Thus far, there was no indication that Schumann knew any more than he had been told by the court.

Their destination in Accra was the The Mövenpick Ambassador Hotel which had been a gift from the UK to Ghana in honour of its independence. Built in 1957, it was a luxurious oasis in an otherwise bustling city. Viktor had explained that because of the sensitive operation, they would not be allowed to go anywhere without Esam. There would be time to enjoy Accra, but only after Schumann was safely in custody.

The next day, the ship began signaling as the shipping lanes drew within visual range of each other. They could see the shore off the port bow and passengers strolled around the deck for the last time before packing their bags. They enjoyed champagne and a buffet of finger foods as their last meal aboard. Some of the passengers were taken aback when some of the crew took up posts around the railing of the main deck carrying rifles. The captain explained that it was just a precaution and that there was nothing to worry about.

Gabby's attendants had been packing her belongings since early morning while she enjoyed the warm equatorial breeze above deck. She held her woven-reed, wide-brimmed hat on with one hand while she toasted her friends with the other. "Let's go make sure that bastard pays!" was Gabby's boisterous response to Freda's somber toast.

The *Zukunft* docked and the captain went to negotiate with the dockmaster who would certainly impose some unknown fee to extort his customer. Freda repeated her warning to Gabby not to appear obviously wealthy. She had dressed appropriately, but there was no mistaking cart after cart being loaded into a rented truck with an armed guard standing watch as anything other than affluence. As the two prepared to disembark, a shadow fell over them from the dock side. The two looked up at a broad-shouldered, dark-skinned hulk of a man. Gabby's thought processes ceased. Freda saw Gabby go silent and decided to take charge of the situation. "Would you be Esam?" she asked.

The man's musical, basso voice was thunderously low but also soft. "I am. Would you be Dr. Dudek and Mrs. Gorski?" He was dressed in loose-fitting black cargo pants like many of the men around the dock. Those men were carrying automatic rifles with large magazines, but Esam did not appear to be armed. He wore a simple raw cotton short-sleeved tunic style shirt and thick veins protruded from his biceps and forearms. Gabby noticed that his arms were almost as big around as her waist. She opened her mouth to speak. Nothing happened.

Freda looked sideways at Gabby to see her seemingly frozen in place, so she responded for the two of them. "Please call me Freda, and this is Gabriella," she said gesturing to the slack-jawed nymphomaniac. Gabby did not even notice Freda's presence anymore. She gazed at him unblinking. He thought her behaviour a bit strange since most people, men and women, avoided him. He knew his physique should be attractive to women, but he did not experience it that way. Women avoided him even more than men did.

Esam gave Gabby a little bow and turned his attention to Freda. They discussed what he expected of them on the way to the hotel. He described what to do if the vehicles were stopped or somehow blocked. Freda acknowledged his instructions and thanked him for protecting them. When he turned to go to the truck being loaded with their luggage, Freda gave Gabby a little slap on the back of the arm and she startled awake. She gave Freda a confused look. Clearly she had not heard a word of Esam's instructions. "I will explain it to you on the way," she said, taking Gabby by the arm.

Albert came up behind them as they headed toward the terminal. Their passports had been collected by the purser when they boarded the ship. The captain had passed them to the dock authorities. They each went to a separate window to answer questions. When Freda was finished, she joined Albert who was waiting near the street exit at the front of the building. They checked their belongings to make sure everything was present while they waited for Gabby, but Gabby did not come. They could see her arguing with an unseen clerk behind a counter. Their view was blocked by the brick arches over each clerk's window, but the way Gabby was gesturing with jerky movements indicated that something was wrong.

Esam's voice was like low rolling thunder that they could feel in their bones, but could barely hear. "Is something wrong?" His unannounced appearance startled them both, but they regained their composure quickly and Freda pointed to Gabby across the room, behind the maze of ropes. Esam did not hesitate. He headed for the counter, then turned right and walked directly toward Gabby. She was too focused on her argument to notice his approach until he was standing beside her. She leaned back to look up into his eyes with an expression of alarm but before she could say anything, he leaned down, wrapped an arm around her waist, and lifted her to his height in a powerful but oh, so gentle embrace. Her alarm melted instantly and she raised one arm over his massive shoulder. She tried to reach around him with the other but it was like trying to reach around a truck. She immediately thought of how his strength might translate to the bedroom and before she realized it, she had forgotten where she was and what she was doing.

He looked deep into her eyes and lifted his free hand to brush her blonde hair over her ear. He said just loud enough for the clerk's supervisor standing a short distance behind the clerk to hear. "Are they giving you a difficult time, baby?"

Gabby batted her lashes and laid a hand over the deep groove in the middle of his chest. "Yes, my love," she whispered. She affected an apologetic demeanor and, stealing a glance at the clerk, confirmed that the set-up was indeed convincing.

Esam turned and fixed his stare on the clerk who recoiled slightly. Esam slowly lowered Gabby to the floor and then turned to squarely face the much smaller man. Esam knew what was happening. This clerk was trying to extort some fee from a vulnerable white woman who had tried to "dress down" to hide the fact that she had money. Esam did not say anything. Neither did the clerk. Almost thirty seconds passed while the smaller man fidgeted, eyes locked with Esam. Esam's only movement was turning his eyes to look at the papers in the clerk's left hand. The clerk extended the papers toward Esam as he parroted, "Passports will be delivered to you at your hotel." Esam turned to Gabby and handed the papers to her. He waited for her to look into his face. She turned her head up and solidified the grift with a look of desperate passion. She apologized in a breathy whisper "I am sorry I bothered you." Esam took her hand and led her toward the rest of the group. A man slipped out the back door after watching the whole scene.

The trip to the hotel was filled with the sounds of a bustling community. Though there were the occasional state-funded buildings housing various governmental departments here and there, the surrounding structures, roads, and people did not match. It was as if the city had been partly-contrived but mostly organic. Each government building was a sterile void in the vital life that thronged around the van and the trucks that followed. The three travelers had never seen so many dark-skinned people. The vibrant colors of the women's flowing wraps and headdresses piled high contrasted with the bland colors worn by the men. When they passed a street vendor cooking beside the road, the van filled with a wonderful aroma.

Esam rode in the front passenger seat with a rifle between his legs, out of sight but strategically positioned so he could shoot anyone who approached the window without them seeing the gun until it was too late. Gabby sat behind the driver who had not greeted them, looked at them, or acknowledged them in any way. His eyes darted constantly making Gabby wonder if they were in danger. Freda sat behind Esam, petrified, eyes wide, saying nothing. Albert had the back seat to himself and he slid from one side to the other, fascinated by the panorama. He had the large eyes of a child seeing a new world and paid no attention to the occupants of the van.

They arrived at the hotel and climbed out of the van while men unloaded the truck that followed with their luggage. When Freda invited Esam to relax with them, he declined but her persistence won him over and he followed them into the The Mövenpick Ambassador Hotel. He handed some cash to the head valet and bent down to have a few words with him. Freda noticed that he was occupied and slowed her pace, waiting for him. The Mövenpick Ambassador had been a gift from the British to the people of Ghana commemorating their independence and had been appointed with all the luxuries one could want.

They walked to the end of the magnificent lobby and took an elevator to the top floor. The valet had to unlock the buttons with a key before he could use them. When the doors opened onto the concierge floor, the valet stepped out and to the side so the guests could exit. They came out into the large space gawking at the opulence of the modern British hotel. Even Esam's eyes were wide.

The architectural elements were stunning and quite futuristic. The valet explained the history of the hotel and how it affected the local area. He told about the recent coup and how there was no reason to worry about security, specifically looking at Esam while he delivered the scripted lines. He introduced them to Piotr, Gabby's personal chef. Piotr presented them with a charcuterie board nearly a metre long containing various aged meats sliced paper thin. Little mounds of various cheeses were paired with fruits and wines as Piotr wove a fascinating story of how the more exotic items were prepared or acquired. The valet excused himself and they began to indulge, but Esam sat off to the side, disconnected from the group, until Freda insisted that he join them.

Reluctantly, Esam joined them. Gabby experienced wanton pleasure each time Esam tried something he had never tasted before. She was not hiding the lust she felt for this man. The elevator dinged. Esam's eyes immediately darted toward the doors and he shoved his hand into a cargo pocket while angling his knee out slightly. The doors opened and the driver of the truck came walking swiftly toward Esam speaking what must be the local language and punctuating his words with gestures. Esam took him aside and they spoke animatedly.

"This does not fill me with confidence," remarked Freda under her breath. Eyebrows raised, she tipped her glass toward Gabby.

Esam finished his conversation with the driver and turned to rejoin them while the driver went back toward the elevator. "Mrs. Gorski," Esam's eyes settled on her and she felt a sense of anguish transmitted through his gaze. "I apologize. I should have stayed with your things." He paused to take a breath and she leaned toward him, putting a hand on his forearm.

"What is it?" Gabby asked, not understanding what she was trying to tell her.

"Your things have gone missing," Esam repeated.

Gabby sat in mild shock. "Well alright then. What does that mean?"

Freda knew. It meant no clothes, jewelry, shoes, or furs. "Sweetheart," Freda interjected, "it means that your luggage has been stolen."

"It *means* I should have stayed where I belong." Esam turned to leave and Gabby sensed from him a deep embarrassment.

Gabby pushed her cocktail away with a finger on its base and rose slowly from her stool. She looked at Esam with her head cocked to one side and an impish grin on her lips. Esam's eyes opened wide in surprise and Gabby might have detected a touch of fear. Suddenly, his formidable size seemed inadequate protection. She stepped slowly toward him, taking her time, examining his expressions. Freda sat watching in silence, wondering what was about to happen.

Gabby stood too close to the hulking man, eyes still locked with his, and poked him as hard as she could in the middle of the chest. He took a step backward toward the elevator. She stepped up to him and again poked him hard in the chest. He took another step back. She closed the space between them again. She pressed her finger into his chest, not poking, but holding a point of pressure which dimpled his skin. Still maintaining eye contact, she said in a voice just low enough so that only he could hear.

"I brought my friends here on Viktor's word that you would protect us. We know we are in danger here. We rely on you to keep us safe while we try to trap a monster." She released the pressure at her fingertip and placed her palm flat against his chest. She could feel his heart pounding. If he weren't a good man, he wouldn't care enough to feel responsible and his heart would be calm. She took a deep breath and let it out slowly, lowering her gaze a moment. Then, looking back up into his eyes, she asked, "How are we supposed to trust you if you can't even keep luggage safe?"

Esam winced as if he had been stabbed. He barely knew these people, but he liked them and Viktor was their friend, therefore, this woman was his friend. He was upset that he had allowed her confidence in him to be soiled. He sighed and placed a hand over hers, pressing her fingers into his flesh. "I am sorry, Miss Gabriella." He sighed, looking down.

Seeing the weight of responsibility on him, she waited for him to look back up into her eyes. When he did, she affected her most seductively breathy voice saying, "We need to trust you, so...you are going to find my luggage. You are going to find it now and bring it back to me." She pressed her hand against his chest, pushing him backward toward the elevator. He retreated another step and then another. "Exactly, what am I supposed to wear?"

At that, she saw the thought flash across his face. He mused as he looked at her body, imagining how her innuendo might play out. She saw desire flash across his face and knew that she had his loyalty. "Don't you look at me like that until you come back with my luggage," she insisted as he backed into the elevator. The chuckling attendant pressed the button to close the doors as Gabby withdrew her hand. Once the doors had closed, she turned to see Freda laughing silently. "What is so funny?" she demanded.

"You just told him he could see you naked if he brought your luggage back."

Gabby's jaw dropped. "I did not!"

"Oh, I'm afraid you did," Freda insisted.

"What just happened?" asked Albert, apparently just looking up from the spread. Freda and Gabby both looked at Albert in disbelief.

Arno began to chuckle. He was leaning back in a creaky old wooden swivel chair pushed to the limit of balance. His feet were crossed on top of the old desk with clumps of dirt on the desk and papers below them. The cigar between his teeth had long ago burned out but he had continued to masticate it until the wet end had become a dark mass of tobacco and saliva. In relaxed Twi Akan, also Esam's first language, he asked, "So you just walked away?" His chuckling redoubled and Arno began to wheeze with laughter. Arno served in the military most of his life, but ever since a serious injury that left his shoulder weak, he was deemed unfit for combat and relegated to the local police force. Like Esam, he made money on the side by guarding the occasional politician or rich tourist. Whenever the opportunity arose, the two of them delighted in slighting each other. A stolen bag or a missing vehicle often left them incapacitated by laughter as they watched the other from a distance trying to find whatever was missing. Despite their friendly rivalry, Arno and Esam knew they could count on each other when the situation demanded.

"Yes. That is how it happened." Esam was embarrassed but he knew that Arno was only relishing the moment. There was no avoiding this particular slight. He had been caught neglecting his responsibilities. It would not have surprised Esam at all if Arno had been waiting for him to turn his attention away so he could snatch whatever cargo he might be guarding. When they found the cases filled with women's clothing, well, there was just no way to resist a little tit-for-tat.

Arno reached up over his shoulder and snapped loudly to someone behind him, out of Esam's view. He brought his hand back down and crossed his arms, making

DIE FOTOGRAFIE

a visual assessment of Esam. He examined the huge man from head to foot, slowly looking up and down. He was obviously trying to prolong Esam's humiliation while he waited for someone to come. Another man dressed in mud-spattered black cargo pants and sweatshirt came around the corner modeling a fancy straw hat wrapped with a flowing silk scarf printed with large orange flowers and green leaves. He walked with a feminine step and one arm stuck straight down with the hand turned level to the ground, fingers hanging daintily.

Esam could not help himself. A smirk flashed across his face and then vanished as he tried to project carelessness by rolling his eyes, but Arno saw the reaction. He would extract every bit of pleasure from Esam's blunder and would reserve his mercy as long as possible. Esam could see in Arno's face that this would be the case. What was he to do? He needed Gabriella's clothes returned. He had trained for over a decade, been shot, stabbed, kidnapped, and tortured. He had traveled to the front line with Nkrumah's freedom fighters and carried wounded men back only to return to the fight immediately. He worked with one of the most expansive Nazi hunting networks in the world and had to kill a man just two days ago to save one of his own, but he would rather have any of those than what was happening right now.

"You want to get these lady things back, yes?" Arno reached back to the man who was mocking Esam and the man gave him the hat. Arno brought the hat before him and turned it around, examining it. He brought the hat to his nose. He gathered a handful of the scarf and inhaled through it. He closed his eyes and inhaled deeply and slowly. He held his breath, savoring having the scent of a woman in his lungs, absorbing her, possessing her. He watched Esam squirm. He took his feet off the desk and stood, taking the single step toward Esam to stand in his face with the hat between them.

There was a tension between them. Esam sensed that it was artificial and nothing to be afraid of, but he should play along to keep his options open. This was not a conflict yet. It was a power play and a tease, but if Arno became embarrassed in front of his men, it could turn sour quickly. Esam looked over Arno's shoulders at the men scattered around the room. None were focused exclusively on them, but each was trying to observe surreptitiously.

Arno saw him looking around the room and raised a finger to touch Esam on the nose, then to touch his own nose, indicating the need for Esam to focus. He was curious why a man as skilled and loyal would let his attention falter as he had. "She smells like a sweet young pussy," Arno said as he returned the hat to his nose for one last whiff. His eyes were closed again and Esam wondered how long it had been since Arno had had a woman.

Arno caught Esam inhaling the scent too and smiled. Esam was trying to hide his attraction to this woman. In that instant, he knew that he had leverage. Esam leaned to the side of Arno's head and Arno leaned in so Esam could speak into his ear. Esam whispered, "She is on a mission to capture a war criminal. The operation is sanctioned by Ankrah himself." Arno recoiled, looking into Esam's eyes to check the truthfulness of his statement. He measured Esam's look and said under his breath, "Shit." He handed the hat to Esam and returned to his desk. He leaned back again and knocked more dried mud off his boots when he raised his feet and dropped them one at a time onto the surface making the previously deposited mud crunch. Bits of dried mud bounced off the desk and landed on the floor.

Esam and Arno now both understood that their rivalry would have to wait, but somehow Arno would have to give their loot back to Esam without capitulating in front of his men. Arno believed in the cause of bringing war criminals from Germany to justice and Esam had relied on him many times. Not all of the men here felt the same way, so their relationship had been kept out of view. Neither wanted to jeopardize Arno's anonymity so they stared at each other, the next move clear to both. Whoever came up with an idea first would speak.

The few seconds that passed felt like an eternity when Arno suddenly raised his voice in anger. "Do you realize what kind of position you have put me in, my friend?" His voice echoed off the walls and was clearly meant to draw the attention of anyone listening. "What do you think Ankrah will say when he hears about this?"

Realizing what Arno was trying to do, Esam cast his eyes on the floor saying, "I am sorry. I should have told you earlier."

"You are damned right you should have!" Arno yelled, his torso contracting with the force of his feigned rage. He spread his arms wide. "So what are you going to do to fix this?" He covertly indicated to Esam that he needed to continue with the farce with an almost imperceptible lifting of one eyebrow and crossed his arms to wait. This would give Esam a few extra seconds to formulate the solution.

"If you return the bags before anyone complains, I can tell him that you and I examined the bags for contraband before returning them. If I am seen bringing the bags back it will look like we were working together and that nothing is wrong."

Arno sat with his arms crossed, dragging out his consideration of the plan so his grudging agreement would seem plausible to the room of eavesdroppers. He displayed a scowl, sat forward taking his dirty boots from the desk and putting his hands on his knees. He gave a deep sigh and came so close that Esam could feel his breath on his cheek as Arno turned his head slightly and called, "Aiye!" The man who teased with the hat earlier came around the corner again. "Load everything back up and make sure it is *exactly* as it was when we took it! I don't want to find *anything* missing! You got it?" He raised his voice at the very end to stress that there would be consequences if his instructions were not followed.

Esam parted his lips slightly and said an unarticulated "Thanks." It was just barely loud enough for Arno to hear and he responded with a slight grunt.

Then Arno raised his voice just enough for others to hear. "I would appreciate it if you don't let this kind of thing happen again."

Esam nodded and turned to go back outside but Arno called to him. Turning back, he saw a man behind Arno slapping a long tube into his hand, raised over his shoulder. It looked like a baton, but it wobbled along its length when it struck Arno's hand. "You will need to return this in person." Arno brought the thing into his lap, then heaved it toward Esam with an underhand throw. As the object arced toward Esam, he began to reach for a point where he could catch it. In mid-arc he realized what it was. He nearly hesitated but he did not want it to be damaged if it hit the floor. As he closed his hand around the floppy rubber phallus, he looked up at the ceiling in an expression of excruciating embarrassment and the entire room erupted with laughter.

Once on the street he could see Arno's men hurriedly stuffing clothing and other items back into the bags as they loaded them onto a truck. One of the men gave a circle motion in the air with his index finger to indicate that he was the driver and that Esam should lead them where they needed to go.

When Esam arrived at The Mövenpick Ambassador's semi-circular drive, he pulled around to the exit and parked to the side. The truck following stopped in front of the door leaving enough space for guests to drive their cars between the truck and the entrance. Esam went inside and retrieved three bellhops with carts. Two men who were riding in the back of the truck began to load the carts, one in the truck heaving bags to the other who caught them and deposited them on the carts. The last out were two trunks that required both men to lift down. Once the carts were full and the men had climbed back into the back of the truck, he gave the driver a two-fingered *clear to drive* gesture and a nod of thanks. He led the bellhops toward the elevators going up to the Gorski suite.

Gabby was content that her gratitude to Esam for rescuing her luggage had been thoroughly expressed. Lying on his heaving chest, Gabby was nearly a half metre off the mattress. His size was not simply thick muscle. He was so tall that his feet hung off the bottom of the bed even when his head was almost touching the headboard. They had cast the covers and pillows aside; too constricting. Two empty champagne bottles were upended in the silver bucket and one of the lead crystal flutes lay in two pieces on a silver tray, a casualty of the evening. The other glass had only a centimetre of flat liquid in the bottom.

A few pieces of luggage stacked around the bedroom suite were strewn across the floor; a result of him carrying her around the room trying creative positions using any surface available. She particularly liked the way he got into a relaxed rhythm while she was face down on the short chest of drawers. With her hips at the edge of the bureau's surface, her feet were well off the ground. She enjoyed the feeling of helplessness as he easily held her weight by the hips and did as he pleased. She relished his power as his forcefulness grew and he growled with pleasure. She knew she had no hope of resisting his wishes given her small size compared to him, but after each change of position he would make certain she was enjoying it too. It was touching to see him being so careful not to hurt her with his immense strength and large endowment.

She lay quietly, listening to his breathing and heartbeat slow, feeling the sweat beginning to cool them both. She still had him inside her and when he had moved to withdraw himself, she had held him down, although willingly, so that she might keep him inside for as long as possible. Since the surgeries only provided a channel that simulated a vagina, she was not able to squeeze him the way a biological woman would be able to. There was also no place for his seed to go since she had no childbearing parts either. She lay there, letting the smell of his body permeate her skin and hair. She was fascinated by his odor. Freshly out of the shower, his body gave off a scent that told her subconscious mind of his strength and virility. She found it exotic and extremely arousing. She would have to ask Anton how he felt about ebony-skinned men for one of their escapades.

She realized that his breathing had become deep and regular. He had fallen asleep. After only a few minutes he seemed to awaken with a jerk. He looked into her eyes. Her smile was the most intoxicating way to wake up he had ever experienced. His emotions began to swell while sleep still clouded his mind, but then he remembered. This woman's heart was unavailable. He could feel that she still held him and his seed inside her and asked if she were comfortable. She admitted that she was cold on one side and still sweaty where their skin met. It was time to move. As she took charge of easing his manhood out of her, he thought he might never get her wonderful smell out of his skin. She was intoxicating.

On the concierge floor above their chambers, the trio would meet for breakfast. Gabby's espresso-brown linen skirt was hemmed below the knee. The top was raw cotton and though the threads were heavy, the fabric was loosely woven. Freda, Albert, and a man she did not recognize in a black beret, black sweatshirt, black cargo pants, and black boots were waiting for her as she emerged from the elevator. The man's skin was so dark that it nearly matched his clothing. One thing she noticed immediately was that his clothes were clean and his boots were polished unlike most of the military men she had seen so far.

Esam came up to the table, thanked them for the opportunity to serve them, and asked them to deliver a message to Viktor when they returned to Germany. He then formally turned possession of the group over to the military commander who accepted with a casual salute. Under President Ankrah, the National Liberation Council would be in charge of the operation in Kumasi. As commander of the unit that would provide support while the Kumasi police surrounded Schumann, he would be responsible for the second ring around Schumann while the local police would approach him. Once they knew he would not attempt escape, the group would be brought into the inner circle to face Schumann while the outer ring defended the position from any outside attack or incursion.

Chapter 42

Dr. Schumann rushed to dress. The call he had just received was urgent. One of the ambassadors, a guest of some politician high up in the new Ghanaian ruling party, the National Liberation Council, had suddenly fallen ill and was complaining of intense pain just anterior and superior of the pelvic bone. Given the intensity of the symptoms, it could only be an appendix that was about to rupture. He advised the nurse that he was on his way to the hospital and would be there shortly. He was concerned that the appendix might rupture before he arrived, so he resolved to take the most direct route to the hospital. Maybe saving a diplomat's life would tip the scales when his appeal to the Ghanaian courts came up.

Ever since Kwame Nkrumah had been deposed in a bloodless coup, he had been a prisoner of routine. The extradition order from the German government had been ignored for over four years and he had expected the Ghanaian government to be in chaos for a while longer. He had been surprised when a travel restriction order had been served to him by the high court. He was to remain in Kumasi and continue his normal duties as a diplomatic national administering at the Komfo Anokye Teaching Hospital which he had helped to modernize.

He grabbed his medicine bag once he finished buttoning his shirt and headed for the door, not bothering to tuck his shirt in. He would tidy up when he reached the hospital and established whether emergency surgery was required. He realized that at sixty he would certainly be out of breath from rushing the half dozen blocks to the hospital, but he was in good enough shape to manage it. He patted the holster hidden under his shirt on his left hip. It was a small Derringer-type gun he had kept as a keepsake of the war. He had meticulously cared for it, cleaned it, and practiced with it, though he had never had occasion to use it. Even though he had become known and respected in the community as a good man, he knew that one could never be too careful. It was prudent to carry protection.

He set his bag down in the hallway and locked his apartment door. His accommodations did not measure up to his standards, but what did in this armpit of the world? He nearly lost his footing taking the steps down to the street at an unsafe pace, keeping a firm grip on the handrail in case he slipped. He wouldn't be able to help anyone if he were injured before he arrived. He rushed eastward down the dusty road sandwiched between wood and mud homes mixed with more modern wood and concrete businesses. He did not see the man on the roof above the door he exited as he sped off toward the hospital.

To get to the hospital quickly, he would have to pass down a short alley that was very narrow. Only carts and people on foot could fit between the buildings there so he was certain there would be nothing. As he came to the corner, an old woman waved and called to him, no doubt wanting to pay her respects, but he did not have time to talk with her so he waved, smiled, and pointed to the watch on the wrist holding up the medicine bag. She understood that he was on a mission and put a palm up toward where he was going, giving him permission to ignore her. She had distracted him just before he was to round the corner into the alley so he was looking the other way.

When he reoriented himself, and was several long paces down the alley, he saw a row of men in black uniforms spanning the other end of the alley. They were evenly spaced and standing at-rest with their hands behind the small of their backs and their elbows touching across the entire width of the alley. He slowed his pace, examining the men's faces. They were devoid of expression but definitely all looking at him. He decided the most prudent course of action would be to back out of the alley and take another street two blocks farther east, then turn north toward the hospital. As he turned and started walking, men dressed in the same black uniforms closed off the end of the alley where he had entered.

As the row of men sealed off his retreat, the last man gave two quick hand signals aimed high. He tilted his head up so he could see past the brim of his hat. Two rows of men stood along the tops of each building. These men were dressed in the gray, green, and black of the military's special operations division and these men were armed with rifles held ready. He knew from his days in the Nazi military that this particular hold meant that the guns were loaded and ready to fire. All they needed to do was aim and pull the trigger. He saw movement at the place where he had entered. Someone was walking behind the men. They stopped at the center of the row of police and the two men in the middle stepped out of the way to let them pass.

Schumann set his bag on the ground slowly. He had not been ordered to raise his hands so he assumed a relaxed stance with his hands at his side. Two large soldiers approached him followed by other people who appeared to be in civilian clothing. The soldiers stopped about three metres away and each stepped to the side. A woman in her early to mid-thirties but dressed older than her years stepped forward between the two men. Her face was beginning to wrinkle with age, but only just. Her woolen skirt seemed out of place in this jungle city. Her dark hair was covered with a macrame scarf or shawl. She was a Jew. He could tell by her dress and demeanor. What would a homely Jew be doing in this part of the world?

A man slightly shorter than she stepped from behind her. He was slight; built like an undeveloped teenager but with a middle-aged face. He seemed timid and his manner also suggested that he was a Jew. The small man wore a simple gray shirt open at the neck and black cotton pants.

Slowly, a woman emerged from the other side of the two Jews. As she came into view, her dress flowed elegantly. *Verdammt*, she was a vision! Her hair shone golden even in the shade of the alley. Her pale skin was creamy and flawless and he could smell her perfume on the air.

The woman in the center stepped toward him and the others came closer on her left and right. She stood before him, looking up slightly, examining his face. She knew him. The recognition was written clearly on her face. So did the other two, but he had no idea who they were.

"You do not remember us." Freda's statement was not a query. "You are Dr. Horst Schumann, *SS-Sturmbannführer* (Major) in the *Schutzstaffel* branch of the *Luftwaffe*, stationed at Auschwitz, Block 10."

"I was stationed in many places, of which Auschwitz was just one." He was proud of his rank and accomplishments and when he heard them spoken so formally, his heart began to pound in his chest and his ears began to ring. He had to remember his blood pressure and try to control himself. Several of the hospital's doctors commented that he might suffer a stroke under great stress. Perspiration began to bead on his upper lip and sweat began to drip down his scalp making his head itch. "What do you want?"

Freda stood and watched the man before her for a few seconds. He had asked her a question, but she was not here for conversation. She was here to ensure that the man taken back to Nuremberg was the correct man and to *know* his fate would be sealed by the three of them. She did not answer. Instead, she said, "You conducted sterilization experiments on prisoners using radiation and surgery." She paused. He did not respond. She continued, "We are three that you mutilated." He still did not respond.

The slight man stepped forward, reaching into his pocket for something. He drew out a square piece of paper and turned it image side up in his palm. He extended his hand toward Schumann who looked down and impatiently took the picture. Examining the picture closely, Schumann squinted. He reached into his shirt pocket too quickly and the soldiers on both roofs aimed their weapons at his head. Startled, Schumann froze with his glasses between his thumb and forefinger. He slowly drew the glasses out so they could see. They returned their weapons to the ready position. He unfolded his glasses and brought the picture close enough to see with his readers.

The emulsion was cracked. One of the corners had been folded so many times that the image had flaked and fallen off. The image was a yellowing black and white print of three emaciated boys. He estimated they would be about ten years old in this picture. All three boys had been surgically emasculated which meant that their penises, testicles, and scrotums had all been removed and the skin closed over the wounds. One of the boys had a strip of bloody gauze protruding from one of the wounds, presumably to help with drainage during healing. He remembered the surgery by the pattern of the incisions. He had pioneered the experimental procedure to see if they could surgically sterilize the males of the Jewish race so that it would die off. The benefit would be that the Nazis would not have to bury or burn the bodies. Instead, they could be released and their families would bear the cost and burden.

He had only performed this procedure sparingly since the subjects usually died shortly afterward, but he vaguely remembered one such procedure. It was just before he was forced to flee Auschwitz. It was on the three boys in this picture. He looked down at the woman before him. For the most part, the bone structure was a match for the boy in the center. He looked to the man beside her, then the blonde woman. Theirs also matched the photograph with latitude for more than two decades of aging.

The woman in the center said, "We are eyewitnesses and victims of your atrocities." Freda paused taking a deep breath and letting it out. Then she added, "You will hang."

"You think an old photograph is enough to convict someone like me? Think again," he jested.

Freda was not phased. She had been through this very conversation so many times in her head that the response came out before she even thought about it. "No. Photographs have not been enough in most cases brought before the courts at Nuremberg." He looked at her with sardonic defiance. She continued, "What we have this time are three witnesses who can identify you first-hand with verifiable photographic evidence of what you did to them, *and* the records of what you did written in your own hand."

Albert took a step forward and reached for the photograph. Taking it by the corner, he flipped it over and laid it back onto Schumann's open hand. There was a message. In jerky script it read "I prayed this day would come. - Maria Stromberger."

"There is no appendicitis case, is there?" he asked, handing the picture back to Albert.

"No."

Freda's answer was final and he knew he had been caught. As he lowered his hand to his side, he caught the front of his untucked shirt with his left thumb. His right hand darted left and grabbed the handle of the Derringer, but before he had a chance to draw it, he felt the impact and knew that he was dead. It was strange. The shot must have grazed him, but he had felt quite a hard hit. There was no sensation of pain in his upper body. He honestly thought they would blow his head off and he would not even see it coming. The gun clattered to the ground, falling from his numb hand. Maybe they had shot him in the arm. He began to feel light headed and a throbbing pain began to mount. His abdomen began to ache and the screaming pain in his right testicle was beginning to mount wave on top of wave.

Gabby had piled all her rage and hatred into the kick. She noticed the way his shirt bulged slightly on the left. That is where a holster would be hidden for a right-handed person so she had been keeping a close eye on his movements hoping she could sense when he would draw. When the moment came, she delivered the kick with all the force she could muster and felt the satisfying crunch of a soft, round mass against her leg. She knew she had done some permanent damage.

Gabby looked around at the soldiers surrounding them and saw that many of them had a grimace of sympathy pain on their faces. She felt a rush of power as she realized that a man could be made to suffer just by seeing another man suffer and a wicked grin spread across her face.

Schumann began to sink to his knees and Albert flipped the wood-handled little pistol out of his reach. His breathing was coming in gasps and he used both hands to grip his balls hoping the pressure would place some kind of limit on the pain. With bloody spittle flying, he croaked in rage. "If you think that punishing me is going to change anything, you are going to be surprised. I am only one man out of many. Hanging an old man will not bring anyone back."

Freda stooped to one knee beside the suffering Nazi. She affected a tone of gentle instruction as one might deliver the moral of a fairy tale to a youngster. "You think too much of yourself, *Herr Schumann*. We are not interested in what happens to you. We are going to use you to send a message to those like you, those who think that they are more worthy of life than others. We will watch you hang and then use your execution to strike fear into the hearts of future generations of Nazis. We will teach them that if they hurt others, if they kill others, they will live in fear for the rest of their lives because we will be coming to hang them too."

Epilogue

In August of 1967, Albert parked around the corner from *Emils Seltene Bücher* (Emil's Rare Books) in Cologne. He hoisted his favourite leather bag to his shoulder and checked to make sure his journal, pens, and various reference materials were inside. He locked the roadster Gabby had loaned him while he was in town, and turned toward the book store. As he rounded the corner, he slowed, amazed. There was a line that stretched the opposite direction, leading into the shop. He took a deep breath and quickened his pace, not wanting to keep Emil waiting. No one recognized him as he approached the door. Some eyed him with suspicion as if to say he should go to the end of the line.

"Come in, my boy! Come in!" Emil met Albert at the front of the shop, helping to clear people out of the doorway. No one had even recognized him as he approached. He felt silly, secretly wishing for that sort of fame, so anonymity was probably for the best. Emil took Albert firmly by the hand and in one motion, shook it and pulled Albert into the store. The heart treatments and futuristic surgeries he had done had given him his strength and vigor back and since Gerta was doing so well with *Kaberett Seks*, he decided to do something he always wanted. The book store was where he and Sofie spend nearly all of their waking hours and it made them happy.

Today would be one of the busiest days the shop had ever seen if the line outside kept growing. Emil paid a couple of the young men that frequented the neighborhood to help move stacks of books toward the table where Albert would be signing and they happily obliged, lifting heavy stacks that were certainly too tall to manage. Albert smiled at the boys as they engaged in energetic competition to see who could do more. Emil showed him where his stool was. Albert set his copy down, various colors of bookmarks protruding haphazardly around the edges.

Once the event started, Emil let in as many people as would fit in the small space to hear Albert speak. Seated on the worn, old carpet in a semicircle around Albert or standing with their backs against the windows, everyone in the store was silent. He told them of his life, his friends, and his motivation behind writing. He read the passage in which the three friends must leave Maria, dying in the hospital, knowing they will never see her again. When he came to the part where Maria reaches out for him one last time, as his character in the book did, he wept openly. So did many of the visitors.

He sat at the table Emil provided, signing books and writing personal messages for what seemed like hours and though his hands ached, he was determined to meet as many people and sign as many books as he could. He wasn't frustrated. He was fascinated that so many people had come to see him. It was surreal.

"Don't let all this go to your head!" A familiar voice called to him as someone made their way around the line. Gabby was smiling broadly as she came around some people who were crowding each other, trying to keep their place in line. Albert looked back down, continuing to sign and converse with people as they filed through.

"Don't worry, old man! I won't!" he called back, smirking.

Gabby mocked irritation at the slight, putting both hands on her hips and pouting as she came to stand beside him. He looked up with a loving smile and someone in the throng stage-whispered, "It's Gabby! That's Gabby Gorski!" Gabby blushed at the recognition, but gratefully smiled and waved as word of her presence spread outside leading some to press against the windows, hands framing their faces to shield their eyes from the glare.

"I think I could get used to this," Gabby remarked.

"You should write a book, then," Albert jabbed, tilting his head in an expectant manner.

"I don't think so. It takes someone boring, *like you*, to sit for months at a time to write a book." The faces of some of the onlookers revealed that they thought their sparring was serious, but Gabby and Albert both knew that each jab was inflicted with love.

As the day wore on, Albert began to grow weary. Several people asked Gabby if she would sign their book too and, though she tried to act demure, she clearly relished the attention. She certainly did not want to intrude on Albert's time in the spotlight, so she politely declined until Albert vocally insisted for the benefit of the crowd. "Please, sit here. I would love it if you would join me," he said, pulling out the chair beside him. She graciously accepted, onlookers impatient for their chance to meet her.

"Somehow I knew you couldn't resist." Gabby and Albert looked up to see Freda standing beside the table, glowering with a playful glint in her eyes. Freda heard her name whispered several times but did not acknowledge the recognition as she continued to stare at Gabby.

Gabby countered, "Would you like to take over?" She feigned getting up from the table until Freda stopped her, waving her hand.

"Oh, no. Not me. I just came so I could bring you the news." Freda paused, stretching out the moment.

Gabby was impatient. "Well?" she asked, prompting Freda with a shrug.

"Schumann has arrived at Nuremberg and is awaiting trial." Even after all the careful arrangements made with the Ghanaian government before their trip, it seemed every politician wanted to interfere with his extradition on the chance that it might bring them some notoriety. All it did was cause delay after delay.

An old woman near the front of the line put her hand to her mouth at hearing Freda's words. She immediately began to weep with happiness and she said in a low voice, "Schumann is in jail." She turned to those behind her and repeated, a bit louder, "Schumann is in jail." Some turned and passed the message. Some patted a hand on their chests. Others nodded in thanks. Someone outside began to clap. More and more began to clap and cheer and the ruckus grew.

As the day went on and afternoon gave way to evening, Gabby and Freda slipped away leaving Albert to talk with his fans. The people surrounding him would listen intently to his answer to one question and then another. As he satisfied their curiosity, they began to meander off, some staying in the shop to browse, others gave their thanks and went on about their business. At some point, Albert looked up and realized that Gabby and Freda were gone. Emil was busily helping customers as

Sofie rang up purchases with a repetitive *ding* that Albert had tuned out hours ago.

Gabby looked around the book shelf nearest the register beckoning to Albert to come with her. He followed and they went through a service door in the rear of the book store. Inside were large boxes and stacks of books, all waiting to be stocked, but as the short hallway opened into the storage room, Albert saw Freda there pouring champagne. Gabby stepped to the side of the table and held up a glass, facing Albert. Freda lifted a glass as well, but hers was clear and bubbly, probably soda water. One glass remained for him. He took it from the table, stepped back, and raised the glass.

"To the success of Albert's first book. May you realize your wildest dreams!" Gabby said bobbing her glass high. The three sipped together.

Freda stepped toward Albert, placing a hand on his arm saying, "I am so proud of you."

Albert indicated that he wanted to toast again by raising his glass higher. "To the continued success of The Weber Foundation." They sipped again.

Gabby realized something with a mumble through a mouthful of champagne, swallowed, and said, "Here's to Freda giving up the juice!" She raised her glass even higher and Freda looked down into her glass of soda, accepting the praise, but continuing to stare into her glass. "What is it?" Gabby asked.

"Viktor once told me that many of the Nazis are hiding in plain sight in Argentina." Freda's mood grew serious. Albert and Gabby waited for her to finish. "Would you two like to go hunting again?"

Even though Dr. Horst Schumann admitted to a court in Frankfurt that he had killed so many Jews that he could not remember the numbers, doctors said that he could not stand trial due to a heart condition. He was released from prison and died a free man on May 5, 1983.

Special thanks to the creators and volunteers of the Remember Me project at the United States Holocaust Memorial Museum for being a powerful source of inspiration. Children are often overlooked when they are victims of war or persecution. The Remember Me project helped reunite children displaced by WWII with their families. May the world never forget their innocence. Visit the project at **rememberme.ushmm.org**.

Thanks to my best friend, Jim Ayres. He was with me twenty-five years ago when we went to the Houston Holocaust Museum. This is where my vision for this book became clear.

Thanks to William (Tom) Loesch, my ghost, my sparring partner, my dear friend. Without his talent, creativity, and late nights, this book would not have been written.

References

This is a work of historical fiction. The story and some of its characters are based on historical figures or events; however, this work is entirely original. The works cited below were used as inspiration for the fictional story.

Atomic Heritage Foundation. (2018). Proxy Wars During the Cold War: Africa. *Atomic Heritage Foundation.* Retrieved from: https://www.atomicheritage.org/history/proxy-wars-during-cold-war-africa

Auschwitz-Birkenau Memorial & Museum. (n. d.). Horst Schumann. *Auschwitz-Birkenau State Museum.* Oświęcim, Poland.

Bellert, J. The work of Polish doctors and nurses at the Polish Red Cross Camp Hospital in Oświęcim after the liberation of Auschwitz concentration camp. Dawidowicz, A., trans. *Medical Review – Auschwitz.* August 12, 2019. Originally published as "Praca polskich lekarzy i pielęgniarek w Szpitalu Obozowym PCK w Oświęcimiu po oswobodzeniu obozu." *Przegląd Lekarski – Oświęcim.* 1963: 66–69. Retrieved from: https://www.mp.pl/auschwitz/journal/english/214760,hospital-in-oswiecim-after-the-liberation-of-auschwitz

Benedict, S. (2006). Maria Stromberger: A Nurse in the Resistance in Auschwitz. *Nursing History Review Vol. 14, pp 189–202.* Retrieved from: https://search.proquest.com/openview/1eadda648ef9f13037c6a16b0e15ad4e/1?pq-origsite=gscholar&cbl=32794

Benjamin, H. (1966). *The Transsexual Phenomenon.* New York, NY. The Julian Press Inc. Publishers. Electronic version: (1999). Düsseldorf, Germany. Symposion Publishing. Retrieved from: https://archive.is/20130105202900/http://www2.rz.hu-berlin.de/sexology/ECE6/html/benjamin/#selection-477.63-477.73

Billings, D., Urban, T. (1982). The Socio-Medical Construction of Transsexualism: An Interpretation and Critique. *Social Problems Vol. 29, No. 3, pp. 266–282.*

Blumenthal, R. (2018). My Decades on the Nazi Trail. The New York Times. New York, NY. Retrieved from: https://www.nytimes.com/2018/08/23/insider/nazi-deportation-josef-mengele.html

Boston Children's Hospital. (n. d.). Vaginal Agenesis. *Boston Children's Hospital.* Boston, MA. Retrieved from: https://www.childrenshospital.org/conditions-and-treatments/conditions/v/vaginal-agenesis

Brooksby, E. P., Brooksby, B. N. (1995). Some Guidelines For Family Research In Ghana. *Ghana Accra Mission.* Retrieved from: http://files.lib.byu.edu/family-history-library/research-outlines/Africa/Ghana.pdf

Carmilly-Weinberger, M. (1986). *The Rabbinical Seminary of Budapest, 1877-1977: A centennial volume.* Sepher-Hermon Press.

Cosgrove, B. (n. d.). A Brutal Pageantry: The Third Reich's Myth-Making Machinery, in Color. *Time Magazine.* Pueblo, CO. Life. Retrieved from: https://www.life.com/history/a-brutal-pageantry-the-third-reichs-myth-making-machinery-in-color/

Deutsch, G., Blau, L. (1901). LANDESRABBINERSCHULE IN BUDAPEST (Országos Rabbiképzö Intézet). In Singer, Isidore; et al. (eds.). *The Jewish Encyclopedia.* Funk & Wagnalls. New York, NY.

Devor, A. H. (2013). Reed Erickson and The Erickson Educational Foundation. *University of Victoria, Canada.* Retrieved from: http://web.uvic.ca/~erick123/

Feron, J. (1972). Doctor Tells West German Jury Visiting Warsaw About Life After the Gestapo Imprisoned Him in '41. *The New York Times.* New York, NY.

Friedländer, S. (1932). *Nazi Germany and the Jews.* HarperCollins. Retrieved from: https://archive.org/details/nazigermanyjewsoofrie/

GhanaWeb Contributors. (n. d.). Lt. General Joseph A. Ankrah Ex-Head of State: 1966 - 1969. *GhanaWeb.* Retrieved from: https://www.ghanaweb.com/person/Lt-General-Joseph-A-Ankrah-119

Ghert-Zand, R. (2019). How historians led a campaign to hunt down, deport Nazi killers living in the US. *The Times of Israel.* Retrieved from: https://www.timesofisrael.com/how-historians-led-a-campaign-to-hunt-down-deport-nazi-killers-living-in-the-us

Gilbert, M. (2005). Churchill Proceedings – Churchill and Bombing Policy. *Finest Hour 137, pp 26.* International Churchill Society. Washington, DC. Retrieved from: https://winstonchurchill.org/publications/finest-hour/finest-hour-137/churchill-proceedings-churchill-and-bombing-policy/

Gross, D. (2017). What to Know About Germany's Legal Prostitution Industry. *Culture Trip.* New York, NY. Retrieved from: https://theculturetrip.com/europe/germany/articles/what-to-know-about-germanys-legal-prostitution-industry/

Ha Galil Staff. (n. d.). Jewish parish hall at Fasanenstrasse: The broken Torah scroll. *Ha Galil.* Munich, Germany. Retrieved from: http://www.berlin-judentum.de/denkmal/fasanenstrasse.htm

Hanink, E. (n. d.). Maria Stromberger (1898-1957), Angel of Auschwitz. *Working Nurse.* Los Angeles, CA. Retrieved from: https://www.workingnurse.com/articles/Maria-Stromberger-1898-1957-Angel-of-Auschwitz

Hillhouse, T. M., & Porter, J. H. (2015). A brief history of the development of antidepressant drugs: from monoamines to glutamate. *Experimental and clinical psychopharmacology, 23(1), 1–21.* https://doi.org/10.1037/a0038550

History.com Editors. (2009). Massacre begins at Munich Olympics. *A&E Television Networks.* New York, NY. Retrieved from: https://www.history.com/this-day-in-history/massacre-begins-at-munich-olympics

Holocaust Encyclopedia. (n. d.). Nazi Medical Experiments. *United States Memorial Holocaust Museum.* Retrieved from: https://encyclopedia.ushmm.org/content/en/article/nazi-medical-experiments

Hospital Staff. (n. d.). A Pest Megyei Szt. Rókus Kórház története (History of St. Roch's Hospital in Pest County). *Szent Rókus Kórház és Intézményei.* Budapest, Hungary. Retrieved from: http://www.rokus.hu/tortenet.htm

Hospital Staff. (n. d.). About Us. *Komfo Anokye Teaching Hospital.* Adum-Kumasi, Ghana. Retrieved from: http://www.kathhsp.org/about-us/

Hospital Staff. (n. d.). Historie. *St. Elisabethen-Krankenhaus Frankfurt.* Frankfurt, Germany. Retrieved from: https://www.elisabethen-krankenhaus-frankfurt.de/ueber-uns/historie

Hospital Staff. (n. d.). Story. *Sächsisches Krankenhaus Großschweidnitz.* Großschweidnitz, Germany. Retrieved from: https://www.skh-grossschweidnitz.sachsen.de/ueber_uns/geschichte/

International Finannce Corporation. (n. d.). The Mövenpick Ambassador Hotel, Ghana, Restoring a Landmark to Former Glory. *World Bank Group.* Retrieved from: https://www.ifc.org/wps/wcm/connect/e9202d1c-ca9e-43c3-ab1b-8618c810ca17/The+Movenpick+Ambassador+Hotel%2C+Ghana. pdf?MOD=AJPERES&CVID=leAOV4S#:~:text=The%20Ambassador%20Hotel%20 Accra%20was,disposed%20of%20by%20the%20state

Jewish Telegraphic Agency Archive. (1966). Nazi Doctor in Ghana Admits Sterilizing 30,000 Jews; Killed 80,000. *Jewish Telegraphic Agency/70 Faces Media.* New York, NY. Retrieved from: http://pdfs.jta.org/1966/1966-10-28_207.pdf

Jewish Virtual Library. (2018). Auschwitz-Birkenau: Nazi Medical Experimentation. *American-Israeli Cooperative Enterprise.* Chevy Chase, MD. Retrieved from: https://www.jewishvirtuallibrary.org/nazi-medical-experimentation-at-auschwitz-birkenau

Jewish Virtual Library. (2018). Irena Sendler (1910-2008). *American-Israeli Cooperative Enterprise.* Chevy Chase, MD. Retrieved from: https://www. jewishvirtuallibrary.org/irena-sendler

Jewish Virtual Library. (n. d.). Horst Schumann (1906 - 1983). *American-Israeli Cooperative Enterprise.* Retrieved from: https://www.jewishvirtuallibrary.org/ horst-schumann

Kukin, M. (AKA: Wiesenthal, S.). (1962). *Humor Behind The Iron Curtain.* Signum-Verlag. Gütersloh, Germany.

Levenson, M. (2020). Judge Orders Deportation of Tennessee Man Who Served as Nazi Camp Guard. *The New York Times.* New York, NY. Retrieved from: https://www. nytimes.com/2020/03/05/us/friedrich-karl-berger-nazi-concentration-camp. html

Lifton, R. J., (1986). *The Nazi Doctors: Medical Killing and the Psychology of Genocide.* Basic Books. New York, NY.

Mayo Clinic Staff. (n. d.). Adenomyosis. *Mayo Foundation for Medical Education and Research.* Rochester, MN. Retrieved from: https://www.mayoclinic.org/diseases-conditions/adenomyosis/symptoms-causes/syc-20369138?p=1

Merrill, A. (2005). In West Africa, a Synagogue Where the Pavement Ends. *The Forward Association, Inc.* New York, NY. Retrieved from: https://forward.com/news/2143/in-west-africa-a-synagogue-where-the-pavement-end/

Newsome, J. (2016). *HOMOSEXUALS AFTER THE HOLOCAUST: SEXUAL CITIZENSHIP AND THE POLITICS OF MEMORY IN GERMANY AND THE UNITED STATES, 1945 – 2008.* ProQuest. Ann Arbor, MI. Retrieved from: https://www.une.edu/sites/default/files/homosexuals_after_the_holocaust.pdf

Nuttbrock, L., Rosenblum, A., Blumenstein, R. (2002). Transgender Identity Affirmation and Mental Health. *The International Journal of Transgenderism (IJT).* Stroud, UK. Hawthorne Press. Retrieved from: http://web.archive.org/web/20070708184313/http://www.symposion.com/ijt/ijtvoo6nooo4_03.htm

Obiorah, C. (2018). 200+ Unique Ghanaian Names. *BuzzGhana.* Enugu, Nigeria. Retrieved from: https://buzzghana.com/ghanaian-names/

Orchard Corset. (n. d.). Corsets and Corseting 101: FAQs. *Orchard Corset.* Wenatchee, WA. Retrieved from: https://www.orchardcorset.com/pages/corsets-101

Queer Cafe Contributors. (n. d.). Old Timey Terms. *Queer Cafe.* Retrieved from: https://queercafe.net/archaic.htm

Rees, L. (2004). Biographies - Auschwitz: Inside the Nazi State. *Community Television of Southern California (KCET).* Los Angeles, CA. Retrieved from: https://www.pbs.org/auschwitz/learning/biographies

Sisak, M. R. (2019). Timeline: Life and death of ex-Nazi guard deported from US. *The Times of Israel.* Retrieved from: https://www.timesofisrael.com/timeline-life-and-death-of-ex-nazi-guard-deported-from-us

Spoliansky, M., Schwabach, K. (1920). *Das Lila Lied (The Lavender Song).* Recorded by Lemper, U. on German Cabaret Songs. London Records. London, UK. Retrieved from: https://www.facinghistory.org/resource-library/audio/lavender-song-das-lila-lied

Stone, D. (2015). The Liberation of the Camps: The End of the Holocaust and Its Aftermath. Yale University Press, New Haven, CT..

u/MetsFinland. (2019). Why would nazi doctor Horst Schumann receive protection of Ghanaian marxist-leninist Kwame Nkrumah? *Reddit.* Retrieved from: https://www.reddit.com/r/AskHistorians/comments/9b0q48/why_would_nazi_doctor_horst_schumann_receive/

United Nations. (n. d.). Auschwitz Birkenau German Nazi Concentration and Extermination Camp (1940-1945). *UNESCO World Heritage Centre.* Paris, France. Retrieved from: https://web.archive.org/web/20191122100906/https://whc.unesco.org/en/list/31/

United States Holocaust Memorial Museum. (n. d.). ANTI-JEWISH LEGISLATION IN PREWAR GERMANY. *Holocaust Encyclopedia.* Washington, DC. Retrieved from: https://encyclopedia.ushmm.org/content/en/article/anti-jewish-legislation-in-prewar-germany

United States Holocaust Memorial Museum. (n. d.). Remember Me?. *Holocaust Encyclopedia.* Washington, DC. Retrieved from: https://rememberme.ushmm.org/

United States Holocaust Memorial Museum. (n. d.). THE NAZI OLYMPICS BERLIN 1936. *Holocaust Encyclopedia.* Washington, DC. Retrieved from: https://encyclopedia.ushmm.org/content/en/article/the-nazi-olympics-berlin-1936

Unknown. (1887). *1887 ECUADOR #12,#13(2),#14 ON 10C REG POSTAL STATIONERY COVER TO GERMANY;RARE*D.* Worth Point Corporation. Atlanta, GA. Retrieved from: https://www.worthpoint.com/worthopedia/1887-ecuador-12-13-14-10c-reg-postal-1925260444

Unknown. (1950). Siamese Twins (1950). *British Pathe.* YouTube. Retrieved from: https://www.youtube.com/watch?v=uT2du_w2z_U

Van der Auwera, G. (2017). Concentration and extermination camp Auschwitz. *Traces of War.* STIWOT. Badhoevedorp, Nederlands. Retrieved from: https://www.tracesofwar.com/articles/4868/concentration-camp-auschwitz.htm

Video. (1966). Ghana: Court Rejects Appeal By Dr. Horst Schumann. *Reuters.* Retrieved from: https://www.britishpathe.com/video/VLVA4MU6S50EOCHC52VJNNJOEBZOY-GHANA-COURT-REJECTS-APPEAL-BY-DR-HORST-SCHUMANN/query/Schumanns

Walter, M., Walter O. Bockting, W. O., Cohen-Kettenis, P., et al. (2001). *The Harry Benjamin International Gender Dysphoria Association's Standards Of Care For Gender Identity Disorders, Sixth Version.* Retrieved from: https://web.archive.org/web/20070610012909/http://www.wpath.org/Documents2/socv6.pdf

WebMD Contributors. (n. d.). Avascular Necrosis (AVN or Osteonecrosis). *WebMD.* New York, NY. Retrieved from: https://www.webmd.com/arthritis/avascular-necrosis-osteonecrosis-symptoms-treatments

Weindling, P., von Villiez, A., Loewenau, A., & Farron, N. (2016). The victims of unethical human experiments and coerced research under National Socialism. *Endeavour, 40(1), 1–6.* https://doi.org/10.1016/j.endeavour.2015.10.005

Wiesenthal, S., Wechsberg, J. (1967). *The Murderers Among Us: The Simon Wiesenthal Memoirs.* McGraw-Hill. New York, NY.

Wikipedia contributors. (2021, January 13). Glossary of Nazi Germany. *Wikipedia, The Free Encyclopedia.* Retrieved from https://en.wikipedia.org/w/index.php?title=Glossary_of_Nazi_Germany&oldid=1000064101

World Professional Association For Transgender Health. (n. d.). Mission & Vision. *The International Journal of Transgenderism (IJT).* Stroud, UK. Hawthorne Press. Retrieved from: https://www.wpath.org/about/mission-and-vision

Yergin, D., Stanislaw, J. (1998). *The Commanding Heights: The Battle for the World Economy.* Free Press. New York, NY.

Your Dictionary. (n. d.). Okomfo Anokye. *Your Dictionary.* Retrieved from: https://biography.yourdictionary.com/okomfo-anokye

Zaltzman, L. (2020). The real story behind 'Hunters,' Al Pacino's new Nazi-hunting Amazon series. *Jewish Telegraphic Agency/70 Faces Media.* New York, NY. Retrieved from: https://www.jta.org/2020/02/21/culture/real-story-hunters-tv-show

Made in the USA
Middletown, DE
11 April 2021

37364190R00205